NAMELESS SOVEREIGN

BOOK 3

A CULTIVATION EPIC

NAMELESS AUTHOR

Timeless
Wind

First published by Timeless Wind Publishing LLC 2024

First edition

Editing by J. Massat and Silas Sontag.

Cover art by Kart Studio. Typography by Lorne Ryburn.

THE STORY SO FAR...

Red, once a young slave toiling in the oppressive depths of the moonstone mines, has clawed his way to the surface. But freedom hasn't come without a price. Red is burdened by a mysterious curse stemming from his time in the mines—a link to a malevolent entity residing on the moon's surface that drains his energy during each new moon.

Red joins the ranks of the Water Dragon Sect, a ragtag group of cultivators in the town of Fordham-Bestrem. There, he trains with the skilled one-armed swordsman Domeron, learns to read from the compassionate Eiwin, and apprentices under the blacksmith Goulth.

Red's arrival on the surface coincides with several unsettling events. Monsters have all seemingly disappeared from the region, leaving the surrounding forests rife with bandits. When venturing into the forest with the warrior Narcha to reclaim his belongings, Red also encounters a zombie controlled by a necromancer and a powerful demon.

Red survives the journey and retrieves his belongings while also bonding with a strange being that appears as a crimson mist. He soon realizes he now has the ability to sense the presence of other living things, as well as gauge their level of strength.

With the help of the insectoid core, Red is able to open enough special acupoints to withstand the moon another month. He deciphers the page he'd torn from Viran's diary, but it only raises more questions about the nature of his former prison and the moon's curse.

To complicate matters further, the Empire, a ruthless power seeking to dominate the continent, has sent a formidable envoy to threaten the kingdom. Allen, the Sect's sheltered Young Master, convinces Red to spy on the imperials staying in the town. They steal an ornate box full of communication talismans, which suggests that the Empire is working with the bandits and Gustav, the corrupt local merchant.

A party is sent out to investigate what the Empire is planning, though Red and Allen are forbidden to leave the Sect by Hector. However, Domeron helps them escape, believing that Hector is too protective of his young protégé. Red is tasked with leading Allen into the forest, where they will meet up with the others.

Things quickly go wrong. Red and Allen are ambushed by a horde of undead animals controlled by the necromancer. They are saved by Reinhart, one of Gustav's subordinates, but are now forced to follow the treacherous knight.

Reinhart reveals that Gustav had previously worked with the bandits. However, upon realizing that they had dealings with the Empire behind his back, the merchant had turned on them. Reinhart is now in the forest to enact Gustav's blood revenge on his former allies.

Red and Allen manage to escape from Reinhart when the demon suddenly attacks them. They soon encounter Rimold, another member of the Water Dragon Sect. Rimold, a thief and a rogue, had disguised himself in order to spy on the bandits. He reveals that the bandits have been using a secret network of tunnels to travel throughout the forest.

They again encounter the necromancer's creatures. One of them speaks to Red, hinting that the necromancer has knowledge about the moonstone mines and the curse. It urges Red to meet in the tunnels beneath the forest to make a deal.

They finally find the hunter Rog, who explains that Narcha and Eiwin decided to investigate one of the bandit tunnels while he stayed behind to wait for Red and Allen. While waiting, he saw Ricard, the leader of the bandits, enter the tunnel, followed by the demon and necromancer's undead creatures. They decide to enter the tunnel in order to help Narcha and Eiwin.

They quickly realize that it is no ordinary tunnel, but an inheritance ground—a labyrinthine trial left behind by a powerful cultivator in order to find a worthy successor. They encounter Reinhart, who has also entered the trial, and agree on a temporary alliance.

After a desperate battle against a Lesser Ring Realm fireleaf stag, Rog is grievously injured. Red nearly dies, but realizes that he can heal by absorbing blood—yet another ability thanks to the crimson mist.

After the fight, they meet a hawk spirit who is overseeing the inheritance trial. It offers them a reward of five Spirit Stones for completing the first part of the trial, which they may trade for spiritual medicines or talismans. They buy medicine to save Rog, but to fully heal the hunter's Spiritual Veins will cost twenty Spirit Stones. Red decides to carry on with the trial in order to help Rog, while Rimold and Allen request to leave the trial. Reinhart also joins Red on the next stage.

Red and Reinhart are teleported to a desolate world of ravines and caves, with lightning flashing overhead. It is even more treacherous than the labyrinth, but with the help of Red's crimson sense, they avoid most monsters. They find more rewards, including a rare Spiritual Fruit that grants Red dark vision by opening a hidden acupoint.

After fighting more monsters, bandits, and imperials, Red finally finds Narcha and Eiwin. Together with Reinhart they encounter the stage's final test—a massive snake that blocks the path forward. In order to continue the trial, one must withstand the pressure of the serpent without showing fear or hesitation. One wrong move, and it instantly kills you with a lightning bolt.

Reinhart and Narcha both make it past the snake, but the crimson mist inside Red makes him tremble uncontrollably while near the creature. To help him, Eiwin teaches Red a meditation technique called Radiant Current. Red quickly masters the technique, allowing him to communicate with the crimson mist, urging it to be calm.

As he nears the snake's powerful presence, Red's senses are overwhelmed, but he maintains his composure. However, the monster's pressure only increases, and despite taking an empowerment pill, Red's progress slows to a crawl. Red pushes onward, even as blood seeps from his pores and the snake prepares to strike him.

Then, a red aura explodes out from him, and the snake begins to move. It slithers away as Red sees a ghostly, reptilian shape in the aura surrounding him. As the aura disappears, Red feels mist within his body stir, urging him to live on and keep fighting—not just for his own survival, but for the mist's as well.

With the snake now gone, the rest of the trial now awaits him.

CHAPTER I

CHALLENGING DEATH

Winds howled over the canyon of the mystical land. Darkness prevailed over the sky, only broken by the occasional lightning strike, but even that had started to die down.

Yet none of this bothered Red.

He was tired, feeling like he could collapse at any moment. But he had made it. He'd endured the lightning serpent's trial.

Red tried to make his way up the ramp to his companions, but his muscles soon gave out and he fell to his shins. He heard footsteps approaching, and when he looked up, he noticed his companions running down the ramp.

Eiwin was the first to reach him. "Red, are you alright?!" She crouched beside him and helped him sit up.

"I should be fine. I'm just tired." Like Narcha, Eiwin, and Reinhart, he'd approached the monstrous serpent that guarded the entrance to the next area of the inheritance ground trial. As the weakest, he hadn't been confident in his chances, even after taking an empowerment pill. Approaching the snake monster had put so much pressure on his body that he'd started sweating blood. He was *exhausted*.

Narcha, who was following behind Eiwin, let out her own sigh of relief. Still, the longer she stared at him, the more fearful she looked.

"What happened, kid?" she asked.

Red hesitated. He'd taken the empowerment pill and approached the snake, but that hadn't been enough to withstand the serpent's oppressive aura. Just when it seemed like it was going to strike, the crimson mist had surged out from his body, sending the great beast into a terrified rage.

"I... tried to use a trick to pass through. Things went out of control after that."

"A trick?!" Narcha frowned in disbelief. "What kind of trick causes a monster like that to go into a rage? Not only that, but how did you come out alive?"

"I don't know."

He was being sincere. While enraged, the monster had lost its focus, its attacks missing their mark. Even then, just the aftereffects of its hissing should have killed him on the spot. Yet Red came out of the ordeal unharmed. He assumed this was the intervention of the crimson aura, but he wasn't certain.

Too much about this situation was odd, but Red looked on the bright side. He had expected to die, but he had survived the challenge.

His response didn't satisfy Narcha, her expression changing from suspicion to resignation. "It doesn't matter. Let's just get out of here before that thing returns."

"Can you get up, Red?" Eiwin asked.

"I might need help."

She didn't hesitate to lend a hand. She held Red by the shoulders as they made their way back up the incline. In the meantime, he tried, and failed, to get some semblance of strength back into his muscles.

When they arrived near the top of the ramp, Reinhart was waiting for them with his arms crossed.

He stared at Red. "You lived."

"I did."

"How?"

Red shrugged.

Reinhart grunted. "Can't you walk on your own?"

"I took the empowerment pill," Red offered.

"That explains it, I suppose. I don't think it was meant to be consumed by kids, or anyone who has yet to open their twelve Spiritual Veins. Even I feel spent after using it."

Despite that, there were no signs of any side effects on his body.

"Either way, we can't take you with us like this," Reinhart said.

Narcha glared at him. "No one asked for your opinion, you bastard!"

"I'm just being realistic. The kid is very useful, so it pains me to leave him behind, but there's no way we can take dead weight with us. We would definitely die."

"Then we wait for him to recover!"

"And how long would that take? Hours? Days? By then, the trial will be over."

Red couldn't help but cringe at his words. He hadn't died in the snake's jaws, yet now he was as useful as a corpse.

"You need not worry about him, Mister Reinhart," Eiwin interjected. "We will take him with us whether or not he's wounded."

Reinhart frowned. "That's a stupid idea."

"If you wish to, you can go on by yourself. No one is holding you here."

Reinhart sighed. "Fine. Just remember that hunter is still waiting for you to save him out there."

"I know." She fetched something from her bag and handed it to Red. "Here, take this."

It was a vial containing a dark, viscous liquid. In fact, Red recognized it. It was the same medicine Goulth had given him to heal his shoulder when he first arrived at the Sect.

"Isn't this a waste?" he asked.

Eiwin smiled. "Not at all. We need your help if we plan on making it further in this trial. Isn't that right, Narcha?"

Narcha looked at Eiwin with fleeting hesitation. She turned to Red and nodded with resolve. "That power of yours is really useful. We might need it."

Red didn't hesitate any longer. He uncorked the vial and downed its contents, the horrible taste and smell assaulting his senses.

A few seconds later, an uncomfortable feeling spread from the pit of his stomach to every corner of his frame. The process didn't last for long, though, and soon the sensation disappeared.

When Red felt the terrible ache disappear from his body, he was able to stand on his own two feet again.

Reinhart seemed annoyed at the sight. "If you planned on giving him the medicine, why bother threatening me?"

Eiwin glared at the man. "My words from earlier still stand, Mister Reinhart. If this were to happen again in the future, we wouldn't leave any of our injured companions behind, no matter how much they may delay us. This includes you too, to some extent, since we are now cooperating. I hope you don't forget that moving forward."

Reinhart winced, but he didn't respond. He turned back towards the ramp. "Let's move. We don't have time to waste."

And he started walking up.

Narcha leered at his back. "Are we really supposed to save him?" she asked Eiwin.

Eiwin nodded. "We agreed to be allies, didn't we? Allies look out for each other, so we need to protect him if it comes down to it."

"Would he do the same for us, though?"

"I don't know, but it doesn't matter, and you should know that better than anyone, Miss Valt. We don't weigh the value of our actions using others' standards."

Her words gave the warrior some pause. A moment later, she sighed. "Fine! But if he tries to backstab us, I hope you won't try to hold me back."

With that conversation settled, they followed Reinhart up the ramp. They found him waiting at the top with his back to them, focused on something in the distance. He didn't even react to their approach.

"Hey!" Narcha cried. "What are you looking at..."

She trailed off as they crested the ramp. What they saw put them in a quiet state of shock.

An endless plain. The flatland stretched as far as the eye could see— desolate rocky ground in every direction, illuminated by the continual lightning from above.

Enormous dust tornadoes on the horizon traveled through the plain, barely moving from the group's perspective but almost certainly racing at incredible speeds. Red counted at least a dozen of them, but every time he turned to a different point in the distance, he spotted even more merging into the stormy clouds up above.

The sight of these gigantic monstrosities mesmerized him.

"What is that?"

"It's a tornado," Eiwin said. "A natural phenomenon that sometimes occurs when warm, humid air clashes with cold, dry air... It's very dangerous."

"So this is all natural?"

Eiwin shook her head. "I don't believe anything in this place is natural."

"Look, there's something else in the distance!" Narcha shouted.

Red saw it—a shadowy shape beyond the tornadoes that even his dark vision had a hard time spotting. Occasional lightning strikes highlighted its rocky form with bright flashes.

"It looks like a mountain," Reinhart said.

"That must be where we have to go, right?" Narcha grunted.

The knight shrugged. "I don't see anything else."

Unfortunately for them, even after exiting the canyon, they hadn't found any direction or clues.

Reinhart looked over at Red. "Do you still see Ricard and the imperials' tracks?"

"It's all been blown away."

"Well, at least this time, our objective seems pretty straightforward," Reinhart said with a sigh. "Shouldn't be a problem to navigate our way around these tornadoes."

Although there were several twisters, they were all relatively far apart. Still, his words convinced no one.

Red frowned. "Do you really think it'll be that easy?"

Reinhart smiled. "Of course I don't. Doesn't hurt to hope, though, does it?"

Red looked back the way they'd come. The canyon stretched behind him, solid ground broken up by large trenches and fissures, as endless as the plains up ahead. Yet something confused him.

"We haven't been struck by lightning."

Narcha blinked. "What do you mean by that?"

"We're at the same height as the canyon walls, but no lightning has struck us."

One reason they hadn't climbed the canyon walls earlier was to avoid the lightning that had nearly killed the bandits. Now, though, they were level with the top of the canyon.

Reinhart laughed. "Is there even any point in trying to make sense of this place, kid? This isn't the real world, after all... Unless you want to try to climb the canyon wall and see what happens."

"Bah!" Narcha snorted. "Stop talking and start moving!"

He didn't protest, and they were soon traveling forward again, noticing new curiosities.

The rocky ground here wasn't smooth. It was cracked, countless small fissures littering the land. Now the word "desert" felt more apt.

Five minutes passed. Even then, the figure of the distant mountain didn't come any closer, proving how massive and distant the peak really was. Still, the group wasn't dissuaded, and they had yet to find any other clues, so they kept walking forward.

That was when the ground beneath them started to rumble.

"Is it that snake again?!" Narcha cried.

Reinhart looked backward and shook his head. "There's nothing there!"

"Stay close to the ground," Eiwin called out. "It's getting stronger!"

Red did as she instructed. The earthquake intensified until they heard the booming sound of the ground breaking apart in the distance.

Ground, dust and detritus spewed out, and the whole group covered their faces. When the dust had cleared up, they noticed a shape coming out from the ground.

It was a colossal monster.

Narcha grumbled, "Fuck me..."

CHAPTER 2
VULTURES

THE CREATURE WAS AN INSECT. Only half of its body was above ground, but that half alone extended well over a hundred meters. Its elongated and plump yellow body made Red guess it was a beetle, but he was quickly proven wrong.

First of all, this monster seemed to have a neck. It extended from its thorax and held a flat head, which bore a gigantic pair of serrated, sickle-shaped mandibles. Curiously, he didn't see any eyes on the creature. The insect's body was covered in countless bristles, each of which was bigger than Red.

While this creature wasn't as long as the snake, it was much wider, and it exuded the same pressure. It dragged the rest of its body out from the ground, revealing all six of its colossal legs. The ground shook with its every step.

The monster raised its head towards the sky. Red held his breath and blocked his ears, expecting a roar comparable to the snake's. It didn't come.

Instead, the creature only opened its jaws. It held that position for over ten seconds, leaving them all confused.

They soon noticed another change.

"The wind is picking up," Reinhart said.

Red felt it too. It was blowing against their backs and towards the creature, dragging plumes of dust with it. He even felt the wind start to pull him along. Thankfully, Narcha grabbed him before he was blown away.

She gaped at the monster. "It's getting stronger!"

The wind was blowing in from all directions, dust gathering around the beast's mandibles. The gusts whipped around them, forming a familiar shape.

Is it making a tornado?

Red's question was answered when the spinning dust tendril extended towards the sky, and the clouds reached down to meet it. Then they connected, and the twister whirled even faster.

The massive insect at the center was unmoved by the extreme winds. Once the tornado formed, it detached itself from the creature's mandibles and found purchase on the ground.

Then the insect, as if satisfied with a job well done, simply turned around and returned to its hole. As it marched off, the ground rumbled with renewed intensity, making Red stumble on his feet. After the insect entered the hole, the quaking soon died down.

Everyone stared at the giant hole and the tornado the creature had left behind.

Reinhart was the first to speak up, raising his voice over the wind. "I guess we found out what was causing these tornadoes."

"What's even the point of doing that?" Narcha cried.

"Maybe it's just instinctual? Or maybe it was ordered by the spirit?"

"But why? It's not like these tornadoes are a threat in this giant desert."

Even now, the tornado was slowly moving away from them. Although the surrounding winds had increased, it wasn't anything dangerous. Avoiding this tornado wouldn't be a big issue.

If anything, the dust getting into their eyes was more of an obstacle.

Eiwin shook her head. "We should not jump to conclusions. The first few trials have already proven that—"

She was cut short by a distant hissing sound. Everyone froze, then turned around. They saw nothing, but the sound grew louder, closing in.

"It's above us!" Reinhart pointed.

It wasn't just one creature. Rather, it was hundreds of them, all joined in a terrible chorus that echoed through the desert. Red looked up to find countless flying shadows highlighted by cracks of lightning against the dark clouds.

And they were getting closer every second.

"Run!" Narcha shouted.

Everyone began to move, but the monsters were much faster than them.

Soon they were close enough for Red to see their true appearance. They were large black vultures, roughly double his size, with wingspans reaching over four meters. While the rest of their bodies were covered in feathers, their undersides revealed reptilian scales.

The monsters themselves didn't seem too menacing—not beyond their numbers. And to their surprise, the birds weren't aiming for them.

Instead, they all flew towards the tornado. Once the horde swooped down, they swerved, diving into the twister, disappearing inside the storm of dust and wind.

Naturally, the group slowed their run.

Narcha frowned at the sight. "What the hell?"

"There's something happening!" Reinhart said.

The birds dove out of the tornado one by one. Far fewer emerged than had entered, but those that came out were covered in strange dust that stuck to their bodies. Their cacophonous cries echoed through the desert, even louder than before despite their lower numbers. They circled the hurricane, unaffected by the strong winds.

Red was curiously watching this strange phenomenon when suddenly one of the birds veered off, heading towards the group. Others joined it until there were dozens of them all making a straight path towards the humans.

Narcha cursed. "Fuck! Just run!"

They broke out into a full sprint again. The dust-covered birds, however, were even faster than before, and soon they had almost caught up.

"We can't escape them!" Narcha grabbed her saber. "Get ready to fight!"

"There's no way we can fight them all," Reinhart interjected. "We need to find cover!"

Although there weren't hundreds of birds anymore, there were still far more than they could handle. Not to mention the increased strength provided by the twister.

"Cover?!" Narcha roared. "Where are we going to find cover here?"

"Agh, goddamnit!" Reinhart whipped out his sword. "Don't stop running!"

Red took out his cleaver while Eiwin readied her fists by his side. Then the first vulture dove at them.

It was swiftly cut down by Narcha's saber, splattering on the ground, dead. Four more came in quick succession, and she didn't have the time to raise her weapon to strike them down. Their large talons aimed for her leather armor, trying to tear through.

Reinhart overtook Narcha and used his sword to bat one of them away. Red and Eiwin were about to join the fray, but the vultures didn't remain still for long, instead flying up and out of their reach.

They hadn't managed to wound Narcha with their talons, but her armor was nearly clawed through. The group had no time to relax as even more birds swooped down—this time, over ten.

Some of them even reached for Red. Eiwin battered two away, but one bird managed to grab his arm. Thankfully, he was wearing his Sect uniform, and although the bird tore the fabric, it let him go unscathed.

Narcha and Reinhart didn't have the same luck. Most of the monsters focused on them, leaving a gash on the woman's shoulder. Her armor fell off, clawed to pieces. The knight, who had no armor in the first place, took even nastier cuts across his back.

They managed to strike down five of the birds, but the rest flew away as another group swooped down to attack.

Red was quick to notice the creatures' strategy. "They're trying to wear us down!"

The birds could have all attacked at once, but they chose not to. Instead, flocks of creatures were striking in volleys while the others prepared the next assault. Red knew bird monsters were strongest in their dives, when they gathered all their momentum to swipe down with their sharp talons and tear at their prey—and these creatures were aware of that. They didn't stay long within the group's reach and cycled between the attackers so they could gather momentum and strike again.

This way, they maximized their strength and avoided unnecessary casualties, all while wearing them down. It was a simple and effective strategy from a group of unintelligent creatures, and there was nothing they could do to counter it.

"I have a plan!" Reinhart said. "Get close and keep them off me!"

Narcha stared at him, but as soon as Eiwin and Red picked up speed to keep pace with Reinhart, she joined them. The birds' next attack came, comprising another dozen.

Red and his companions did their best to fight them off, but all of them took damage. Eiwin's uniform sleeves were ruined, blood pouring down her arms. Narcha suffered the worst of it as one of the birds managed to swipe at her face, leaving a deep cut in her forehead. Red was mostly unaffected, since his height meant few of the birds aimed for him as the group clustered together.

Meanwhile, Reinhart activated a talisman. Right before the next attack came, it glowed, and a round translucent barrier surrounded the group, moving with them. The creatures, undeterred, continued to dive and attack.

They crashed against the barrier, their talons unable to sink in. The monsters cried out in anger and continued to swipe at the shield, but to no avail. More birds from above joined in after seeing their brethren's frustration, and soon the group was surrounded by birds all trying their best to pierce through.

Reinhart turned to Red and the others. "Remember—stay close to me and don't stop running! I don't know how long this barrier will last!"

Narcha gritted her teeth and nodded. She looked over at Red. "Kid, do you have any plans?!"

Why are you asking me?

Red couldn't imagine how they would be able to escape. Perhaps they could stand and fight, and with all their talismans and pills, maybe they could win. Even then, they would definitely come out with serious injuries. It wasn't an optimal solution, much less so considering the rest of the trial awaited, but it was better than dying.

Right as Red was about to make his opinion known, he felt something shake in his pouch. He looked down in confusion before searching for the cause. His hand grasped an object, dragging it out into view.

It was the compass they had gotten from the imperials, glowing with a faint white light.

CHAPTER 3

MAUSOLEUM

RED FLIPPED the lid of the compass open. It was pointing in a different direction, to their right.

"The compass is doing something!"

Narcha, just ahead of him, blinked back at Red. "What! How?"

"I don't know! It started glowing, and now the arrow is pointed in another direction!"

He had checked the compass in the canyon and noted the direction it pointed to. He knew it would help them orient themselves in an illusion, but perhaps not surprisingly, the item from the imperials seemed to have another use.

"Where is it pointing?" Reinhart cried over the noise of birds scratching at the barrier.

"There!" Red gestured with his hand.

It was pointing southeast, away from the distant mountain they had been walking towards.

Narcha groaned. "There's nothing there!"

"There's nothing in any direction, Miss Valt!" Eiwin shook her head. "Let's move, quickly!"

They needed to stay together inside the transparent shield. This cut down their running speed, but it was better than exposure to the birds' attacks. The beasts were relentless, never pausing for even a second.

Soon enough, small cracks appeared in the barrier. "It's not going to last much longer!" Reinhart warned.

The cracks seemed to motivate the vultures to redouble their efforts, and half a minute later, the minor fracture had spread across the entire shield.

Narcha gritted her teeth. "What about the compass, kid?! Anything?!"

"It stopped glowing!" Red said.

"What?!"

It had stopped emitting light, and now it was pointing in another random direction.

"What happened, kid?"

Red frowned. "How would I know? It's given us a direction, so just follow it!"

"Agh, damn it all!" After some hesitation, Narcha pulled out a talisman from her bag.

"Stay close to me!" she said.

Everyone stayed close. Then, right as the barrier verged on collapse, she activated the talisman. A few seconds later, the shield shattered, much to the joy of the vultures surrounding them.

Just when they were about to swoop down and tear their prey apart, another barrier emerged in the place of the first one, and their talons all clashed against it, deflected.

They cried out in anger.

Narcha had used the barrier talisman they had acquired from the imperials, buying the group even more time. "Let's be quicker! I don't have another talisman!"

But they were already running as fast as they could in their awkward formation. At most, this talisman would buy them a couple of minutes.

As the first few cracks appeared in the barrier, Reinhart finally spotted something ahead. "There's a building!"

A mirage shimmered in the air, becoming more solid the closer they came. Within a hundred meters, it became fully clear.

It was an enormous temple built from black stone bricks. There were no visible windows, and the walls were smooth and bare, devoid of symbols. All they could see was a wide stone door with two circular rusted handles attached.

Narcha didn't hesitate. "To the door!"

Everyone followed her. To their surprise, though, the birds were growing reluctant to attack. Once they reached the black temple's doors, the monsters' assault had stopped completely. Instead they circled the area, observing the group.

This gave them some time to relax and collect themselves—and right as their second shield was about to break.

Red watched the vultures overhead. "They're afraid of the temple. Or of whatever's inside it."

It was common for lesser monsters to avoid places where stronger beasts dwelled. It was instinctual.

"Do you sense anything, kid?" Narcha asked.

"Not from this position."

This temple was at least two hundred meters wide and over thirty meters tall. It was a massive construction, even Red couldn't cover it all with his crimson sense in one go.

"Let's move around, then," Reinhart said. "Doesn't look like the birds are eager to attack, and I'd rather not walk into another horde of beasts."

They circled the building, finding similar stone gates on each end. By the time they returned to their original position, Red had yet to detect any fluctuations.

"Really?" Narcha was baffled. "Are you sure there's nothing inside?"

Red shrugged. "I can't say with complete confidence. There are blind spots I might not have been able to detect, but it's unlikely."

"If that's the case, why are those birds so scared of it?"

"Other monsters aren't the only things creatures like this are afraid of," Eiwin said. "They may also avoid dangerous natural places, or perhaps there is a formation that keeps them away."

"So do you suppose this place is safe, then?"

Eiwin shook her head. "I didn't say that. There might be dangers here that aren't monsters."

That wasn't reassuring, Red thought.

Narcha seemed to agree. "What are we supposed to do in that case?"

Eiwin gave her a helpless smile. "Just continue being careful, I suppose."

The warrior gritted her teeth and turned to Reinhart. "Are you going to open the door, or do you want me to do it?"

By this time, the shield they were using had worn off, and the group was back to keeping a certain distance from Reinhart.

He smiled. "I'm on my way."

Reinhart walked over to the door and pushed against it. To their surprise, it barely moved.

Turning around, he gave Narcha a sly grin. "I might need some help here."

Narcha glared at him. "Just move aside!"

He did as he was told. Narcha set both of her hands on the double door and started to push. It clearly took a huge effort, but she made quicker progress than Reinhart, and soon enough, the doors were open wide enough to let them through.

Narcha stepped back and wiped the sweat off her forehead. "Gods, why would they make a door so heavy?"

"Maybe it was meant to keep people from going in," Red suggested.

She grimaced. "If they didn't want people going in, why make a door at all?"

Red didn't have a response to that.

Their attention turned back to the building as they filed in. The place was thick with pure darkness, and while Reinhart and Red could see, the same couldn't be said for Narcha and Eiwin. After confirming with Red that there were no monsters lying in ambush, Narcha lit a torch.

They entered a large stone corridor.

As soon as Red looked around, he noticed something strange. "This isn't right." He pointed upward. "The ceiling is way higher than it should be."

From the outside, the building looked around thirty meters tall, and yet now Red felt the distance to the ceiling was well beyond that. This alarmed the entire group.

"Were we teleported somewhere else?" Narcha asked.

"I don't think so," Red replied. "The outside world is still there."

The door behind them remained open, and the desert and its tornadoes still waited beyond it.

"Another illusion, then?" Reinhart suggested.

"Not necessarily," Eiwin said. "Certain extremely powerful cultivators can manipulate space to some degree. Making a space bigger on the inside than it seems from the outside is not entirely unheard of in the world."

Narcha scoffed. "You talk about it as if it's common! I've only heard of a few places like that before, and they're all in the holy lands of the Sects!"

"As I said, I don't know for sure." Eiwin sighed. "Whether it's an illusion or some other thing, it doesn't matter to us, does it?"

The group kept moving forward, examining their surroundings. The inside was as devoid of symbols or decorations as the outside, and this corridor gave them no clues. Red also saw no signs of footprints, which came as a relief.

As they delved deeper into the temple, the smell of stale air became even more pronounced.

Narcha rubbed her nose in discomfort. "How long has it been since this place has been opened? No wonder there's nothing alive in here!"

The corridor led them well past one hundred meters, over half the length of the temple from the outside, until they finally arrived in a large circular room. To call it a room, though, would not do it justice.

An indoor amphitheater stretched a hundred meters in diameter. Steps connected the circular floor where they had emerged to towering bowl-like walls, and in the middle of the central floor was a platform. The chamber surrounding it all went well beyond what Red could see with his dark vision.

But that wasn't all.

Hundreds of segmented squares made up the "seats" of this place, all with nameplates Red couldn't read from a distance. In fact, the more Red looked at them, the more they resembled drawers.

"This isn't a temple..." Eiwin said, voice shaking. "This is a crypt."

Red frowned. "What's a crypt?"

"It's where people's remains are buried."

"Oh..." Red nodded in realization. As he stared around, the weight of her words hit him. "Wait, are those..."

"Graves." Reinhart was the one to respond. "Every one of these drawers probably has someone's bones inside it."

The revelation shook Red. The drawers numbered in the hundreds, even thousands. And from what he could see, there were names written on all of them. He couldn't imagine why something like this would be inside a trial.

"Fellow cultivators... Please, help me." A voice sounded from the center of the chamber.

Everyone's hands flew to their weapons.

"Who's there?!" Narcha cried.

"I'm here, fellow cultivators," the voice responded. "Don't be alarmed."

The central platform shimmered, and a translucent figure appeared out of thin air.

Narcha took a step back. "A g-ghost?!"

CHAPTER 4

DISEMBODIED SOUL

THE FIGURE FINISHED TAKING SHAPE—AN old man sporting a short beard and long white hair reaching to his knees. He wore a black robe that covered the entirety of his body as he floated in the air.

The old man smiled at them. "I wouldn't call myself a ghost, fellow cultivator. I am simply a soul that hasn't been allowed to move on to the afterlife."

His voice was almost magical, and he spoke with such serenity that the startled group calmed down almost instantly. But it wasn't enough for them to drop their guard.

I can't feel his presence.

Red wasn't sure what that meant.

Eiwin was the first one to regain her composure. "Might I ask what this esteemed elder is doing in this place?"

The spirit shook his head with a sad smile. "Must you ask questions that you already know the answer to? I have been imprisoned in this place by the creator of this mausoleum."

"Don't talk to him, Eiwin!" Narcha threw her hand on her companion's shoulder in a show of courage. "He's a ghost! He'll try to trick you with his words!"

"I understand why you would think so, but I can guarantee you I am not a ghost," the elder said. "Ghosts are creatures corrupted by undead forces,

17

and they have both their appearance and personality distorted during their transformation."

She gnashed her teeth. "Bullshit! Even if that's the case, there are plenty of intelligent ghosts that can change their appearance!"

The old man continued to smile. "You're from the barbarian tribes, aren't you? They have always been superstitious when it comes to matters of the soul."

His words upset Narcha even more. "What do you mean by that?!"

"It's a simple difference. Once a cultivator reaches a certain level, their soul can remain in the mortal world for long periods of time without a body, unlike a mortal soul which dissipates mere moments after death. Of course, a disembodied soul can do little without a body, and it will eventually also dissipate and enter the Nether Realm, but it may still be kept alive by some special means..."

"And you're saying this is what has kept you alive here?" Eiwin asked.

He nodded. "I'm imprisoned in a formation that was especially designed to keep my soul from dissipating—to torture me. It's the only reason why I'm still alive."

"You don't look like you're being tortured," Reinhart said.

"I'm only putting on a brave face in front of my juniors. In truth, every moment spent inside this prison is a living hell..."

It was hard to match his grim words with his composed appearance.

"Why are you imprisoned here?" Red asked. His eyes were examining the rest of the chamber.

The smile disappeared from the old man's face as he looked at his surroundings. "I was killed by the man who built this place. He was a demonic cultivator who killed my countrymen and fellow Sect members. He imprisoned me in the middle of their graves as a punishment for my failure..." He trailed off, eyes scanning over each and every grave. "... Every single moment I'm inside this place, my soul is tortured by the invisible flames of this formation and by the monuments of my defeat—their graves."

Reinhart laughed. "Weren't you smiling a minute ago? Don't seem like someone who's saddened by the death of all their friends."

The old man turned to him and grinned again. "I had a long time to mourn them. I am saddened by their deaths, but I know they died fighting for everything they believed in. We all knew this was the most likely outcome in the end, when we decided to fight against that fiend."

While the spirit talked, Red walked up to some of the nameplates.

Ealdwulf Thane - 45 - a husband, a father, and a son. Burned alive.

Annel Evet - 37 - a wife, a mother, and a daughter. Burned alive.

Gylew Alard - 7 - a son. Burned alive.

This common theme didn't change even as he read nameplates by the dozen.

"Might I ask what Sect you are from, elder?" Eiwin asked.

"I'm from the Hidden Flame Sect," the old man said. "My name is Loran, but they called me Purifying Flame."

These words piqued Red's interest even as he continued to read.

Eiwin frowned. "I've never heard of you."

"That doesn't surprise me. I'm certain the fiend destroyed any traces of me and our Sect after my death."

"Who's this fiend you're talking about?" Reinhart asked.

"They called him the Dread Viper. He was a demonic cultivator who shook the world and made every Sect cower in fear."

"Dread Viper?" Narcha scoffed. "If this guy was such a big deal, why have we never heard about him?"

It was the old man's turn to be surprised. "You've never heard the name?"

Eiwin shook her head. "Neither your Sect nor this so-called Dread Viper have ever come up in any history books I've read."

He sighed. "This can only mean the other Sects directly interfered to wipe any mention of this fiend from history."

"When exactly did this happen?"

"I wouldn't be able to tell you. I have lost any notion of time since I've been imprisoned here. It might have been hundreds of years ago, or maybe even a thousand. It's hard to tell."

He said such outrageous numbers so nonchalantly. Red could barely wrap his head around such long lengths of time.

Reinhart coughed loudly. "This is all very interesting, but you still haven't told us what you want."

"I don't know why we're even listening to him!" Narcha interrupted. "Ghost or not, it's still too dangerous to even interact with him!"

The elder laughed. "I assume we are in a trial for an inheritance ground, correct?"

No one responded, but their silence must have been enough of a confirmation.

"Demonic cultivators have always had a habit of guarding their inheritances with these types of challenges." He sighed again. "Since that is the case, I'll get straight to the point—I want your help in freeing my soul from this formation."

"No way!" Narcha cried.

"Please, listen to my offer before—"

"I said no! This is what ghosts *do*! They lie and trick you!"

"Please, Miss Valt." Eiwin's words held her back. "Let's hear him out."

Narcha's eyes widened. "Are you insane, Eiwin?!"

"Miss Valt." She held her gaze. "Please, trust me."

Something in her eyes inspired a change in Narcha. She clenched her teeth in anger, but still fell silent.

After getting her companion's approval, Eiwin looked back at the old man. "I also happen to know that one way for a disembodied soul to come back to life is to possess another body. Isn't that right, elder?"

He grinned at her. "You are very smart. That is indeed the case, but it's hardly a solution. One's soul is made for one's body, and the chance to find another body compatible with it is very low. Even if a lost soul does possess anyone, there would be a myriad of problems to deal with that would eventually lead to their eventual death."

"But it would still be better than the situation you find yourself in, wouldn't it?"

"You're correct. However, my soul has long since passed its time. Once the formation is destroyed, the forces keeping me together will cease to be and I will be allowed to pass on to the afterlife."

"And what do we gain from that?" Reinhart asked.

"I could inform you of the location of my Sect's hidden treasury."

"Hidden treasury?" The knight frowned. "Who knows how long it's been since your Sect was destroyed? What makes you think it's still there?"

"The location of our hidden treasury was only ever known to two people —our Sect Master and the Grand Elder. Both of whom happened to be killed by that fiend, and one of whom is right in front of you. It was kept in a pocket dimension that only we knew how to access, so even if anyone else were aware of its existence, they simply wouldn't be able to reach it. The treasury contains the most valuable items our Sect accumulated over hundreds of years, and they are worth more than any inheritance this fiend could ever offer you."

"Those sure are some fancy words," Reinhart said dryly. "Still, you're just giving us an empty promise. Seems hardly worth it for your soul's salvation."

"I also have my knowledge to offer. I was the Grand Elder of our Sect, and one of its most powerful members. The techniques and secrets I know are invaluable to cultivators like you. Even if they are not of any use to you right now, merely selling some of this knowledge could provide you with enough riches to propel your cultivation forward for decades to come. Breaking into the Spirit Core Realm would be just a matter of time, and even the Spiritual Awakening Realm wouldn't be too far off."

Red had to assume the Spiritual Awakening Realm was the fourth realm of cultivation. Judging by his companions' expressions, they were also hearing about it for the first time.

Those words finally caught Reinhart's attention. "Go ahead, then, tell us some of that knowledge."

The elder laughed. "Do you think I'm stupid, child? First, you need to agree to help me."

"Sure, sure." The knight nodded. "Whatever you say—we'll help you!"

Narcha seemed about to protest, but Eiwin held her back again.

The old man shook his head. "Your word alone won't do."

Reinhart furrowed his brow. "What else do you want, then?"

"I need you to sign a contract."

At those words, Reinhart hesitated. "What kind of contract?"

"A blood contract," the old man said. "Haven't you heard of that? It's a technique cultivators use to make sure there is no treachery of any sort in their business dealings."

Reinhart didn't respond, falling into pensive silence.

The elder looked pleased as ever. "You needn't worry about any treachery on my part. I'll make sure the terms are clear so as to leave no room for doubt. I trust that won't be of any issue to you, right?"

The knight still didn't respond.

Frowning at his silence, the elder looked over at the others. "I understand your distrust, but I can assure you that I—"

"Why do all the nameplates of these graves say they died by being burned alive?" Red interjected.

Narcha and Eiwin turned to him in surprise. They had been so absorbed in the discussion that they hadn't attempted to read the nameplates, and this new information gave them another reason to be suspicious.

Reinhart dropped the act. He smirked back at the elder, all pretense of an internal struggle over whether or not to trust this spirit disappearing from his face.

The elder looked over at Red with a sad smile. "This is the way that fiend found to taunt me even after death—by burning all of our Sect members to ash."

Red frowned. "This seems strange, though. I thought cultivators at your level lived up to hundreds of years, but none of the ages on these nameplates seem to be older than a hundred years."

The old man's face grew hard. "There are hundreds of my compatriots buried here. A few of them would be over that age, of course."

Reinhart laughed. "So I suppose if we search long enough, we'll eventually find some of those dinosaurs' graves, will we?"

The elder fell into silence. The air surrounding him changed, and a few seconds later, Red could have sworn he was looking at an entirely different person. He emanated a dangerous pressure rivaling that of the colossal serpent.

"You insects should consider your next few words very carefully," he said. "Just because I'm in this formation doesn't mean you're safe from me."

CHAPTER 5
A TROUBLING REVELATION

ALTHOUGH THE PRESSURE the old man emitted was strong, Red didn't feel the same sense of danger as from the snake. His companions were likewise shifting on their feet under the pressure, but mostly unbothered by the threatening display.

Eiwin looked at Red and nodded, as if to reassure him. She then glared at the old man. "If you can hurt us, why bother asking for our help?"

The elder smiled. This time the expression looked deranged. "If I kill you, who is going to free me? Of course, if I know you are going to leave without helping me, then I won't hesitate to attack."

"What about these people?" She pointed at the surrounding crypts. "Did you kill them?"

The old man scoffed. "How would I know? I never bothered to commit to memory the name of every cultivator I killed, much less mere mortals."

Eiwin narrowed her eyes. "Don't you feel any remorse for it?"

He laughed. "Remorse? Why would I? The path of a cultivator is carved into a mountain of corpses—if I had stopped to cry over them, I would never have reached the level I did."

"Perhaps—but you wouldn't have ended up here either, would you?"

Her words silenced him.

"Is anything you told us true?" Red asked. "Were you really a member of a Sect?"

The old man frowned. "I would never lie about that, brat. My Sect was one of the most powerful in my era, and I was leading it towards greatness."

"If you were so powerful," Reinhart said, grinning, "how did you end up being destroyed?"

The elder's expression twisted in anger. "I've had enough of your questions! Either you help me or your lives will be forfeit!"

His voice boomed over the crypt, echoing around its walls.

Eiwin seemed unshaken. "You cannot harm us, lost soul. You put on a confident front, but your actions speak louder than your words. You are desperate. You are not in control, and you will remain here to pay for the sins you've committed."

"Do you know who I am, you insignificant insect?!" His voice grew even louder. "My name inspired fear and respect in the hearts of mortals like you! People lined up at my gate to pay their respects! I ruled this world!"

She turned to her companions. "We should move."

Narcha, who had been uncharacteristically quiet, nodded in response. Even Reinhart sighed and offered his silent agreement. Red kept watching the raging spirit, noticing he never stepped past the central circle of the room.

The elder stared at the group with increasing madness in his eyes. "Where are you going? Do you hear me? If you turn your backs to me, all of you will pay!"

Eiwin ignored him, and immediately moved towards another corridor. The others followed.

"You bastards! Idiots! If I ever get out of here, all of you are going to pay!"

No one responded.

The elder's anger was replaced by desperation. "I wasn't lying about my treasury, you know? If you let me out, I can take you there!"

Still no response.

"What I can offer you is more valuable than anything that fiend could possibly give you! I can take you on as my disciples! We can restore my Sect together!"

The group finally reached the threshold.

Once the old man realized his pleas were falling on deaf ears, he gave up. "You do not know what you are doing... I admit I was never a good person, but the master of this place was much, much worse."

His words finally gave them some pause. Narcha stopped walking and turned around to stare at the old man.

He brightened at the attention. "I wasn't lying about his name earlier, either. The Dread Viper. He was a devilish cultivator, and not only that, but he was the most hated man in the world."

Narcha snorted. "You expect us to take your word on other people's morals?"

"Miss Valt..." Eiwin looked crestfallen.

The elder laughed. "You may think what you want from my words. The Dread Viper made an enemy of the entire cultivation world—so much so that according to you, they wiped any mention of him from history. Yet do you think that he has been forgotten? The damage he caused, the people he killed—I wasn't there to see the end of it all, but I can assure you that is something the Sects will never forget... Tell me, is the Crystal Sky Sect still alive?"

Narcha's frown deepened.

This was all the confirmation he needed. "Haha, of course they are! That Sect survived all the biggest hurdles humanity has ever faced. From the Beast Wars to the demon invasions and the very Queen of the Dead herself! But do you know at whose hands they suffered their biggest loss?"

This time, it wasn't just Narcha who felt the shock.

The old man laughed. "That's right! They lost to this damned fiend! Tell me, what do you think will happen to you if they ever learn that you came in contact with his inheritance? You are doomed! All of you are doomed!"

Narcha seemed about to talk back before Eiwin put a hand on her shoulder.

The younger woman shook her head. "Miss Valt, let's leave."

The warrior gritted her teeth and nodded.

Soon the group was walking out of the chamber, hearing the old man's maddened laughter grow faint.

Only when they couldn't hear the old man anymore did the whole weight of the interaction dawn on them all.

Reinhart sighed. "Fuck, what an experience! That old man must have been someone really strong in the past to be imprisoned here!"

No one responded, contemplating in silence.

The knight seemed oblivious to that. He looked over at Red. "So do you think he was telling the truth?"

"I don't know. This whole forgotten history seems too convenient of an excuse, since there's no way to verify his claims."

Reinhart smiled. "And yet if he is telling the truth, looking into it might get us killed."

"I guess he wanted us to suffer with the uncertainty, since he couldn't harm us physically," Red replied.

The knight shrugged. "I'm not too worried myself. As long as no one goes snooping around, no one's at risk, are they?"

Red supposed he was right.

"His words were troubling, but there is something else that's bothering me," Eiwin said.

Red stared at her. "Are you wondering why the owner of this trial put something like this here?"

She smiled. "Exactly. If this man is at all who he claims to be, then running the risk of setting him free seems absurd."

Narcha scoffed. "Was there even a way to set him free? I scanned the whole room, and I saw no signs of a formation. Unless it was hidden in the dark or something, I don't know how we would have done it." She looked questioningly over at Red and Reinhart.

Both of them shook their heads, showing they hadn't seen any such thing with their dark vision.

Eiwin nodded. "This still doesn't explain what he was doing here."

"It's a trial, isn't it?" Reinhart asked. "Maybe they were just testing us to see if we were going to release this evil spirit or not."

Narcha snorted in frustration. "You'd have to be stupid to take his words at face value! No one with a brain would ever release that man!"

"You're right," Eiwin said. "So maybe it wasn't about whether or not we would release him, but more about judging our interaction with him."

"That's good and all, but if this really was a test, shouldn't we have a reward for passing it?" Reinhart asked.

She shook her head. "I think we should be thankful we escaped from those birds with our lives for now."

Reinhart grumbled to himself.

The group walked through the corridor for a fair distance, still baffled by the strange spatial properties of this mausoleum. They expected to arrive at the other exit of the building at some point, but instead they came across a small room.

Reinhart's eyes widened at the sight. "Spirit Stones!"

"Wait, what?!" Narcha, blind beyond the torchlight, was surprised. "Don't even think of rushing ahead, you bastard!"

After some arguing, the group entered. It was a small square chamber, no more than five meters across. At the back wall stood a stone desk decorated with unlit candles and all sorts of jewelry, urns, and gold coins. The real treasure was the copious amount of Spirit Stones gathered on top of silver plates.

There were about thirty.

Reinhart laughed. "We're rich!"

Narcha couldn't hide her good spirits either. "We have enough stones to trade for Rog's pill with this!"

Eiwin smiled. "Indeed. But be careful, we don't know if there are any traps in this place."

"Right, right!" Narcha nodded. "Do you sense anything, kid?"

Red shook his head.

The warrior sighed in relief. "There, we're safe!"

Both she and Reinhart went about uncovering the desk and gathering its valuables. It took them no more than two minutes to set everything apart. What they found were thirty-three Spirit Stones, three strange purple arrows, and a large amount of jewelry which, while still valuable, paled in comparison to the Spirit Stones.

"Look, we got some special arrows for you, kid!" Reinhart said.

Red regarded them skeptically. "How do you know they're special?"

"I mean, look at them! They're purple! They have to be special, right?"

He supposed Reinhart had a point. He grabbed an arrow and tested its sharpness. They were made of a slightly coarse metal, and Red couldn't feel any Spiritual Energy flowing through them. In fact, the arrows were no sharper than his common ones, but he still decided to keep them on hand. He knew some magical items had more to them than met the eye, so he could use these in a pinch and hope for an effect or explosion.

After that, the group divided the Spirit Stones four ways, with Reinhart taking nine instead of eight. When all was said and done, Red's group had thirty-six Spirit Stones total, sixteen more than they needed for Rog's pill.

It immediately lightened Narcha and Eiwin's mood.

Now that they were done looting the place, the group found themselves at a dead end, as there were no other passages other than the way they had entered.

Narcha looked around. "So what do we do now? Do we just go back..."

As she trailed off, they all turned around.

The corridor they had just come from had disappeared, and in front of them stood a closed stone door instead. The building had shifted and transformed, with none of them even noticing as it happened.

Reinhart smiled. "Well, I guess that's our cue to leave, right?"

CHAPTER 6
DESERT ENIGMA

REINHART STEPPED up and pushed against the double door. Just like before, though, the gate was too heavy, so Narcha helped him. It cracked open, and the familiar flashes of lightning hit their eyes. Once the gate was fully open, they knew.

They were back outside.

Reinhart smirked. "Well, ain't that a surprise?"

The group filed out. The ground was cracked, and there were dozens of tornadoes traveling in the distance—they were still in the same region. When they looked back toward the room they had just exited, though, the temple had disappeared, and instead a small cube-shaped building stood in its place. They had left through an entirely different building than the one they had entered.

Narcha frowned. "So we got teleported?"

"Makes no difference. We're still in the middle of an endless desert." Reinhart looked up. "At least those birds aren't around anymore."

Narcha didn't seem too happy about that. "It feels like we're being led around rather than exploring on our own."

"Doesn't matter to me as long as we're getting rewards... Wait, that's right!"

"What is it?"

"We forgot to check the crypt drawers!" Reinhart said, his eyes flashing with greed. "What if there was something valuable inside?"

Narcha glared at him. "Didn't you see what happened to that ghost? If we went grave robbing and disturbed those corpses, I bet we would've ended up like him!"

Reinhart sighed. "Who knows? If that guy is really a demonic cultivator, maybe he would've respected us even more if we did it."

She ignored him and turned to the horizon.

"There, that mountain is still there!" She pointed.

Red squinted. "It seems a bit closer."

They had traveled for quite a while before entering the building and, back then, had yet to make any noticeable progress towards the peak in the distance. Yet now after being teleported, they were closer than before.

"Did we get teleported closer because we passed the test?" Narcha wondered.

"This trial may be similar to the labyrinth," Eiwin said. "We may only be capable of making progress by passing through the challenges the trial throws at us."

Narcha frowned. "But isn't that ridiculous? If we didn't have that compass, we would never have found that temple. That's not fair!"

Eiwin seemed thoughtful. "It seems strange, yes. Stumbling upon these disappearing buildings in this enormous desert would normally be a matter of pure luck. However, when you think about it, that compass isn't an item the trial gave us, but something we found on those imperials."

"The imperials seemed to know what these trials were going to be and came prepared," Red added. "Anything else would be too much of a coincidence."

"And how would they know that?" Narcha said. "This is a cultivator's inheritance ground! If people know the challenges in advance, there's no point in making a trial at all!"

Red didn't respond. He recalled what a bandit from earlier told him, that the imperials claimed this was the tomb of one of their ancestors. Reinhart had dismissed it as nothing more than an absurd idea, yet it didn't seem as far-fetched anymore.

Red looked over at Reinhart. The knight, however, just smirked back.

"Is the compass working again?" the man asked. "If it's really so important, we'll need it."

Red shook his head. The object had been completely ordinary since it had pointed them towards the temple.

Reinhart sighed. "I guess we have no choice but to keep walking, then. Watch out for the birds and giant insects burrowing underground this time around!"

No one had any other suggestions, and the group walked towards the mountain at the horizon again.

"Why is this place so fucking empty?!" Narcha's angered words echoed through the desert.

They had been walking for almost an hour already, and they had yet to find anything notable. That mountain didn't seem any closer, either. By now, they were certain they were under some kind of illusion or spatial distortion. Either that, or the mountain was so large and so distant that it would take an unimaginable amount of time to reach it.

In either case, now they had definite proof that just walking towards it wouldn't get them anywhere anytime soon. Unfortunately for them, Red's compass had yet to reveal anything, so they had no other leads.

"We're missing something..." Reinhart said.

"You think?" Narcha glared at him.

He threw his hands up. "Hey, I'm just trying to start a discussion, okay? If we know we're missing something, let's think about it... What exactly are we missing?"

"Maybe we should stop heading towards the mountain and walk in other directions," Narcha said. "Perhaps that's exactly what this trial wants of us, and the only way to go on."

Reinhart seemed skeptical. "That doesn't seem right. What's the lesson in that? To stop heading towards the one obvious goal and look for invisible things in random directions?"

"Who says there needs to be a lesson in this?! Not everything is done for some obscure reason!"

"Please, Miss Valt," Eiwin said. "Mister Reinhart has a point. I doubt the solution is that easy."

Narcha gritted her teeth. "What else are we supposed to do, though? We know walking towards it doesn't work, so the only other option is to walk away!"

Reinhart smiled. "You have a point. But first"—he looked over at Red—"have you managed to make it work?"

"Not yet," he said.

Red hadn't been idling this last hour. He kept examining the compass, hoping to find some hidden mechanism, but to no avail. He assumed that the item might need Spirit Stones to work. This would explain why the imperials had almost no Spirit Stones—they had been using them to power the compass.

However, upon touching the item with a Spirit Stone, nothing had happened. Red tried it many ways, but no matter which part of the compass he touched, nothing seemed to happen. If the item could absorb the Spiritual Energy from the stones, it wasn't by contact.

When he thought about it further, it made sense that this method wouldn't work. After all, wouldn't it be very inconvenient if your magical item just so happened to absorb the Spiritual Energy of anything it touched? What if it made all your other magical belongings useless in the process? It would be a terrible design flaw.

Unfortunately for Red, it meant he couldn't get the compass working.

The news didn't surprise Reinhart, but he still looked disappointed. "I was hoping you'd be able to work a miracle, kid."

Red frowned. "I know nothing about magical items."

"Maybe you should learn about them when you return—could be useful. In the meantime, do you have any other brilliant ideas about how we should proceed?"

"If what Eiwin said earlier is true and we need to find these invisible buildings to proceed, then there must be a way to find them other than just hoping to stumble on one. I doubt the creator of this place would design it in such a way that you would need to rely on an external item to succeed."

"Then what do you suggest, kid?" Narcha asked. "There's nothing around us! Nothing but dust and those damn tornadoes!" She waved her hand, punctuating her words.

Her complaint, however, gave Red some pause. An idea struck him.

"The tornadoes," he said. "They're the answer."

"What do you mean by that?"

"It's the only thing we haven't explored," Red said. "If we want to proceed, we must face them directly."

Eiwin and Reinhart's eyes shone with realization.

Narcha, however, looked at the boy as if he were insane. "Are you out of your mind? Those things will rip us apart! We'll die!"

Red responded with a question of his own. "When you entered this place, did you see a sentence written on a wall?"

She nodded. "There was something like that."

"Do you remember what it said?"

"Do I remember it?" Narcha fell silent in deep thought. A few seconds later, though, she had the same realization. "You mean...?"

Red nodded. "Only he who knows death as a friend may go further."

She hesitated. "Isn't that too much, though? I mean, how do we know this is what he meant by that sentence?"

"We'll never know for sure, but if you consider the labyrinth trial, it makes sense," he said. "We tried to avoid the rooms with the monsters back then and focus on finding our way out. However, we ended up getting lost, and only after we decided to fight against the monsters did the true path reveal itself. Then there's also the giant snake, which we had to pass without faltering."

His words further convinced Narcha. Still, she looked troubled. "This is too dangerous."

Reinhart laughed. "You just sneaked past that giant snake! What could be more dangerous than that?"

"That's because back then, we knew that was what we needed to do!" Narcha snapped. "Right now, we are taking a shot in the dark! If we're wrong about this, we'll die!"

"How about this, then?" Reinhart pointed at himself. "I'll go first, since you're too scared."

"Who said I'm scared, you bastard!" she growled.

Reinhart smirked. "If that's the case, do you want to go first?"

Narcha paused, seriously considering his suggestion.

But Red interjected. "You should go first, Reinhart. Since you still have your defensive talismans, you can survive the tornado if something goes wrong."

Narcha looked shocked. "You still have more defensive talismans?"

Reinhart didn't reply, instead looking at Red, his smile twitching. "You're right, kid. I should go first, just in case."

Red nodded. "Since we have that settled, we should get going."

He looked around, spotting the closest tornado well over a kilometer away. The spinning funnel of dust and wind extended high above, merging into the clouds.

A monument to the destructive power of nature.

And they were headed right towards it.

CHAPTER 7

STORM CHASERS

It took them no more than a few minutes to approach the twister. They still had a considerable distance to reach it, but about fifty meters out, the winds picked up and grains of dust peppered their skin.

Reinhart stared at the tornado, looking troubled. "Suddenly I don't feel too confident about this idea."

Narcha scoffed. "What's the issue? Didn't you sneak by that snake already? What's there to fear about a little tornado?"

He grinned at Red. "How exactly are you going to be able to tell whether this plan succeeds? I mean, if I get sucked into that thing, will you even be able to see what happens to me?"

Red frowned in thought. "I don't know for certain. If I'm correct, then once we're close enough to the tornado, it'll draw us in and we'll be teleported, so it would be best to see how close we can get before the winds grow too strong."

The tornadoes themselves weren't that wide, so Red hoped he could get close enough to still detect Reinhart with his crimson sense. He wouldn't find out until they tried it.

Reinhart nodded. "Then let's not delay any longer."

The man led the charge, a talisman in his hand. Red guessed this must have been one of the few remaining talismans he had received from trading with the hawk spirit.

Thirty meters out, the winds hit harder. They pushed Red back as he walked forward, the gales blowing against his side making it hard to breathe, the dust blocking his view. The others weren't as affected by the strong winds, but clearly it wore on them all as they neared the spinning monstrosity.

Narcha looked at Red, shielding her eyes. "Is this close enough?" She had to shout to be heard over the shrill sounds of the wind.

Red shook his head. "Let's go closer!"

It was hard to tell how distant they were from the actual tornado, especially as the twister blended with its surroundings in his vision. Plus, the tornado never stayed still, and they struggled to keep up with it.

The group followed Red's command and continued to push forward. Soon enough, even Narcha and the others struggled against the pressure of the wind. Eiwin grabbed onto Red's arm so he wouldn't be blown away.

"This... do!" Reinhart said.

Red couldn't hear his voice anymore over the wind, but he'd heard what he needed to hear.

Red looked over at him and nodded.

Reinhart stared straight ahead and clenched his teeth. "... fucking... insane!"

The last traces of hesitation fell from his face. The talisman in his hand started to glow, and he stepped forward.

Red saw the barrier forming around his body as he struggled to maintain his balance against the gale. Soon enough, Reinhart's figure was swallowed by the dust at the tornado's base and disappeared.

Red then focused on the knight's fluctuation with his crimson sense, using its strength and direction to gauge his distance. Though he had expected it, Red was still amazed as he sensed Reinhart's presence lifting itself from the ground and away from him.

Then, a few seconds later, his presence completely disappeared.

That fast?

Red wasn't sure whether the fluctuation had simply left his detection range or Reinhart had been teleported like he'd guessed. To be safe, he decided to remain close to the tornado, as he expected that if Reinhart was floating around the twister, he would eventually make another pass above his head and be detected by his crimson sense.

That didn't happen, though, even after almost a minute had passed. Red was still uncertain, but he decided it was best to retreat for now.

He pulled at Eiwin's sleeve, motioning with his head. She understood, and likewise informed Narcha with a nudge of her feet.

Soon enough, the group had distanced itself from the tornado.

Narcha frowned at the column of spinning dust. "Do you guys see anything?"

Eiwin shook her head. "There's no sign of him."

Not even Red with his dark vision could spot Reinhart. Either he was concealed by the tornado's dust, or he had been blown very far away. The latter scenario didn't seem likely, as only flatland surrounded them and they should have spotted him from miles away.

Narcha turned to Red. "Do you think he was teleported?"

He nodded. "Still, I'd rather wait and see if anything else happens."

And so they waited. After five minutes passed, they were certain that Reinhart wasn't coming out of the tornado.

"We should go," Red finally said.

Narcha stood up. "I'll lead the way."

"Wait!" Eiwin held her back. "We need to do something first."

She took a length of rope from her bag before throwing it towards Red and Narcha.

Red frowned. "You want us to tie ourselves together?"

"It's for the best," Eiwin said. "That way, if anything goes wrong, we'll still be together."

If anything were to go wrong, he wasn't certain they would survive even with this rope. Still, he wouldn't complain, considering his weight meant he was the one most likely to be affected by the strong winds.

Narcha had no complaints either, and soon they were all tied up together by their waists, with Red being the middle link.

"Try to cover yourselves," Narcha said. "There might be a lot of detritus closer to the tornado."

Unfortunately, they didn't have a defensive talisman like Reinhart, so they could only rely on their armor to protect them.

Narcha led the way, and soon the group had caught up to the tornado again. The winds picked up, blowing in their faces and threatening to take Red off his feet. Eiwin held his arm once more, though, and soon they were as close to the heart of the twister as before.

This time they didn't stop. Narcha forged ahead, one step at a time, fighting against the tormenting winds to keep her balance. Red had no such luck and was lifted up again and again, only the rope and Eiwin's grip keeping him from being swept away.

A few steps further and they reached the base of the tornado. The dust covered their vision, and Red couldn't see anything else. He jerked fully into the air. Eiwin had also lost her fight against the winds.

The rope tying them to Narcha, the only thing keeping them from flying off, was yanked taut. Although Red couldn't see her, he knew she was doing her best to keep her balance. But against the might of the tornado, there was nothing a simple cultivator could do.

He lurched again, a signal that Narcha had lost her balance too. He was sent adrift along the strong winds, forces he could do nothing to resist. A terrible feeling of helplessness attacked him.

He had no grasp on direction, and all of his senses were overwhelmed. Still, Red focused on keeping his breathing steady.

Every breath that he drew was a struggle, but worse was the pounding, unending dust and debris that, at these speeds, felt like a hail of pebbles. His uniform deflected most of the impact, but it wouldn't hold out. The force increased with every second.

Red didn't know how much time had passed when suddenly the wind pressure around him plummeted. Before he could even process what was happening, he hit the ground with a thud.

The shrill sound of the tornado disappeared, along with the dust shrouding his view and pelting his body. As Red collected himself, he heard the groans of his companions by his side.

A familiar voice greeted them. "You're finally here! I really thought you'd decided to abandon me back there."

Red looked up and saw Reinhart sitting against a wall, regarding them cheerfully.

Wait, a wall?

They were inside now?

Reinhart laughed. "You were right, kid! The tornado was the answer after all!"

Narcha stood up, cradling her head. There was a trickle of blood running down her temple. "Yeah, good job, kid... Just hope we don't have to do that again."

Eiwin shot to her feet. "Miss Valt! Are you alright?!"

She shrugged. "This is nothing. I think a big rock hit me inside that tornado... Else we could've made it even further in."

Red shook his head. "I'm not sure how that would have helped."

Narcha ignored him and looked around. "So, we're in another one of those invisible buildings?"

Reinhart nodded. "I haven't explored too far, but this one seems a bit different."

Red knew what he meant. This place was in ruins. Cracked walls, fallen debris, dust everywhere. He could even see hints of a storm outside through the cracked ceiling.

The room seemed to be made of a similar black rock as the mausoleum, and just like that place, it lacked any decoration or notable details. The only path was a long, narrow corridor on the other side of the room.

Narcha frowned. "Great. More corridors..."

"I'd wager it's better than being lost out there." Reinhart rose, patting the dust off his clothes. "So, should we get going?"

"Sure. No point in waiting around."

"Wait!" Eiwin held Narcha back. "Are you sure, Miss Valt? I know you might not think the injury is anything serious, but blows to the head can't be overlooked, even in cultivators."

Red could understand her worry. A hit to the head from tornado-propelled rock would have killed any normal person, and he doubted even someone like Narcha could ignore it.

She shook her head in annoyance. "I already told you I'm fine. Besides, we don't have time to wait, do we? We have to catch up with those bastards!"

Eiwin sighed. "Fine. Just don't push yourself if you feel anything's wrong."

Soon the group was walking through the dark corridor with Reinhart leading the way. They had decided not to use torches here because the lightning pouring through the cracks overhead provided some illumination.

Red half expected this corridor to stretch for a long while, considering the way the creator of this trial seemed to enjoy warping space. To his surprise, though, that didn't happen.

Instead, they came upon another room in less than a minute. This chamber was around thirty meters wide, and hundreds of meters long. Possibly even more than that, as Red couldn't see the wall at the other end.

Granted, there were also many obstacles in his way. Ruined pillars lined one side of the room, and large boulders littered the long room. But none of this stood out.

There was a monster in their way. A giant lizard resting by one of the pillars.

No, it's not just one.

There were countless lizards spread throughout. In fact, the more Red looked, the more monsters he spotted, hidden in crevices and behind cover.

Ten seconds later, he'd counted dozens.

And all of them, without exception, were staying eerily still.

CHAPTER 8
REPTILE MINEFIELD

RED THOUGHT at first that these lizards were all dead, as they didn't even blink. Upon closer observation, however, he could see their midsections rising and falling as they breathed. They were anything but dead.

These lizards were even larger than the ones Red had fought earlier. They were well over five meters long from head to tail, covered in gray scales, with a crest running down the back. Unlike their smaller siblings, they were bulkier, with a large midsection that exuded a level of brute strength. Their claws, close to shortswords in size, looked extremely sharp, and the scratch marks around the room were a testament to that.

What really stood out were their white, blank eyes. He guessed this pointed to blindness, but he wouldn't make a premature judgment.

Red and his companions all stood stock-still, observing.

"How many do you two see?" Narcha asked in a low voice.

Reinhart shook his head. "Too many to fight."

Red didn't respond, instead taking a few more careful steps forward so he could bring them into his crimson sense detection range. It didn't take long before he felt a fluctuation from one of the lizards.

He winced. "There's something weird about them."

"What do you mean?" Narcha asked.

"I... don't know how to explain it. They don't feel like normal monsters, though."

Just like humans, monsters had a vibrant presence in his crimson sense, and each individual person and creature had their own peculiarities. Undead, on the other hand, conveyed a strange stillness.

These lizards' fluctuations were similar to an undead's, but in no other way did they seem like zombies. This revelation left Red stumped.

"Is this something to be worried about?" Reinhart asked.

"I don't know."

The man looked over at Eiwin. "Any idea about these monsters?"

Eiwin gave him a helpless smile. "Please, don't take me for a monster expert. All I can tell you is that they're probably from the Great Serpent Canyon."

Reinhart grunted in disappointment. "So, what do we do?"

Narcha glared at him. "We should be asking you. You're the one who can see in the dark. What does the rest of the room look like?"

He gave the room another look and relayed everything he could see.

"Is there a way to sneak through without a fight?" she asked.

"Without them noticing? Seems almost impossible. They're everywhere."

"They seem to be blind, though," Red pointed out.

"Doesn't mean we can sneak by them. Blind animals tend to develop their other senses even more. They might spot us just by smell or sound."

Narcha frowned. "So what you're saying is, there's no other way?"

Reinhart nodded. "Seems to be the case."

"But you just said there are too many to fight."

He shrugged, making Narcha even angrier.

"There's no need to jump to conclusions yet," Eiwin said. "Every trial we've gone through thus far has always had a solution, so why would this one be any different?"

"We could test their senses," Red suggested. "They might not be as developed as we think."

Eiwin grinned. "It's a good idea." She picked up a small rock off the ground. "Be ready if anything happens."

Everyone nodded. Then she leaned back and threw it.

The pebble flew through the air like a bolt, shattering against a pillar. Almost immediately, the lizards moved. At first, just the creatures close to the stone sprang into action, blindly charging towards the source of the noise. However, just like a ripple traveling through a pond, this agitation spread to the surrounding creatures, and soon enough, the entire room was shifting.

For such large creatures, they moved quickly on their four legs. To make matters even stranger, none of them made a single sound—all Red could hear were their claws scratching against the stone floor. The creatures bumped into each other, even climbing over bodies in alarm.

This agitation didn't last for more than ten seconds. One by one the creatures calmed down, realizing there were no intruders, and they once more fell still.

Their near-silent movement, their sudden burst of speed, and how quickly they stopped again—the scene was extremely eerie for Red. These creatures didn't behave like any he'd ever seen before, and his companions shared his discomfort.

"I guess you were right," Reinhart said. "There is something weird about them."

Red nodded. "I think we can also confirm they're blind."

"They do seem to be sensitive to noise, but it doesn't approach the level of super hearing," Eiwin said. "That rock sound should have reached pretty far, but at first only the lizards near it reacted."

"So they're blind and their hearing isn't even that good?" Narcha said. "This doesn't seem right. What about their sense of smell?"

"We can test that too." Eiwin took out a piece of dried meat. The smell of the food wasn't strong, but it was distinct. If a normal human could smell it from only a few meters away, so would a below-average monster.

She leaned back and threw the sizeable piece of meat towards one of the lizards. This time, she didn't throw for power or distance. The dried meat slid across the ground, landing not too far from one of the closest lizards. They waited for a reaction.

Even after a minute had passed, the lizard showed no sign of having smelled the meat. This left the group puzzled.

Reinhart frowned. "So they can't smell very well either?"

"Either that, or they have no interest in the meat," Red said.

"That seems strange for a monster."

"We know by now this is not a normal type of monster," Eiwin said. "It might have been specially prepared for this trial. In any case, this is favorable for us."

"So you want to sneak through?" Reinhart asked.

"Indeed. If combat is not an option, this seems to be the only way to pass through the chamber."

"Are you sure about this?" Narcha said. "If we get caught up in the middle of those monsters, we'll have nowhere to retreat."

Eiwin gave her a comforting smile. "We already have nowhere to retreat, Miss Valt."

Narcha winced, looking around. "We could try breaking the walls. This place doesn't look that sturdy."

"First thing I tried when I got here," Reinhart said. "Made some scratches on the stones, but it would probably take a long while to get one of these walls down, even with your strength."

She sighed in defeat. "I guess sneaking through it is, then."

"There is still a problem, though," Reinhart added. "Even if these creatures don't have good hearing, we'll still be moving right by them. There's a lot of dust and pebbles in the ground, so it's likely they'll be able to hear our steps."

Red had an idea. "We can use the thunder as cover. As long as it's loud enough, it should mask the sound of our steps."

Reinhart regarded him with skepticism. "And if we have no thunder? Are we just supposed to wait in the middle of those lizards without moving a muscle?"

"As long as you don't panic, it should be fine."

Reinhart smiled. "You really are insane."

It was decided that Red would lead the party, with Reinhart and the rest right behind him. His detection abilities would be of extreme importance, since they would need to determine their route in advance, and only he could tell whether creatures were hiding behind giant rocks or pillars.

Sneaking in silence, they would lose most of their power to communicate. While Red and Reinhart could see gestures and read lips, to *send* a message, Red would have to wait for a burst of thunder.

Narcha had reservations about Red showing his back to Reinhart, but they had no better options. Not to mention, if the man tried something, he would probably die as well.

Red took the first few steps towards the lizards, already having a mental image of his route in mind. Thankfully, they all remained still, so he wouldn't need to change his course.

He approached the monster minefield with quiet and measured steps, prepared for all their testing to be for naught and for the beasts to react as soon as they came close. It didn't happen, though, and the lizards were oblivious to their presence.

Once he was within twenty meters of the creatures, he stopped in his tracks and looked back at his companions. The room was dark between the flashes of lightning, but not impenetrable. He pointed up to show he was waiting for the thunder.

The others nodded, and they waited in absolute silence. It took fifteen seconds before a peal of thunder rolled in, and Red took a few quick steps towards the lizards, stopping five meters away.

His companions followed his steps perfectly, advancing and stopping with him. Not that Red expected anything less from three seasoned cultivators.

The next thunderclap came faster, and he pushed forward, now completely in the lizards' midst. In fact, one of the creatures was no farther than three meters from him. This close, Red was afraid to even breathe too loudly. But as he stood frozen, no lizards were alerted, and soon enough the next thunderbolt came, urging them on.

The entire process went smoothly over the course of the next ten minutes. Red had to stop and turn around when they came upon a dead end or when too many monsters blocked their path forward, but these were hardly nuisances. Even when they had to step over a tail, the creatures showed no reaction.

It was slow going, but it was safe and steady, and they made significant progress.

Red could even see the other end of the long room, and an exit seemed to lead into another corridor. He prepared for the next peal of thunder, and once the rumbling sound came, he advanced. But he had taken only a few steps forward when he felt something with his crimson sense.

He froze, raising his hand to halt his companions. They came to a quick stop, staring at Red in confusion.

What is it? Narcha mouthed the words to him.

Red only frowned as he focused on a new fluctuation. It stood out amidst the sea of strange lizard fluctuations, as it seemed to belong to a regular monster. It wasn't yet at the Lesser Ring Realm, but its presence gave him a bad feeling.

What was it doing amid these strange creatures? Could it sense them?

When he looked around, all he saw were the giant gray lizards and ruined stones, and no sign of anything out of the ordinary. If there was another creature here, it was hidden.

Red focused on the source of the fluctuation, hoping to spot the hiding place of this creature before it spotted him. There was a lizard there, right by the side of a pillar—a blind spot for the group where another monster might be hidden.

The moment Red considered how to tell his companions about this, he noticed movement out of the corner of his eye. He squinted, eyes glued to the spot with that lizard and pillar. Nothing strange was there at that moment, but he kept his gaze steady, ready to catch what had moved.

Then it happened again, and this time Red spotted it.

The lizard had blinked.

This wasn't cause for alarm in any normal animal. Yet in the sea of dozens of lizards, this was the only one Red had seen blink.

And he felt the monster's pupil-less eyes staring right at him.

CHAPTER 9

DISGUISED

RED SHOOK OFF HIS SURPRISE, looking away from the monster.

Did it notice me?

He wasn't sure. This lizard seemed blind, like all of its brethren, but his crimson sense told him he was being observed, and he knew it wouldn't lie to him. There was something off about this creature.

His companions weren't saying anything, but he could feel their questioning gazes on the back of his head. He faced them, wondering how to explain what he had detected with nothing but the big gestures his whole group could see.

Thankfully, his posture told them something wasn't right.

What is it? Narcha mouthed the words again.

Red pointed toward the strange lizard. His companions made to look at it, but he held his hand up to stop them.

They all looked back at him, even more confused than before.

Red pointed at the lizard again, then at his eyes, and then to himself. He repeated the same motions a few times until he saw understanding dawn on their faces. He was trying to say that the lizard could see them, and it seemed they understood.

Narcha frowned and mouthed, *Are you sure?*

Red hesitated. Still, he nodded. He was almost certain.

He wasn't sure by any means, but it was better to be safe than sorry. There was no way to explain to them what exactly he had seen.

His warning worked, worry settling on his companions' faces. Reinhart pointed back the way they'd come with a questioning gaze.

Neither Narcha nor Eiwin responded. Instead, they looked to Red.

After a few seconds of thought, Red shook his head. There was no point in retreating, since this was the only way forward. They had to go through the lizards, and they had gone too far to turn around now.

Red made a circling motion with his hand, showing his intention to avoid the area with the strange lizard. The others nodded, and they prepared to move on.

Red had already mapped an alternative route through the ruined room and frozen monsters, and he did not look at the lizard again, afraid the creature might detect his eyes. Thunder came rolling in again, and the group moved.

Red tried to stay as far away from the blinking lizard as possible, but the room was still only thirty meters wide. He would need to pass relatively close to the monster, but he planned to use the ruined pillars as cover, which this place had in abundance.

As he came closer, he monitored the fluctuation with his crimson sense and watched for any movements out of the corner of his eye. To his surprise, nothing happened, and as the next bout of thunder rumbled from above, they passed through the lizard's vicinity with no fanfare.

Was I mistaken?

Perhaps there was indeed something special about that lizard, but it might not involve having any better senses than its brethren. Still, Red maintained his vigilance as they got ever so close to the other end of the room.

He waited for the next roll of thunder. A few seconds later, the rumbling arrived, and Red moved, stepping around a few lizards.

The strange fluctuation moved in sync with his steps.

He froze. His companions stopped in time and avoided bumping into each other. Before they could give him any silent questions, Red held his hand up, motioning for them to remain still.

Red focused on the fluctuation. It had stopped moving as soon as the group froze. If Red hadn't been paying attention, he might have missed it amidst the dozens of presences around him, but he had been waiting for something like this to happen.

He turned around, giving a quick glance behind him, but he couldn't spot the lizard among the cover blocking his way and all its identical brethren.

His crimson sense was a powerful ability, yet it also had its limitations. When there were too many fluctuations all around him, they blended together in his consciousness, and he couldn't parse which fluctuation belonged to what. This was exacerbated when all the monsters looked the same. Still, he took a mental note of the positions of all the lizards surrounding them.

Red looked at his companions. He made a wide motion with his hand, miming grabbing his weapon.

Be ready, he mouthed.

Narcha winced, but she knew this wasn't the time for questions.

Half a minute later, the next thunder came, and Red moved. He felt the fluctuation moving along with him, quickly closing the distance between them. He froze where he stood, this time giving ample warning with a hand sign.

I can't hear its steps, he realized.

This wasn't surprising, considering the thunder muffled their hearing as much as it did that of the surrounding lizards.

The fluctuation also stopped moving, and he could sense it was no more than fifteen meters behind them. He turned around to a sea of sleeping creatures. Then he compared this image with the positions he had previously memorized in his head.

Red quickly spotted a creature that shouldn't have been there. It was partially hidden behind the body of another lizard, and if not for having memorized their positions before, he would have missed it. The strange fluctuation was coming from that exact direction, so he was certain he'd found the culprit.

It's not even looking at us.

It was as if the creature were doing its best not to be spotted. This wasn't the type of intelligence Red was used to seeing in monsters, and it made him even more wary. He shifted his gaze away.

What now?

He hesitated. The lizard was stalking them, possibly waiting for the right moment to strike. Yet considering how fast it had moved, Red knew they couldn't outrun it while sneaking either, and if they ignored it, it might take one of them down.

His struggle was obvious to his companions.

Narcha seemed to understand his concern. She pointed at herself and at the ground. *I'll watch our back.*

In the lightning's illumination, Eiwin frowned, but Narcha's resolve made it clear she wasn't putting this up for discussion. The younger woman relented.

Reinhart also had no reason to protest the idea, seeing as it didn't involve putting himself in the way of danger.

With a plan settled, Red shared the general location of the lizard with Narcha through gesture. She nodded, her hand hovering over her saber's hilt.

As the group got ready to move, however, a low groaning sound started to rise in the room.

Anywhere else, it would have been easy to miss, yet it stood out like a sore thumb in the silent chamber.

Red had a bad premonition.

He looked over at the strange lizard. It had raised its head ever so slightly, and the flaps under its neck were growing bigger as it released the strange sound from its mouth.

Red felt the air around the chamber change as all the lizards shifted. Then, all at once, they turned their heads to stare directly at the group with their milky white eyes.

Reinhart gritted his teeth. "Fuck."

Without the need for anyone's prompting, they all ran. The lizards were spurred into action at once, charging straight at the group.

The first lizard closed in, and it was already swinging its claws at Narcha guarding the rear. She barely had time to pull out her saber and block the blow. Sparks flew upon impact.

She prepared to counter, but no sooner had the first lizard attacked than another one stepped over it and clawed at her. Narcha was forced to keep her weapon up to parry yet another blow as they ran.

"I thought they couldn't see!" she screamed.

No one had the time to respond to her.

Eiwin ran ahead. "Red, step back!"

Red didn't complain, letting her take the lead. A lizard was quick to step up to her, sweeping its tail like an enormous whip. Eiwin was just as quick to jump out of the way, and Reinhart used his sword to cut the monster's tail off as it rolled by.

The creature didn't even seem to notice the injury. Curiously, no blood spilled from its wound, and none of the monsters were deterred by the injury. The group didn't have the time to consider this detail. They focused on running away.

"Weave through the pillars!" Red shouted.

The creatures were closing in by the second, and if they stayed out in the open, they would be quickly overwhelmed. Eiwin did as Red suggested.

She dashed behind a pillar, slowing the creatures by forcing them to turn. But it only worked for a moment, and more ran around the obstacle to attack the group.

Eiwin and Reinhart did their best to clear their way forward, but these creatures were not normal monsters. No wounds or lost limbs dissuaded them from attacking their targets, whom they could sense with precision despite their lack of eyesight.

The group halted their progress as they moved themselves into a circle of ruined pillars, focused on keeping the monsters at bay. Clearly, this position was untenable.

"Shit!" A curse came from Narcha.

Red turned and saw a large streak of blood flowing down her shoulder. She was keeping most of the monsters off them, but one had just slashed its huge claws through her shoulder.

Narcha hissed in pain, but didn't falter, using her sword to beat them back. More came forward, though, replacing their incapacitated brethren, climbing over their bodies. The room, narrow and debris-ridden, was the only reason they hadn't been overwhelmed by so many enormous monsters.

Red grimaced. He was doing his best to shoot at the lizards, but his arrows barely affected them.

"Use the talisman!" Reinhart bellowed. "In the pouch on my waist!"

Red rushed toward the knight. The man had abandoned all semblance of skill and was swinging his sword wildly, battering scores of lizards away. Red pulled his pouch off, spilling several items on the ground.

He was quick to spot the right talisman in the midst of the unidentified ones.

He has another shield talisman?

Red didn't have time to confront Reinhart about it. He reached for the talisman and hurried to activate it.

He shouted at his companions. "Close to me!"

They all came closer. Seconds later, a translucent shield formed around the group. The lizards didn't stop their attack, but their claws now scratched at the barrier.

Red knew from experience that it was only a matter of time before the shield was destroyed with so many monsters attacking it. All his companions, even Eiwin, had been wounded in the conflict. A large bloody scratch ran down her arm, though she suffered through her pain in silence.

As they considered their next steps, the lizards froze. All attacks stopped. Then, as one, they started to step back, moving away from the group and their shield before stopping once more and staring at them with their blind eyes.

"What... What are they doing?" Narcha asked in between her heavy breaths.

A lizard stepped forward from its brethren, and Red was quick to recognize its fluctuation. It was the monster that had spotted them.

It walked right up to their shield, seemingly examining the humans hiding behind it.

"What is that..." Narcha trailed off as the monster changed.

Its milky white eyes bulged out of its head, more than doubling in size. Veins popped out of the orbs as they grew, until they suddenly exploded in a shower of blood. Then, beneath the gore of its now-empty eye sockets, something stirred.

Small red tentacles emerged where its eyes had once been, dripping blood and pieces of flesh along their length. Each of the dozens of tentacles moved individually, but they all reached for the translucent barrier.

They slithered across, smearing it with blood, as if searching for an opening. Then the group heard the same low droning that had alerted the lizards to their presence, but this time it wasn't coming from the creature's mouth.

Rather, it was coming from inside its head.

CHAPTER 10

PARASITE

As the droning sound went on, the lizards around the room charged. They threw themselves at the shield while the monster with tentacles in place of its eyes retreated, disappearing in their midst. The barrage of attacks resumed.

"What the fuck was that?!" Narcha cried.

Eiwin frowned. "It must be a parasite! It should be the one controlling these monsters!"

Reinhart looked at her expectantly. "So if we kill it, will they stop attacking us?"

She hesitated. "I don't know, but it's worth a try!"

"But how do we reach it?" Narcha asked, eyes locked on the monsters. "How do we even spot it?! It's hidden in the crowd!"

At this point, the lizards were going berserk. They were even crawling above them as their claws slashed against the invisible barrier, which already showed signs of cracking.

"I can single it out!" Red said.

"You can?!" Narcha asked, turning to Red in surprise.

He nodded. "I can lead you to it, but it's behind a lot of the other lizards. You'll need to clear a path to it!"

She gritted her teeth. "I don't know if we can do that in our state!"

"We can use the pills," Reinhart said.

"That still won't be enough."

More cracks appeared every second.

Eiwin looked at her companions with a resolved expression. "We'll just focus on opening the way! Red, you strike the monster once you spot it. Here." She tossed him an item from her pocket. "Use this."

Red grabbed it—the fireball talisman.

He stared at Eiwin. "The whole place might collapse if we use this."

"I know, but it's the strongest attack we have. If we don't kill this thing in one blow, it might escape. Besides, we don't know if the lizards will stop attacking us once this parasite dies, so this fireball might afford us the chance to escape."

Red nodded, convinced. At that moment, yawning cracks appeared in the shield, the telltale sign of its imminent collapse.

"Eat the pills, quick!" Reinhart urged.

The knight did as much himself, and Narcha and Eiwin weren't far behind. While the effects made their way through their bodies, Red held onto his talisman and located the lizard-parasite's location with his crimson sense.

"It's over there!" Red pointed.

The lizard hadn't moved much since it retreated, and he wondered if this was because of its absolute confidence in its strength. In any case, the monster couldn't have known about the group's abilities, and this was working to their benefit.

Narcha looked at Reinhart and Eiwin. "You two, take my flanks! Red, stay close to my back!" The warrior glared at the lizards on the other side of the barrier. "I'm not waiting until this collapses! We're breaking through right now!"

There was no time to protest before she swung her saber against the inside of the barrier. Her blow was strong enough to shatter it at the point of impact.

The saber passed through the fractured barrier, brutally strong now that she had consumed the Empowerment Pill. Two lizards attacking the shield were cut in half by the sword's path. A few others were knocked back as Narcha struck again, the weapon now serving more as a club than a blade.

"Now!" Narcha roared.

The group dashed forward as Narcha led the way. Lizards poured in from the sides, but Eiwin and Reinhart held them off with quick and precise attacks. If the empowerment was reflected in Narcha's sheer strength, then in Eiwin and Reinhart it took the form of overwhelming speed.

Monster limbs went flying everywhere, but the lizards continued to scramble over the bodies of their incapacitated comrades to strike. Yet the group's path would not be impeded, and they made fast progress mowing down any creatures in their way.

Red was focusing on the lizard-parasite's fluctuation. It was only twenty meters away until he noticed it retreating again. "It's running away!"

"Then kill it quickly!" Narcha shot back.

He thought to ask her how he was supposed to do that, but there was no time to argue. Beyond his crimson sense, he still couldn't spot the parasite amid the dozens of other creatures in the room.

He had an idea, though.

"Stay still!" he said to Narcha. "I'll jump on your shoulders!"

"You're going to what?!" she cried in disbelief as she batted the lizards away.

Red didn't respond. He put a hand on her shoulder and used it as leverage to jump up in a single fluid motion. Then, with his feet settled on Narcha's shoulders and one hand grabbing onto her head for balance, he looked around for the parasite.

Red heard some cursing from beneath, but he tuned it out. He looked in the fluctuation's direction, hoping to spot the retreating beast.

It was the only monster running away from the group while all the others charged at them. Red spotted it easily. He activated his talisman without hesitation.

"Stay still!" he warned Narcha again.

Another wave of curses came at him, but he ignored it. A few seconds later, the talisman was on the verge of activating, glowing with an orange light. The lizard-parasite looked back at Red, as if sensing the sudden disturbance of Spiritual Energy.

Unfortunately for the monster, it was too late.

Red waved the talisman, and a scorching ball of flame materialized out of thin air, hurling toward the monster. The flaming sphere was about the size of an adult's fist, and yet the power packed within it wasn't to be underestimated.

It crashed near the monster, and a shockwave rang through the room.

Red lost balance from Narcha's shoulders and fell back onto the ground. Hot air blasted against his face as a cloud of dust spread through the space.

He heard the crashing of stones, and he could feel the ground rumble as the fragile building collapsed in on itself. Before Red could stand up to find cover, a hand grabbed him, lifting him off the ground.

He couldn't tell who it was, but he let himself be dragged like a sack of potatoes as the person ran. Debris continued to fall all around him, but by this point the person had stopped running, seeming to find some cover.

Only now, after some of the dust subsided, did Red see that the person who had dragged him away was Reinhart. He didn't see any signs of Narcha or Eiwin. Searching for them with his crimson sense, he found they were within twenty meters of him, though in what condition, he couldn't tell.

The collapse of the building stopped a few seconds later, and their vision slowly cleared. A section of the ceiling and nearby sections of wall had collapsed, revealing the desert and stormy sky of the outside world. Much to Red's delight, the lizards had all collapsed too, unmoving. They weren't even breathing this time around.

"Seems your friend was right, kid," Reinhart said, surveying the rubble.

Red nodded, but he didn't let down his guard. For some reason, he could still feel the lizards' strange fluctuations, which shouldn't have been happening if the creatures were truly dead. To his surprise, he could also feel the parasite's presence, although it was severely weakened now.

"It's still not dead," he said.

"Are you sure?" Reinhart looked surprised.

"It's wounded, but still alive."

"Then let's hurry and kill it!" The knight hurried off.

Red followed him. Not too far away, the figures of Narcha and Eiwin revealed themselves from behind a partially collapsed pillar.

"What are you doing?!" Narcha asked the two of them.

"It's still alive!" Red answered.

"Shit!"

Narcha and Eiwin joined behind them without hesitation.

As they approached the center of the explosion, their path was soon blocked by the ruins of the building and the dozens of lizard corpses buried beneath the debris.

The fluctuation stirred.

"It's moving!" Red said.

The group tried to hurry, jumping and climbing over the rubble. Soon enough, they saw the scorch marks of the explosion, as well as the charred remains of those lizards unfortunate enough to be caught in its radius.

"There!" Reinhart pointed.

Something moved from the midst of the ruins. A small red blob of tentacles.

Narcha charged without hesitation. "Come here, you little shit!"

As if comprehending her words, the blob sped up, disappearing within the rubble.

"Fuck!" Narcha looked toward where it had escaped. "Red, where did it go?"

"It's going that way!" Red pointed to the other side of the room.

They all continued to give chase until Red's crimson sense felt the creature go still.

"It stopped moving!" he said. "It's hiding over..."

Red felt something weird with his crimson sense.

"Over where, Red?!" Narcha urged.

He didn't respond, instead looking around. He felt the fluctuations of the supposedly dead lizards stir.

"Something's happening to the lizards!"

There was no need for his warning, as it soon became clear to them all. The eyes of the dead lizards burst, one by one, and out from their now empty eye sockets crawled more red tentacles. There were ten to fifteen tentacles for every lizard, far fewer than the original host, but across every monster in the room, they numbered in the hundreds.

Then they climbed out of their monsters' eyes, and one by one they slithered away like worms. They were all moving in a single direction—toward the parasite they had just been chasing.

"They're trying to merge!" Red realized.

The shock of the situation wore off, and the whole group moved to stop these disembodied tentacles. They stomped, slashed, and tried everything to kill them. For the most part, it worked, as the crushed tentacles spewed out a strange bright-red blood and stopped moving.

However, there were too many of them, and the survivors all moved between the cracks in the ruins and stones to avoid their attacks.

"It's not going to work!" Eiwin shouted. "Focus on the main body!"

Yet the creature was hidden beneath tons of rubble, and not even Narcha could clear it fast enough. They still tried their best, shoving and lifting stones, killing small tentacles along the way before they could join the main body.

It was to no avail.

More tentacles slipped by them, and Red felt something change in the parasite's fluctuation. The creature was getting stronger.

"Move away!" he warned.

The group had learned to trust him, and they all stepped back without hesitation. A few seconds later, the rubble they had been digging through rumbled, then exploded in a shower of dust and rock.

Then it climbed out.

It was the blob of tentacles, but this time much bigger than before, roughly as tall as a human adult, with more and more tentacles joining its mass. Red sensed it had already reached the power of a Lesser Ring Realm creature, and judging by the expressions of his companions, they also felt the pressure it emitted.

The creature hoisted itself up by grabbing onto nearby rock surfaces, then went still. From beneath the ball of slithering appendages, a new body part appeared.

A single, dark human eye, rolling around before settling in place.

It stared directly at Red.

CHAPTER II

PEST CONTROL

For a brief moment, everyone in the group was mesmerized by that eye. A voice snapped them out of it.

"Shoot it!" Narcha screamed at Red.

He took the bow from his back and aimed an arrow at the creature. Yet the eye retracted into the parasite's body before he could shoot.

Red still let loose, but the arrow was swallowed by the mass of tentacles, causing no apparent damage. The creature, aware that it was under attack, moved away from the humans.

"It's running!" Narcha warned the group, chasing after it.

"Wait—" Red, feeling the monster's fluctuation, tried to stop her.

But Narcha was already swinging her saber against the monster's "back." It turned and its body writhed and parted, avoiding her blade by changing its own form. Then several tentacles shot out at Narcha, like arrows released at point-blank range.

Narcha was taken by surprise. She could only turn her own blade to protect her midsection from the appendages. The tentacles clashed with her saber with incredible force, pushing her back. And she couldn't block all of them.

Three spouts of blood shot out of her body as the tentacles pierced her shoulder, arm, and leg. The ones that missed wrapped around her weapon, trying to wrench it from her grip.

Even injured, Narcha acted fast. She struggled to pull herself away by marching backward, sword held as rigidly to her torso as possible, but the appendages hooked into her flesh and stretched along with her. At the same time, the creature tried to drag her closer, and the two of them fell into a tug-of-war.

"Miss Valt!"

Eiwin rushed ahead to help her, but more tentacles shot out in her direction, forcing her back lest she end up in the same situation.

"Red, Reinhart, help her!" Eiwin cried, her eyes searching for a better path.

Red dropped his bow and took out his cleaver, rushing towards Narcha. Reinhart hesitated, but followed with his sword.

The parasite sent even more tentacles to block their way. Red sliced them, but the appendages were slippery, and for every one he cut, two more shot out to keep him at bay. Reinhart didn't seem to fare any better as the monster used clusters of tentacles to hold him off.

Meanwhile, Narcha was doing her best to resist the monster's pull. The two of them seemed to be in a deadlock, neither gaining ground on the other. Still, by Narcha's expression, it was clear her injuries were taking their toll.

She gnashed her teeth, fighting through the pain of the tentacles hooked into her flesh. "You fucking bastard... Let go!"

The monster did not. In fact, even more tentacles wrapped around her saber. Slowly Narcha was dragged towards the blob. But she refused to let go of her weapon, the only thing keeping the appendages from piercing her organs.

Eiwin grew more panicked. "Narcha!"

"Lady, listen to me!" Reinhart called out. "We need to—"

Before he could finish speaking, Eiwin charged ahead. A rush of tentacles came for her, but instead of dodging, she spun around and let them hit her body. They tore at her Sect uniform, drawing cuts and blood, but failed to pierce her flesh.

Eiwin used this small sacrifice to approach Narcha with a jump. Her hands became chopping knives as she struck the tentacles binding her companion's weapon, breaking them apart in a single blow.

Narcha took notice, using this window to cut the appendages hooked into her flesh with her now-freed saber.

The creature didn't remain still either, and it sent a barrage of tentacles to pierce through the women.

They were ready for the attack this time around. Narcha stepped forward, drawing a wide arc with her blade to swipe the attacks off, while Eiwin stood by her side to grab and snap any tentacles that reached her. Then they retreated.

Still, the creature's entire attention was on them. An endless tide of tentacles hurtled towards them, leaving them no choice but to focus on defense.

Reinhart grumbled, "Fucking idiots!" He looked over at Red. "Come on! We need to help them!"

Red was surprised that Reinhart of all people was the one to urge him on. He simply nodded. "Let's flank it!"

"Does this thing even have a flank?!" Reinhart didn't linger on the details, running to circle the creature. Red followed him, cleaver in hand.

Unfortunately, the knight was right: the monster had no flank or front. Though still lashing at Narcha and Eiwin, it sensed their approach, and dozens of tentacles flew to stop them.

Red and Reinhart stepped back, dodging the blow. But it didn't seem interested in pursuing them, simply holding its tentacles in the air to keep them away.

Why isn't it attacking?

Red and Reinhart kept pushing forward, cutting the tentacles that got too close, but the creature seemed to have an endless supply to throw at them. It still refused to push its attack, though.

Red had an idea.

"I'm going to try something!" he said to Reinhart. "Cover me!"

"What are you going to do?"

Red was already moving away. He stepped back a good distance and pulled a talisman from his pouch—his last one.

The creature's reaction was instant. It stopped attacking Narcha and Eiwin and charged at Red with pure madness—or at least madness was what he sensed in the bumbling mass of tentacles.

Like I thought!

Red guessed he'd put the creature on its guard when using the fireball talisman earlier. Now, as it saw the human pull out another slip of paper, it attacked him out of desperation. But this talisman was just a lure, an attempt to give some breathing room to his comrades.

Reinhart tried to put himself in between the monster and Red, but its tentacles twisted together, creating a club that threw the man aside like a rag doll. Red turned to retreat, but he underestimated the monster's agility.

Its speed skyrocketed, and a mass of tentacles shot toward Red. He jumped away, but one of them wrapped around his leg, making him tumble to the ground before lifting him upside down. More tendrils swept forward, and he held his cleaver up to block.

The weapon shattered like glass, and one of the tentacles pierced his abdomen. Blood poured down his chest onto his face, but Red saw even more tendrils just about to stab him.

A sword flew out of nowhere and cut apart the tentacles holding onto him. He dropped to the ground, the other tendrils missing him by a small margin.

"Red!"

He had a hard time recognizing the voice. He tried getting up, but his strength failed him and he slipped back on the floor. His hand reached down, feeling warm blood spilling out of the hole in his stomach. The hook of the tentacle was still inside.

The sounds of battle intensified. Red looked up, his head dizzy from the effort. He was surprised to see Reinhart standing close by, fighting off the reaching tentacles with his sword. The man had just been clubbed by a force equivalent to a battering ram, yet now he was standing again and fighting.

When did he...?

The question died in Red's mind as he heard a guttural roar from the other side of the room.

An intense silver light streamed from behind the creature. It ceased its attacks on Reinhart, as if sensing a sudden danger. Red's crimson sense also picked up a change. He looked past the tentacle mass and saw that both the roar and the light originated from the same person.

Eiwin.

Her skin was glowing silver, and her fluctuation was intensifying. Like she was growing in power by the second. For a second, he thought she was breaking through to the Lesser Ring Realm.

No, that's not right. It's something else.

The glow subsided a few seconds later, and yet Eiwin's fluctuation remained the same. Narcha stood beside her, staring with worry but not surprise.

Eiwin's eyes were trained on the parasite, full of anger. Then her body tensed in preparation. The creature took notice, and streams of tentacles flew towards her.

But Eiwin didn't move, letting the tentacles strike her body. Even Narcha didn't attempt to help her companion. Red was baffled by this and braced himself for the worst.

Yet as soon as the tendrils came into contact, they all bounced off her skin with loud thudding sounds. It was as if they had struck metal. Eiwin didn't even flinch, and finally, she moved.

She grabbed the tentacles that tried to attack her, ripping them apart in a single fluid motion. Then she charged forward, nearly closing the distance to the monster in a single moment.

The creature seemed to panic, and dozens of its tentacles hurtled forward to block her path. But Eiwin was unstoppable. Her hands resembled blades as she swiped through the tendrils, cutting them off with ease, ripping apart those that tried to wrap around her. There was no dodging involved as she approached the creature step by step.

The parasite, apparently knowing that there was no stopping Eiwin, ceased its attacks and tried running away. As soon as the pressure was off her, though, she jumped forward, bridging the gap.

Her fist struck the ball of tentacles, and an explosion of tendrils erupted. The monster was sent flying, splattering into the wall, but it wasn't dead. It staggered off the wall, trying to run away.

Eiwin was soon upon it again. She jumped on top of the writhing mass, punching again. Another explosion of tendrils burst forth as the monster crashed down onto the floor. Eiwin followed up with another punch, and at that point, the creature had lost more than half its mass.

Its struggles weakened. Still, Eiwin didn't relent. She punched it more, each impact louder than the thunder from outside, until there were almost no tendrils remaining on the parasite. Then, once there was nothing left in her way, she reached down into the wriggling mass and pulled something out.

It was a strange, wormlike being with a single human eye on one of its ends, no bigger than a human forearm. It struggled under Eiwin's grip before she squeezed. The creature exploded, and unlike its tentacles, a gush of blood flew out, splattering her face and clothes with the crimson fluid.

All the remaining tentacles stopped moving, and Red felt their fluctuation slowly disappear. He wasn't focused on that, though.

He was staring at Eiwin.

She smiled at him, her face still smeared with blood. "Are you okay?"

CHAPTER 12

BATTERED

EIWIN'S FLUCTUATION plummeted just as quickly as it had risen. A few moments later, it was even weaker than it had been originally.

She lost her balance, falling down to one knee with a grunt.

"Eiwin!" Narcha ran towards her.

Red tried getting up to follow, but he felt a pain spreading through his midsection.

That's right... I was stabbed.

He'd almost forgotten after witnessing Eiwin's transformation. He reached down, feeling the wound. Blood was still pouring out. Red considered himself lucky that the tendril hadn't pierced his chest. Nonetheless, this was still a serious injury.

He didn't pull out the tentacle piece embedded in his wound, as that would only increase the flow of blood. How was he supposed to fix this?

While he was focused on his own wounds, he heard the women's conversation on the other side of the room.

"I'll survive!" Eiwin said. "Go help him!"

"R-right!" Narcha stammered.

A few seconds later, Red heard approaching footsteps. He looked up and noticed Narcha crouching down by his side.

"Still conscious? Great! How's the wound?"

Red grunted in pain as he shifted around. "It... It didn't pierce through. It's still bad."

Narcha frowned. "Let me see."

Red did as he was told, shifting his hand away from the wound.

She cringed. "You're leaking blood!"

Narcha's hand flew to the wound, pressing around it to stop the bleeding. She cursed as she looked closer. "It might have pierced an organ! We need to add pressure!"

"I... I can do that myself."

"No, you can't! You just got stabbed in the stomach! You're going to bleed out if we don't treat you quickly!"

Now that she mentioned it, Red noticed he had lost a substantial amount of blood. More than a normal adult could afford to lose, much less a child. Yet while he was weak, the wound didn't feel nearly as bad as it should.

"Agh, I need to find something to staunch this..." Narcha looked at the bag over her shoulder, as if to reach for an item, but she was reluctant to release the pressure on his wound.

Then she spotted Reinhart. He was standing to the side, observing curiously.

"You!" Narcha howled at him. "Aren't you going to help?"

"Hm?" Reinhart looked surprised. "You didn't ask!"

"You fucking bastard! Just get me a cloth or some gauze to apply pressure here!"

He nodded. "Right away."

Reinhart pulled some white cloth out of his own bag and approached Narcha.

She extended her hand. "Give it here!"

He handed it over without protest. Narcha put the cloth over the wound, and it quickly became drenched in the crimson fluid.

"We need to keep pressure on this for a while until the bleeding stops," she said to Red. "After that, we can clean up and dress the—"

"Hey," Reinhart said.

"What is it?!" Narcha glared at him with hateful eyes.

"Your other friend doesn't seem to be doing too well."

"What?!" Narcha looked over in Eiwin's direction and saw she had collapsed to the ground.

"Gods fucking damn it!" She gritted her teeth. "Eiwin, are you awake?!"

No response. Narcha hesitated.

Red reached over her hands to hold the cloth down. He nodded at her. "I'll live. Go tend to her."

All reluctance disappeared from her face. She stood up and turned to Reinhart. "Look after him!"

The knight nodded, and Narcha was off to tend to Eiwin.

In the meantime, Red did as he was told and applied pressure to his bleeding. Still, he already had other ideas.

"Help me up," he said to Reinhart.

The man frowned. "Why?"

"I need to do something."

"You're bleeding."

"I won't die. Bring me to where they are."

The knight sighed. "Fine."

Reinhart walked over to him and grabbed his shoulders before helping him up. Red felt unsteady on his feet, but the man helped him keep his balance.

They walked over to Narcha and Eiwin. The warrior looked worried as she examined her companion's body. There were no signs of serious injuries on Eiwin, and although she was unconscious, she was still breathing.

Still, Narcha's expression told Red that things were not as simple as they seemed.

"What's going on with her?" he asked.

Narcha looked up in surprise. "What are you doing here, you moron?" She glared at Reinhart. "Why are you holding him up?"

The man shrugged. "He asked."

"I'm... I'm fine," Red told her. "Trust me."

"Trust you? You're bleeding to death!"

"I'm still standing," he said between heavy breaths.

"Ugh, fine! If you want to kill yourself, at least don't bother me!" Narcha turned back to her unconscious companion.

Red pulled himself out of Reinhart's support and sat on the ground with some difficulty, still holding onto his wound.

"What is going on with her?" he repeated.

Despite her harsh words, Narcha still answered. "It's a side effect of what she did."

Red could tell she was being deliberately vague, so he didn't push the matter. "Is she going to live?"

"She will, but..." Narcha winced. "It'll take a bit for her to recover."

"Don't you have any more of that medicine?" Reinhart asked.

She cast him another glare. "If we had any, do you think I would be waiting around?"

He shrugged, then looked at Eiwin. "How long until she's conscious again?"

"I don't know... Hopefully soon."

The room fell silent as Narcha continued to monitor Eiwin's situation.

Red, in the meantime, scanned their surroundings.

He was indeed worried about Eiwin's state, but this wasn't the reason he'd asked to be brought over. A few seconds later, he spotted some small streaks of blood not more than three meters away.

It was the parasite's blood. Red intended to use it to heal himself.

He was aware his injury wouldn't be life-threatening if given proper treatment, but it would certainly be debilitating for a long time. He couldn't afford to be this weak at this point in the trial, so he decided to use his recently discovered power to heal.

This decision wasn't made on a whim. In truth, Red would rather not use the power at all before he understood it, but he simply did not have any choice, as they had no more healing medicines with them.

Red took advantage of a moment when Narcha and Reinhart were looking away and slid himself over to the pool of blood. Then he reached into it with one of his hands.

The reaction was immediate. A burning sensation spread over his hand, up his arm and into the rest of his body. Unimaginable pain assaulted his senses, reaching into the very core of his being, into parts of himself Red had never sensed before.

He couldn't hold back. He let out a scream of agony.

Narcha and Reinhart looked up in shock.

"Kid, what is going on?" Narcha rushed over.

Red didn't respond. In fact, he couldn't respond. He curled up on the ground in torment, feeling the horrible sensation spreading to every part of him. He fought to focus on the area around his abdomen, where his flesh shifted and mended itself.

The reaction subsided after ten seconds, but it felt as if an eternity had passed. When his senses recovered, he felt Narcha shaking his shoulders and glaring at him.

"You little shit, tell me what's going on!" she said. Her gaze flew down to the wound. "You need to keep the pressure in your wound, or it's going to... It's going to..."

Red followed her gaze, knowing what had caught her attention.

Beneath the blood smears on his abdomen, the wound had disappeared. The tentacle that had been stuck in his injury had fallen out, bringing bits of flesh and blood with it. His wound had completely healed.

Narcha was shaken by the sight. "H-how?"

Before he could reply, another voice interjected. "R-Red, are you okay?" Eiwin had recovered consciousness and was sitting up.

"Eiwin!" Narcha let go of Red and ran to her companion.

"W-what about, Red? Is he okay?" Eiwin asked in a weak voice.

Narcha nodded. "He's fine! But what about you?! You shouldn't have done that!"

The younger woman shook her head with a smile. "If I hadn't done that, we might have died."

"You still look like you could die!" Narcha glowered at her.

Eiwin's countenance was pale. And her fluctuation was faint, no stronger than a normal individual's. Whatever price Eiwin had paid, it was reflected within Red's crimson sense.

This was an important clue, but not something he was interested in looking into right now. He walked over to her.

"Are you okay?" he asked.

"I'll be fine." Eiwin nodded, her smile frail. "W-what about your wound?"

He hesitated. "I'll... explain it later."

"I see..." Her attention shifted to Reinhart, who looked deep in thought. "What about you, Mister Reinhart?"

"Me?" He was caught off guard. "I'm fine. I was just wondering..."

Eiwin shook her head and sighed. "If there's something you wish to ask, go ahead, Mister Reinhart."

Reinhart smiled. "Oh, I'm not going to pry into your secrets. I was just wondering, shouldn't this parasite have a monster core? It seemed to be in the Lesser Ring Realm, but I found nothing of the sort."

She frowned. "I'm not too certain myself. I know little about parasite monsters, but they should still have monster cores."

"Shut up, the two of you!" Narcha interjected. "You shouldn't even be talking in your condition, Eiwin!"

"I said I'll be fine, Miss Valt," Eiwin said, taking a deep breath. "I might not be of much help moving forward, but I'll live. We still have to find your pill, don't we?"

Those words stung Narcha, who clenched her teeth in anger and shame.

Eiwin didn't pay attention to her reaction. As the seconds passed, she recovered her composure and strength bit by bit, but Red could tell from her fluctuation that she was far from healed.

Still, she tried to stand up. Narcha seemed like she wanted to protest, but one serene look from Eiwin was enough to make her swallow her words. The warrior just helped her companion to her feet.

Once Eiwin was up, she looked over at Reinhart, who bore a thoughtful expression.

"So, have you decided to abandon us?" she asked.

He smiled, but didn't deny her accusation. "You're wounded."

"I am."

"You will hold us back."

"I probably will."

Reinhart shook his head. "I've gotten too far to be held back at this juncture."

Narcha scoffed. "I knew this would happen. This is who this man is, Eiwin! We should be thankful he didn't stab us in the back before leaving!"

He laughed. "I didn't say anything yet. I would like to continue working with you lot, but we can't do it with an injured person holding us back."

Narcha narrowed her eyes. "What are you trying to say?"

"It's simple. Leave her here, where we know she will be safe, and let the rest of us continue in her stead."

"It's not happening," Narcha said bluntly. "She's coming with us."

Reinhart sighed, as if expecting this reply. He looked over at Red. "What about you, kid? You should be more reasonable than these two, right?"

Red shook his head. "I can't leave them."

They had done too much for him. Although he knew Reinhart was being logical, Red was no ingrate, and he would never turn his back on people who had helped him again and again. It just wasn't the type of person he was.

Reinhart sighed again, this time disappointed. "I expected more from you, kid."

"You have your answer," Narcha said. "Now, are you leaving or not?"

The man shook his head. "I guess I'll stay with you until we leave the building. After all, we aren't done exploring this place, right? Who knows if there are still any dangers around?"

Narcha glared at him. "We don't need your—"

"We'll be thankful for your help, Mister Reinhart," Eiwin said.

Narcha stared at her, but fell silent under her companion's gaze once again.

Reinhart smiled. "Great. So, should we see what's beyond that corridor, then?"

CHAPTER 13
PARTING SEA PILL

RED SIGHED, looking over at his now-ruined weapon. His cleaver had been utterly destroyed by the parasite's tentacles.

Eiwin tried to comfort him. "We'll get Goulth to craft you a new one once we're out."

He nodded. The cleaver had been with him since he escaped from the underground, and although he wasn't necessarily attached to the weapon, he still lamented the loss of a good tool.

There was no point in dwelling on it, though.

The group moved down the room, with Reinhart leading the way. Narcha helped Eiwin walk while Red focused on his crimson sense and kept a close watch on their surroundings.

On the surface, nothing had changed. But their group dynamic felt different, as the seeds of resentment had been planted. This mostly came from Narcha, who glared at Reinhart, as if expecting him to turn around and attack them at any moment.

Red didn't blame her. Now that the battle had ended, he had time to contemplate what had happened.

Reinhart had another shield talisman.

This by itself wasn't surprising. If it were Red in his place, he would also have kept his most valuable defenses for a worst-case scenario, or in case his "comrades" tried to attack him. What made him suspicious had happened during the fight.

He'd seen Reinhart get battered by the monster—a clubbing attack that would have shattered Red's bones. However, the man didn't seem injured, and a few seconds later, he'd already been back on his feet, helping Red against the parasite. Was the blow not as strong as Red thought, or did Reinhart have something to protect or heal himself?

Red wasn't sure. He had been too busy fighting for his life to observe what the knight was doing. It was a reminder that Reinhart wasn't one of their Sect members, and he had no reason to be honest or trust them. No matter how much he had helped the group, Red doubted Reinhart would ever put himself in a hopeless situation for them, which meant the man had still been confident he could save his own life throughout this fight.

He was almost certainly hiding something.

Red asked himself whether he was being too suspicious of Reinhart. After all, the man did save his life, didn't he? However, Red took no one at face value. Reinhart in particular had given him plenty of reason for suspicion in the past, and their alliance was nothing more than a matter of convenience, so Red doubted he had saved them out of the goodness of his heart.

Did this mean Reinhart would betray them? Not necessarily, but it didn't inspire confidence in Red.

At the very least, he seems intent on parting ways after this.

It would be for the best, since Red wouldn't need to monitor everything Reinhart did moving forward.

The group walked in silence through the empty ruins. They entered the corridor connected to the destroyed chamber, stepping over the corpses of the lizards.

The rest of the building was identical to the room where they had just been—cracked and ruined rock surfaces without so much as a hint of decor or symbols. Something changed soon, though.

"There's a light ahead," Reinhart said.

Narcha merely grunted in acknowledgement.

The knight looked back at Red. "Tell me if you sense anything, will ya?"

He nodded.

They walked until the source of the light became clear.

Lamps emitting white light lined the hall, which led to another room. Curiously enough, this section of the building wasn't damaged or worn-down. It was as if they had crossed an invisible line beyond which the place was protected against the elements, never approaching a state of disrepair.

None of this surprised Red anymore. He was already numb to the strangenesses of this trial.

The corridor continued for a few dozen meters more until they arrived. This chamber was just as well-lit, with lanterns hanging from pillars along either side of the spacious room.

In the center was a raised altar, which held a large, charred cauldron. The object stuck out in the pristine chamber, but what caught their attention was the round object above it.

It was a blue pill, floating in the air and emitting a soft blue light. The pill didn't look remarkable in any way, but the more Red looked at it, the more he felt a stirring within his body. A few moments later, he started to sense things.

First were the sounds. Waves crashing against the coast—a sea disturbed in the middle of a storm. Then came the visions. He saw the faint image of watery streams floating around the pill. A tingling sensation hit his skin, the sign of a high concentration of Spiritual Energy in the air. All coming from the pill. A sense of craving sparked from within his body, from a place Red had never felt before, begging him to consume the pill.

He didn't need any explanation to understand what this item was or what it did, and, from the looks of it, neither did his companions.

Narcha stared at the pill. "It's... It's..."

"A Parting Sea Pill," Reinhart said.

This was a cultivator's dream item. A pill that could open a person's Spiritual Sea, no matter how poor their talent might be, and allow them to break through into the Lesser Ring Realm. It was such a rare and precious item that not even cultivators already in the Lesser Ring Realm could afford it, and only the strongest organizations in the world had the method and means to produce it.

And yet, here it was. A genuine Parting Sea Pill, right in front of them.

It all felt like a dream. At least until they heard hurried footsteps.

Reinhart was dashing straight at the pill.

"Wait!" Narcha panicked and chased after him, dropping Eiwin on the floor.

She was too late. Reinhart jumped over the cauldron and grabbed the pill. Immediately, all the otherworldly phenomena disappeared. Rage built up inside of Narcha as she whipped out her saber.

But Red noticed Reinhart fishing in his pocket as he retreated. He had a terrible feeling about this. "Narcha, be careful!"

That gave her pause.

Reinhart was pointing the talisman at her. "Not one step further!" he cried. The item was already glowing orange as his fingers hovered over its design, ready to trigger the spell.

She froze, glaring at Reinhart. Both she and Red recognized the talisman he was holding. Another fireball talisman, the kind he had used in the forest against the demon and Red had just used against the parasite.

Reinhart looked over at Red. "Don't reach for that bow, kid. You know better than me what will happen if I activate this talisman."

Red winced, but stopped moving.

Narcha, however, raised her saber towards Reinhart, trembling with anger. "If you activate that talisman in here, you won't escape unscathed."

Reinhart smiled. "Maybe, but what about your companions? Do you think Eiwin could survive the flames in her state?"

"I'll kill you!" Narcha growled.

He laughed, waving the talisman in her face. "Will you really?"

Narcha seemed on the verge of losing her mind, and her trembling intensified.

"Miss Valt!" Eiwin cried.

Her words, which always calmed Narcha, fell on deaf ears. Narcha was poised to attack Reinhart, regardless of the talisman he held.

But he continued to smile. "Come on, Narcha. There is no need to be this angry. I don't want to fight, I just want to negotiate."

His words gave Narcha pause. She glared at him with hateful eyes. "Give me the pill."

Reinhart frowned. "Is that what you call negotiation?"

Narcha gnashed her teeth, but Eiwin chose that moment to interject again.

"What do you want from us, Mister Reinhart?"

Reinhart beamed at her. "See? It's always easier to speak with reasonable people."

Eiwin frowned and repeated the question. "What do you want?"

He shrugged. "It's simple, really. I'm willing to give this pill to you for a certain price."

Narcha's eyes widened. "You expect us to believe that after you tried to get one over us, you bastard?"

"Now, don't say that. I just had to take the initiative. After all, if you had gotten your hands on this pill first, would you have been willing to listen to me?"

"So what? You're just willing to hand over a priceless pill like that and not use it for yourself?!"

"I didn't say I was just handing it over. Of course, I would love to keep this pill for myself, but... Let's just say there are things I care about more than breaking through."

For a moment, Reinhart almost looked sad. But the face was gone just as quickly as it had appeared.

"As long as it's within our Sect's capabilities," Eiwin said, "we can repay you in any way you choose, Master Reinhart."

He laughed. "Now, don't be ridiculous. We both know that your entire Sect's treasury wouldn't be enough to trade for a pill like this." He looked at Narcha. "And to someone like you, this pill is more precious than anything, isn't it?"

Narcha's eyes twitched. "Just tell us what you want, you fucking bastard!"

"It's simple. I'm not willing to trade with your Sect, but I am willing to trade with the three of you... I need you to do something for me."

His smile disappeared.

"Help me kill Hector, and I will give this pill to you."

CHAPTER 14

BETRAYAL

KILL HECTOR?

THE WORDS DIDN'T REGISTER for Red and the others at first.

Even Narcha, fueled by her hatred, was taken aback. "Is this a joke?"

Red was half expecting Reinhart's serious demeanor to drop and the man to laugh again, to talk about how that was all an elaborate joke. It didn't happen.

"No," Reinhart said. "Not this time. My offer is genuine."

Narcha glared at him, still not convinced. "Then let me rephrase. Are you insane?"

He grinned. "Me, insane? I actually think this is a great plan. Hector is very strong, so you can't really expect to overpower and kill him. You need to use subterfuge and strike him from where he least expects it... And who else is more suited for that than three of his own Sect members?"

Another extended silence settled in the room.

"... You're actually being serious, aren't you?" Narcha stared at him as if he were mad.

"Of course I'm being serious. Do you think I would just steal this pill and threaten you as a joke? That's too risky, even for me."

"So, this was your brilliant plan? To take the pill you knew I was looking for and compel us to betray our Sect in exchange for it?"

"I know what you're thinking. But trust me, I would never try something like this if there was no chance to succeed."

Narcha shook her head in disgust. "There is no chance. The answer is no."

He sighed. "This is why I don't like speaking to headstrong people." He turned to look at Red and Eiwin. "The two of you are much more reasonable."

"Our answer is the same, Mister Reinhart," Eiwin said. "We would never entertain the thought of betraying our own, no matter how valuable of an item you offer us."

"Of course, I expected that. But what if I gave you a good reason to betray that old man?"

Eiwin frowned. Red could see that she was debating whether they should waste more time engaging Reinhart in conversation.

Red spoke up on her behalf. "Why are you doing this?"

"For Gustav, of course," Reinhart said. "I'm sure he would be very thankful to be rid of Hector."

Red didn't believe him for one second, but he knew better than to try to pull a straight answer out of the man.

He moved on to the matter at hand. "What reason could you possibly give us to betray Hector?"

Eiwin's hesitant gaze lingered on Red for a moment, but she didn't speak up.

Reinhart was delighted by Red's question, and he gave him his full attention. "Because he's a horrible person, that's why."

"What has he done?"

"He was part of the Ocean Bearers Sect, kid. Has anyone in your group ever told you what that Sect did in the past?"

Red narrowed his eyes. He noticed that Eiwin was troubled, but neither she nor Narcha seemed surprised.

Reinhart laughed. "Of course they wouldn't tell you! Those people drowned entire countries during their wars! They were absolutely ruthless!"

"Master Hector had left the Sect long before it was destroyed," Eiwin said. "He was never involved in the atrocities they committed."

"So you say." Reinhart shook his head. "Hector might not have been involved in what happened back then, but he still did plenty of horrible things on his own. I mean, he still keeps in contact with the survivors of his Sect, doesn't he?"

She didn't deny his words. This was old news to her, but to Red, it was a revelation.

"Have you ever heard of a technique called Sea Extraction, kid?" Reinhart asked him.

He shook his head.

"This was something Hector and his fellow Sect members invented." Reinhart pointed at his chest. "It consists of extracting an individual's Spiritual Sea to be used as an ingredient for Spiritual Forging. They say the more talented that person is, the more useful their Spiritual Sea becomes once it's taken out of their body."

Red understood where this was going. "Is this what happened to you? Did Hector extract your Spiritual Sea, so now you want revenge?"

Reinhart grinned. "No. It wasn't Hector who did it."

"So why do you want to kill him?"

"Because the people who did this to me are already dead and Hector was the closest person to them I could find."

"You are out of your fucking mind!" Narcha shouted. "You don't even know if Hector did all those things you're talking about, and you *still* want to kill him just because he knew those people?"

Reinhart smirked at Narcha. "Not just related. He was their master."

His words left her speechless.

"Of course, I don't really know if they learned that technique from him." He shrugged. "Still, he's the closest person I got, so he will have to do."

"You're willing to go against him just for that?" Red asked.

He had a hard time reconciling these words with what he knew about Reinhart. For a man as logical as him to go to such lengths just for revenge against someone tangentially related to those who wronged him—it made little sense to him.

"You wouldn't understand, kid. I've had to live with this burning desire to get back at those people for decades. I will take what little relief I can."

Red examined his face. Reinhart's expression didn't match the weight and passion of his words. The boy wasn't sure if he was lying, but Eiwin and Narcha's silence hinted that there was an inkling of truth to what he said.

"Of course, don't think you're safe, kid." Reinhart put on a pitying expression. "If Hector really does know the Sea Extraction Technique, then he may use it on any of you one of these days. Who knows, maybe he's rearing that Allen kid for that reason."

"Silence!" Narcha roared.

Reinhart, however, just smiled at her. "You're almost twenty-six, aren't you? Even if you break through soon, you'll never amount to anything as a cultivator."

Narcha's saber hand shook with fury.

Reinhart continued with his taunting, waving the blue pill in her face. "This pill can be useful to you, but why were you even forced to go to such lengths in the first place? Hector still has contact with some of his surviving Sect members, so why was he unable to secure a pill for you? I mean, sure, they might be nowhere near as strong as they were in the past, but one Parting Sea Pill should have been no problem for them." He shrugged. "Especially if someone like Hector asked for it... Oh, wait!"

He put on a mask of feigned realization. "It must be because your talent is terrible, isn't it? Why would he waste favors on someone like you? On the other hand, I'm sure he has one of these pills lined up for Eiwin. I mean, after seeing what she did against that parasite, I can tell you she definitely doesn't have a simple background. That's someone worth nurturing!"

Narcha looked down, her trembling spreading to her whole body.

Eiwin noticed and glowered at Reinhart, even with her pale face. "We know what you're doing. Those lies would never—"

"SHUT UP!" Narcha's booming voice interrupted her.

Eiwin looked at her companion's back in disbelief. "N-Narcha, you..."

"I don't need you to speak for me!"

Eiwin fell silent, shaken.

Reinhart, on the other hand, was delighted. "Now, isn't that unfair, Narcha Valt? How many years of your life have you spent serving this little Sect of yours? And yet when you need it the most, Hector refuses to offer his assistance... Doesn't that make you angry?"

Narcha raised her head, looking at him. "... Are you done?"

"That depends... Are you willing to help me?"

She let out a small laugh. "What do you think?"

"That's a shame." Reinhart shook his head, turning Red. "What about you, kid? Are you also going to stand by them? Aren't you afraid that Hector will use you in the future just like he did this poor woman?"

"They're part of my Sect." Red made his stance clear.

Although what Reinhart had revealed did alarm him, Red had never once entertained the thought of betrayal. Whatever actions he'd take in the future after what he had learned, they wouldn't start with backstabbing those who had helped him.

"Shame." Reinhart sighed. "So it seems we've arrived at an impasse, haven't we?" He looked at the pill and glowing talisman in his hands. "Now, what should I do about this pill? I can't use it, so should I take this back to Gustav or try to sell it myself?"

"Are you still in the mood to joke around, you bastard?" Narcha cried.

Reinhart ignored her. He shook his head. "No, I can't bring this outside. If word got out about it, I can't imagine how many people would try to kill me for it."

Red and the others stared at the ridiculous display in silence. He continued to argue with himself out loud until he finally arrived at a conclusion.

Reinhart huffed. "I guess there's no other way, then." He raised the hand holding the pill towards Narcha. "Here, you can have it."

She was shocked. "W-what are you—"

She didn't get to complete her sentence.

Reinhart squeezed the pill with all his strength. A cracking noise came from within his closed fist, and a soft blue light slipped from between his fingers. Then he opened his hand and let the ruined remains of the pill fall to the ground.

He smiled at Narcha. "Here, I said you can have it."

"I'LL KILL YOU!"

Narcha charged.

CHAPTER 15
GUILT

NEITHER RED nor Eiwin had time to react as Narcha hurtled forward. Powered by nothing but her own anger, she sought to close the distance between her and Reinhart in an explosive sprint, but he had been waiting for just that.

The glow of the talisman in Reinhart's hand intensified as his finger crossed over the last line and triggered it. Rather than throwing the talisman at her, he tossed it up towards the ceiling.

The fireball formed just as Narcha swung at him. It crashed against the ceiling, and an explosion of flames and debris shook the room. The impact reached Red, and the force of the blow threw him backwards against the wall with incredible force.

A wave of heat singed his legs, but the flames didn't reach him. His ears rang from the explosion, and he couldn't see anything through the smoke and dust.

He tried to focus on his crimson sense.

They're moving.

Red felt Narcha and Reinhart's fluctuations. Reinhart was moving away while Narcha seemed to be searching blindly. Her movements were slow.

She's wounded.

This wasn't surprising, considering she had been close to the explosion.

Reinhart, on the other hand, didn't seem affected by it, and soon enough his presence moved out of his range.

There was also the third fluctuation, which didn't seem to be moving at all.

Eiwin!

Red went towards her, legs aching. As the dust settled down, he spotted Eiwin on the ground, unconscious. Although she was still breathing, her fluctuation was even weaker than before. When he looked her over, though, he couldn't find any injuries or wounds on her body.

He called out to Narcha. "I need help here!"

She didn't seem to hear him and continued to rage. "WHERE ARE YOU, YOU BASTARD?!"

Red grimaced. "Eiwin is dying!"

"I'LL— What?" Narcha looked over at him.

When she spotted Eiwin's unconscious body, her expression softened.

"Eiwin!" She dropped her saber and ran towards them.

There were burn marks running down Narcha's left arm and the side of her head, where most of her hair had been burned off. She looked better than Rog, but even then, a burst of flame to the face was beyond what a normal person could survive. The fact she was still standing was a testament to her strength.

Narcha crouched by Eiwin's side, examining her. There were no obvious wounds in her companion's body, but it was clear her condition was critical. "What is going on, kid?"

"Her fluctuation is getting weaker," Red explained.

"Fluctuation?! What does that mean?"

"It's how I can detect people." He tried to be as concise as possible. "I don't know what it detects, but once someone dies, their fluctuation disappears from my senses."

"Shit, shit, shit!" Narcha cried. "Do you have any pills to heal her?"

He shook his head.

She gritted her teeth in frustration. "What about pills with Spiritual Energy? Do you have any?!"

This time, he nodded. He took out his box with the Burning Vein Pills. "These are special Vein Opening Pills I got earlier. How is that supposed to help, though?"

"Just give it here!"

Red passed one to Narcha. She then forced it down Eiwin's throat and made sure she swallowed it.

Eiwin broke out in a sweat—Red assumed this was a side effect of the fire-attribute Spiritual Energy contained in the pill. To his surprise, Eiwin's fluctuation stabilized, which was reflected in her relaxing face.

Narcha let out a sigh of relief.

Red stared at her. "What happened?"

"The ability she used is a Body Refinement technique that's meant to be powered by Spiritual Energy," Narcha said. "But there are other ways that it can be powered if someone hasn't yet opened their Spiritual Sea. The technique she uses keeps draining her vitality even after it wears off, though. We can fight it off by using healing medicine that Goulth made for us, but..."

"But she used the last bottle on me, didn't she?" Red realized.

Narcha nodded. "It wasn't your fault... I thought we had enough time to leave this place and get her some treatment, but I didn't consider the fact this was the second time she used that ability today. Even if it didn't look like it, it must have taken a toll on her body."

She looked crestfallen.

"But why did the Vein Opening Pill help?" he asked.

"The technique she used is based on opening special acupoints. When she injects her body with Spiritual Energy, these acupoints start absorbing this energy instead of her vitality... But it's not a solution." Narcha shook her head. "We still need to get her healing medicine or she won't get better."

It sounded awfully similar to Red's situation with his own special acupoints.

He frowned. "How long does she have?"

"I don't know. I've never been in this situation. Eiwin only explained to me what I had to do if something like this happened."

"I have two more of those pills." Red handed the box over to Narcha without hesitation. "You can give them to her if she gets worse."

She accepted the box. "I will..."

A heavy silence fell over the room as Narcha looked over Eiwin's unconscious body with a look of defeat. Red had never seen her in such a state before.

She smiled weakly. "I'm really pathetic, aren't I? I was meant to come here to save Rog and get my pill, but look at what happened... Now we have another companion at risk of losing her life."

"You're not the only one who took on that responsibility. It's not all your fault."

Narcha laughed. "Not all my fault? If I didn't rush Reinhart back then... If I wasn't lost in rage, none of this would have happened. The truth is that I didn't consider the consequences before acting, and now Eiwin is paying for it."

Red didn't know how to respond.

"The thought of risking it all crossed my mind even while we were talking," she said. "I thought that maybe whatever risk you and Eiwin would face from that talisman would be worth it for the pill, even if I could die too... But I suppressed it. I said to myself there were more important things at play here, that nothing was worth sacrificing your comrades over. And yet when he crushed that pill... I was too weak. I gave in to my anger, and Eiwin got hurt because of it." She looked away in disappointment.

"Can't we still use the pill, though?" Red asked. "Even some of its remnants?"

Narcha laughed. "That's not how it works, kid. Even if you got every little piece, it would have lost its essence... Besides, can you find any of it?"

He looked around. After the explosion and all the stone detritus and dust, he saw no signs of the pill anywhere.

"It's just as well that I never got that damn pill. I don't deserve it," she said.

"Maybe you don't."

Narcha looked at him with a smirk. "Isn't this the part where you're supposed to comfort me?"

He shrugged. "I don't know how to do that. I can only say that from my brief experience, nothing in this world is about deserving."

"That's not a very pleasant way to look at things."

"You're right," he said. "You made a mistake, but there's no point in letting yourself be dragged down by it if you want to be a cultivator. Eiwin told me how much that pill meant to you, and that she was willing to risk herself by your side to help you acquire it. She knew the dangers of this place and she still went ahead with it. I don't think she would blame you for what happened."

"Maybe you're right. Eiwin is a very understanding and kind person, but... That only makes things worse."

"And why is that?" Red asked.

She sighed. "You really don't know how people work, do you, kid?"

"I suppose not."

"... Then there's no point in explaining it to you." Narcha went quiet again, looking back at Eiwin.

"Will you stay here?"

"Someone needs to look after her... and I'm too wounded." Narcha looked at him. "Why do you ask? Do you still want to continue?"

"I do. The earlier this trial ends, the earlier you can bring Eiwin back to the Sect."

Narcha scoffed. "And so what? Do you intend on winning against Ricard and those imperials?"

"I do. That way we can save Eiwin, and I can continue my path as a cultivator."

She hissed out a breath. "You're not even trying to deny that you're also doing this for your own benefit?"

"Why would I? Eiwin helped me in the past, so I'll help her when she needs it. But I want to be a cultivator, so my focus will always be on that."

Narcha smiled. "I guess we know which of us is better suited to be a cultivator, then, don't we?"

Red didn't know how to reply to that, so instead, he took a few items from his bag.

"Here." He handed his Spirit Stones to Narcha. "Keep these, in case I die on the way."

"Are you sure?" Narcha asked. "If the trial ends and you're still alive, you can use these to trade for some treasures from that bird."

"It doesn't matter. These stones might help me, but they won't change my fate in the long run," Red explained. "I have to keep aiming for the highest prize if I want to continue on this path. Besides, you might need them to trade for medicine for Eiwin and Rog, and you can still use what's left to get something for me."

Narcha gave him a weird expression, but accepted the gift. "I guess you're right." She stored the stones in her bag. "You need to be careful about Reinhart, Ricard, and those imperials. They're still out there."

"Reinhart knows my powers, so I doubt he'll risk attacking me. As for Ricard and the imperials... I guess I'll need to improvise."

Red still had the wind bestowment talisman, but he doubted it would be enough to defeat Ricard and the imperial agents, considering they were probably armed with even better equipment.

"Just be careful, kid," Narcha said. "You're smart, but with some opponents, no amount of planning will help you."

"I know." He recalled the spiders in the underground and the insectoid he and Viran had fought. No plans or clever ideas could help you against overwhelming strength. Thankfully, Red had some powers of his own to rely on.

"Then I'll be going," he said.

"You do that."

Red collected his things and turned to walk towards the other exit of the room, which he assumed Reinhart had escaped through.

"Oh, and kid..." Narcha called out to him before he could leave.

Red turned around. "What?"

"Make sure you kill Reinhart if you see him."

He frowned. "I'll probably just avoid him."

"Agh, you little shit!" Narcha glared at him. "Just get the hell out of here!"

Red obliged and left without turning back.

CHAPTER 16

SANDSTORM

ALTHOUGH RED HAD SAID he had no intentions of fighting Reinhart, he was still on the lookout for him. He focused on his crimson sense and examined the tracks the man had left behind.

Thankfully, Reinhart wasn't waiting in ambush. Red reached the end of the corridor without incident and found an open door leading back into the desert.

With one last careful search, he stepped outside.

Nothing seemed different about the desolate land, except that the mountain was much closer than before. It looked no farther than a few kilometers from him, but Red wouldn't let himself be deceived by his eyes again.

Only, upon closer examination, he noticed something was missing.

The tornadoes have disappeared.

Although the storm still raged above, there were no signs of the twisters. Red felt lost for a second.

His gaze wandered back to the mountain.

Does that mean I can walk towards it now?

Red wasn't sure, but it seemed the only option left to him.

He took one last look at the building behind him before stepping forward.

Red tried to search for signs of Reinhart, but even though the tornadoes were gone, the winds on the plain were still strong, and they had wiped away any tracks. What confused him was that even though Reinhart had quite a few minutes of advantage over him, it should still have been possible to spot his figure from afar across the desert. No such thing happened.

It was as if the man had disappeared.

To Red's surprise, he made progress toward the mountain over the next ten minutes. It was nowhere near as fast as it should have been, considering the time that had passed and his perceived distance from the peak, but all the same, the mountain grew closer to him ever so slightly.

At this distance, Red noticed more details. The mountain had a dark, rocky surface, and its triangular shape seemed perfectly symmetrical, reaching into the sky. He had never seen mountains before, but even he could tell that the peak wasn't natural. More interesting was how the storm behaved around the mountain.

A perfect circle of clear sky had formed around the apex of the mountain, and the tumultuous clouds and lightning never trespassed this invisible boundary, even as they roiled across the rest of the desert. Of course, although Red interpreted it as clear sky, what he saw was a simple absence of the storm.

There was no sun, blue sky, or stars beyond the clouds in that disc, only pitch-black darkness that not even his improved vision could pierce through. It was nothingness. Red felt as if he were staring into the abyss—what lay beyond the edge of this strange world he had been teleported to—and it filled him with unexplainable dread.

He averted his gaze, deciding it was best to focus on the path ahead.

And it was good that he did.

Something seemed to be moving at the foot of the mountain. Red squinted, trying to discern what he was seeing. It was an indescribable mass, too small for him to make out from this far. Red hesitated, and he stopped walking, contemplating what it could be.

Soon it made itself evident on its own.

The stirring mass grew in his vision little by little until it occupied the whole horizon. It was then that Red recognized it.

A dust storm. And it was heading right for him.

He cringed, wondering what he was supposed to do. It didn't take him long to admit defeat.

What a joke... There's nothing you can do against something that big.

Red could only hope the sandstorm didn't kill him on impact as he made what preparations he could.

He covered his face with spare clothes, hiding ears and keeping only a slit open for his eyes—for whatever good they would do him in there. He also made sure all his equipment was tied to his body so that none of it would fly off when the strong winds struck.

Then there was nothing left but to brace himself.

The dust storm continued to grow in his vision, seemingly conjuring more dust out of thin air. Soon enough, it reached the stormy sky above. It became a monster of untold proportions, swallowing everything in its path and reaching beyond where Red's eyes could see.

Out of all the natural disasters Red had seen today, this certainly took first place when it came to sheer size—and yet here he was, walking right towards it, and possibly towards his own death. At this point, though, he began to feel numb.

When someone risked their life so often in such a short period of time, the fear was bound to lose its effect on them.

Maybe that was the point all along...

The dust storm grew until it swallowed the boy.

The first thing Red felt were the strong winds battering him. With his small size, every step in the gale was orders of magnitude more difficult.

Then there was the worst part—the dust. Red felt countless particles pepper his body, giving no respite. His uniform, although damaged, still absorbed most of the impact, but the sand still hurt him, much more whenever it slipped past the cloth he'd wrapped around his head.

Red couldn't use any of his senses. He couldn't see, hear, or smell anything. His crimson sense was also useless for navigation with no life-forms around him, so all he had to rely on was his body and trained sense of direction as he kept marching forward under the unceasing barrage of the storm.

It didn't take long for the difficulty of the situation to wear on him.

His steps were slow. His breathing was labored. His body was aching.

Red didn't know how much time had passed, nor how much progress he had made. All he could see around him was dust, and even his hands blurred out in the storm. Still, he weathered it, remaining steadfast even as his body started to give out under the strain.

This wasn't even among the hardest things he had gone through today. There was no way he would allow himself to falter here.

Finally, after ages, the storm abated. The winds slowed down, and the dust stopped pelting his body.

Am I through?

Only now did Red dare to fully open his eyes. To his surprise, his vision was still blocked. This time, it wasn't due to the dust storm, but a thick gray mist.

What is this?

Red waved his hand through the fog. It parted with his movement, but soon more mist slipped in to occupy the empty space. He frowned, feeling the damp air around him.

It's just water.

Red had learned to expect the worst in this place, but it didn't seem like there were any tricks to the fog. Still, although he wasn't in danger of suffocating, he couldn't see more than five meters around him.

He looked at the ground under his feet. It was still the cracked desert floor, so he was still outside. Strangely, he couldn't hear the thunder from the storm any longer.

Red pushed his doubts to the back of his head and focused on the task at hand.

Am I still moving in the right direction?

He had tried to keep his path steady in the storm, but there was no way he could guarantee he hadn't deviated. Red tried to use the compass to check, hoping its normal function could still help him orient himself.

But the arrow was spinning around every which way. Red frowned.

Useless thing.

He pocketed the compass and looked around. Since there was nothing he could use to navigate, he decided to just trust his instincts and keep heading in what he thought was the direction of the mountain.

Yet Red soon found out this place was just as desolate and endless as the rest of the desert. Even after half an hour passed, he had yet to see any change in his environment.

Then there was also the silence.

There was no ambient noise of wind and thunder, and an eerie stillness settled around Red. He could only hear his own footsteps.

This directionless search lasted for almost an entire hour before he encountered a change.

A fluctuation!

His joy at finally making progress soon died out. It was a monster's fluctuation, and it wasn't a weak one either. It was stronger than that of any Lesser Ring Realm beast Red had ever seen, but still much weaker than that of the lightning serpent.

Is this a monster in the Greater Ring Realm?

Red didn't know for sure, but he did know there was no chance he would survive an encounter with it. He still held some slight hope of outwitting a Lesser Ring Realm monster with his remaining talisman, but against something even stronger than that? There was no chance.

He only hoped this wasn't another one of the trial's tricks, that he wouldn't need to head towards the monster that would probably kill him to advance. This was something he could only find out in time.

Red circled around the creature, avoiding it entirely. Thankfully for him, its fluctuation wasn't moving, and neither did it seem to notice him. Even as he was passing by, he didn't hear or see anything else to indicate its presence.

If it wasn't for my crimson sense, I might have walked straight into it.

Soon enough, Red had walked past the creature. Whatever had been waiting for him in the fog, he wasn't too keen on finding out.

To his dismay, only five minutes later, he sensed another fluctuation entering his detection range. It was just as strong as the first, but moving rather fast. Red heard nothing, but he could feel the ground tremble underfoot even from a hundred meters away.

Without hesitation, he turned and ran in the opposite direction. It was then that he felt another fluctuation appear out of nowhere, heading straight for him with incredible speed.

Red panicked and dove to the side.

A moment later, a gigantic hoof stomped down where he had just been. He looked up, spotting the shadowy figure of a four-legged monster.

But the creature ran past him without even noticing him—or making much noise for a beast of that size, for that matter.

Red sighed in relief once the monster's fluctuation disappeared. A few seconds later, however, even more fluctuations entered his range.

There were ten of them, all in the Lesser Ring Realm, running in the opposite direction of the previous monster.

A low roar joined them.

He whirled around and fled.

CHAPTER 17
MONSTROUS FOG

As soon as Red retreated, he detected even more fluctuations. Whatever creatures these were, they were just as strong as the ones he had felt moments before, and moving just as frantically.

Red stopped.

The monsters passed by without noticing his presence. He couldn't even see their shapes, and other than his crimson sense, the only thing that indicated their presence was the rumbling of the ground as they ran past.

Noise doesn't spread in this fog, he realized.

This told him there was no relying on his ordinary senses to detect the monsters. Although that went both ways, by the looks of it. The monsters didn't react to his presence, even while walking by his side. It was no wonder they wouldn't notice him, since they seemed to be constantly running from each other.

This was a death field for just about anyone, where bumping into anything would mean death. Red, however, had something he could rely on that no normal person had—his crimson sense.

He waited in place until the creatures had left, opting not to hurry and possibly bump into one. His patience paid off.

Soon the monsters dispersed. Red waited a bit longer, but no other fluctuations entered his range.

They're gone.

Red then decided to move.

This time around, he braced himself against any sudden stampedes, ready to dive out of the way in a heartbeat. Although he could still detect the monsters with his crimson sense, these creatures were much more powerful than him. They could cross one hundred meters in a matter of seconds, and if one of them just so happened to be heading in his direction, he could end up run over if he didn't react fast enough.

But over the next leg of his journey, no such thing came to pass.

Red still detected more fluctuations—each stronger than the last—but most of them were either lying still or moving at a leisurely pace. Sometimes, the presences bumped into each other, which gave rise to a panicked chain reaction in the surrounding monsters.

That was when he had to react quickly. With his crimson sense, he was more than capable of moving out of the way in time. His journey thus continued with no trouble, even as he passed by many powerful monsters.

After Red felt another hour had passed, though, he began to worry.

How do I get out of this place?

Everything looked the same. Fog blocked his view in all directions, and nothing stood out. He had been trying to head in the same direction, but at this point, it had been so long with no change in the environment that he was losing confidence in his plan.

He decided to take a risk.

Red had been counting how many monsters he'd come across—about a hundred of them. Of those, thirteen were in the Greater Ring Realm while the rest were all in the Lesser Ring Realm. It was a massive collection of powerful beings all gathered in one place. If they were released on the town of Fordham-Bestrem, they would raze everything to the ground.

However, now that Red paid attention, he noticed they didn't fight each other. He'd found no blood or signs of struggle around the areas where these fluctuations met, which left him curious.

If they're not fighting, why are they so panicked?

Were they afraid of something? That would explain their behavior. But to be so scared that just bumping into another monster was enough to make them run away? That didn't make sense to Red. It wasn't how monsters were supposed to behave—they were very territorial.

Maybe they're afraid of something else.

This didn't help Red.

So he decided to take an ever bigger risk.

Red headed for the weakest fluctuation he could find. It belonged to a Lesser Ring Realm monster, a beast that could easily kill him in a single strike.

He had his reservations, but he approached the monster.

The creature wasn't moving, so he could come very close. Once he was within thirty meters, Red took out his bow and aimed at the monster through his crimson sense.

Then he loosed an arrow.

Red couldn't see if his arrow hit. But a moment later, the monster's fluctuation stirred, and an angry feline roar echoed through the mists. Much to his surprise, he could hear the noise quite clearly.

Then the presence moved.

It's coming right at me!

Red turned and ran. Unlike what he was used to coming across, this creature didn't seem to be in a panic. Instead, it roared and paced around the area where he had just been.

Red had already dashed out of the way, observing the scene from a safe distance. Although the monster was aware it had been attacked, the fog still inhibited its senses. It couldn't spot him.

But Red wasn't willing to risk it, and ran as far as he could from the monster.

So they still react when attacked.

This was a valuable discovery, but it didn't answer his original question. Why were the monsters so panicked when they ran into each other, but still willing to retaliate against an attack from him? Was this just how they'd been taught to behave?

It made little sense, but Red knew no answer was forthcoming in his situation. All he could do was continue forging ahead.

His situation soon worsened.

As time passed, fluctuations appeared more and more frequently in his crimson sense. It reached a point where Red couldn't walk without being surrounded by dozens of extremely strong monsters. His crimson sense was growing overwhelmed.

By now he had counted five hundred different creatures, and the number was only growing. It was then that he saw the true danger.

If any of these monsters started a panic, Red would be caught in the middle of a stampede. By then, even with his crimson sense, he wouldn't stand a chance of surviving.

Luckily, the monsters stayed still, or at least moved slowly. This way, Red could either weave around them or predict when two fluctuations were about to collide and flee in a different direction.

With this enormous advantage, he was able to make his way through the monster-infested fog with little hassle. The fact that the challenge was getting harder only made him more confident in his progress.

Then Red felt a familiar presence enter his crimson sense.

He froze.

Why is it here?

Red didn't wait. He turned around and tried to distance himself from this being. However, right as he'd detected it, the creature also seemed to have felt his presence. It moved in his direction.

Red broke out in a full sprint.

His pursuer wasn't to be outmatched. It sped up and bumped into several other fluctuations. These monsters then entered a state of frenzy, colliding with even more beasts.

Soon a chain reaction broke out around Red, and the whole world came alive with the roars of monsters. His blood ran cold, and without missing a beat, he took his last talisman from his pouch—the wind bestowment talisman.

I hope this works.

Red activated it according to the spirit's instructions. Once it glowed, he pressed it into his own chest. A surge of energy surrounded him, and he felt light as a feather.

He kept running.

His speed had increased several times, and with each step he grew even faster. But with the stampede already spreading ahead of him, he still needed to avoid rushing beasts.

A giant foot, almost two meters wide, appeared above his head, threatening to stomp him down. Red tried to dive out of the way, and to his surprise, the energy around him responded to his intent.

Wind lifted his body, and as he tilted to the side, the wind carried him with it, saving him from the monster's foot. It crashed down a moment later, making the ground around Red rumble like an earthquake as another monster, a crazed elephant beast, ran toward him.

He didn't have time to marvel at the talisman's abilities. More monsters appeared in his way, and to make matters worse, Red could still feel his pursuer hot on his trail.

Even with his impressive boost in speed, the raging monsters could still keep up with him. It was a grim reminder that these talismans didn't give him an advantage—they merely evened the odds.

How can it detect me?

Red wasn't sure. Unlike with his insectoid core, he didn't think his crimson mist emitted any energy signals. Clearly, he had been quite wrong.

The distance between him and his pursuer decreased by the second. Red tried to pass close by other monsters, hoping they would prove a distraction.

But nothing seemed to work, as the being's speed never fell. This pursuit continued for several long seconds until Red felt the density of rampaging monsters around him decrease.

He wasn't happy about it.

His talisman wouldn't last much longer, and that creature was still gaining on him. If he were left out in the open against it, what could he do?

Red decided to take yet another risk.

He located a fluctuation charging at him, another Lesser Ring Realm monster, and dashed towards it. Then he slowed down, allowing his pursuer to catch up to him.

Now sandwiched between two murderous beasts, he took a deep breath and steeled himself. It took only a split second for both monsters to close in, and that was when Red picked up speed again.

The winds carried him forward, and the silhouette of another monster, something deerlike, appeared in front of him. With hardly a glance, he dove in between its legs.

The beast's hooves almost smashed Red, but with the help of the Wind Energy surrounding his body, he spun out of the way and past it. Then he heard a roar from behind, and like two speeding carts, the beasts crashed into each other.

Red turned around just in time to see a blur of crimson scales tear at the deer's throat with knifelike claws. The prey didn't even have the time to scream before the attacker had ripped through its neck. Unable even to bellow in pain, the deer fell on its side, its life slipping away from its body.

The other creature wasn't interested in finishing it off. It turned to Red, revealing rows of sharp teeth and a menacing stare.

Red could finally lay eyes on his pursuer. It was the lizard demon he had seen in the forest with Reinhart and Allen. It had grown even taller, now almost four meters high, and judging by its fluctuation, it was on the verge of a transformation.

Is it about to break into the Greater Ring Realm?

This seemed inconceivable. It had been barely a day, yet the monster had already advanced that much? Was this the power of a demon?

Red didn't know, and he didn't have time to think about it. He nocked one of his purple arrows to his bow and aimed.

It didn't even bother moving out of the way, slowly stalking towards Red. Perhaps it thought he had no chance? Or maybe it thought the seemingly common arrows weren't any danger to it?

It may be right about that.

In any case, at least Red had a clear target.

He released it, and the arrow impacted the demon's chest.

A purple light exploded from the tip, consuming everything in his vision.

CHAPTER 18
BLOOD RITUAL

THE ARROW'S purple light pierced even the fog surrounding Red, and for a second it was all he could see. He closed his eyes to avoid being blinded.

He almost expected the creature to roar in pain, or to charge at him through the light. Nothing of the sort happened, and instead there was complete and eerie silence. When Red opened his eyes again, the scene shocked him.

The fog had retreated under the purple light, leaving behind a pocket of clear air. The demon stood frozen in place, transforming.

A festering purple substance was spreading across its body. Scales and flesh rotted every part it touched, and soon most of the demon's chest scales had rotted away into a putrid pile of dark fluid.

The creature stumbled, letting out a low bellow of pain.

It's poison?

Red wasn't sure. He noticed, however, that despite the demon's wounded state, it didn't seem about to die. It remained standing, its hateful, rage-filled gaze fixed on him.

He nocked another purple arrow and pulled back, his movements aided by the Wind Energy around him. The demon had wised up to the danger of his arrows, though, and it dashed forward before he could shoot.

Ten meters were covered in the blink of an eye. Even with the help of his talisman, Red didn't have time to move out of the way.

The demon's claw slashed through his bow and arrow. Red tried to pull his bow-holding hand out of the way, but to no avail. It sliced his left hand in half, taking three of his fingers clean off with it.

Red didn't even register the pain. He pulled back, trying to distance himself from the monster, but he was too close. Grabbing onto his flesh and bones to hold him still, the demon's other claws stabbed him in the side.

He struggled against the demon's grip, but it was no contest. His opponent was far too strong for him, and his strength was quickly leaving his body as the beast's claws dug into his insides.

Red wasn't resigned to his fate, though. As the demon lifted one clawed limb to finish him off, Red's right hand grabbed the remaining purple arrow in his quiver.

Just as the demon slashed down, he stabbed its neck with the arrow. Another blinding flash of purple light blasted forth as the head of the arrow exploded against the beast's body.

Then everything went dark.

Huh?

Red's eyes flew open. The pain had disappeared, and he could feel his own left hand again. He examined his limb. All his fingers were back in place.

I survived.

He felt dizzy and confused. He couldn't remember what had happened moments ago, only fighting against that lizard demon and being close to death.

As his senses recovered, Red found he was lying on his back on the ground, staring at the sky above. But something was wrong.

There were no stormy clouds or lightning anymore. There was only the crimson-colored firmament and a dark star that bore down upon his very psyche, threatening to devour him if he continued to stare.

Recognition crossed his mind. He was back in the world of the crimson mist—the first time in a long time.

Did I die? Or am I just dreaming again?

Just as Red thought this, he heard the shuffling of feet behind him. He sat up and his head swiveled around, searching for the source of the sound. His eyes widened in shock.

"W-where am I?"

There was a person standing right there.

A frail man. He was almost skeletal in appearance, his skin pulled taut against his bones, and whatever patches of white hair remained on his head seemed ready to fall out. What surprised Red, though, was his heavy plate armor. It was wrought with symbols and decorations Red didn't recognize, yet it struck him as rich or noble.

As Red spotted this man, the man also noticed him.

"Y-you!" The knight pointed at him with a trembling finger. "Tell me! Where are we? Where did you bring me?"

He spoke with a commanding voice, but Red could see it was all a facade. His eyes betrayed the pure terror he felt.

Red felt at a loss for words.

"You, I told you to..." The man's gaze wandered to the sky above.

As he spotted the crimson sky and dark sun, he froze. His pupils dilated, and the fear he had been trying to hold back poured forth all at once.

He fell to his knees, his gaze locked onto the firmament.

"N-no, no... This can't be."

He grabbed his head as terror seemed to consume him.

"T-this wasn't supposed to happen!" He shook his head in denial. "Y-you promised me! I-I... Oh gods, my Mikaila!"

Tears of realization streamed down his face.

"I didn't mean to! Please, please, forgive me..." He wept, slamming his fist onto the ground. "I must... I have to..."

His eyes wandered back to Red, and a glimmer of hope returned to his face.

The deranged man smiled. "You! You have to help me!"

He crawled up to Red and, on his knees, held his hand.

Red was too taken aback to even react. "Who are you?" he asked.

"You have to help me!" The knight didn't seem to hear his words. "I saw you! It was just a glimpse, but I saw you!"

"What do you—"

"You need to take me back! I have to warn my lord! I can't let them..."

Before he could finish speaking, his tongue fell out of his mouth. He didn't even seem to notice, as he kept babbling incoherently and looking at Red with pleading eyes.

Red could only stare in horror as even more of his decrepit flesh fell off his body. His skin melted and evaporated into nothingness. All while the knight was completely oblivious, still trying to communicate with Red.

He only slowed down when his muscles melted. A few seconds later, there was nothing left of him but his skeleton and his shining armor.

Red looked down. The man's now-skeletal hand was still grabbing onto him.

He didn't even have time to process what had just happened before a wave of pain spread through his body. Red fell to the ground as his skin began to burn.

Then everything went dark again.

This time, Red's senses didn't take long to return, but he could see nothing, and a numbing weight like a boulder was pressing him down into earth. The first thing he felt was pain.

Unbearable pain.

He felt as if he were being boiled alive. Every centimeter of his body, every pore in his skin, was screaming. And Red felt everything with an acute awareness he had never thought possible.

A croak of agony came from his mouth as his whole body contorted. He tried to escape from this torture, yet there was no escape.

It enveloped his being, leaving nothing untouched. There was only agony, and Red's expanded awareness to experience it all in excruciating detail.

After he realized there was no stopping this sensation, he tried to use what little he could of his working mind to identify the cause.

It didn't work.

He only knew something was making its way inside of his body, and even that took a lifetime to figure out. The pain wasn't getting any better, either. In fact, every second, the agony grew worse.

Red knew he had to act, but his mind seemed incapable of acting or thinking under the torment. He kept doing his utmost, and almost subconsciously, he found something to grasp.

Radiant Current.

The meditation technique.

His mind repeated the words he had been taught not too long ago by Eiwin. He tried to speak them out loud, but only an incomprehensible croak came out.

Without the words, it was an exercise in futility.

Still, his mind was set on the task at hand, and Red didn't give up.

With what little control he kept over his body, he repeated the movements Eiwin had taught him. He focused his entire being on the mudras and mantras, pressing on even if all that came out was a scream or a twitch of his fingers. His single-minded devotion to the task eventually paid off as he regained his concentration.

His awareness expanded to the edges of his body, still experiencing the excruciating pain, but this time able to bear it and act despite it. What he felt in his core, though, scared him.

The tendrils of Red's crimson sense had expanded within him, reaching into nearly every corner of his frame. It was injecting some kind of atmospheric energy into his veins, pumping it in at innumerable points.

He immediately recognized this as the source of his torture.

Red's expanded awareness reached for the crimson mist as it had done before, trying to make it stop. But the entity didn't listen to him, continuing to absorb this energy and spread it through his body.

An incredible anger rose within Red, and he once more reached for the mist, commanding it to stop. This time, the entity reacted. Instead of obeying him, it protested.

He was about to lose his mind. The rage continued to rise, the indignation at being challenged by this being that had invaded his body and did as it pleased.

Almost out of instinct, Red tried something. Instead of commanding the mist with his expanded awareness, he tried to attack it from within. Like an ocean wave, his formless awareness washed over the invader.

The crimson tendrils recoiled, wounded by his blow.

Red didn't know how, but whatever he had done was working, as if his expanded awareness of the meditation technique had taken physical form and lashed out at the entity. However it happened, it came naturally to him, as if he had known how to do it his entire life.

The injections paused, but the mist didn't retreat. It reached out again, hoping to absorb more of the energy.

But Red, now armed with this new weapon, struck out again with his formless consciousness. The mist tried to retaliate, but against his blows, it could only fall back.

Eventually, the mist gave up and retracted to its original state in his core.

Red felt some semblance of control return to him as the pain faded away, but the consequences of what had happened still lingered in his body.

He could still feel this strange energy traveling through his blood vessels. His body was practically bursting from the saturation of energy. He had to drain this somehow.

He tried to move, but something was lying on top of him, weighing him down and blocking his vision. Red pushed against it, but it was too heavy to push aside.

Then he tried to slip away, and after some effort, he wrenched his upper body free.

Finally able to look around, he found himself back in the trial, surrounded by fog. When he saw what had been lying on top of him, he froze.

It was the corpse of the lizard demon, and Red was resting in a large pool of its blood.

CHAPTER 19

BLOATED

BEFORE RED COULD PROCESS what had happened, another pang of pain wracked his body. He gritted his teeth and looked down at his arms.

His missing fingers had regenerated, but he had no time to be happy about it. His veins bulged as whatever energy he'd absorbed while unconscious looked for an outlet. It wasn't just his arms, either. The energy traveled all over his body, pumped by a heart ready to collapse under the strain.

From one hell to another.

Red groaned. Before he could do anything, he had to move this giant corpse lying on top of him.

Eventually, he managed, but his situation worsened. The bloating became unbearable, and Red couldn't even see properly as blood blocked his vision.

He knew what he had to do. He had to get this energy out of him, and for that, he needed to provide an outlet.

Red reached for the knife at his waist, blindly grabbing before feeling the cold handle of the blade. Then, quickly, he slashed at his wrists with the knife.

A jet of blood left his body, sizzling as the crimson fluid evaporated a moment later. He felt some relief, but the wound closed in the blink of an eye, and pressure continued to build.

Red winced. He had never expected his own regeneration to work against him.

He made another cut, but it closed again. Another jet of blood spewed out, transforming into a mist before dissipating into the fog. This time, he didn't relent and continued to cut.

Attempts at keeping the wound open didn't work, his body doing its utmost to keep him healed even from the inside, and he could only repeat the same desperate slashing movement over and over. Red didn't even register the pain any longer.

After slicing himself dozens of times over the course of a few minutes, he felt the pressure inside his body diminish. Yet the effect was so small that it hardly made a difference.

The method worked, but just barely.

This will take too long.

He hadn't forgotten where he was. This was monster territory, and more than that, he was still racing to complete this trial before Ricard and the imperials. He couldn't afford to waste time.

Red got up, collected his things—including the remaining half-broken purple arrow—and looked around. He couldn't hear or see any monsters, and his crimson sense wasn't detecting any fluctuations, either.

After falling unconscious, Red had completely lost any sense of direction —for all the good it did him in this fog anyway. He picked a direction—the one he assumed he'd been heading towards earlier—and began to run.

The energy in his body was debilitating, but as soon as Red moved, he felt an explosive energy course through his muscles. The wind talisman had long since run out, but he was running as fast as he had before with its help.

He didn't stop trying to eject the energy from his body, though. Red tried cutting veins on other parts of his body along the way, but all the wounds healed just as quickly. Still, the experiments were having a positive effect, as the pressure in his body shrank ever so slightly.

Red had barely run for a few minutes when he felt more monster fluctuations enter his crimson sense. He froze in surprise.

The range of his crimson sense had increased. He wasn't sure by how much, but he was certain that the ability had improved. The fluctuations of the monsters also felt clearer in his mind somehow, but Red couldn't pinpoint what that meant, and neither did he have the time to experiment with it right now.

The creatures weren't moving, but they were still blocking his path like before.

What am I supposed to do?

Trying to sneak past these monsters while spewing blood mist from his body wasn't a good idea, but what choice did he have? Wait until the bloating passed? That wasn't an option.

He clenched his teeth and made a decision.

I have to risk it.

He crouched and approached the monsters through the heavy fog. As soon as he came within thirty meters of the beasts, their fluctuations stirred.

Red froze again, staring forward in disbelief. The monsters closest to him moved, and soon enough, another stampede of dozens of monsters in the Lesser Ring Realm was stirring around him.

Did they smell my blood?

He didn't have the time to consider the question as he braced himself, preparing to dodge the stampeding monsters. A few creatures charged in his direction, the ground rumbling before them.

Red prepared to move out of the way, but to his shock, the monsters changed directions as soon as they reached him, stumbling over themselves to avoid his path. Something was wrong.

... Could it be?

Red continued to run forward, ready to dodge the monsters. But there was no need, as they all avoided him as soon as they got close, with no need to even lay eyes on the human.

He confirmed it. This was the work of the crimson aura.

It had happened with the snake too, once enough blood had poured out of his body. Red imagined this was the same phenomenon, except this time he couldn't see any signs of the crimson aura surrounding him.

Could this be something else?

Red wasn't sure, but it didn't matter. The effects were still very real.

He abandoned all pretenses of sneaking and ran right into the middle of the rampaging monsters. Each of them could kill him with a simple swipe of their paw, but as soon as Red came close, they avoided him in terror, as if driven by a primal fear.

More and more fluctuations entered his crimson sense, and without exception, they all avoided him. Soon enough, Red felt as if he had stirred the entire world into chaos.

But he didn't forget the danger he was still in. He continued to cut himself as sprays of bloody mist spewed into the fog.

Red didn't know how much time had passed in this state. An hour? Two hours?

All Red focused on was running and easing the pressure inside his body. He felt inexhaustible in this state, and even moving at max speed for hours on end didn't drain his stamina.

And yet the fog seemed endless. Monster continued to pour out and run from him, and Red was quite certain the number of Lesser Ring Realm creatures he had come across was in the thousands.

The pressure had fallen by more than half under Red's efforts and constant running. He gradually grew worried of what would happen if he ran out of the energy—but thankfully, the fog finally changed.

It thinned, and Red could see the world more clearly. The giant monsters all running from him were revealed, creatures he had never seen before in his life.

Of course, once he could see them, the beasts could also see him. Their panic was intensified—now they knew the source of their terror. The monsters avoided him even before getting close, and a few minutes later he couldn't feel even a single soul with his crimson sense.

He didn't slow down, though.

As the fog dissipated, a gigantic shadow appeared before his eyes.

The mountain!

His objective was now within reach. It was there, only a few kilometers away from him. When Red laid his eyes on it, he knew something was different about the peak. Its pressure bore down on him, threatening to crush all that approached it.

He became certain that it wasn't an illusion.

Red's eyes wandered down to the foot of the mountain. There he saw a large stone gate, over thirty meters high, embedded in the rock.

What caught Red's attention, though, was the being that stood in front of it.

It seemed to be a giant lion, a creature he had only read about in books, sporting a mane and almost as tall as the gate itself. Yet as he ran closer, he noticed something off about the creature.

Its skin was stone, and it appeared totally motionless in its seated position. Red almost thought it was a statue, but he could swear the creature was staring right at him.

Within a couple hundred meters of the monster, Red slowed down. By now, the pressure had lowered enough that he no longer felt he would explode, so he kept whatever energy remained inside him in reserve.

He looked the creature over, unsure of what to do. Not even being this close to the stone lion made it clearer to him whether or not it was alive.

That was, until its mouth moved.

"You made quite a mess of this place, didn't you?" A deep voice resounded from within the creature, reaching Red's ears with a profound echo.

Red frowned. "You can talk?"

The lion scoffed, displaying a humanlike expression and disposition. "Of course I can. I'm a construct, not a monster."

Red had never heard the term before, but he felt somewhat relieved that he wasn't facing another monster. The fact a statue was speaking to him didn't faze him either.

"Don't try to change subjects." The lion glared at the boy. "You caused so much chaos in the fog that I had to interfere to keep things under control."

"It wasn't my intention," Red admitted.

"And?" The lion frowned. "Aren't you going to apologize?"

He shook his head. "I did what I had to do."

The lion fell silent, its unfriendly eyes still examining Red.

"Do I need to defeat you to continue?" he asked.

The lion sneered. "Defeat me? You think you'd be able to do that?"

Red considered the question. "Probably not."

This was a thirty-meter-tall monster made of stone. He couldn't imagine himself being able to kill it.

"To proceed, you must pass the test," the lion said.

"What test?"

"It doesn't matter... You don't need to undergo the test. You pass."

He stared at it in surprise. "I pass?"

"I have been observing you, and I judge you worthy to continue," the lion said. "Of course, under other circumstances, I would have been stricter, but...

It has come to our attention during these trials that some competitors have been given an unfair advantage over others. As such, the playing field must be leveled to a certain extent."

Red came to a realization. "The imperials?"

The creature shook its head. "This doesn't concern you. You should just be happy that you'll be able to advance to the last part of this trial."

Although Red was still curious, he didn't press the matter.

The lion stood up, the ground rumbling beneath its feet. It moved out of the way of the stone gate before sitting back down.

Then the gate opened on its own, just enough that a small slit formed for Red to pass through.

The lion looked back at Red. "Go ahead, cultivator... In the end, the ultimate rules of this trial can't be changed. You must rely on yourself if you want to win our master's inheritance."

Red contemplated the golem's words before nodding.

Then, with a mind fully focused and prepared for the task ahead, he stepped forward.

Towards whatever awaited him at the heart of the mountain.

CHAPTER 20
MEETING THE LEADER

BEYOND THE GATE was a large stone corridor. It was lit up by the lamps Red was used to seeing in the trial, and it seemed to lead deep into the mountain. He found no decorations along its walls other than the simple markings of stone bricks.

He tried to see what awaited him at the end of this corridor, but the passage stretched into the distance.

Red frowned. *This again?*

His curiosity about these endless corridors had long since faded. Now he wondered why the creator of this place needed to make everything so long. There was no point in complaining, though.

Red took a deep breath and walked down the corridor.

He focused on his surroundings, expecting the next trial to have begun without his knowledge. But nothing out of the ordinary happened, and to his surprise, the long corridor did eventually have an end.

Red arrived in a large circular room. There was nothing of note inside, other than a massive spiral stone staircase carved along the walls of the room. The steps looked quite crude, and there were no railings along its length. He had a hard time believing a person had built this, no matter how strong. Still, who else but a cultivator could have carved out a mansion in a mountain?

He looked up, hoping to see where the stairs led, but all he saw was an endless spiral of steps. Whatever the next trial entailed, it might lead him straight to the apex of the mountain. Before climbing the stairs, Red looked around, hoping to spot anyone else's tracks.

There was nothing. He sighed and started running up the stairs.

Even with his improved speed, it didn't feel like he was making any progress.

After ten minutes of running without pause, the ground below had become nothing more than a tiny speck. Yet when he looked above, he could still see no end to the stairs.

Red was forced to slow down as he sensed the extra energy in his body running thin. Eventually, he finally spotted a ceiling above him, as well as an opening.

He pushed himself through this last leg of his journey, afraid that he was already too late. As he got close to the end, though, Red heard something.

Someone's fighting.

Who was it? Ricard? The imperials? Reinhart?

He couldn't tell, but he slowed down as he neared the end of the stairs.

What do I do?

Only now did Red realize how ill-equipped he was for fighting. He had lost his cleaver and his bow, and had used up all his talismans. The weapons he had left were a knife, the purple arrowhead, and a few empowerment pills. Even with those items, he would be hard-pressed to win against any of those people in a fight. Without them, he'd simply have no hope.

I need to wait for my chance.

As he ascended, the noises of battle came closer. It sounded like metal clashing against metal. Were they fighting amongst themselves?

His crimson sense detected a handful of fast-moving fluctuations. There were three of them—one of which seemed to be in the Lesser Ring Realm, all of which belonged to humans.

Ricard and the imperials.

Other than those fluctuations, he felt nothing more. Which confused him.

Are they fighting with each other?

Red didn't know for sure until he finally reached the last section of stairs leading up to the opening in the ceiling. He caught a glimpse of the dark abyssal sky overhead—this opening led to the outside world.

He carefully approached the opening before trying to see what was going on outside.

These stairs didn't lead to the peak. They led to an open-air platform lower on the mountain's side, surrounded by tall, sharp stones. He couldn't see much around him, as the many large rocks spread around the platform blocked his vision.

No, that's not right.

Red looked at said "rocks" more closely. They were broken-down statues of monsters, similar to the lion he had seen at the foot of the mountain. Many were shattered, with marks of charring and weapon damage. There were more of them than he could count.

He quickly connected the dots about what had been happening above his head.

Red walked further out of the opening, hiding behind one of the large statues. On the other side of this platform, he saw the three individuals whose fluctuations he had detected.

Two of them were sporting armor like that of the imperials he saw earlier, and wielding longswords glowing with golden light. A man and a woman, both blonde and far taller than the local folk of Bestrem. They carried themselves in combat as soldiers, and everything about them left no doubt as to their identity.

In fact, Red even recognized one of them. It was the man he and Allen had stalked and stolen from in town.

The third one, whom he assumed was Ricard, wore simple leather armor and wielded a spear. He also wore a dark hood and mask around his head, hiding his face from Red. Yet from what he could see, he was much younger than Red had assumed.

Their opponent was a large creature made of stone. It stood on two legs like a human, but that was as far as similarities went. A distorted torso and broad belly were carried by muscular arms and legs with vicious claws jutting out. With a monstrous head and horns, it resembled the crimson demon Red had fought earlier.

Despite its movements and expression, it was not a living creature, but rather a construct, as Red now knew. That was why he couldn't detect its fluctuation as he approached.

The demon construct also seemed close to defeat. Ricard circled around it, moving faster than any cultivator Red had seen before. The construct tried to strike at him, but the man had no issues dodging its attacks. He dove back as the stone beast tried to claw him down and, in the same movement, stabbed forward with his spear.

Pale-green energy gathered at the tip. When the weapon clashed against the construct's side, there came an explosion of wind blades. Countless shards of stone shattered as a huge chunk of its frame dissolved.

Spiritual Arts.

This was the first time Red had ever seen one in person, and he couldn't help but stare in awe. The creature didn't seem to feel pain, keeping up its offensive. The bandit leader, however, had already retreated with surprising swiftness, and the construct's head swiveled, unable to find him.

"Do it now!" Ricard shouted, his voice authoritative and hoarse.

The imperials closed in.

The woman took out a talisman and shouted out its trigger while her companion dashed forward with his glowing sword. The man's weapon struck the construct's leg with another explosion of golden light and stone.

At the same time, the woman waved her talisman toward the construct. A wind blade formed, then shot forward.

It crashed straight into its chest, bringing an even bigger explosion of detritus. A cloud of dust formed across the battlefield, and a few seconds later, a thud echoed.

When the dust cleared, Red saw that the construct had collapsed, unmoving, the upper half of its body completely missing.

He hadn't even had time to consider interfering in the fight before it was over.

The imperials gave a sigh of relief while Ricard surveyed the platform.

"Is that all?" the bandit leader asked.

"It should be." The male imperial nodded. "From here on out, you shouldn't find any more resistance in the trial."

"Good." Ricard stowed away his spear on his back. "Then you should wait here while I finish this."

The female imperial frowned. "Wait here? This wasn't the deal you made with our captain."

"Your captain isn't here." Ricard glared at them with emotionless eyes. "Besides, there are still some insects you need to take care of."

As he spoke, he looked over at the exact spot where Red was hiding.

He felt a shiver run down his spine. He tried to hide more thoroughly behind the rocks, but he knew it was too late.

"What do you mean by that?" the imperial asked.

"You heard what I said. I thought no one else would be able to make it this far."

"There's no way anyone else could have survived—"

"Enough," Ricard said. "Just come out, I've already seen you."

Red knew the bandit leader was speaking to him, but he didn't move from his hiding spot.

"Would you prefer I drag you out myself?" Ricard asked impatiently.

Red sighed. He knew he had no choice.

He stood up and walked out from behind his cover.

The imperials' expressions twisted in shock.

"This... This isn't possible." The female imperial was staring at him, mouth agape.

"I know you," Ricard said as eyed Red. "You're part of that Water Dragon Sect in town, aren't you? You and your friends have been killing quite a few of my men over the last few months."

"How did you spot me?" Red asked.

The bandit pointed at his eyes. "I have a special technique I learned in my army days. It was taught to Lesser Ring Realm cultivators specifically so we could spot hiding cockroaches like you." He lowered his hand. "What about the rest of my men? Have any of them lived?"

Red shook his head. "Maybe a few are hiding around the trial, but most of them died."

"That's unfortunate." He took the news well. His tone betrayed no sadness or turmoil. The bandit leader looked over at the imperials. "So? Didn't you say no one else was ever going to be able to pass those trials?"

The male imperial winced. "No one should have. Without proper preparation, it should have been nearly impossible to make it to the mountain."

"And yet here he is." Ricard looked over at Red. "A kid, no less. What do you suppose happened?"

The imperial's expression grew ugly. "I... don't know."

"Well, make sure you find out." Ricard patted his shoulder. "In the meantime, I'll be finishing up this trial."

He walked away without sparing another glance at the imperials or Red.

The boy couldn't see much from his position, but behind all the detritus of the constructs, he saw another set of spiral stairs climbing up the side of the mountain that led up to the very peak.

Before long, Ricard had disappeared from view.

Red was left alone, facing two imperials who stared at him with murderous eyes.

CHAPTER 21

FACE TO FACE

"Are you the brat who stole from me?" the male imperial asked, voice threatening.

The question did not surprise Red, considering Reinhart had also been aware of the theft. He nodded. "It was me."

The man smiled. "And did you make good use of those talismans?"

"We used some of them to kill your other companions."

"You what?!" The female imperial glowered at him.

She was about to charge, but her companion held her back. He measured Red with a skeptical gaze. "There's no way they would lose to someone as weak as you."

"You're right," Red admitted. "I had help, though... Here, I can show you proof." He took the compass from his pouch. "This is what you were using to navigate in the trial, wasn't it?"

The woman's face twisted in anger. "You cultivator scum, I'll kill you!"

"Enough!" Her companion once more held her back. He also looked hostile, but he wasn't about to lose his cool.

"What do you expect to do by telling us this?" the imperial asked. "Just anger us and make the few remaining minutes of your life that much more painful?"

"I was hoping to learn why you were here," Red answered. He was actually trying to buy time as he came up with a plan, but he wasn't about to let the imperials know that.

The man shot him down. "You are not the one asking questions here. Tell us how you got this far and we'll make your death as painless as possible."

"Sure, what do you want to know?"

Red put on a cooperative guise, but his mind was brainstorming countless plans for escaping this situation. Unfortunately, the two imperials were watching him like hawks, and Red knew the slightest misstep would leave him dead.

What do I do?

"How did you get past the snake?" the man asked.

"One of the bandits told us how to do it."

"Useless scum." The man grimaced. "And how exactly did you manage to get to the mountain this quickly?"

"I used the compass," Red said.

"Don't lie to me." The imperial pointed his glowing sword at him. "You have no idea how to make it work, and the others would never tell you."

He wasn't wrong about that. Red thought about lying further, but he didn't want to enrage the man.

"I used the tornadoes," he confessed. "They were the solution to finding those invisible buildings."

"I see..." The man looked satisfied. "And the fog? How did you pass it?"

"I sneaked through."

The man's face fell again. "If necessary, we can wring the information from you by force."

Just as Red hesitated, a familiar fluctuation entered his crimson sense. He felt compelled to look in its direction, but he didn't want to give it away to his opponents.

"We're wasting our time," the female imperial said. "We should just torture him until he speaks."

Her companion considered the idea, but didn't act on it. Red guessed he was afraid the boy might be hiding something, or that someone else might be around to support him. It was a reasonable assumption. After all, someone who had made it this far in the trial would have their own powers to rely on.

Red decided to play on those fears. "The spirit let me through," he said.

"The spirit?" The man looked surprised.

Red nodded. "It said you had an unfair advantage over the other competitors, so it let me through the last few trials."

"The spirit would never do that!"

"I thought so too. But it was apparently angry at how you were using those compasses and how you knew all the trial's challenges before coming in."

What Red said was half-true. The lion at the gate had said something to that effect. He just decided to embellish the truth.

The imperials' reaction was immediate, their faces filling with doubt. In the meantime, the fluctuation was coming closer. Red didn't know if the return of this individual would benefit him or not, but it was his only hope of surviving.

The male imperial became grave. "How do we know you're speaking the truth?"

"I would have never made it this far without their help," he said. Red had actually passed through the fog on his own, but he wasn't certain he would have made it inside the mountain if the stone lion hadn't let him through.

This seemed enough to convince the man, whose face was overwritten with concern.

"This is not right, Dumas!" the woman cried. "The ancestor would never do this to us. He sent us his visions!"

He appeared conflicted, but after a moment's thought, the man grew resolute. "There is no room for doubt, Vega. We don't know if this child is telling the truth, and even if he is, there must be a reason for the ancestor's actions."

"R-right!" The woman flushed and nodded. "I will not doubt the ancestor's will again!"

Red observed the whole interaction with slight curiosity. His primary concern was getting out of this place alive. The fluctuation had stopped moving and was within fifty meters of them, seemingly unnoticed by the imperials.

Red didn't know what it was waiting for, but he knew he had to buy more time.

"You said you're from the Water Dragon Sect, correct?" the male imperial asked him again.

Red nodded.

"Red hair, no older than ten... You're the kid that arrived in town a few months ago, aren't you?"

Red didn't like where this conversation seemed to be headed.

The woman looked taken aback. "Dumas, are you suggesting...?"

The man raised his hand to interrupt her. He examined Red with a steely gaze. "Are you the slave we've been looking for?"

Red's stomach sank. He refused to respond, but that was enough confirmation for the imperial.

"In retrospect, we should have looked further into you," he said. "We were quick to dismiss you, since the information we were given mentioned that the slave was a powerful and dangerous individual... We thought a child like you didn't fit such a description, and yet, here you are—one of the only survivors of this trial."

"What do you want from me?" Red asked.

"We have been ordered to capture you and bring you back to our superiors—if that wasn't possible, to exterminate you by any means..." The grip around his sword tightened. "It just so happens there's no real way to imprison anyone inside this trial, is there?"

Red knew what he meant. The hawk had said that once the trial was done, it would teleport everyone back to where they'd entered. This meant the imperials couldn't force anyone to remain their prisoner once this trial was done, leaving them no other choice.

Red tensed, his hand hovering over the purple arrowhead in his pocket.

"You shouldn't fight back," the man said. "Since you cooperated, I promise to make the last moments of your life as painless as possible."

He stepped forward while his companion took out a talisman. She stared at Red, watching for any sudden movements.

Red braced himself, prepared to put up one last struggle against the imperials, when he felt the fluctuation behind him move. A shrill laughter followed.

"Ack! Look what we have! Foolish imperials! All lost, far from home!"

"Who's there?!" The man swiveled in search of the source.

A small monkey hopped out from behind a pile of rocks. Its body was rotting, and yet it could still move and talk.

"Undead!" the female imperial barked.

She threw her talisman at the monkey. Another blade of wind formed out of thin air and shot forward. The animal didn't even have time to move before its body disintegrated in the gust in a shower of gore.

Red's eyes twitched. Was his supposed savior dead just like that?

A moment later, another fluctuation entered his crimson sense. A vulture similar to the ones they had fought in the desert landed on one of the rocks up above, screeching in anger. This beast, too, was partially rotted.

"Rude, rude!" the undead vulture screamed at the imperials. "Idiot! Savage! Don't interrupt when I speak!"

"This... How..." The woman stared in disbelief.

"It's a necromancer," her companion said, his voice grim.

Her face paled with caution and fear.

The vulture laughed. "That's it! Fear me, flee from me! Ants should know superiors!"

"Undead scum!" The woman glared at the undead. "Creatures like you are a violation of life itself! You shouldn't be permitted to live!"

The bird continued to laugh. "Then kill me! Kill me! Waste another talisman! How many you have?!"

She seemed on the verge of doing just that, but her companion held her back.

"We need to run," he said.

She hesitated, but ended up nodding.

They ran towards the stairs Ricard had just ascended.

"NO! NO!" the bird screeched. "Was not done talking!"

Even more fluctuations entered Red's detection range. From behind the stone walls surrounding the platform, dozens of undead vultures appeared out of nowhere, swooping toward the imperials.

"The other way!" the man cried, and they both headed towards the other set of stairs, towards the foot of the mountain.

At the same time, the female imperial activated another talisman, and a dome barrier appeared around them. The undead vultures clashed against the shield, scratching at it with their talons.

The imperials, safe for now, ignored Red on their way out. Red simply watched.

The vulture perched on top of the rock screeched as it watched the imperials try to escape. "Said I was not done talking!"

More fluctuations appeared around Red as undead vultures joined the fight. Some were markedly stronger than the others, and when they appeared before his eyes, Red confirmed it by their enormous size.

These were vulture zombies in the Lesser Ring Realm. Almost a dozen of them, too.

These birds came crashing down onto the shield. Soon, Red couldn't even see the imperials under the countless birds all pecking and clawing at their protection. The imperials weren't advancing any longer under the overwhelming siege.

The screeching from the undead vultures was deafening, and Red had to cover his ears. He couldn't see what was happening to the imperials, but within seconds he heard their labored breaths and saw the light of another talisman from beneath the bird pile.

It was to no avail. As some of the monsters fell, more flew from beyond the stone wall—reinforcements. It was a ruthless strategy of throwing bodies at their opponents, and there was nothing the imperials could do to fight back no matter how many talismans they had.

Almost a minute later, the sounds of struggle stopped. The zombie birds flew back, landing around the platform and away from the center of the struggle.

Red could finally see what had become of the imperials. Little more than unrecognizable bits and pieces of gore were strewn across the ground. Even their plate armor and equipment had been torn and destroyed, only unrecognizable scraps remained. The undead army had left nothing behind.

The vulture perched atop the stone wall laughed. "It's what you get! Be more respectful next life!"

At this point, the zombie vultures surrounding Red didn't give him the slightest bit of apprehension or fear. After all, what could he do against this kind of opponent?

"Long time no see, kid!" the vulture said. "Knew you'd come! Now... let's talk!"

CHAPTER 22

TO THE LAST

RED STARED at the undead vulture with caution. "What do you want?"

"What I want?" The creature beat its wings in indignation. "You came here to negotiate, right?"

He frowned. "I had no intention of meeting you when I stumbled on this place."

The vulture squawked at him. "It matters not! Matters not! Now that you here, we can make deal, correct?"

Red hesitated. He didn't feel like making a deal at all with this necromancer, but he was hardly in a position to deny them.

"Is this about the entrance to the underground?" Red asked.

"Yes, yes!" The vulture gleefully flapped its wings. "You saw it too, right? Big scorpions with green eyes!"

He nodded. He'd seen the creature back at the canyon, but he hadn't had time to study it, and he wasn't confident it was a monster from the Moonstone Mines. But the necromancer seemed to be giving him confirmation.

"This place, this man... He knows! He knows a way in!" the vulture said. "It's how he brought that thing! Yes, yes!"

Red narrowed his eyes. This revelation came as a surprise to him, but something else confused him. "Earlier you said you wanted me to take you to the entrance of the underground I exited from. When did your intentions change?"

"They didn't change!" the vulture squawked. "I searched entire forest already! Found way you came from! Imperials got to it first! Blocked it, closed it! Bastards! Unforgivable!"

"So what you said earlier was a lie?"

"Not all! Still need your help! Need you to win trial, get information, then lead me to entrance! In exchange, I help you with curse!"

"Why me, then? If you don't need my information or my crystal, couldn't you have made this deal with anyone else? Or better yet, can't you just win the trial yourself?"

The vulture raged. "Not allowed! Stupid bird won't let me! Besides... There's something else."

"This is quite enough." A new voice echoed through the platform. "I won't allow you to interfere with this trial any longer, necromancer."

Red turned towards the source. In the center of the platform, out of thin air, a figure emerged. Its body was translucent, and yet the being's shape formed a familiar outline.

It was the hawk spirit, floating.

"You!" The vulture pointed at the hawk with one of its decrepit wings. "What now? Come to spoil plans again?!"

"We had a deal, necromancer," the hawk said in its impassive tone. "I would allow your minion to roam free on these grounds as long as you didn't interfere with the trials. Yet not only have you killed two competitors, but you wish to influence another one."

"Hypocrite!" the vulture spat. "Could have stopped me any time, but didn't! Gave silent approval! Now try to blame me?! Bastard! Liar!"

"As you said, I gave you my approval to kill these individuals, but that is as far as your interference goes." The hawk pointed a wing at Red. "If this child wishes to beat this trial, then he must do it on his own. Likewise, I won't allow you to reveal sensitive information or influence his decisions in case he was to win."

"Bastard! You used me! Couldn't kill them yourself, so let me do it! Let me finish job, at least! Still one cheater left!"

"I will not." The hawk lowered its small head. "Although that person cheated, he is still worthy of winning this trial, unlike the others."

Red could only assume they were talking about Ricard.

"You insane! Stupid!" Wild with fury, the vulture thrashed its wings. "He still working with imperials! What difference it makes?!"

"I am under no obligation to explain my decisions to you, necromancer," the hawk said. "I am wasting time explaining this much to you merely in exchange for the help you provided. Must I remind you of the situation you find yourself in?"

The vulture fell silent. It stared at the hawk. "What about after? Can I speak with child?"

"Whatever he does after the trial is none of my concern."

The vulture perked up. It looked over at Red. "Quick! Go! Run! Don't let cheater win before you!"

The army of zombie vultures stepped back, opening up a straight path towards the stairs leading up the mountain.

But Red hesitated. He looked over at the hawk, who had shown itself to be a less-than-impartial judge. This entire situation and conversation was too much for him to process in such a short amount of time, and he felt like a pawn in a game whose stakes he didn't understand.

It made him suspicious.

The hawk noticed his hesitation. "If you have made it to this place, through whatever adversity, you may consider yourself judged and found worthy of winning this trial. You must only scale the last step before your competitor... And I can promise you that whatever awaits the victor ahead will only benefit them."

Red nodded. He was already on a path with no return—what was one more step into the abyss?

The vulture continued to urge him on. "Go, go! You already behind!"

He obliged the necromancer. He ran towards the steps, hoping to catch up to Ricard before it was over.

Red felt the gazes of two strange and incredibly powerful beings boring into his back, both heavy with expectation.

Red walked up the steps of the spiral staircase. It was carved into the mountain, corkscrewing up to the peak hundreds of meters above. The steps were narrow, too, and there was no rail to speak of, meaning that if he slipped, he would fall kilometers below to his death.

Yet when Red looked down, he didn't see the expanse of the desert. Instead, he only saw endless fog in every direction.

Above him, the view wasn't any more comforting. There was only darkness, no signs of stars or moon, and he feared looking up more than he did looking down.

Once more, Red's sense of space was distorted as he ascended the stairs for far too long, all while the peak of the mountain remained ever so distant.

He saw no signs of Ricard, either. He'd run for the first several minutes, expecting the man to appear so he could overtake him with a final burst of speed, but he never had. So he'd slowed down, conserving his energy, knowing there would be another layer to this trial.

Thankfully, the steps eventually had an end, and he saw the top of the mountain approaching. With a few more rounds up the spire, Red finally crested the peak.

The top of the mountain was surprisingly flat, so he could walk on without having to worry about stumbling and falling down. The entire area was only a few dozen meters of rather narrow rocky terrain, and Red still saw no signs of Ricard.

The only thing he saw at the peak was a stone archway standing right at the edge.

It had no markings and was on the verge of falling apart. Red looked through it, but there was only the endless fog and an inevitable fall for those that tried to step through the archway.

But how could the prospect of death scare Red at this point? Since this was the only thing at the top of the mountain, it was the only path that made sense.

Red took a deep breath and stepped through the stone archway, his eyes wide open the entire time. He felt his feet stepping on nothing but air, and for a single moment, he worried he was truly going to fall to his death. But he followed through with his stride, passing through the archway in one go.

He blinked his eyes. When they opened, everything around him had changed.

Dozens of water droplets pelted his skin. A deluge of rain and strong wind drenched him. Thunder rumbled from above as he protected his face from the sudden assault on his senses. His body would be taken away by the winds if he so much as stumbled.

Where am I?

Red collected himself and tried to observe his surroundings. He saw nothing but dark-gray fog and the endless flashes of thunder from above.

His eyes shifted toward the ground, but he couldn't even see his own feet. Even his hands were only visible if he held them right up to his eyes.

With the storm bearing down on him and his senses useless, Red decided to take a step. He almost tripped as his feet came down onto a raised platform.

A step?

Red tried to confirm this by feeling with his feet, slowly waving them forward. Another hard surface blocked his way. He then tried to plant his foot on top, and sure enough, he started to ascend yet another set of stairs.

This time, Red couldn't see whether anything was in his way, so he took a slower approach. He ascended a dozen steps in this manner until the sounds of the storm started becoming more muffled and distant.

Is it subsiding?

Red didn't know, but he still felt the winds and heavy rain peppering his body.

As he scaled another few steps, the noise of the storm continued to fall away. This had to be wrong.

He brought his right hand to his ear, snapping his fingers. He barely heard anything, and the noise that came through sounded like it was underwater.

His heart sank. *I'm going deaf.*

After the shocking realization, Red composed himself. He assumed this was part of the trial, so he didn't panic. Even if he was deaf, there was nothing to fear. All he needed to do was to keep walking, right?

He soon learned things weren't as simple as he thought.

Another handful of steps up, and his entire world became silent.

After a few more steps, his field of vision narrowed. Even though he had been seeing nothing but fog and lightning, he was quick to notice the loss.

Red grimaced, focused, and discovered even more was off. The smell of rain had faded. He couldn't feel the cold wind and rain against his skin. The pain and strain of his body was fading away.

It was then that he knew.

With every step he took, he was losing more of his senses.

CHAPTER 23

VOID

IT WAS STRANGE. Red didn't feel any type of pain or danger, and yet as he climbed the stairs, his steps weakened, his vision faded, and the world seemed to recede.

Dread crept in. He wasn't fighting a monster, or anything he could see or touch. Instead, Red was combating this unknown force that took away his sense of awareness little by little—and he didn't know what to do about it.

He was losing awareness of his own body.

Instinctively, he slowed to a dead stop. Red hoped to find a way to stop this phenomenon from happening, yet not even pausing afforded him the chance to think. The feeling of doom was growing stronger, clouding his very mind.

I can't stop moving!

Thinking on the problem was pointless. Red decided to hurry through this storm. He hoped there was an end to this fog and that once he left it, his senses would return to normal.

Yet while his aim was well-founded, it was already too late.

Every step weakened as all feeling in his skin disappeared. He ordered his body to move, but he could not tell whether he was making any progress or simply lying still on the ground. His hearing was gone. Blindness crept in, and what replaced his clear vision wasn't darkness as he had expected. Instead, it was nothing—a complete lack of existence or substance.

NAMELESS AUTHOR

An unknowing void.

Red felt he had conquered his fear of death. He still hesitated in the face of overwhelming danger, but he could act in spite of that, no matter how risky or certain death might seem. In a way, he had won against death itself.

And with death defeated, what else was there to be afraid of?

He had never been so wrong before.

This loss of control of his own senses, this silent descent into an abyss of nothingness while still being completely aware of his own thoughts—it horrified him.

To die, to feel pain, to be hurt both physically and mentally—these were things that Red understood very well. Pain was something he had experienced and learned to resist. Yet to be stripped of all his connections to the world, helpless as awareness of his own body disappeared, unable even to resist, was the most terrifying thing he had ever experienced.

He could no longer sense. Could he even move? With his whole body numb, his perception all faded, he could tell his legs to move, but he had no way to tell. He was functionally immobile.

No amount of struggle helped.

I can't... I need to do something!

Red had forgotten about the trial at this point. He focused on regaining control of his dwindling senses. First he tried the Radiant Current technique. After all, it had worked before when he couldn't move.

He repeated the mantras in his mind, commanding his hands to repeat the mudras even if he couldn't tell whether his body was executing the movements. To his surprise, Red felt his mind settle into that expanded awareness that helped him in the past.

When he tried to use this awareness to inspect his body, though, he was dismayed. There was nothing but void.

Red tried again, hoping to find something his mind could grasp.

It didn't work.

It was as if his entire body had disappeared. Neither his own mind nor his magical technique could detect even the slightest sign of his physical form. Red didn't know what to do.

What is going on?

He no longer had any sensation in his body, so he couldn't tell what was happening. Was his body truly gone? Why could he still think and sense his own consciousness, then?

Despite being numb to his physical functions, Red still felt panic. His emotions were still there, all the terror and anxiety he had been left with. In fact, he could feel them even more clearly now.

His consciousness stewed in the nothingness of the void, with no way to resist, no way to escape.

There was no pain in here. No suffering, no struggle.

There was nothing in here.

Only silence.

Red didn't know how much time passed. Perhaps a few seconds? Or maybe a year?

Time had no meaning when one couldn't sense its passing. To Red, it felt like both an instant and an eternity had passed at the same time.

He still felt as terrified as when this had first begun, and yet he had tried everything to escape with no success.

Red had tried to communicate with the crimson mist. He'd tried to use his crimson sense. He'd tried to expand his awareness with the meditation technique multiple times.

Nothing worked.

Red had nothing to grab onto. Nothing to help him out of this situation other than his own thoughts.

And so he thought.

He tried to figure out what had happened to him. Was his consciousness separated from his body? Were his bodily functions blocked by some kind of special technique?

There's no point in this.

In either scenario, what could he do to reverse the situation? Consciousness, Spiritual Arts—they were beyond his understanding.

Yet... Wasn't this a trial? If there was an issue in front of him, there was always a solution.

That was what Red had learned in this inheritance ground, so why would this be any different? There had to be a way out—he just had to find it.

Red reined in his mounting panic and focused on his thoughts.

He had to expand his search.

He reached into the depths of his memories. He considered the strangest possibilities, the most outlandish ideas. He tried to invoke the oddest beings and sights he had ever seen before, hoping any of them could bring him out of this situation.

Nothing worked.

It's useless...

Was he hoping for a miracle? For another otherworldly being or ability to appear out of nowhere and save his life?

He didn't know.

Maybe there was no way out. Maybe this trial had been a sham to give cultivators like him hope and then take it away at the very last step. It wouldn't be strange for a cultivator to do that.

Or maybe I'm just not good enough to beat this trial.

Red felt his efforts slip bit by bit. His thoughts slowed down, and the silence of the void grew inside his own mind.

He felt he was becoming part of the nothing. Maybe this was what awaited those who failed.

"Hm?! Turns out it was you reaching out!"

A familiar childish voice invaded his mind. The mysterious blob who had offered him a deal in the moonstone mines.

Red was shocked. He tried to open his eyes and look toward the voice before remembering he couldn't see anymore.

"There's no point in looking for me. There's nothing to see or feel in this place."

He tried to reply before remembering he had no voice.

The being discerned what he was thinking. "Are you surprised?" it asked in a mocking tone. "You shouldn't be. I told you our fates were tied back then!"

Red's mind trembled.

"Now look at what you've done to your body! As if that curse wasn't enough, now you also have demonic energy running inside your veins... My, my, it's like only one impending doom wasn't enough for you!"

He felt the being probing his mind, and he could do nothing to resist it.

"Ah, no wonder I felt you reach out to me! Turns out you're right on top of a gate to the void..." The being gazed into his mind. "This place looks interesting! Maybe I should pay it a visit once I get out."

Red struggled, trying to expel the voice from his consciousness. It didn't work.

"Now, why are you being so uncooperative?" it asked testily. "Weren't you the one who reached out for help in the first place?"

He didn't deny its claims. But he'd been desperate, and hadn't thought that recalling the blob in his mind would have any effect.

"So, have you thought about it? I can help you if you accept that deal."

Red's struggle intensified. He hadn't changed his mind. In fact, after the sheer terror of losing control over his senses, he was even more against that idea than before.

He would rather just fade away right now than go through that experience again.

"Ah, that's a shame!" the voice said. "Well, I wasn't expecting you to change your mind so soon anyway, so I guess I can't be that sad. Either way, good luck with this trial! I'm sure we will meet again in the future!"

The probing force in his mind disappeared as the voice faded away.

He was once more alone, but after the encounter with the dark being, his resolve had actually been reinforced.

I can't give up right now... I won't let it win.

Red focused on his thoughts again, searching for a way out. He went back to the voice's words. It had talked about his body and the demonic energy running through his veins.

It could feel my body.

This brought Red to one possibility. Maybe his mind and consciousness weren't split after all.

Even so, what can I do with that information?

Perhaps his body was still there, but did that make any difference? He couldn't move it.

No, that's not right.

Red had assumed he couldn't move his body at all because of this complete lack of senses. Yet there was nothing that indicated that for sure. Losing the feeling of touch didn't mean one was incapable of touching.

Or at least that was what Red liked to think. Without being able to feel any pressure against his skin, Red couldn't imagine walking or moving around properly.

Yet what did it matter?

As long as Red could move, he could still make progress. Even if it was by crawling, by spasming, by rolling his body, or by any other means. Even if it took an eternity to reach his goal.

Even if I'm wrong and I can't move at all... I can't give up.

As long as his mind was still there, Red would never give up.

He tried to make his body move, his mind sending the orders as if he could still sense his physical form. There was no feedback to tell him whether he was successful, but it didn't matter. He tried to push his feet, one after the other, as if he were walking.

He also used his hands to crawl forward in case he was on the ground. Then, to be sure, he moved the rest of his body, trying to make any movement or commotion he could to awaken himself from this nightmare.

Time blurred together. He began to lose faith in his plan, but there was nothing else he could do in this situation, so he kept sending orders to a body he didn't even know was there.

Then, all of a sudden, Red felt it.

A fluctuation entered his crimson sense. Ricard's fluctuation.

It seemed there was one thing in his body this place couldn't affect.

CHAPTER 24
THE LAST OBSTACLE

I NEED TO REACH HIM.

Red had no plan, and neither did he know what would happen if he reached Ricard. But the bandit leader's fluctuation was the only beacon of light in the darkness of the void, so Red had to grasp it with all his strength.

He continued to command his body to move.

To his surprise, the bandit leader's fluctuation inched closer.

I was right.

With his crimson sense, Red regained some sense of space. His body was still there and responding to his will. The only caveat was that he had no other sensory input, so he couldn't tell whether he was moving or not.

With the fluctuation as reference, though, Red believed he could still make progress.

In this manner, he approached Ricard. The progress was slow—so slow that Red felt he had only covered a few meters even after concentrating on the task for over ten minutes.

He couldn't tell whether this was because Ricard was also moving away from him, or because of his poor travel speed. Red was unable to sense his movements, and he couldn't even feel what position his body was in, so even if he could still move, it was evidently slow.

Still, he made progress. After what had to have been hours, the distance between him and Ricard was less than one hundred meters. It was then that he felt something.

This is...

Yes. He felt something.

A pressure against his skin. It was so slight and small that Red could have missed it, but in the endless nothing, he could feel it as clear as day. And it didn't stop there.

This same pressure splattered and retracted against multiple points in his body. Red had a hard time telling what he was feeling and where he was feeling it, but just this much progress was more than enough for him to grow hopeful.

As he moved forward, the sensations intensified. Cold, dampness, and even the slightest bit of pain returned to him, and Red welcomed them all with open arms.

Finally, he regained some awareness of his body. What he felt left him baffled.

I'm still standing?

Red expected to be on the ground, crawling around as he tried to inch forward. Yet he was still steady on his own two feet.

He felt this wasn't right, but just as he was contemplating it, Ricard's fluctuation began to fade from his crimson sense. The bandit leader was indeed moving, just like him.

I need to hurry.

Now that he'd recovered some feeling, Red increased his pace. He was bridging the gap, but he struggled to speed up further. His body was still unstable, and the relentless storm was still beating down on him.

Thankfully, it didn't seem like Ricard was moving any faster.

This chase continued for another hundred meters until even more of Red's senses returned. The noise of the water droplets striking his body, the smell of the rain, his foggy vision. The senses weren't fully functioning yet, but regaining control gave Red a sense of confidence and relief he had never felt before.

As his vision returned, he saw something through the fog—a blue light that pierced even the rain and mist. Without his knowledge, Red had been heading toward it the entire time as he pursued Ricard.

How did Ricard know that was there?

Was he not affected by the loss of his senses? Had the imperials given him another item to help him through this last trial? Only that made sense.

Red felt this whole situation was unfair.

Still, to his surprise, the distance between them was falling exponentially. This wasn't because Red was moving fast, but rather because Ricard was moving slowly.

In any normal situation, a Lesser Ring Realm cultivator could outpace a boy with no issues. Something was off.

As Red's senses recovered, he discovered the reason. A strong metallic smell reached his nose even through the rain.

Blood. Ricard was bleeding. Heavily, too.

What could have inflicted that injury? Did he fight someone inside this storm? Red didn't know, but he wasn't about to let this opportunity go to waste.

The light grew even stronger, and the storm and fog abated as he approached it. Through the fading mist, he saw the shadow of Ricard less than fifty meters away.

The rain weakened, and the pressure on Red's body all but disappeared. His vision cleared up, showing him the source of the blue light.

It was a large floating orb filled with currents of extraordinary water. Inside this translucent sphere, between the flows, Red saw sparkling blue dots, the source of the light. He thought these were glowing gems at first, but the more he stared at the orb, the more perplexed he became.

As the currents drifted by, the dots dissipated, only to reform into small crystals in a different section of the sphere. It was a mesmerizing sight, and Red felt his skin tingle from the Spiritual Energy within.

He wasn't the only one staring at it. Ricard had stopped moving too, similarly mesmerized by the sphere.

Red turned to him. Blood dripped down his armor, creating a long trail on the stone ground.

Ricard didn't seem to have noticed him.

Red took a deep but silent breath.

This is it, then.

He took out the empowerment pill bottles, his hand brushing the few weapons he had left.

"You made it here?" Ricard asked without turning around.

Red wasn't surprised the man could see him, considering what had happened earlier. He ignored his question and swallowed all the empower-ment pills—three in total.

"How did you do it?" the bandit asked. "I had to use the method those imperials gave me, but what did you have to fight through that? If I hadn't known what this trial would be about, I would have lost to despair."

Red ignored him, feeling the power of the pills coursing through his veins. How could he answer that question? He still wasn't sure what this trial had been about. All he'd done was experiment with everything that he could, and it had eventually paid off for him.

Ricard faced him. "Unfortunately, you made a mistake in challenging me. Even in this state, you don't really stand a chance."

His mask had slipped down, and Red could see a seasoned and scarred face beneath his hood. He didn't spend much time looking at it, though.

He crouched down, as if preparing to sprint forward.

Ricard observed him keenly. He took out his spear, preparing for Red's charge.

He didn't take the initiative.

This was already telling. His wounds were definitely more serious than they looked at first glance. Perhaps that was how he had escaped that void in the first place. Even so, it didn't mean Ricard was wrong about his chances of winning.

Which was why Red smeared his hand in the man's trail of blood as he crouched down. The burning sensation hit him not as strongly as he'd expected, but still filling his body with energy in a matter of moments.

This blood energy, coupled with the effects of the empowerment pills, made Red feel ready to explode from the power circulating inside him. But he didn't flinch. He grabbed his two remaining weapons.

In the next second, Red charged forward.

First, he threw his knife at Ricard, trying to imitate Rimold's movements. The blade flew straight for the man, but he parried it with his spear in a short and fluid motion, snapping it in half in the process.

Then, following the first projectile, Red threw out his next weapon. A dark-purple arrowhead flew at Ricard, who swatted it away as he had done with the knife. But when his spear hit the purple projectile, it exploded in a blinding purple light.

Ricard covered his eyes and jumped back, just in time to avoid a mist of poison that would have eaten away at his body. His weapon wasn't so lucky, though, as the corrosion tore into it.

Ricard simply threw the spear away as he prepared for Red's next attack. While he was distracted by the purple light, though, the boy had changed directions and circled around him.

Red was heading straight at the orb of crystalline water.

He heard a curse from behind him, but he didn't stop to look back. He expected Ricard to chase him, yet that didn't happen. Instead, there was a shrill sound, and something pierced his back and straight through the other side.

His blood energy sought to close the wound as he continued to run, trying to ignore the pain. Yet the next second, even more piercing shots drilled into his back, puncturing straight through his organs in quick succession, destroying his body from the inside.

Red's strength was rushing out, despite all the pills and the blood he had consumed. However, by this point, he was already within ten meters of the orb of water.

I won.

These were the last words Red thought as he dove towards the sphere.

CHAPTER 25
THE TRUTH OF THE TRIAL

WHEN RED CAME TO, he found himself lying on a cold, hard surface. His hands instinctively reached for his midsection, feeling for the puncture wounds he'd suffered before touching the orb. They weren't there.

Did my power heal me?

Red doubted it. He hadn't absorbed that much blood, and even then, he'd never suffered a wound that grievous. He took a risk by showing Ricard his back, and whether or not he'd reach his target, Red hadn't known if he would survive. He didn't even know if he would win by touching the orb.

He'd still gambled on it. Red knew he couldn't hesitate against someone like Ricard, and he hoped that when he won the trial, the hawk spirit wouldn't let him die to his wounds.

His bet had paid off.

"Clever," a voice called out to him. "It was a risky plan brought about by your own weakness, but it befits a true cultivator. The costs for your healing will still be detracted from your final reward, however."

"That's fine," Red said, sitting up. "It's better than nothing."

He looked over toward the voice. The hawk spirit was floating, staring down at him.

Red was also sitting on air, and around him were countless currents of water releasing blue light as they traveled, forming a sphere around him and the hawk.

He felt as if he were inside a dream. He extended his hand to touch one of the water currents, but it simply passed through his palm like he wasn't even there.

"Are we inside that water orb?" Red asked.

"We are."

"What kind of water is this?"

"Water refined by a Primordial Ocean Crystal," the spirit said. "It's among the most valuable belongings of my master. It can be used to cultivate the purest Water Spiritual Energy in the world."

"And you just placed it here? For anyone to touch?"

The hawk shook its head. "Even if someone managed to get their hands on it, they wouldn't be able to store it without the proper equipment. This water can pass through almost every kind of physical matter."

"Is it mine now?" Red asked.

"Sure. As long as you are able to keep it all inside your body, you can take it."

Red frowned. He obviously had no idea how to do that.

"Why did you help me?" Red asked again.

"I didn't help you. All I did was make sure that this trial was fair to all competitors. Besides, you still had to prove yourself to come this far."

He still wasn't convinced. "Were you the one who placed that demon in the fog?"

The spirit lowered its head. "That was a mistake on my part. I was aware of the demonic energy you carry inside your body, but the restrictions inside the fog should have suppressed it. I am still uncertain how the demon was able to detect you. I could not interfere to help you due to the nature of my existence. Yet you came out alive in the end, and that is all that matters."

"What if I didn't? Were you going to let the others win?"

The hawk went silent for a moment. "I... would have been forced to, despite my unwillingness."

Red decided to ask a question that had been on his mind this entire time. "Why were you unwilling? Because they cheated?"

The hawk nodded. "They knew about certain aspects of this trial, something that shouldn't have been possible, and even then, I could do nothing but watch as they used their knowledge to traverse the obstacles that my master had placed. It is an absolute disgrace to his name, and it's not something that I would never have allowed, were I able to do something about it."

Red followed his logic. "That's why you used that necromancer."

The hawk sighed like a human. "I was forced to, despite my reluctance. They were not restricted by the same laws that bind me. I was split between my duty of finding a deserving disciple as quickly as possible and my urge to punish those who would sully my master's name... It was not a simple decision to make."

Red frowned. "Why did you need to find a disciple as quickly as possible?"

Since the hawk was willing to tell him about these matters, he continued to throw questions at it.

"The ones who invaded this trial were mere proxies of an outsider's will," the spirit said. "Behind them are strong cultivators specialized in divination who have been trying to locate this inheritance ground for decades already."

"Divination?"

"It's the ability to gain insight into matters by reading the threads of fate. The specifics do not matter, but all you need to understand is that these cultivators found out about the existence of this inheritance ground, as well as some of the trials prepared for it... Which was why I had to hurry to find a worthy disciple."

"So, you chose to open up the trial."

Things started to connect in his mind. The sudden disappearance of the monsters, the hidden tunnels located throughout all the forest—they were all caused by this spirit. However, there were still matters that didn't make sense to him.

"Isn't opening up the trial even more dangerous if they're looking for it?" Red asked.

"The opening you went through is merely a portal to the inheritance ground. If a cultivator stronger than what my master allowed tried to enter, a mere thought on my part would be enough to sever the connection from the inheritance ground to that entrance. It is not a foolproof method, however, and I still took on a risk by revealing the entrance to the trial. All the same, it was necessary if I wanted to find a true inheritor for my master."

"But you ended up attracting some of their forces to the location, then," Red surmised.

"Indeed. I was fully prepared to sever the connection to that entrance, but thankfully, they didn't seem intent on invading and perhaps thought they could acquire the inheritance through normal methods."

What the hawk said made sense, but Red was more aware of the situation outside than the hawk. If it was the Empire that was searching for this trial, then of course they wouldn't send strong forces to the entrance, considering it was in the middle of enemy territory. A stealthy operation would avoid bringing attention to the inheritance ground, considering the Sects were monitoring their movements.

"What about the necromancer?" Red asked. "Why did you let them enter the trial?"

"I did not let him enter the trial. He was already inside it."

He frowned. "What do you mean?"

"I said the method for stopping cultivators' invasions wasn't foolproof. Long ago, that necromancer also tried to invade this inheritance ground through one of its entrances."

Red's eyes widened.

The hawk continued. "Luckily, my master had prepared some defenses in case that happened, so in the end I was able to imprison him inside a formation. Unfortunately, I had to spend a lot of resources to accomplish that, and I sincerely doubt this world could sustain other attacks on such a level."

"If that's the case, how can he still control his undead from the outside world?"

"That's because I allowed him to do it," the spirit said. "Although I had opened the entrance to this trial, that did not mean proper candidates would reach it in time before those crooks. So I made a deal with the necromancer —he would help me scout the outside world for proper candidates, and in exchange, perhaps he wouldn't end up under the control of another powerful cultivator from the outside world once they conquered the inheritance ground."

"He agreed to that?" Red asked in disbelief. That seemed like a terrible deal. "Didn't he try to negotiate for his release?"

"He did, but I would never accept such terms," the hawk said. "I would rather raze this whole place myself than risk releasing someone like him with knowledge of these grounds into the outside world. In the end, he accepted the deal. In his mind, he must have thought it would be easier to convince a weak and naïve cultivator to free him than someone who was as strong as him."

Dots connected like lightning inside Red's mind. "So that's why he helped me. He wanted me to free him."

The hawk nodded.

Red hesitated. "He offered me a deal. A beneficial deal."

"He did."

"Aren't you worried that I'll agree to it?"

"Why would I be?" The hawk shook its head. "You would need to be a fool to think that freeing someone countless times stronger than you and expecting them to hold up their end of the deal would turn out well for you. Since you won this trial, I know you are not a fool."

The spirit wasn't wrong.

"Besides, these are problems you must deal with by yourself in the future," it went on. "That formation won't keep him imprisoned forever, and you'll eventually have to decide what to do. Perhaps making a deal with him once you're stronger would be in your best interest."

Red couldn't imagine how he would face this problem in the future, but there was still an even more pressing matter he needed to address.

"The necromancer said the master of this place knows about the moonstone mines." He looked at the hawk with a meaningful gaze.

"He does," it said. "However, he hasn't found a way to deal with the curse, if that's what you're asking."

Red's brow furrowed. "You know about the curse?"

"I do. My master managed to lure a handful of creatures from one of the entrances of the moonstone caves. They were all very weak and mostly unremarkable, but the Spiritual Energy they kept inside their bodies was unlike anything my master had ever seen before. Unfortunately, on the night of a new moon, they all perished without exception."

"This..." Red was baffled. "If that's the case, how was that scorpion still alive?"

The hawk answered his question with a question of its own. "You come from that place too, right?"

Red hesitated. Still, he nodded.

"My master experimented countless times on those creatures, trying to find ways to stop this curse from taking effect," the hawk said. "He studied the moon, the energy, the pieces of moonstone these monsters brought with them to the outside... All except entering the caves himself. He eventually reached two partial solutions for keeping the creatures alive."

The bird waved its wing, and a translucent image of a scorpion formed in front of it. "If a creature was kept in a deep hibernation, then the curse wouldn't take effect."

Red immediately eliminated that option. What difference was there for him between being dead and being kept in a coma to stay alive?

"The second solution was a formation he developed." The hawk waved its wing again, and complex symbols appeared above the scorpion. "He tried to imitate the underground environment of these monsters by using samples of soil and moonstones. He achieved some success and was able to create a formation that could block the absorption force of the moon from reaching these creatures for at least a few years."

A few years wasn't a permanent solution, but it was better than nothing.

"Can I use this formation?" Red asked eagerly.

"If you remained in this place for long, sure. As for creating this formation in the outside world? Maybe only when you reach the fourth realm."

He felt instant disappointment.

"I can teach you a simplified formation you may be able to use once you reach the Lesser Ring Realm, though," the spirit offered.

Red stared at the hawk, waiting to hear more.

"First, however, I must ask you..." It stared back at the boy with sharp eyes. "Do you even know what this curse consists of?"

Red hesitated. In his eagerness to find a solution, it had completely slipped his mind that he didn't even understand this curse.

He shook his head.

"The moon, or whatever being is on the moon, absorbs the energy of creatures that have come into contact with the moonstone caves," the hawk explained. "Death comes when said creatures can't provide enough energy to this being and it starts absorbing the creatures' vital energy instead."

A shiver ran down Red's spine. He recalled the very first time he had suffered the absorption of the new moon. The creature had taken all the Moonstone Energy from his acupoints, and when that had run out, it had started taking something else.

Red never knew what had been taken from him, but hearing the hawk's words left him with a horrible inkling.

The hawk sighed. "It happened to you too, didn't it?"

Red nodded. He stared at the spirit, looking dour. "How bad is it?"

It hesitated.

Under his unyielding gaze, however, it relented. "In your current condition, you won't live beyond thirty years of age."

CHAPTER 26
ENEMY OF THE WORLD

You won't live beyond thirty years of age. Those words were a heavy blow.

"That is not all, either," the hawk said. "My master found out that the absorption grows stronger over lunar cycles, which is why even if a cave monster in the Lesser Ring Realm could recover their Moonstone Energy, they would still die all the same in a matter of a few cycles."

This didn't surprise Red. He'd doubted that avoiding the curse would be as simple as that, or else he wouldn't have needed to worry about opening any more of the special acupoints with Viran's technique.

"I see you've come up with a clever method to store Moonstone Energy in your body despite not having opened your Spiritual Sea," the spirit said. "Unfortunately, that doesn't solve the root of the problem, and you're still at risk of having more of your life essence absorbed."

"Is there really nothing I can do about what I've already lost?" Red asked.

"You don't need to despair yet," the hawk said. "Although your life essence has been drained, as long as you break through into higher realms, you will live for much longer."

"Maybe, but life essence is an important factor in a cultivator's breakthrough," he reasoned. "How hard will it be for me to open my Spiritual Sea?"

"For a normal cultivator? It would be nearly impossible. But you are now my master's disciple, and nothing is out of his reach."

"Will you be giving me a Parting Sea Pill?" Red asked. That would certainly solve the problem of opening his Spiritual Sea.

The hawk shook its head. "I will give you something better."

Red stared at the spirit in suspicion. "What is it?"

"I will explain it later." The hawk waved its wings, dispersing the images of the scorpion and the formation. "Before you receive your rewards, we need to talk about some conditions."

Red's suspicions were raised even further. "You never said anything about any conditions."

"That's because that is the concern of the winner of this trial alone. If you don't agree with these conditions, you will still receive rewards, but you will not be acknowledged as my master's disciple."

Red narrowed his eyes. "Is there a difference?"

"There is. My master prepared different rewards for the individual who agrees to become his disciple, since this would incur greater risks to this person."

Red sighed. He could already imagine where this was going. "Does this have to do with what that ghost told us?"

"Indeed. I will now list the conditions my master put forward for one who would like to be his disciple."

I hope there are no more impossible promises involved.

He braced himself.

"First of all, by winning this trial, you only receive some of the rewards my master has prepared for you," the hawk explained. "The entirety of the knowledge and treasures my master left behind for his disciple will only be available to you once you reach the Spiritual Awakening Realm."

Red frowned. "The fourth realm? Isn't that too far?"

"It is very far. However, this is the condition my master put forward. He wanted his disciple to reach the Spiritual Awakening Realm without relying on the riches he left behind. It was how he reached that realm, too—by relying on himself and the opportunities he carved out through his suffering and hard work. He was a rogue cultivator and had no backing from large factions or stronger cultivators. It is only natural that his disciple should be able to do the same."

With my talent, I don't think I need to worry about any large factions backing me.

Red had little understanding of how hard it was to reach the fourth

realm, so he couldn't judge this "master's" decision. He could also understand the man's perspective, though—a master would always want their
disciple to at least measure up to what they themself had accomplished. If
Red couldn't do even that, how could he be deserving?

"Finally, to the first condition." The hawk looked at Red with a piercing
gaze. "By accepting your master, you inherit both his riches and his enemies
in the outside world."

Here it comes.

"So that ghost wasn't lying?" Red asked.

"That man told a lot of lies to you, but on that topic, he was being honest.
My master was at war with almost every Sect in the world by the time he set
up this inheritance ground. Of course, he still had allies, but his enemies
heavily outnumbered his supporters."

Red started to feel the weight of the situation. "What did he do to
warrant that?"

"He did nothing." The hawk shook its head. "He was merely repaying the
wrongs committed against him. They slaughtered his people by the
hundreds of thousands when he was young as a result of their wars."

"So he attacked them in revenge?" It was a simple motive, as far as Red
was concerned, but an understandable one.

"You could say that. My master's heart, however, was always set on
pursuing his path as a cultivator above all else. He only sought to punish
those involved with killing his family and people, and wasn't seeking to
declare war against the rest of the Sects. Yet things developed outside of his
control, and soon enough he found himself at war with almost the entire
cultivation world in his quest for revenge."

Red couldn't imagine what could have happened for a simple revenge
quest to devolve into a world war against one man. He was even more
impressed that this one man had stood alone against the forces of the
Sects.

"Many of the Sects tried to paint my master in a poor light, even
branding him as a demonic cultivator despite the fact he practiced orthodox
arts," the hawk said. "This was how that foolish alias of 'Dread Viper' came
to be."

"Did he win that war?" Red asked.

"Of course he did," the spirit replied. "It was close, but my master still
won in the end. If he hadn't won, then you would probably have read the

story about how the Sects all banded together to kill this terrible demonic cultivator by the name of Dread Viper."

That was almost inconceivable to Red. A lone cultivator winning against the absolute behemoths that Sects were supposed to be? On top of that, this same cultivator was now supposed to be his master. It was too good to be true.

"Suffice it to say that my master chose to spare some of the Sects he was at war with," the hawk continued. "He was afraid that their fall would be too heavy of a blow to humanity and would give the opportunity for demonic cultivators and other evil forces to rise in their place."

What kind of power did one need to consider the fate of humanity as a whole?

"I sincerely doubt that any of those Sects were grateful for his mercy, though," the spirit said. "Most of them likely still hold grudges, which is why if you accept to be his disciple, you should be careful about letting this kind of information slip out, or else you'll be hunted down and killed."

Red realized there was a problem. "What about the others in the trial? Couldn't they leak this information?"

"They could, which is why I will wipe most of their memories about this place," the hawk said. "But it's not a perfect method, and if any strong cultivators get curious, they could notice traces of my technique. It is of little importance, considering there are others out there who know about these grounds already, but it should protect your identity for the time being."

He nodded. "Are those all the conditions?"

Although he was intimidated by the prospect of being an enemy of the Sects, how could he pass up such an opportunity to change his fate? He hadn't even considered refusing it yet.

"There is another condition," the hawk said. "As long as you accept him as your master, you are not allowed to join any Sects. Should you do so, you'll renege your claim to his inheritance even if you reach the fourth realm."

"But I'm already part of a Sect." He thought it was better to come clean with such matters.

"Are you?" The hawk seemed surprised. "What Sect took someone like you with such poor talent?"

"I don't think it can be considered a proper Sect," he said. "The Sect

Master is an eleven-year-old kid and the Grand Elder is in the Lesser Ring Realm. However, they have connections with a destroyed Sect."

The spirit considered his words in silence. "What is the name of this Sect they have connections with?"

Red recalled the name Reinhart had mentioned to him. "The Ocean Bearers Sect."

The hawk sighed. "That was one of the Sects my master was at war with. It is surprising that they have been destroyed even after my master spared them."

"Will that be a problem?"

"As long as you limit your relations with them, it shouldn't be." The hawk shook its head. "My master doesn't seek to limit who you interact with, even if they happen to be in Sects. You may even work together with them in the future, should you so wish. The only thing you won't be allowed to do as his disciple is take their oath."

Red nodded. "That shouldn't be a problem."

With his talent, what Sect would have an interest in recruiting him? There was another thing bothering Red, however.

"Those people that came in with the compasses..." He thought about how to approach the subject. "They said they were descendants of the creator of this place. Was your master a member of the Empire?"

The hawk shook its head. "There were a handful of empires in my master's time, but he was most definitely not a part of any of them. My master didn't leave behind any descendants either, and most of his fellow countrymen died during the Sect wars. It could be that some have lived to this day, but my master never left a faction behind or any inheritance other than this one. Even if that was the case, none of them would have any more of a legitimate claim to his legacy."

"Your master... what happened to him?" Red asked.

"... I don't know."

"You don't know? Isn't he dead?"

"Not necessarily. One of the last things my master did in this world was create his inheritance. After that, he left to attempt his trial for ascension. Whether or not he succeeded, I do not know, but what I can tell you for sure is that he is no longer in this world."

"Ascension?" The term confused Red. "What is that?"

"This is not something you should concern yourself with right now," the hawk said. "If you're truly worthy of being my master's disciple, one day you'll learn more about it on your own."

Although Red was disappointed, he didn't push the subject. "Are those the only conditions?"

"They are," the spirit said. "Do you accept them?"

"I do."

"Then from this day forward you can call yourself a disciple of Silas and will bear everything that title carries," the hawk said. "Now I will distribute your rewards."

The spirit waved its wings, summoning several shining lights.

CHAPTER 27

WINNER'S PRIZE

"FIRST, YOU WILL RECEIVE THIS." With a wing, the hawk directed one of the shining lights to fly towards Red.

He touched the glowing orb. It disappeared, and a leather-bound book appeared in his hands.

A Primer on Arcane Script.

"Is this a manual?" Red asked with interest.

The hawk nodded. "It should teach you what you need to know about Arcane Script and its applications up to the Spirit Core Realm. My master focused on formations, however, so the manual has a larger focus on that practice."

Red frowned. "I thought one needed to be at least in the Lesser Ring Realm before learning Arcane Script."

"That's not necessarily true. The truth of the matter is that many advanced manipulation techniques in Spiritual Crafting require one to use Spiritual Energy, and crafting certain items without them is nearly impossible. However, that is for advanced recipes. On the lower end, one may still be able to craft basic Spiritual Items with enough practice and the right resources. It is hard, but not impossible."

Red nodded in understanding. He recalled how Goulth could make powerful medicines even without having opened his Spiritual Sea. But the man also said that Arcane Script was much harder to learn than alchemy at that level.

"Is the formation against the curse in this manual too?" Red asked.

"It is, but that will be harder for you to build before you're in the Lesser Ring Realm. Right now, you should focus on learning the basics of Arcane Script. Once you're done with that, you will need to familiarize yourself with formation building. When you are finally confident in your own abilities, there is one formation in particular you should focus on learning."

The hawk waved its wings, and the book in Red's hands levitated. It swung open, flipping to a specific page before falling back into his hands again. On the open page was a magical circle with so many fine details that Red felt a headache coming on from simply looking at it.

On the top of this drawing, there was a title.

He read the words out loud. "Parting Storm formation..."

"This is a formation my master came up with," the hawk said. "As long as you can build it and have enough Spirit Stones to fuel it, you may use this formation to open your Spiritual Sea."

Red was baffled. "Can you use it multiple times?"

"You can."

He was even more shocked. Wasn't this basically a reusable Parting Sea Pill?

"You shouldn't be too happy about it, though," the spirit said. "Not only are the materials for building and powering this formation expensive, but its effects differ from a normal Parting Sea Pill."

Red reined his excitement in, paying close attention.

The bird continued. "The Parting Sea Pill is so valuable because it does two things. It provides a large amount of harmonious Spiritual Energy to one's body, and it also helps a cultivator to open their Spiritual Sea with no effort on the individual's part. It is a foolproof method, and the rate of success is almost one hundred percent. The Parting Storm formation almost does the first thing—it provides you with even larger amounts of harmonious Spiritual Energy to open your Spiritual Sea, but it doesn't help you control it."

Red's initial excitement deflated. "Isn't that worse than the pill, then?"

If he still had to do the hardest part, controlling the Spiritual Energy, what was the point of the formation?

"It depends on how you look at it," the hawk said. "If you're only interested in opening your Spiritual Sea, then the pill is better. However, there is more to opening the Spiritual Sea than you think. Cultivators who managed to open their Spiritual Sea by themselves claim to have felt a moment of enlightenment once they succeeded. The vast majority of this time, this doesn't result in anything special, and the feeling of enlightenment slips away in a split second. However, some cultivators claim to have deepened their understanding over certain aspects of Spiritual Energy after accomplishing that feat... You could say they improved their own talent in a way."

Red's eyes widened, but he didn't let himself be swept away by his excitement again. "How likely is that to happen?"

"Very unlikely," the hawk said. "But my master learned that chances may differ from individual to individual, and it mostly has to do with their previous experiences and understanding of the world before opening their Spiritual Sea. Of course, that was mostly conjecture on my master's part, and there was no way for him to confirm it. However, this might prove to be an invaluable chance for you with your low talent, which is why you should strive to open your Spiritual Sea without the help of a pill."

Red hesitated. In the end, he nodded. "I'll do my best."

He was being sincere. He couldn't pass up such a good opportunity, no matter how difficult it might prove to be. After all, his ambitions didn't stop at just the Lesser Ring Realm.

"Good. The materials required for the formation are relatively rare for a cultivator at your level, but they were still obtainable while my master was alive. The hardest part will be setting up the formation, but I trust in your skills."

Red didn't know why the hawk would, considering he had yet to even learn the slightest thing about Arcane Script, but he didn't question it.

"Suffice it to say, although this formation may still be inferior to a Parting Sea Pill in many ways, it would still cause quite a commotion if it were to be revealed to the outside world. You should be careful about how you handle it."

That went without saying. Yet Red felt every secret he was coming into contact with in this place was like a bomb waiting to explode.

"Then... Your next reward." The hawk waved its wings.

Another of the lights shot towards Red. He extended his hand, hoping to catch it, but instead it plunged into his chest, disappearing without a trace.

"What was that?" he asked, trying to keep calm.

"An anti-divination technique," the hawk said. "The people who have been prying into this inheritance ground might find out about you in their divinations, so it's necessary to protect you in some ways."

This concerned Red. "They can find out about me?"

The hawk nodded. "Now that you have come into contact with this place, your fate is connected to it. Inevitably, you will appear in their divinations too."

Another bomb waiting to explode, then. Red had so many knives hidden in the dark waiting to stab him that he was numb to the addition of one more. It didn't make him any happier, though.

"If it makes you feel any better, they probably already knew about you from the moonstone caves. It is very likely they would have found you eventually, even if you hadn't come into contact with this trial. With this anti-divination technique, you get protected from their divinations on two fronts."

Red nodded in agreement. He supposed that was a fair point. "How long does it last?"

"It depends," the spirit said. "It might last you hundreds of years if no one tries to probe into your identity. However, if these oracles continue their investigation of this place with the same intensity as before, then your protection will last at most twenty years."

Red frowned, thinking over what he'd learned. "Is that enough to reach the fourth realm?"

"It is a very quick pace... My master reached that realm when he was twenty-nine, though."

So, I have to be at least as fast as he was if I want to keep my identity secret.

Another urgent goal Red had to accomplish.

"This anti-divination technique doesn't feel like much of a reward," he said. Indeed, it was more like an absolute necessity if the spirit didn't intend to lose its inheritor as soon as they stepped out of this trial.

"You're right, it isn't. So let's move on."

It waved its wings again, and another mote of light flew towards Red. It hovered above his hands, and he reached out for it. A small glass bottle fell into his hands.

Red saw hundreds of tiny pellets inside.

"These are Vein Opening Pills," the hawk said. "More than enough to open all twelve of your veins."

"These are pills?" He frowned.

They were miniscule compared to the pills he was used to seeing.

"Cultivators care little about practicality on this level, but my master was an exception," the hawk explained. "If he could make medicines as small as possible so they might all be stored inside one vial, then he would do it."

Red kept examining them, transfixed by the tiny pills. "I suppose that makes sense."

"You should already know this, but these pills are meant to complement your normal cultivation," the spirit said. "You shouldn't consume too many of them at once, or the toxins will accumulate in your body and will affect your future cultivation."

Red already knew this—Hector had explained to him how to use Vein Opening Pills.

"Then, the next reward." The bird waved its wings again.

Red touched the next mote of light, and when the glow disappeared, he noticed he was holding a bracelet.

"A magical treasure?"

"Indeed. It's a low-level treasure, though."

"What does it do?"

"It masks your appearance."

"... Why do I need to mask my appearance?"

The hawk didn't respond immediately, staring at him with its piercing eyes. A few moments later, it sighed. "Have you looked at your own reflection since you entered the trial?"

"I don't think so." Red was always too focused on other matters to take note of his own appearance.

"Then have a gander." The hawk summoned a stream of water in front of Red. It circled in the air before forming into a round, flat mirror.

What he saw in the reflection left him shocked.

Red's general features looked the same as ever—his sharp features, red hair, and emotionless eyes and expression. But then he examined his left eye.

His iris had changed colors—becoming a deep, dark crimson. His pupil had become more elongated too, resembling a lizard's. And that wasn't all. A few red scales were growing on the left side of his face.

Red traced his fingers over them, feeling the coarse and hard surface of this new skin.

"Demonification," the hawk said.
The word made Red's blood run cold.

CHAPTER 28
A TRUE CULTIVATOR

"THIS," the hawk explained as Red stood dumbstruck, "is a side effect of your blood absorption powers. It is a clear sign of demonification. Once you put on that bracelet, your appearance should return to normal—but be aware that is only an illusion. The scales and red eyes will still be there."

Red was still examining his face in disbelief. "When did it become like this?"

"When you killed that lizard demon, your body underwent significant changes. I was afraid you would die if you did not wake up in time."

Red's face fell. "The imperials and the necromancer... They didn't mention anything about this."

These changes in his features were quite obvious. He couldn't imagine they would fail to comment on it.

The hawk sighed. "That's because I hid it. If the necromancer had noticed that his supposed savior was under demonic influence, then he might have reconsidered his plans."

"Is there a way to reverse it?" Red asked.

"There is, but..." The hawk hesitated. "The process of demonification you're going through is something I've never seen before."

Red felt like his situation only kept getting worse. "How so?"

"Bodily changes like this only happen during the second phase of demonification. First, an individual will go through severe personality

159

changes, which you seem to have entirely skipped... That is, unless you are adept at hiding your state of mind and tricked me."

He shook his head. "I don't feel any different."

"Then it is as I thought," the hawk said, its expression severe. "I can't tell you exactly what is happening, but a force beyond my understanding must be controlling your process of demonification."

Red's mind shifted to the crimson mist inside his body. He decided to tell the truth to the spirit. "I have something inside of me. It's a sentient mist that I took with me to the outside world when I left the underground... My power of absorbing blood comes from it."

The hawk fell silent in contemplation. Its gaze wavered. "You said you took it from the underground?"

He nodded. "It was in another monster's core... I feel like it didn't really belong in that place."

"You would be correct. My master's research into those caves was limited, since he never dared to explore them himself. However, he never came across any type of demonic influence from that place... Did anything else happen since you came into contact with this mist?"

"I also started to have strange dreams about a different world." Red described the endless plains of black sand, the giant bones, the crimson sky, the dark sun, and the behemoth creature he saw in those dreams.

The hawk shook its head. "I have no knowledge of such a place. If I had to guess, however, it seems you have been dreaming about the Infernal Realm."

Red frowned. He knew little about this Infernal Realm, but it was common knowledge amongst the people of the outside world that this was the home of demons. A place of despair and evil.

He had obviously considered the possibility but hearing it from the hawk made it much worse. "What do you think those dreams mean?"

"I don't know. I cannot interpret your dreams, but I can tell you with confidence that you should be careful how you act inside that place. Although you may think of these forays as mere dreams, nothing is ever so simple in the world of cultivation. The Infernal Realm is a land of horrors and nightmares, and they may reach you even through your dreams."

Another danger to worry about.

"What about the mist?" Red asked. "What can I do about that?"

He had decided to confide in the hawk. This was his best opportunity to learn about these otherworldly matters, and the spirit was willing to share what it knew.

"The best course of action would be to remove it entirely from your body, but I'm afraid it won't be that easy," the hawk said. "Unlike your moon curse, I know nothing about this force living inside your body. Demons from the Infernal Realm that can reach through dimensions and exert their influence on our world are rare, but they are all extremely powerful. I fear that if I try to remove it from your body, I might kill you in the process and attract the attention of a being beyond what I or these grounds can possibly contend with."

Red grimaced. "Then what should I do?"

"Refrain from using those blood absorption powers. They seem to be the catalyst for your demonification, so you should never use them unless absolutely necessary. You may also take solace in the fact this demonic influence inside of you seems to have no interest in taking your body over at the moment, since it has most likely kept your mind in a sane state. However, it is still a demon, so never be fully trusting of it. As for the future..." It paused, weighing its words. "The most important part is that you must take control of your own fate."

Red was bewildered. He had been trying to do that the entire time. It was why he had risked so much to win this trial. Yet this mountain he sought to climb seemed to get taller and taller with every step. How was he supposed to reach it like this?

"I am limited in the ways I can help you," the hawk admitted. "However, I have judged you worthy of being my master's disciple, so that alone makes you qualified to take on anything this world can throw at you. A true cultivator creates opportunity out of adversity, and you must tackle all obstacles with such a mentality in mind. The forces you are matched against might seem beyond what you can deal with, but there is no such thing as impossible for a cultivator. Seek every opportunity to climb even one step further on this ladder to the top, and your horizons will grow. The world will be revealed before you, and more opportunities to climb even further will appear."

As Red listened to the spirit, he felt a deep resonance within himself.

"Analyze your problems with an open and rational mind. Be aware that even the hardest puzzles have a solution, and that there is nothing in this world that cannot be solved by an ambitious individual. This demon, this curse... Seek to understand them. If you cannot be rid of them, then seek to use them to your advantage. If that isn't possible, then seek to suppress them until there comes a day where you can either use them or finally be rid of them. Gods, demons, sects, empires, cults—nothing is ever beyond you. Understand that this is the spirit of a true cultivator, and that it's more important to grasp this with all your heart than to have the best talent in the world..."

The spirit fell silent, and Red contemplated its words.

Finally, the hawk spoke up again, this time with a lower tone. "These aren't my words. They're what my master said to me before he departed. He told me that this was the most important lesson to his future disciple, more valuable than any treasure he could possibly give you... I never agreed with him. I thought, if one was allowed to live a peaceful and happy life, why seek more? Who cares about the world? About power? Ambition is the downfall of great men, and yet they all throw themselves into this abyss without a second thought." It stared at Red. "But you aren't any different from them, are you?"

He shook his head. "I suppose not."

"Indeed. Which is why you won this trial, after all."

The spirit waved its wings, and the last mote of light flew towards Red. He touched it, and another manual fell into his hands.

Storm's Blessing.

"This is a cultivation manual that my master created for his disciple," the hawk said. "It consists of a set of circulation techniques from the Lesser Ring Realm up to the Spirit Core Realm. It also has multiple Spiritual Arts, and a vein opening technique that you must use if you seek to practice them in the future. You can take this as a comprehensive inheritance for cultivation up to the Spirit Core Realm, and you will not lack for techniques or knowledge as you progress towards the fourth realm."

Red examined the manual like it was the most valuable treasure in the world. He didn't know how much this was worth in the outside world, but it was still priceless to him.

"The *Storm's Blessing,* as my master named it, consists mostly of water, wind, and lightning techniques," the spirit continued. "You may practice any of these elements and its techniques individually, but their true strength only manifests when all three of them are combined."

"What if I don't have any talent for one of those elements?" Red asked.

"It shouldn't matter. There is also knowledge in the book about how to increase your elemental affinity. These methods are extremely rare, but I know you can accomplish them."

He nodded. These were techniques he would only need to worry about in the future.

"Is that it?" he asked.

"For rewards? Yes," the hawk told him. "Why? Were you expecting more?"

Red didn't deny it. "I was."

Although all of these treasures were extremely valuable, he had definitely expected something that would increase his power right away.

"My master was clear in his instructions. He didn't want to give his disciple anything too valuable that would make their journey too easy. He said that the knowledge and manuals he has imparted unto you are the tools you will use to obtain those things yourself. The hard part will still be up to you."

Red sighed. "Does everything have to be so difficult?"

He didn't disagree with this rationale, but he thought he had proved himself plenty already.

"It must be. My master said hardship builds character... I don't agree with him, but I am not the one who made this place."

Red didn't push the subject. "So, what now?"

"Well, that depends," the hawk said. "Do you have any more otherworldly secrets you wish to tell me?"

He hesitated. "I have a few, but—"

"Do they concern your immediate safety?"

"I... don't think so."

"Then don't bother. Sometimes knowing too much about something can be very harmful—in literal ways, too. Certain beings in the world can feel when someone talks about them, and getting their attention is the last thing I want to do right now. If it weren't for the fact your life was on the line, I wouldn't have even mentioned anything about that demon."

That was understandable. Red would need to keep information about the blob to himself.

"How do I find this place again?" he asked.

"Once you reach the Spiritual Awakening Realm, a mark will activate on your body," the hawk said. "By that point, you will know how to enter these grounds again."

"What about the bracelet?"

"Wear it around your wrist and it will do its job without any need of activation," the spirit said.

"Then I guess this is it."

"So it is. I will be sending you out with your companions."

"Are they still alive?" Red asked.

"They are. In fact, since you won this trial, not even a second has passed."

Red was stunned. "How is that possib—"

The hawk waved its wings, and everything went dark.

CHAPTER 29
OUTSIDE AGAIN

THE FIRST THING Red heard when he came to was birdsong. The sunlight shone from above, the sudden influx of brightness making him squint.

It's already been a day?

He wasn't surprised. He had lost track of time inside the hidden realm, but he had been certain at least a day passed.

Red was surrounded by trees. This alone told him nothing about his location, though, and he couldn't see any signs of the hole he'd used to enter the underground.

The hawk had said it would teleport them back to a safe spot away from prowling bandits, yet it never said where that would be. Red could only hope that Narcha and Eiwin were nearby.

Before anything, though, he gathered his rewards from the trial and then put on his magic bracelet. He felt nothing change, and when he ran his hand over the side of his face, he could still feel the scales. However, using the reflection of the shiny silver bracelet itself, Red saw that his appearance had returned to normal. Satisfied, he hid the bracelet beneath his uniform's sleeve and moved forward.

He walked in a random direction, using his crimson sense to scout the way. His detection range had increased to just over two hundred meters since he'd entered the trial, and he could pinpoint even more fluctuations, distinguishing them much more effectively.

It didn't take him long to notice a handful of human presences. They weren't the ones he'd been expecting.

What are they doing here?

Red was puzzled. As he approached their location, a frantic conversation reached his ears.

"Quick, young master! We need to bring him back to the Sect!"

"I'm trying my best," a child shot back.

Red approached until he finally spotted them. Rimold was carrying Rog's unconscious body on his back while Allen struggled to keep up with his pace.

They all froze as they came face-to-face with Red.

"Y-you..." Rimold looked as if Red had risen from the dead. "What are you doing here?!"

"Red!" Allen cheered, but his joy quickly disappeared. "Wait, Red? H-how can you be here?! You said you were going to help Rog and the others!"

Red frowned in confusion. "What do you mean? The trial has already ended."

"What do you mean, you bastard?" Rimold glared at him. "We just left that place! How could it have ended?"

Red's frown deepened. Something strange was at play here. How could Rimold and Allen still be in the forest so many hours after leaving the trial?

He recalled the hawk's words.

"I'm telling the truth," he said. "The trial has already ended. I was inside there for more than half a day since you left."

The rogue's anger faltered. "But how is that even possible?"

"I don't know, but you saw it yourself," Red insisted. "I told the spirit I was going to continue the trial, so why would I leave immediately after?"

"It must be temporal magic!" Allen cried. "I've heard about it before!"

"Ugh, listen, none of this matters right now! I believe him." Rimold shook his head. He looked at Red with anticipation. "Did you get the medicine?"

The young master also remembered something. "What about Narcha and Eiwin? Did you find them?"

"I don't have the pill," Red said. "I gave all the Spirit Stones I collected to Narcha and Eiwin, though."

"And where are they?" Rimold asked. "Shouldn't they have left with you?"

"We got split up. It's hard to explain right now, but... they should have the pill. As long as we can find them, then we should be able to give it to Rog."

Allen showed genuine joy again. "That's great! We should hurry!"

Rimold sighed with relief. "Let's do that. The sooner we find them, the sooner we can heal Rog and leave this cursed place behind." He narrowed his eyes at Red. "You seem to be in very good condition, so why don't you lead the way?"

Rimold and Allen hadn't had time to heal any of their wounds from the battle with the fireleaf stag. In contrast, Red didn't seem to have suffered the slightest injury, despite his torn uniform.

He nodded. "Follow me. I think they should be nearby."

Red moved ahead while his companions hurried behind him.

Allen was far too curious to remain silent. "What happened in there, Red? Did you fight any more monsters? Did you win the trial?"

"I fought plenty of monsters. No, I did not win the trial." Red didn't hesitate to lie. It would be far too troublesome to reveal this information to his Sect members, much more so after what he had learned about Hector.

Allen barraged him with questions. "What kind of monsters did you fight? Were they as strong as that stag? Did you go through any more labyrinths? Wait! What about Reinhart? Do you know what happened to him?"

"It's not convenient to talk about this right now." Red shook his head. "We can talk about it once we return to the Sect."

Allen was disappointed, but he kept silent. As for Rimold, he gave Red a meaningful gaze, but Red ignored it. There were still certain things he wanted to confirm before talking about anything in the trial.

The group continued through the forest, Rimold carrying Rog on his back. It didn't take long for Red to detect the fluctuations of the rest of his companions.

"They're close," he said.

"Then let's go!" Allen urged them on even in his limping state.

Red considered warning him about what state he might find Narcha and Eiwin in, but he thought better about it. They soon found the women sitting against a tree side by side, tending to their wounds.

Much to Red's surprise, Eiwin was conscious.

Allen's face lit up. "Eiwin, Narcha!" He ran towards them.

"What— You brat!" Narcha scowled as he threw himself into a hug. "We're injured! Be careful—"

"I-I was so worried..." Allen trembled, on the verge of tears.

The warrior grunted, some of her anger subsiding. "Worried for what?"

"I-I thought I was going to die, b-but then when I heard you two were still there... I wanted to keep going, but... I was too weak."

"It's fine, young master." Eiwin patted his back. "You did your part, and that's all that matters."

Allen nodded and stepped away, holding back his tears. He tried to put on a brave expression. "N-next time I won't run away... I learned a lot from Red. I-I will be prepared."

Rimold cleared his throat. "I'm sure this is all very emotional, but must I remind you lot about the unconscious hunter I'm carrying on my back?"

Narcha gave him a look of contempt. "Ugh, it's you."

"Didn't you mean to say, 'Thank you for saving the two kids, Mister Rimold?'" he spat back.

"If anything, I bet it was the kids that saved you."

"Please, Miss Valt, Mister Rimold," Eiwin interrupted. "Let's tend to our wounded companion before devolving into another argument, shall we?"

None of them complained. Rimold stepped forward, laying the unconscious Rog on the forest floor.

Eiwin approached the hunter, examining his wounds. She looked sorrowful. "Thankfully, you managed to save him. We should have stayed behind with him instead of rushing into that cavern."

Behind her, Narcha's expression softened, but she remained quiet.

From her pouch, Eiwin took out a bright-red pill. She fed it to the unconscious Rog and made sure he swallowed it. Once finished, she stepped back.

Complete silence settled around them as everyone waited with bated breath. Still, even after a minute had passed, Rog showed no signs of waking up again.

Rimold frowned. "Is that it? Wasn't something else supposed to happen?"

"Stop yapping." Narcha glared at him. "Not every medicine has a showy effect."

Rimold gritted his teeth, but didn't respond.

"This pill is meant to expel the hostile energy lingering inside his body and repair his crippled veins," Eiwin said. "The spirit didn't specify a time frame for this recovery, though, and there are a lot of pills with slow acting effects—"

"ARGH!"

Rog lurched up, eyes wide open as he grabbed his chest in pain. He took a few deep breaths before devolving into a coughing fit.

Everyone watched the hunter in shock, afraid to even breathe too loudly. Finally, Rog calmed down as his coughs ceased. He looked around, surprised to have so many people staring at him.

"Where are we?" he asked.

"In the forest." Red was the first one to recover from his shock. "You were wounded in that fight against the deer. We had to carry you out and get a special pill to heal you."

"Huh." Rog moved to scratch his beard, only to notice an absence of hair on his chin. "... Where did my hair go?"

"It got burned off," Red explained. "Most of your body was burned, actually."

"I see." The hunter nodded sullenly. "Thanks for saving me, I guess."

"There's no need for thanks," Red replied. "If it wasn't for you, I would be dead."

"Hey! This brat wasn't the only one that helped!" Rimold interjected. "We all did our part! Narcha and Eiwin even had to exchange twenty Spirit Stones for a pill to save you!"

Rog frowned. "Spirit Stones? Exchange? What do you mean?"

"It doesn't matter," Eiwin said. "What matters is how you feel right now. Can you walk?"

"Should be able to. I feel weak, but it's not immobilizing."

"Good. We can explain everything once we get back to our Sect." She looked over at Red. "How did it go?"

He shook his head. This was to indicate he hadn't won—an absolute lie, but he wouldn't entertain telling them the truth until he had weighed all the risks involved.

The others observed curiously, everyone but Narcha, who was still sulking on the sidelines, stewing in her own thoughts. Most of her wounds had healed, which Red assumed was due to some pill she had received in a trade with the spirit, but he wasn't going to ask about it at this moment.

"Then let us be on our way," Eiwin said. "Even with the trial done, there are many dangers still remaining in this forest."

The others were quick to agree. They didn't know whether or not there were any more bandits around—or imperials, for that matter. Not to mention, Red also knew Ricard hadn't died at the end of the trial, and although he was grievously injured, the boy would rather not cross paths with him again.

They were about to continue walking when Red felt several fluctuations enter his range.

"Someone's coming!" he called out.

Their hands all flew for their weapons, but before they could even draw them, the newcomers had already arrived.

"Worry not, friends," a man's voice called out. "We are not here to fight. We merely wish to ask you some questions."

A man covered in dark plate armor from head to toe stepped out from behind a few trees. There was a strange symbol of a golden sun on his breastplate, and a large hammer strapped to his back. Behind him, four others with similar equipment stepped out on his sides.

They didn't surround them, but their mere presence was more than enough to intimidate Red's group. Red examined their fluctuations. Each of them, without exception, was in the Lesser Ring Realm.

"Cursebreakers," Rimold whispered.

Red recognized the name. They were the undead hunters.

CHAPTER 30
CURSEBREAKERS

"HA! Does our name invoke such reactions these days?" the knight in front said.

"No, no!" Rimold raced to correct himself. "I mean, we are all very grateful for your presence in our province!"

This reaction only made the man laugh louder. One of his subordinates didn't seem as happy.

A woman's muffled voice spoke from beneath another suit of armor. "Hmph, how soon do mortals forget. When undead were rampant on the continent, they sang our praises and cooperated with us at every opportunity. Now that they think the threat is gone, they dread our very presence."

"That is not what I meant—not what I meant at all!" Rimold cried. "I mean, it's just that your presence here took us by surprise... Right, guys?"

He looked back at his companions. Narcha was readying herself for a fight while the others all looked sheepish, except Rog, who seemed distracted as he continued to scratch at his naked chin.

"There is no need for such theatrics," the leading knight said. "We know our reputation in the mortal world. Still, we must do our job."

Narcha frowned. "And what is your job exactly? Are you intent on razing our town to the ground too?"

"Hold your tongue, mortal!" The female knight stepped forward, her hand grabbing the hammer on her back.

Red and the others felt a deadly pressure. Danger radiated from the woman's figure, and none of her companions seemed intent on stopping her.

"Enough." The leader pulled her back. "We don't want to scare them, do we?" Red could imagine his smiling expression, even though he couldn't see his face.

Eventually, Eiwin stepped forward to speak for the group. "We understand your duty, fellow cultivators. We are not seeking any conflict. We were merely surprised to meet you in the middle of the forest after everything we have gone through."

"I see." The man nodded. "And might I ask what you were doing in the middle of the forest? You seem to have gone through some fighting yourself."

Eiwin hesitated. "We... were pulled into a hidden realm as we were investigating the bandits."

Red cringed. Some of his companions stared at her dubiously, but none of them interrupted her.

"A hidden realm in this place? Was it an inheritance ground?"

"It was indeed an inheritance ground." Eiwin nodded with no apprehension.

"That is surprising..." The Cursebreaker contemplated this. "Do you know which cultivator it belonged to?"

"I'm afraid that..." Her face became confused. "I'm afraid that... I don't remember."

He was taken aback. "Hm? You don't remember?"

An air of suspicion rose amidst the knights.

"I'm being truthful." She shook her head in disappointment. "Now that I think about it, there is very little I can remember about that place... It's like there's a fog covering the trials I went through in there. Even the appearance of the place."

Allen yelped, then slapped the top of his head. "I-I can't remember it either! There was that stag, but... I can't remember what it looked like!"

The same realization came to the others. Narcha and Rimold's expressions turned ugly—they had missing memories too. Rog continued to show no reaction.

So the hawk really did wipe their memories...

Red was not sure how the process worked. His companions seemed aware they had been in a trial, but their recollections were fuzzy. In fact, they hadn't even noticed there was anything amiss with their memories until Eiwin tried to think back on the details and brought it to their attention.

He would need to pay attention to his companions so he could act convincingly.

"None of you remember it?" the leading knight asked warily.

"I'm... afraid so." Eiwin admitted, looking resigned.

The man went silent. He looked over at his left-hand companion. "What do you think?"

"They seem to be telling the truth," another grave male voice replied. "These types of techniques are not uncommon, either. The owner of the trial might have been trying to hide their identity."

"Hm, that's unfortunate. You think it could be connected to the necromancer?"

His subordinate shook his head. "Unlikely, or else I doubt they would be alive."

The leader sighed from beneath his armor. "What a mess... Still, it is none of our concern."

He looked back at Red's group.

"The tall woman and the child with the red hair." He pointed at Red and Narcha. "Tell me about your encounter with that zombie."

Red shivered, and Narcha's expression soured further.

"How do you know about that?" she asked.

"Some bandits survived the encounter in the dead section of the forest," the knight said. "It was a simple matter getting this information from them, considering how much your appearances stand out. Of course, I never really expected to run into the two of you in this forest, but our investigations led us to this place, so..."

"Answer the question," the female knight interjected, showering the group with another powerful wave of pressure.

Narcha clenched her jaw, glaring furiously at the knight.

Red spoke up before anything else could happen. "We spotted some of the bodies that zombie had killed and followed its tracks to the dead forest. We saw it fighting against a few bandits there and noticed it wasn't moving like a normal undead. It noticed us from miles away and we were forced to flee. It eventually caught up to us, so we fought it a bit before running away."

"And?" The leader stared at him from beneath his visor. "Is that it?"

Red nodded. "That's it. We later assumed it was a necromancer, but we weren't willing to investigate it further."

"I see..." The man grew thoughtful. "How old are you, child?"

"Ten... I think."

"You seem to be very well-spoken for such a young child," the knight said. "Did the zombie say anything to you? Did it do anything strange? We would appreciate anything you can give us."

Red shook his head. "It didn't say anything of importance."

The leader looked back at the subordinate on his left, who nodded.

Why is he looking at that man for confirmation?

A grim possibility crossed his mind. The knight might be using divination or a different technique to tell if Red was lying. He couldn't tell whether any of his companions had noticed this too, since they were all so tense. Only Rog continued to act absent-minded.

Red focused on Allen and Rimold, however. *I can't let them speak. I need to take the initiative.*

These two had been present for Red's interaction with the necromancer, so they could implicate Red and perhaps the entire group by revealing what the necromancer had said. He couldn't allow that to happen.

"We found a bunch of undead animal corpses around the forest," the knight said, turning back to the group. "Do any of you know about it?"

"Allen and I ran into some of them while making our way through the forest," Red answered. "We were saved by someone else, though."

Eiwin and Narcha were surprised, but they didn't interrupt him. He had been afforded a certain amount of trust by his companions.

"Who's Allen?" the knight asked.

"M-me..." The young master raised his trembling hand.

"I see." The man looked back at Red. "Did you have any more encounters with the necromancer or his undead while you were inside this forest?"

Red replied instantly. "No." He didn't look at Rimold and Allen, as curious as he was to observe their reactions.

The leader looked at the knight on his left. He didn't respond right away. A few seconds later, though, he nodded.

Red was relieved, but he didn't let it show in his expression.

Before the leader could turn back, the subordinate spoke up. "This boy has a strong will."

Those words, confusing as they were, gave him an awful sinking feeling.

The leader hummed. "It certainly seems to be the case. Thankfully, he's not the only one in this group."

He shifted his focus to Allen, and the young master shivered in apprehension. Red was alarmed, but he couldn't do anything about it, or else he would raise even more suspicion.

"What about you, Allen?" the knight asked. "Did you encounter any more of those nasty zombies while wandering around this forest?"

Allen shivered. "I-I..."

Red braced himself, prepared for the worst.

But someone interrupted Allen. "I saw them."

The leader turned to Rog. "You did?"

"I did. They were waiting inside that hole in the ground for the bandits—a whole army of them. I think they were inside the trial too, but I didn't meet them there."

The knight went silent for a moment. "... They were inside the trial?"

"I think so." Rog shrugged. "Never saw them there, though. Got hit by some flames and was unconscious."

The air around the Cursebreakers changed. They looked at each other, and an entire silent conversation seemed to happen between them.

A moment later, the leader looked back at the group. "We'll need you to take us to this hole."

Eiwin frowned. "And afterwards? Will you let us go?"

"Certainly. As soon as we've properly interrogated you about what happened inside the trial, that is."

Narcha glowered. "You're going to do what? Do you think we're lying about our memories being wiped?!"

"Not at all. I believe you. However, there are ways to recover memories from individuals. Some of the higher-ups in our organization are specialized in said interrogation techniques, so if we judge the danger of this necromancer to be high enough, we could enlist their help."

"You!" she growled. "You can't do this!"

He laughed. "Of course we can. If it's necessary to expunge this world of the undead, we can do much worse. You need not be afraid, though. This technique is quite safe, and as long as we can confirm nothing is wrong with your memories, you will all be allowed to go free."

Red knew he had to do something to stop this. If they interrogated him and looked into his memories, they would find all his interactions with the necromancer. By then, it wouldn't be just him, but their entire group would be doomed.

Just as Red was thinking about what to do, Eiwin looked back at them. "There's no need to be afraid," she said. "I already warned him when we got out of the trial. He should be on his way."

Although she seemed to be saying that to everyone, Red felt her eyes focus on him.

"Hm?" The leading knight turned to her. "Are you talking about that old man? He's in the Lesser Ring Realm, but you mustn't get delusional. Against the Cursebreakers, there is nothing that he can—"

A shrill sound echoed through the forest. The man looked up, his hand going to his hammer.

"Watch out!"

He and his subordinates jumped back. A spear of ice crashed down where they'd just been standing, shattering into countless pieces. The shards pelted their armor with incredible force and threw them back even further. Somehow, none of the ice shards flew toward Red and his group.

"What gall!" cried an old man's voice, full of rage. "You think I'm afraid of some declining organization?!"

Red and the others looked toward the source.

"Hector!" Allen yelled with glee.

CHAPTER 31

BACK IN TOWN

THE KNIGHTS STARED Hector down from under their visors.

The female knight was the first to react, flinging her hammer off her back. "You dare to attack—"

Another ice spear formed on Hector's fingertips and shot at her. Her hammer bashed it, shattering the projectile, but the impact was enough to send her flying against a tree.

"Out of the way!" Hector ordered Red and his companions.

They obliged him.

The knights had all recovered from the elder's surprise attack and wielded their mauls. Runic symbols glowed on the heads of the hammers, emanating a purple aura.

None of them stepped forward to attack Hector. The old man likewise stopped walking once he came within ten meters of them. A tense staredown followed.

"I would advise this senior to not interfere in our organization's matters," the leader said in a measured tone. "We do not intend any harm to those people, and merely wish to get to the bottom of the necromancer's presence in this forest."

Hector scoffed. "I don't care what you intend to do. You tried to cross me and abduct my Sect members. That is enough to warrant your deaths."

The leader stirred, the grip around his weapon tightening. "Would this

177

senior really wish to feud with our organization? Our superiors would not stand for others meddling in our affairs."

The elder cackled. "What is this? Trying to hide behind the name of your organization? Are you so certain that you will lose to me in combat that now you're trying to intimidate me?"

The air around the knights became tense, charged. Yet none of them spoke up, not even the female knight, who struggled to breathe after taking a hit from the ice spear.

"What?!" Hector roared. "Are you just going to stand there and stare at me? If you don't want to fight, then don't waste my time and scram! Your superiors know where to find me if they want to repay their subordinates' grievances."

Two of the knights trembled, about to attack the old man. Red could tell that after what had happened to their companion, there was reservation in their actions—an uncertainty that came with facing someone stronger than you. Hector's display of power had done its job.

"We won't fight." The leading knight lowered his weapon. "I only hope this senior is ready for the consequences of his actions."

Hector spat on the ground. "I don't need a coward to tell me about the consequences of my own actions."

The man shook his head. "Let us retreat. We are returning to our base."

One by one, the other knights all lowered their weapons. Then they all left the scene quickly, eager to distance themselves from Hector.

Red was both awed and confused by what had happened. Hector could cast an ice spear similar to the one from the talisman Allen had used before, but even stronger, and with a much shorter activation time. In fact, the elder formed these spears in an instant. It was beyond compare.

Yet he did not understand why the knights retreated so promptly. They were all in the Lesser Ring Realm, and he could feel from their fluctuations that they were close in strength to Hector himself. So why were they afraid? There was some secret Red couldn't see from a brief clash alone.

"Hmph, cowards, the lot of them," Hector said. "No wonder their organization has fallen so far."

"We appreciate your timely arrival, Master Hector." Eiwin gave a grateful smile. "If it wasn't for that, I'm afraid we would have all been captured."

"Do not be too happy, girl. I was already in the forest searching for a certain runaway when you used the talisman to call me. If it wasn't for that, I wouldn't have arrived in time."

Allen shivered, but he didn't say anything.

Hector looked over at Rimold. "I see we also have a new arrival."

"Master Hector." Rimold bowed, showing respect Red had never seen from the crass man before. "I happened upon them in the middle of the forest... I had to reveal my identity amidst the bandits to help the children."

"There is no need for concern," Hector said. "After today, Ricard and his band are not long for this world. The Baron and Gustav have both agreed to move against him. Even if we do nothing, that man is doomed."

"We might not even need to worry about that," Narcha said, grinning.

The elder frowned. "What do you mean?"

"It is not convenient to explain these matters right now, Master Hector," Eiwin said. "It's best we return to the Sect before we explain everything."

Hector hesitated. He looked over the group carefully, noticing all the wounds they had accumulated. His gaze lingered on Rog in particular.

"What happened to your hair?"

"Got burned," Rog said, looking down in embarrassment.

"Ugh, fine." Hector shook his head. "Let's return to the Sect. I need to have a discussion about your actions too... Or do you think I've forgotten you went against my explicit orders?"

His aura changed as he stared down each and every one of the Sect members. They all shifted on their feet uncomfortably, even Rimold, who had done nothing to deserve it.

The group had almost forgotten that what had taken them here was an act of defiance against the elder's will. They couldn't be blamed for forgetting, either. After the trial, such considerations and conversations seemed to have come from a lifetime ago.

"No matter." He waved his hands. "We can settle this once we're back."

He led the way through the trees. Every one of the Sect members looked concerned. Among them, Allen was the most troubled.

I guess it's time to see if you learned anything, Allen.

Red sighed and followed his companions.

Night arrived an hour or so into their long trip back. Red felt the gaze of the moon settle upon him again, but this time he didn't feel nearly as much intensity. Whatever had happened inside the trial had reinforced him mentally, making him more resilient against it, but he found no comfort in that. He knew such respite would be short-lived, and that in the future, the curse would only grow stronger.

From Hector, Red also learned that this was still the same day he and Allen had left the Sect. The events inside the trial had happened over the course of days from Red's perspective, and yet only a few hours had passed in the outside world.

As they approached the town, they came across many soldier patrols. These men were moving deeper into the forest, and they all greeted Hector with reverence and fear as they passed. The elder just gave them a nod and continued on his way.

Soon enough, they could see the town on the horizon lit up by countless white lanterns. Walking the main road, even more soldiers passed them by. Red counted hundreds, some even mounted on horses.

All of them, without exception, gave way to Hector and his group. This respect was only exaggerated once they entered the town proper.

Although it was already night, the town was still active, the streets packed. Once people spotted Hector, though, a hubbub spread through the crowd, and they all parted in fear and awe.

Red and his companions were suddenly under the scrutiny of countless eyes, and the subject of odd conversation.

"It's Hector..."

"What do you think he was doing out here?"

"It's his entire guild!"

"Did he kill someone this time?"

"Shut up! He's a cultivator! He can hear you!"

Red cringed. He was uncomfortable, but he did his best to ignore these people. Whatever happened next, he supposed it would be impossible for him to maintain any level of anonymity in this town. Now his identity was tied to the Water Dragon Sect for good.

As they moved up the hill towards their Sect, Allen appeared by Red's side.

The young master came close to his ear and whispered, "R-Red... W-what do I do?"

Red frowned. "What do you mean?"

"I-I mean Hector..." Allen trembled. "H-he's going to punish me, isn't he?"

"Probably."

The young master paled. "A-and what do you think I should do? I don't want to be punished."

Red shook his head. "You made your choice once you decided to flee. What else is there to do but own up to the consequences of your actions?"

Allen looked defeated. "I... I suppose you're right."

"Just make sure not to back down this time. Hector will try to intimidate you and break your will, but you made your choice as a cultivator. Whatever comes after it, take on the repercussions of your actions with the same courage you had when you decided on those actions in the first place."

"R-right!" Allen regained his spirits slightly. "I won't cry this time!"

This loud sentence earned him a few quizzical looks from the rest of the group, and Hector's steps faltered for a moment. They all ignored it, though, and continued on their way.

Once they reached the Sect, the chatter of the crowds was distant. This was Hector's territory. No one dared to trespass on his turf.

At the Sect's main building, the elder waved his hand and a gale of wind forced the gate open.

"To the hall!" Hector ordered. "Now!"

His attitude changed as soon as he arrived. Gone was the image of a hero who appeared just in time to save them, and back was the bearing of a relentless tyrant.

Red saw the hesitation on Allen's face, but none of them had any choice.

One by one, they filed into the hall. Not even Rog tried to slip away this time. Red, who had already sensed two familiar fluctuations inside the building, was not surprised to see his master Goulth and Domeron already sitting at the table.

Neither of them said anything once they saw the group enter. Goulth glared at Red, while Domeron looked serene—which certainly didn't fit a man who had betrayed Hector's trust and sent Allen out on a suicide mission earlier that day.

Hector sat at the head of the table and waved his hand. "Sit!"

They all followed his orders. Red sat between Eiwin and Allen, bracing himself for whatever came next.

"So..." Hector crossed his arms and stared down his Sect members. "Are you ready to talk about your crimes against the Sect?"

CHAPTER 32

DISCIPLINARY ACTION

THE HALL WAS DEAD SILENT. Hector had indicted the whole table and no one spoke up. To his surprise, among those who had gone against his orders, none showed any remorse or backed down from his gaze.

Narcha stared at Hector with defiance. Rog's mind was clearly elsewhere. Eiwin carried a peaceful look. Domeron, who had put this all into motion in the first place, kept his eyes closed as a smirk formed in the corner of his lips. Allen was shivering, but seeing his companion's reactions, he kept his calm.

Only Rimold shifted in his chair. "Might I speak, Elder?" he asked.

Hector frowned. "What is it?"

"I was really not involved in any of this." Rimold looked around at his companions. "This punishment does not involve me too, does it?"

The elder just narrowed his eyes at the rogue. Rimold gulped and fell silent again.

"So..." Hector faced the rest of the Sect members again. "Is no one going to speak?"

"Might I ask what crimes we have committed against the Sect, Master Hector?" Eiwin asked.

"You went against explicit orders from your Grand Elder to not investigate the imperials," he spat back. "Is that enough of a crime?"

"It might indeed be," Eiwin acknowledged. "But according to unspoken cultivation tradition, if the majority of the Sect members disagree with their

183

superiors' decision, they may reserve the right to act in spite of their commands if a dire situation were to arise. It happened multiple times in the Crystal Sky Sect, and remnants of the Sect only survived to this day because of the judgment and decisiveness of those people."

Hector scoffed. "Hmph, don't presume to speak of cultivation tradition to me, girl. This was a custom made in times of war and calamity. After those times of crisis were over, it was used as a pretense to overthrow their superiors and cause civil wars inside their own Sects. It has long since been outlawed."

"Yet is Master Hector truly worried that we were planning rebellion?" Eiwin shook her head. "You know us better than anyone, and you are aware of our loyalty. We were worried the imperials were planning something that would be detrimental to our Sect. We went against your orders for the sake of investigating and stopping it if necessary."

Narcha laughed. "And turns out we were right all along."

Hector was ready to lash out, but he closed his mouth at Narcha's words. He looked at her. "What did you find out?"

"The imperials found out about an inheritance ground with the bandits' help," Narcha said. "We followed them into it."

"An inheritance ground? In this place?"

Eiwin nodded. "I was skeptical at first, but we later confirmed it. The creator of that hidden realm was very adept in spatial manipulation, so it's likely that we were teleported into another place altogether for the trials."

A flash of excitement crossed Hector's face. "Spatial manipulation?! Then that must have been the realm of a very strong cultivator! The fact all of you came out alive is a wonder too!"

"It was more or less a miracle." She lowered her head.

"And?! What did you come across inside that realm? What rewards did you acquire?" The elder seemed unable to contain his joy at the news.

Domeron laughed. "What is this now, old man? Weren't you about to punish them?"

Hector waved him off. "That can be left for later! We need to address more important matters now!" Gripped by the news of the trial, he wasn't even trying to put up an authoritative front anymore.

"We came across some rewards, but..." Eiwin trailed off, hesitating.

"What is it?" Hector's face fell. "Did you lose them?"

"No, old man." Narcha glared at him. "We almost died trying to acquire them, but that's not the problem. The problem is that we've forgotten almost everything about the trial."

"What do you mean?"

"It is as she says," Eiwin replied. "Someone or something seems to have wiped our memories of the trial. No matter how much we try to recall it, specific details about the environment and monsters we faced in the trial are simply out of our reach."

Hector sank into thought. "Explain what you remember. From the beginning."

And so they did. Their entrance into the underground, the labyrinth, the canyon, the desert, and all their fights and travels there. Of course, although they recounted these events, they lacked many details.

As Eiwin had mentioned, they couldn't recall the appearances of the areas they had traveled in—only their feelings and experiences in these places served to describe them. The labyrinth, for instance, invoked feelings of being lost and confined. They remembered that they fought a few monsters and gained a few rewards, but couldn't recall their exact opponents.

Even in the canyon and beyond, only certain words and images came to their mind—like thunder and tornadoes, sneaking past a being of pure lightning, walking for hours on end. It was a brief and lackluster recounting, and yet every single one of them could remember the danger and dread they felt throughout.

There were no mentions of the hawk spirit or the ghost inside the mausoleum.

Some things they remembered almost vividly. Their interactions with each other, or any other human for that matter, were still fresh in their minds. They told Hector about their cooperation with Reinhart and about their fights with the bandits and the imperials. Once the conversation headed towards the end of the trial, though, Narcha and Eiwin were both reluctant to continue.

They threw uncertain gazes towards Hector, and in a rare display of tact, he didn't push them on the matter. Their reluctance wasn't unnoticed by the rest of the Sect members, who all acted concerned. Perhaps they thought that Reinhart had betrayed them, and while they weren't wrong, this wasn't why Narcha and Eiwin were hesitant to elaborate. What Reinhart had revealed about Hector still weighed heavily on Red.

Red didn't take an active role in this discussion. He could still remember every detail of the trial, and he was afraid that he would slip up and reveal something he shouldn't have remembered. He replied with similarly vague descriptions when prompted, and didn't seem to rouse any suspicions from the others.

Of course, some new revelations caught Hector's attention.

"You can feel other people's presences?" Hector asked, surprised.

"I can," Red admitted.

"Unfaithful disciple!" Goulth slammed his hand on the table and glared at him. "You could have at least told your master about it!"

Red bowed his head. "I'm sorry, I should have told you about it."

"Um..." The blacksmith was taken aback. "It's fine, it's fine. I can see why you would like to hide it. Next time, just make sure to tell me the truth, alright?"

"I will."

Goulth smiled. "Good."

This sudden change in attitude earned the giant man more than a few judging looks, but he simply acted like nothing had happened.

Unlike Red's master, Hector wasn't angered by this revelation. "It's a very useful skill. And from what I understand, without it or your quick thinking, none of your fellow Sect members would have made it very far in the trial."

"Maybe. But without their help, I wouldn't have gotten very far either, even with my powers."

Hector looked satisfied. "It's good that you understand that."

Red didn't really understand the praise. He was just being sincere. Still, he didn't protest.

"So, by the looks of it, the creator of this trial wanted to keep his identity hidden, which is not uncommon in the cultivation world," Hector said, addressing the group. "Many cultivators leave enemies behind after their deaths, so it makes sense that they would like to conceal certain things. The fact the imperials knew about this place and actively sought it out is the part that interests me the most. It hints at there being something larger behind those trials..." He looked over at Red. "Do you still have that compass?"

Red tossed it over.

Hector examined the item. "Interesting design. I could take it apart and inspect it, but I'm afraid that might destroy it in the process." He passed the compass over to Goulth. "Anything you can do?"

The blacksmith frowned as he looked it over. "Hard to tell without careful inspection... If this is really from the Empire, though, I doubt a mortal like me would be able to take it apart."

Hector sighed. "Just do your best. See what you can learn."

Goulth nodded and pocketed the compass.

"Now, what exactly did you acquire at the trial?" Hector looked back at his Sect members with unconcealed eagerness in his eyes.

They all put forward what they had acquired. Five Spirit Stones, two monster cores, a few medicine bottles from the imperials, a handful of unidentified talismans, and the Dark Iron nuggets.

Goulth's eyes widened at the sight of the ore. "Is that..."

Red nodded. "Dark Iron."

"Great! Perfect!" The blacksmith snatched them up and set about inspecting them, seemingly forgetting about all the other items on the table.

Hector winced at the other treasures. "Is that it?"

Narcha scoffed. "Why? Is that not enough for you?"

"That's not it. I was under the assumption you had acquired more than this."

"We did, Master Hector," Eiwin said. "We had to exchange most of the Spirit Stones we acquired in the second part of the trial for medicines to heal Rog and... me."

She caught the attention of the whole table.

"W-what happened to you, Eiwin?" Allen whimpered.

"Nothing that matters now, young master." She shook her head regretfully. "I'm just sorry to say that because of our wounds, we couldn't bring back as much as we wished to the Sect."

Hector sighed again. "There is nothing to worry about. These Spirit Stones alone are more than enough to sustain our growth for months to come. Each and every one of you is entitled to rewards and will have a say on how we spend these resources. Is anyone against me putting all these treasures into the Sect vault after they've been inspected?"

No one protested. Red wondered if they were being intimidated into accepting this, but their expressions told another story. At the very least, the group trusted the elder not to swindle resources from them, so Red didn't speak up.

"Since that's settled, let's return to the matter at hand..."

Hector's countenance became serious again. The rest were surprised, but no one dared to say anything.

The elder opened his mouth but stayed silent, as if considering what he was about to say. "... I was wrong."

Everyone was dumbfounded.

"Can you say that again, old man?" Narcha asked.

Hector groaned. "I was wrong about the imperials."

Domeron laughed. "Who would have thought I'd live to see the day the great Hector admitted he was wrong to his juniors?"

"Shut up, you bastard!" the old man shouted. "I have been hiding for too long inside this town, and I was too comfortable with the safety this place provided. I ignored the fact that the true meaning of being a Sect cultivator is taking risks for the Sect's future! I was too old and cowardly and didn't want to risk upsetting the status quo, while you, the young, were right in taking a stand and fighting for your own ideals and future! Is that enough for you?!"

Everyone stared at him. Even Domeron's laughter faded away as he looked on in disbelief.

Hector scoffed. "I am not beyond admitting my own faults. I am still upset that you disobeyed me, but the fact you did it for the right reasons forces me to put that indignity aside. In the future, I promise you I won't be so hesitant to take a stand against our enemies, no matter the risks. At the same time, I won't be so forgiving of blatant disrespect for the rules. Is that understood?"

Eiwin smiled. "It is, Master Hector."

"Good. However, there is another breach of the rules that needs to be addressed."

Narcha frowned. "Bah! I knew this was too good to be true! What did we do this time, old man?"

"Not you." Hector shook his head. "He did it." He pointed at Allen.

All eyes shifted to the young master, who trembled in his chair.

CHAPTER 33

A SECRET REVEALED

"You, Allen, have gone against my explicit orders not to leave the Sect grounds," Hector said. "And unlike the rest of your fellow Sect members, your offense is by far the most severe."

Allen shifted in his seat. "I-I don't..."

"Silence!" Hector cut him off with a wave of his hand. "I was not done speaking."

The young master hastily nodded.

"By putting yourself in danger," Hector said, his face severe, "not only have you risked your own foolish life, but the lives of your companions as they tried to protect you and almost wasted all the resources and time the rest of the Sect has put into your growth."

"B-but I didn't..."

Hector threw him another glare, and Allen fell silent.

He continued. "I care not what notions of grandeur you had, or how much you might want to experience a life of adventure—your responsibility lies with the Sect. Everything else is secondary, even your own aspirations and desires... Do you understand?"

Allen looked down.

Hector frowned, repeating his question like a threat. "Do you understand?"

"Master Hector," Eiwin intervened. "Young Master Allen didn't—"

"Enough!" The elder raised a hand, stopping her. "I asked him a question! I will not allow anyone else to answer in his stead!"

Allen stayed silent. He clenched his fists against his pants and looked around the table. His eyes lingered on Red, but Red pretended he hadn't noticed the boy's pleading eyes.

His intentions were clear. *You have to rely on yourself here.*

Red didn't know if Allen understood the meaning of his actions, or if he simply felt betrayed by his companion's attitude. In any case, the young master looked back at Hector with a shaky gaze.

"So?" The old man stared at him. "Must I ask you the question again?"

Allen's expression hardened. "N-no..."

"Good. Then what is your—"

"I don't understand it!" The young master slammed his fist against the table.

Silence reigned in the room as everyone stared at Allen, stunned. Hector looked as if he had just seen the most preposterous scene in the world.

His eyes twitched. "What did you say?"

"I-I said I don't understand it!" Allen found his courage. "Why do I have to remain here while everyone else risks their lives out there? Who cares about my duties to the Sect? I never asked for any of it!"

"You!" Hector stood up and pointed a quaking finger at him. "Take back what you just said!"

Allen hesitated for a second, but his resolve quickly returned. "I won't! I'm a cultivator too! If being the Sect Master means I can't be out there helping my friends, then I don't want to be the Sect Master at all!"

"I... I..." Hector stumbled on his feet before falling back onto his chair, pale.

"Master Hector!" Eiwin cried.

Hector didn't seem to hear her. He held his head in his hands in dismay. "All my years wasted raising a successor, only to come up with an ingrate... Oh, what would my fellow Sect members say if they could see me right now."

Red marveled at the strange display. No one around the room knew how to react to the elder's sudden despondence. They could only exchange looks with each other in silence.

Allen, on the other hand, immediately regretted his words. He gave Hector a troubled look. "I didn't really mean to…"

"Enough!" Hector cut him off. "I know what you mean to say! You've made that very clear!"

"B-but I—"

"I SAID ENOUGH!" Hector slammed his fist down, cracking the whole table into splinters.

Red and the others jumped back, stumbling between themselves to avoid the wooden shards and items sent flying. The larger remains of the table fell with a slam as the treasures they had brought to the Sect scattered across the ground.

Only Hector remained sitting. He heaved large gulps of angry air, and no one dared to break the heavy silence that had settled in the hall.

Hector waved his hand at them. "Out! All of you!"

Not even Narcha dared to disrespect his commands as they shuffled out of the hall.

"No, wait!" the elder called out.

Everyone froze.

"Narcha, Eiwin, Red and Domeron," Hector said. "You stay. I still need to clarify your reports."

Red hesitated. He didn't want to be near the elder in his moment of rage, but he didn't think it wise to go against his order, either.

The others were all too eager to leave the hall. Goulth was still enthralled with the ore and couldn't wait to go back to his workshop, while Rog and Rimold likewise wanted to be as far away from a mad Hector as possible. Allen feared that the elder would change his mind and punish him, so he ran out behind his companions.

Finally, several long seconds later, there were only five people in the hall.

Domeron looked down at the pieces of wood. He frowned at Hector. "You broke our table."

"So what?!" The old man glared at him. "We can just have Goulth build another one."

"You also broke the pill bottles."

Hector waved his hands dismissively. "Bah, it doesn't matter! Someone will gather them later." He turned to Eiwin, Narcha and Red. "So, what is it that you wanted to tell me?"

Narcha hesitated. "That depends... Will you lash out at us again?"

Hector scowled. "Are you going to betray my trust too?"

"I don't think so."

"Then it doesn't matter. Just spit it out!"

So Narcha did. She told him about what Eiwin had done to defeat a certain monster whose details they couldn't recall, about how they had found a Parting Sea Pill and how Reinhart had chosen to backstab them. She trailed off once she came to the conversation that had followed.

Even Eiwin looked down.

"What is it?" Hector, already flush with anger, looked at the two women with suspicion. "I assume you didn't manage to get the pill, is that right?"

"He tried to blackmail us," Red said. "He wanted us to help him kill you."

Both Domeron and Hector's eyes widened.

"He wanted you to betray the Sect?" the swordsman asked in disbelief.

Red nodded.

"Did he give you a reason?"

"He did." Red looked at Hector. "It was for revenge against you."

"Revenge?" The old man's brow furrowed. "Revenge for what?"

"For what your Sect did," Red replied. "He said you and your Sect created a technique to extract a cultivator's Spiritual Sea... He said that you were the master of the individuals responsible for taking his own Spiritual Sea, and the closest person to them he could kill to get revenge."

Hector's face fell. Eiwin and Narcha looked apprehensive, but neither tried to stop Red as he spoke. Domeron sighed, remaining silent.

"Is that true, then?" Red asked. "Did you really come up with such a technique?"

Hector hesitated, but still ended up nodding. "I did. It wasn't just me, but my research played a large part in the technique's invention."

Red frowned. "I assume the part about your disciples taking his Spiritual Sea is true too?"

Hector's expression soured. "How would I know? But I know for a fact my disciples took more than their fair share of Spiritual Seas, so it is obviously plausible."

Red was relieved by his honesty, but the information was still alarming. "Did you take any of them yourself?"

Hector shook his head. "My role in my Sect was not what you might think. My realm was very low compared to my companions, so my interactions in the field were very limited. However, when it came to understanding the fundamentals of our Sect's techniques and their applications, not even individuals dozens of times stronger than me could compare."

The others in the room quietly observed. It was clear they already knew most of this information and weren't surprised by it.

Red, on the other hand, was unsure what to think.

"Are you worried I will take your Spiritual Sea from you?" Hector went straight to the heart of the matter.

"I am." Even if Red had lied, he doubted Hector would have believed him.

"It's not an unfounded worry," Hector admitted. "I too would be concerned about my superior holding the power to take my Spiritual Sea from me at any point in time."

"That's not doing much to assuage my concerns."

"Nothing I say will completely assuage your concerns, so why bother?"

Red supposed he had a point.

"If it makes you feel any better, one of the reasons I left my original Sect was precisely because of this technique," Hector said. "Our Ocean Bearers Sect was always focused on healing arts, and one of the biggest conundrums of our research was how to heal a wounded Spiritual Sea, since interacting with it while it remained inside a cultivator's body was almost impossible. We reached a consensus that taking it out of one's body, fixing it in the outside world, and then reintroducing it into the body was the only possible way to do it. It was a three-step problem—which we never got past step two."

"Why is that?" Red asked.

Hector sighed. "Because taking out a cultivator's Spiritual Sea from their body brought about unexpected changes. Loss of the cultivation base kept inside their Spiritual Sea was one of them, but there were also problems with the individuals themselves that appeared once they were separated. Problems with their spirit, which turned out to be much more severe than whatever wound we were trying to heal in the first place. As such, the idea of the technique stopped in the first phase, but some people within the Sect found other uses for it."

"They used the Spiritual Seas as treasure ingredients, I assume," Red said.

"Indeed. It was an unexpected use of a technique I myself had a hand in inventing, as they were now able to extract the equivalent of extremely rare ingredients from the bodies of cultivators to use in many ways. They also found that the quality of the Spiritual Sea didn't depend on cultivation, but rather on talent. You can imagine what happened from there..."

Red could indeed imagine it. Taking talented cultivators off the street, perhaps by force or simply by promising them a spot in their Sect, only to stab them in the back and take their most important possession. It was an ingenious and devious plan.

"I protested the use of my technique in this manner," Hector said. "At that point, it did not differ from a demonic technique, and we were one of the seven Orthodox Sects! We were supposed to fight against those practices... Unfortunately, on the face of such benefits, my protests availed to nothing, and the rampant use of the technique continued... Does that explain everything to you?"

Red nodded. "Kind of."

"And do you believe me?"

"Partially." People who told a story often made themselves out to be the good guys. This was merely the account of one man, and while Red appreciated his attempt at honesty, he would be foolish to trust it wholeheartedly.

"There is one thing that confuses me, though," he said. "Reinhart said you were the master of the cultivators responsible for taking his Spiritual Sea. If you were against the use of this technique, why did your disciples use it?"

Hector's face fell. "Who do you think discovered that demonic use of my technique in the first place?"

"I see. Are they truly dead, then?"

"They are," Hector said. "Killed by the Empire for all their foolishness... However, they left something behind."

These words piqued the interest of not only Red, but also Eiwin and Narcha. Domeron, on the other hand, closed his eyes as if knowing what was about to come.

"What I'm about to tell the lot of you is confidential." Hector stared at them, his face grave. "If it wasn't for what you told me, this would have remained a secret, but considering the urgency of the situation, I have no other choice but to reveal it."

Narcha began to worry. "What is it, old man? Does this have to do with those disciples of yours? Did they leave behind any more cultivators looking for revenge?"

"Oh, I have no doubt they did, but that's not the point." Hector shook his head. "It's about Allen."

"What does this have to do with..." The realization hit her. "Oh no."

"Indeed. Allen is what my disciples left behind. He is their son."

CHAPTER 34
A TRUE SECT

HECTOR'S REVELATION shocked the room. Neither Eiwin nor Narcha knew how to react, and Red simply went silent, thinking over what they'd learned.

"Does the young master know about this?" Eiwin asked.

Hector shook his head. "He knows his parents were part of the Sect and that they were killed by the empire. He doesn't know about the more... questionable practice they had a hand in."

"Questionable practices?" Narcha cried. "Earlier you made it sound like they were engaged in demonic cultivation!"

Hector pursed his lips but didn't deny it.

"Besides," she went on, "do you think it's a good idea to hide this from Allen?"

"And what would you do? Tell him his parents committed atrocities and slaughtered innocent cultivators for their Spiritual Seas? What do you think that would do to the psyche of a child?"

Eiwin huffed. "You might be right, but you know you can't hide this from him forever."

"I don't intend to. I will tell him when he's ready." He didn't sound as confident as usual, and Red wasn't the only one who picked up on it.

"When do you think he'll be ready?" Narcha pressed. "The more you wait, the more damage you'll do when he learns that the parents he looked up to and sought to avenge weren't so good after all!"

Hector glared at her. "Don't act like you don't understand it yourself, girl! Although his parents weren't the heroes he thinks they were, this doesn't change the fact that Allen's quest for revenge towards the Empire is just! Or what, do you think the people from your tribe were all saints too?"

Narcha gritted her teeth and fell silent.

Red finally spoke up. "Why are you telling us this? Are you afraid of Reinhart seeking revenge against Allen?"

"Of course I am," Hector said. "Not so much of Reinhart, but of the people that might be behind him."

"You mean someone other than Gustav?"

The old man grunted in agreement. "I doubt Reinhart could have acquired this intelligence about me so easily. Even when my Sect was still alive, I didn't have any reputation to speak of and was only known to my fellow Sect members... Which is why I believe he must be working with someone else who could acquire that type of information."

"The Empire, then?" Narcha said. "Or maybe a surviving member of your Sect?"

Hector nodded. "Either is possible. In fact, I wouldn't be surprised if it's both. There was no lack of cultivators that joined the Empire once they noticed the tides changing. They must have placed Reinhart in this town as a spy."

"At least he doesn't know about Young Master Allen," Eiwin said, relieved.

"It doesn't surprise me. My identity was known to quite a few people inside the Sect, so it's not a shock it could have leaked. Allen's parentage, however, was only known to a scant few, who are all dead right now or in this room." He stared at each and every one of them, his face dire. "Suffice it to say, I expect absolute secrecy on your part regarding this, and for the three of you to alert me to any signs of Reinhart's presence in the town."

Narcha scoffed. "You don't even need to say anything, old man. After what Reinhart did in that place, I would be searching for him even if you hadn't said anything."

Eiwin and Red both nodded, although Red was still confused about a few matters.

Hector seemed satisfied. "Good. I have entrusted you with the weight of the truth due to what Reinhart revealed to you, and I expect you to wield that power with responsibility. The consequences of letting this leak could be disastrous for the Sect and everyone related to it." He waved his hands. "Now, begone! I have many matters to think about."

The three of them turned to leave.

"Not you, boy!" Hector shouted. "I need to speak with you."

Red paused. Both Eiwin and Narcha looked uncertainly from him to Hector.

"I said you two can leave!" Hector scowled. "I won't take his Spiritual Sea, if that's what you're concerned about!"

Narcha scoffed and walked out while Eiwin turned to Red. "We'll be waiting for you outside," she said.

He nodded, and then she followed Narcha outside.

The hall door closed behind the two women, leaving Red and Hector alone. At least that was what Red thought until he remembered there was someone else in the room who had been uncharacteristically quiet.

"I thought this was only between me and Hector," he said, looking at Domeron.

The swordsman smiled. "I am Hector's right hand. My presence anywhere he goes is a given. He trusts me implicitly. Isn't that right, old man?"

Said old man ignored his question.

Red frowned. He returned his attention to Hector. "What do you want to talk about?"

"You said you continued on with the trial after the others, right?" Hector asked after some contemplation.

"I did. I don't remember much, though. All I can recall is having to avoid very dangerous monsters while relying on my detection power. After that, the trial ended."

The elder grunted. "And you didn't meet anyone else? No imperials, no Ricards, no Reinhart?"

Red didn't hesitate to lie. "No one."

"I see..."

A silence settled. For a second, he thought the elder would accuse him of lying, but thankfully he changed the topic instead.

"You helped Allen escape, didn't you?"

Red nodded.

Hector scratched his beard in thought. "And? What did you think about his performance? Did he show any signs of growth?"

The question surprised him. Red had been fully expecting to be punished for helping Allen escape, but Hector was now asking about Allen's skills, and without any signs of his earlier anger.

Red looked towards Domeron, who was simply smiling at him with his one arm crossed over his chest. A possibility came to his mind.

He looked back at Hector. "Did you know about Allen's intentions of escaping?"

Hector hesitated, but still answered. "I did."

Red frowned. "And you still allowed it?"

He nodded again.

"Why?"

"Because I needed him to grow," Hector said as if the reason were obvious. "Of course, if I knew he would be sent to a life-or-death trial, I would have thought twice about it, but in the end, it all worked out."

Red looked from Hector to Domeron. "You two were in on everything."

Hector knew about it. Allen's escape, the Sect members' imperial investigation. He was aware of it from the start.

This revelation shocked Red to the core.

"I had to tell Hector." Domeron shrugged. "He isn't stupid. He expected something like this from his Sect members as soon as he imposed those limitations."

Hector let out a dry laugh. "How could I not expect it from a group of stubborn mules like them? I was not only expecting it, I was counting on it."

Red was still puzzled. "If you wanted it to happen, why all the theatrics?"

"Because I wanted to test them," Hector said. "I wanted to see how far they were willing to go to resolve their own personal vendettas. I wanted to cultivate their hatred for the Empire towards a common goal and to see them all grow because of it."

"This all sounds so unnecessary." Red couldn't believe it. "Couldn't you just have told them?"

The old man scoffed. "It was a test... You see, a few months ago before you came about, I had never seen Eiwin disobey my orders even once. She stuck to the rules and principles of the Sect, even if it was to the detriment of her companions. Yet in you came, and then suddenly she is challenging me to my face. I was angry at first, mostly at you, but then I realized this was true growth on her part, and I was happy about it. Then she did it again, this time to help Narcha against the Empire."

Red was baffled. "Didn't you tell us how the Sect rules and principles were important to you? Why would you be happy about her violating them?"

"A Sect isn't about rules and traditions," the elder explained. "It's about the spirit of the Sect and how the people seek to fulfill it together. That's something a lot of Sects nowadays have forgotten about. They stick to their old-fashioned customs and ideals, following the rules established by their ancestors without a second thought. Their members are willing to do anything to rise in position inside their Sects, even sacrificing their integrity and companions for the sake of a hollow title and prestige. It's a mockery of the bastions of humanity these Sects were in the past, and it's why I left my Sect in the first place."

Red couldn't say he understood this ideal Sect Hector spoke about, but he could understand the disdain in the old man's words.

Hector continued. "Narcha, Eiwin, and Allen hold the idea of a Sect on too high of a pedestal. One day, once they are out exploring the world, they will understand how treacherous and petty Sect cultivators are too, how they are no heroes to be celebrated. Even the Crystal Sky Sect these days is infested with infighting, though the mortal world at large may be unaware of it. These are not the examples I want them to follow. I want them to challenge the rules and authority imposed over them, to stand up for each other and carry the spirit of the Sect with themselves, not bound by traditions or petty worries. I want them to rely on each other, to put their own lives on the line for their companions and reach as one for that ultimate goal of all cultivators—immortality! This is what a true Sect is and what I want this Water Dragon Sect to become in the future... For that, though, they must prove themselves willing to challenge the judgment of the ones they fear and respect the most."

Red was starting to understand. "Is that why you're putting up this act? To raise a rebellious and cooperative spirit in them?"

He wasn't sure how that would turn out, and yet judging by what he had seen from the others, it was working. He had lost count of how many times his fellow Sect members had risked their lives to save each other. Even Red was no exception to that.

Hector grinned. "It sounds ridiculous when you put it that way, but it's just how I like to teach. There is no point in spelling things out to my students—either they grasp these concepts on their own or they die trying. It's the cultivator way."

Hector and Red's new master were of the same mind on these matters. There was, however, still one thing Red was confused about.

"Why are you telling me all this?" he asked. "It seems risky to entrust me with this information."

Red had barely been part of this Sect for a few months. How could he be trusted with so much delicate knowledge?

Hector scoffed. "That's because you're a cynic, boy. I told you all of this, but did you feel moved at all? You probably spend every hour of the day wondering how people around you can betray you, how you can be stabbed in the back at your most vulnerable moments, how you can come to only rely on yourself... Isn't that right?"

Red didn't respond, but he knew the answer to the elder's question.

"In some ways, those are the markings of a true cultivator, but I'm trying to build a Sect, not create a bunch of independent and arrogant rogue cultivators," Hector said. "Still, there is at least one admirable trait to you—you have a sense of honor. There were times when you put your life on the line for your companions, even if you were unwilling and knew how detrimental it would be for your future. You might have had an ulterior motive behind those actions too, but what matters is that you saw them through. This is why I know I can trust you."

Hector took out a badge and handed it to Red. It was a bronze medallion, depicting a large-beaked and slender bird in astonishing detail.

"This is why I have a new position for you inside this Sect."

CHAPTER 35
RAIN DANCE

RED REGARDED THE MEDALLION WARILY. He looked up at Hector. "What kind of position?"

The elder smiled. "Have you ever heard of a heron?"

Red shook his head.

"They are adept and stealthy hunters," Hector explained. "Yet they don't stalk and search for their prey like you might think. Instead, they wade into shallow waters using their long legs and remain still and observant, waiting for a fish to come by so they may catch it. Sometimes they even use bait to attract their prey. They are incredibly patient hunters, and many cultivators have studied these beasts' behaviors to develop their own techniques."

"What are you trying to say?" Red was always interested in learning more about beasts and other matters of the cultivation world, but right now, his priority was to understand what Hector wanted of him.

"Some cultivators who studied these herons were from my Sect. They incorporated their observations into their weapon techniques and became some of the most adept assassins in the cultivation world. They hid in plain sight, waiting for their victims to wander by. Then, in the blink of an eye, they struck, and suddenly our Sect had one less enemy to worry about. Most of the time, the people nearby didn't even see what happened before our assassins left the scene."

Red sighed. "So that's what you want me to be? An assassin?"

"I think it fits you," Domeron piped up. "This practice requires patience, ruthlessness, and an eye for opportunity. Out of everyone in this Sect, you are the only person who has all three of those traits in abundance."

Red wasn't sure whether he was supposed to be flattered or offended.

"Of course, I don't intend to send you on political assassinations like my Sect did," Hector said. "What I want is for you to protect and watch the backs of those three. They lack the resolve and ruthlessness required to thrive in the cultivation world, and although I hope one day they will grow up too, I must have someone willing to do what's necessary for them."

"You mean you want me to kill everyone who threatens them?" Red asked.

Hector nodded with a grin. "More or less. Of course, I don't mean to trick you. You would still be an assassin, trained to get rid of the enemies of this Sect. However, you may rest easy in the fact that you are doing this for your companions and not for my own personal interests."

"That doesn't sound very convincing."

The elder sneered. "Nothing I say will be fully convincing to a paranoid child like you. How about a promise, then—if you do not agree with a mission I assign you, you may refuse it. How does that sound?"

Red hesitated. This was an extremely important decision he was about to make, and he wasn't willing to rush into it unaware of all the benefits and dangers involved.

Domeron seemed to read his mind. "Your training will also change. I will not only teach you how to fight, but I will also teach you how to kill. This will involve teaching you the weapon arts of the Great Heron School of the Ocean Bearers Sect."

Red's interest was piqued. "You mean like a Spiritual Art?"

"More or less. It's something you'll be able to use in the future if you break into the Lesser Ring Realm."

"Then I'll do it."

Hector glared at him. "What, was the prospect of helping your companions not attractive enough for you? All I needed to do was to offer you a reward for you to do something?"

"Yes." He couldn't deny it.

"Bah, get out of here, you greedy brat!"

"What do I do with the medallion?"

"Just take it with you! I don't care!"

Red examined the lump of metal. "Can I sell it?"

Hector's eyes twitched. "If you sell it, I'll skin you alive!"

Red supposed that meant no.

Domeron sighed. "Just go rest. Your training will begin tomorrow, and I'm sure Goulth will also want to talk your ear off."

Red nodded and exited, leaving behind a fuming Hector and a smiling Domeron.

Outside, Narcha and Eiwin were waiting for him near the fence. He wondered whether they had heard any of his conversation with Hector, but he didn't think the elder would be so careless with so much important information.

Narcha waved him over. "Come here, kid!"

Red walked over to them.

She smiled. "You're still alive, huh?"

He frowned. "Were you worried Hector was going to kill me?"

"Well—"

"We were not," Eiwin said hastily. "We were simply worried Hector was going to punish you for bringing Allen out... Wait, did he?"

Red shook his head. "He just wanted to talk about the trial."

"Talk about the trial?" Narcha narrowed her eyes. "What else could you tell him we didn't already?"

"He thought I was a more impartial witness to the events and could give him a more reliable account of what happened. He told me he couldn't trust you because you were too hotheaded, and he couldn't trust Eiwin either because she always covers for you."

He lied as naturally as he breathed, and the two women seemed convinced.

Narcha gnashed her teeth. "That bastard! That's exactly what he would say!"

I know, which is why I came up with it.

"Enough, Miss Valt," Eiwin said. "It is understandable that Master Hector would be wary of us after what happened. Besides, we didn't omit anything in our report, so there is nothing he could fault us for."

Narcha nodded reluctantly. "I suppose you're right..."

"Is that all you wanted to ask about?" Red asked. "I'd like to rest, if that's okay."

"Wait!" Narcha said. "There's something else." She handed Red a glass vial from her pouch. It was full of dozens of green pills.

"What is this?"

"Wood-Attributed Vein Opening Pills," Narcha said. "I got them in a trade for the remaining Spirit Stones we had."

Red frowned. "Why didn't you give this to Hector?"

"Because it belongs to you. You gave out all your Spirit Stones to me to exchange for the medicine and couldn't trade for anything for yourself. It's only fair I got something for you."

Red didn't know how to respond.

Eiwin smiled. "You don't need to hesitate, Red. These pills will be very useful for you in opening the rest of your veins. Wood is the gentlest of elements, too, so the energy in the medicine will be easy to control."

Red nodded, storing the vial in his pocket. "Thank you."

Narcha rolled her eyes. "There's no need for thanks. If it wasn't for you, we wouldn't have gotten very far in that trial."

"She's right," Eiwin said. "You have helped us in more ways than you can possibly know, Red, so it's only fair you're rewarded for it."

"Now, go and have your rest!" Narcha waved him off. "We're tired too, so we'll be going to our own rooms."

Red nodded again and walked away.

At this point, his crimson sense encompassed the entire Sect, so he knew there was no one waiting for him near his room. That was ideal. He needed time to think.

Red entered his shack, closing the door. He didn't even bother turning on the lantern, as his improved vision allowed him to see in the room's darkness. He sat on the bed, taking out the bottle of pills.

He was conflicted.

Do I tell her about the Parting Storm formation?

Red didn't know. There were too many complications with this matter. On one hand, it was the best way he could make it up to Narcha for lying to her, but on the other hand, he would be taking an enormous risk.

First of all, he couldn't reveal this formation to any specialists, considering its value. He needed to build it himself, but he didn't know how long that would take him. Narcha only had a few years left to open her Spiritual Sea, and Red had no guarantee he could learn it by then, much less gather all the supposed rare materials. And this formation wasn't a pill—it didn't guarantee you could open your Spiritual Sea. For Narcha it was better than nothing, but was it worth it to give her false hope?

Maybe it was the only chance she had, but Red needed time to do his research first. If he felt it was possible to build this formation within two years, then he would tell Narcha about it. If it was impossible, then there was no point in giving her hope only to waste her time.

At this moment, he was too mentally tired to go through the Arcane Script book. There was, however, one manual he was keen to try.

He took it from his pouch.

Storm's Blessing.

It was a curious name. Could a destructive storm ever be considered a blessing? Perhaps there was a deeper meaning, but Red wasn't in the right mindset to think about it.

He opened the book, and right on the first few pages, he found what he was looking for—the Vein Opening Technique the hawk had spoken of. Once he read its name, though, his face fell.

Rain Dance?

Since when could a dance help you open your veins? As Red continued to read the instructions, he grew even more perplexed. The manual depicted a set of ridiculous and exaggerated movements, which it called "dance moves." Apparently, Red was supposed to repeat this dance until he felt the spirit of the rain calling for him, and by then the blessed Spiritual Energy would be entering his body. Not only that, but he had to repeat the same sentence the entire time he danced.

Oh rain, bless your lost child.

He almost thought this was an elaborate prank, but he doubted the hawk would spend so much effort just to trick the trial's winner. So Red decided to put the manual down and imitate the movements.

As soon as he did the first steps, he hesitated.

This is ridiculous.

Red sighed and put such thoughts to the back of his mind. He repeated the movements many times, diligently, even though he found them silly. The dance itself was simple, with many hops and arms raised as if praying to the skies.

He repeated the sentence out loud, knowing through his crimson sense that no one else was close enough to hear it. This went on for almost ten minutes, with nothing happening.

Just as he was thinking he was doing something wrong, he heard the boom of thunder. His movements faltered as he stood stunned.

Is it raining?

Red looked at the sky outside his window. It was a clear night, with no signs of clouds.

What is going—

Before he could complete his thought, another boom sounded, and a raging tide of energy entered his veins.

CHAPTER 36

TAKING STOCK

RIGHT AFTER THE Rain Dance's storm began, Red sat down to focus on the energy entering his body. Although this took him by surprise, he didn't panic. It wasn't the first time he'd dealt with rampant forces inside of him.

This Spiritual Energy, however, was unlike anything he had ever encountered.

It was strong, far thicker than the Spiritual Energy Red was used to cultivating with. Yet his veins seemed more than capable of bearing the brunt of it. The true challenge was controlling the energy.

Every time he exerted a little bit of control to direct the energy, it slipped away from him, diving into another part of his body. It was like trying to direct a stubborn animal to its pen—it did the exact opposite of everything you ordered it to do.

Red winced. *Since when is cultivation supposed to be like this?*

He struggled again and again, to no avail. Five minutes passed before the energy dissipated from his veins, with Red unable to use even a thread of it to open his acupoints.

His mind was exhausted, but still pondered what he'd experienced.

The manual said nothing about this.

Red started to have doubts. With the technique he learned from Viran, there was no need to exert fine control over the Spiritual Energy. In fact, the threads of energy would naturally travel towards his unopened veins. All he needed to do was give it a push.

This energy from the Rain Dance was quite literally the opposite. It ran wild inside his body, not stopping in one place for more than a moment. It was impossible to use it to cultivate unless he controlled it, and yet Red didn't see how he *could* control it when he didn't even have his Spiritual Sea open.

I have to be missing something.

He doubted the spirit would give him a faulty technique. Yet no matter how many times he read the explanation in the manual, he found no guidance of any sort.

I suppose this is something I'll have to figure out on my own.

Red had a few ideas already, but he didn't dare try them in his current state. This being the case, he put the book aside for now. There was no reason to rush it.

His mind wandered to the other manual. Pushing past his tiredness, he pulled it out. *A Primer on Arcane Script.*

"Arcane Script is the true language of the world."

This was the first phrase Red came across. Unlike the cultivation manual, the writings in this text were more like diary entries, and he could feel the writer's feelings and personality through these words.

The manual then explained what Arcane Script was.

"It consists of all symbols that, once taken shape, may evoke a reaction in the world around them."

The deliberate words left Red curious. He had been led to believe that Arcane Script could only be represented through drawings and etchings, but the more general phrase "taken shape" suggested otherwise. No explanation seemed forthcoming, though.

"It is used in four different areas: formation-building, talisman-drawing, rune-carving, and the execution and creation of spells. This means that by mastering the basics of Arcane Script, one will also achieve initial proficiency in any of those areas. This makes it by far the most useful trade skill in the cultivation world, and it can earn an individual a large amount of riches to help them on their journey."

Red frowned. Why did the manual put such emphasis on earning money in the explanation? Did his master predict that his disciple would be poor?

Not that he was complaining. He would need a large amount of resources if he planned to build the Parting Storm formation.

He was also curious about the spells the manual mentioned. He had not been aware that Arcane Script was also tied to such an integral part of high-level combat. Did this mean Hector also had some mastery over Arcane Script?

That doesn't make sense.

If that were true, then why would the elder throw the responsibility of studying Arcane Script to Goulth? Red felt compelled to find the answer, but the book didn't broach this question just yet, and he had no intention of skipping any explanations.

"Humans first discovered Arcane Script by observing certain natural phenomena at the very dawn of cultivation. The shapes of a storm, the veins of a leaf, the arc of a lightning bolt—arcane symbols can be found all over the world. Yet no one knows for certain how the practice itself originated and who was responsible for coming up with the idea of utilizing these symbols for other purposes. Over tens of thousands of years, humans have developed the Arcane Script to serve many ends, and they have even managed to create symbols not found in nature, which expands the practice to new horizons."

The explanation sounded familiar. Red recalled what Eiwin had told him about Spiritual Energy—how humans were able to create previously unseen types based on abstract concepts such as swordsmanship, order, and virtue. It seemed this concept extended beyond just pure energy.

The manual didn't delve deep into these interesting matters, only establishing a basic understanding before diving straight into the practice itself.

It explained the materials Red needed for Arcane Script, a fine-point pen and paper—at least for the basics. More complex arcane symbols would require much more expensive material, but right now, this wasn't his concern. The manual said that his first goal should be to familiarize himself with the fundamental arcane symbols and how to draw them.

Said fundamental symbols consisted of 496 complex drawings that Red had to master before even beginning his study proper. Some of them represented basic elements—such as fire and water—while others represented concepts and connections—such as expand, retract, retain. Many of those basic symbols also had variations depending on their use, which meant that there were more than simply 496 drawings he had to memorize.

Red knew at a glance how daunting the task ahead of him was. No wonder this was such a difficult practice. His head hurt just by looking at one of these symbols, and now he was supposed to draw and memorize almost five hundred of them.

How long would that take?

He was not discouraged, though. He was not afraid of hard work; he was afraid of having no path forward at all.

Red closed the book and made up his mind.

I will need to ask Master Goulth for help tomorrow. He must have proper paper and pens for this.

Revealing his intentions to learn Arcane Script to the blacksmith didn't worry him. The giant man had always kept secrets for him. What worried him was how Goulth would react when he learned he intended to focus on something other than blacksmithing.

Would the man be happy that he could lighten Red's burden? Or would he be angry at him for splitting his attention with another practice?

Red didn't know, but he had to find out one way or the other.

After addressing his two most immediate concerns, he pulled back his sleeve, revealing the silver bracelet wrapped around his wrist. No one could see it before, but now the treasure stood out on Red's arm.

Yet how long could he keep it hidden? The chances of someone spotting it during his day-to-day life in the Sect were too high for him to risk it. Red didn't think they would push him about the bracelet's function if he wasn't willing to talk about it, but he would rather not arouse any suspicion in the first place.

He took it off his wrist and tried to put it around his ankle. Red was expecting it to be a tight fit, but to his surprise, the bracelet changed sizes on its own and strapped around his leg perfectly. He then pulled both his pants and his sock over it so it would be better hidden.

There was still a risk others would find out about it, but this was the best Red could do.

An hour had passed since he had entered his room, and even with his curiosity sated, there were still so many things he urgently needed to address.

He sat down cross-legged on his bed and used the meditation technique Eiwin taught him. Expanded awareness came to him even more easily now that he was out of danger, and Red inspected his own body.

Nothing seemed out of the ordinary, which was a relief. He had felt nothing weird in his transformed eye either, meaning the demonification hadn't gone past the surface level.

Red then focused on the mist suffusing every corner of his body. The strands didn't stir like they had the last time they'd come into contact with his awareness, which left him confused. He tried it again a few times, but the mist remained silent.

This made him suspicious. Yet there was nothing he could do about the strange being inhabiting his body right now other than cautiously observe it.

He let the expanded awareness dissipate, focusing again on his surroundings. More specifically, he focused on his enhanced crimson sense.

Back in the trial, Red didn't have the time to inspect it thoroughly. Now he could examine its new limits in the comfort of his room.

Like he had thought before, the range of detection of his crimson sense had doubled to around two hundred meters. All things considered, this wasn't a major increase in a plain environment, but in the town and forest, with countless buildings and trees for him and his adversaries to hide behind? It was invaluable.

There was also the matter of precision. Red could discern the fluctuations of others better, even in a crowd. Not to mention, when he inspected his Sect members earlier, he could feel more details about their fluctuations. He didn't know what they meant, but his experience in the trial had offered him deep insight into how his power worked.

First, he felt confident that what his crimson sense detected had to do with blood. It could not feel any non living beings, such as the hawk spirit and the statues, and his other "demonic" powers had to do with blood too. It was just conjecture at this point, but Red felt he wasn't too far off mark.

There were, however, some problems with that theory. If what he felt was blood or related to blood, why couldn't he feel it once it left an individual's body? He couldn't pick up the fluctuations of puddles of blood, or any dissected flesh, for that matter. This left him confused.

But there was an even more puzzling matter.

Why can't I feel my own fluctuation?

CHAPTER 37
THE DARK STAR

RED HAD ALWAYS THOUGHT of his detection power as a sixth sense, hence the name. Yet if the crimson sense could detect living blood, why couldn't he detect himself with it? He could see himself with his vision, smell his own odor, and hear his own voice, so why would this be an exception?

Perhaps he had the wrong idea. He understood little about the power, so it wouldn't be surprising for him to be off the mark with his conjectures. Yet this detail left Red both curious and unnerved.

What would he feel if he could detect his own fluctuation? Would he be able to detect the mist? Would he feel his own dwindling life essence?

Its usefulness couldn't be understated. It had saved his life countless times, and Red felt he had barely scratched the surface of what it was capable of.

Yet it still worried him. He was wary of its demonic origins, and he wasn't sure whether using it contributed to his demonification. But he couldn't "turn off" the ability. He decided to take the hawk's advice and work towards understanding this power in the future.

Red spent the next half an hour studying his companion's fluctuations as he lay in bed. Already he found out details he couldn't pick out before, including one specific rule.

It seems the younger you are, the more active your fluctuation is.

It was easy to miss this at first, but the more he observed, the more easily he could feel it. There was a certain vibration to every signal. It didn't seem to be tied to the strength of the fluctuation itself, yet it hinted at a potential strength hidden inside the body of each individual.

The most active fluctuation in his range was Allen's by far, followed by Eiwin, Narcha, and Rimold in that order, which just so happened to match with their ages, as far as Red knew. Then there were the other ones whose fluctuations were slower—those being Rog, Goulth, Domeron, and Hector.

In fact, Hector's fluctuation was much more inert. Each "wave" coming from the elder was dozens of times stronger than the others, yet they were nowhere near as frequent.

I wonder how old he is?

Was he close to death? You never knew with a cultivator. If he wanted to know, he would need to experiment with others around town.

Still, the little time he spent studying his companions yielded him far more knowledge than he'd expected. Perhaps in the future he could tell much more about an individual than just their strength and age.

Not now, though... I need to sleep.

Red laid his head down and closed his eyes. For some reason, as darkness started to take his consciousness, he had a strange feeling that something was waiting for him.

These thoughts had no chance to develop as his exhaustion carried him to sleep.

Cold, hard ground.

This was the first thing Red felt. He immediately knew where he was.

He opened his eyes.

Endless black sand. Giant, jutting bones. A blood-crimson sky. A dark sun.

He was in hell again.

So that's what was calling for me...

Red found no comfort in knowing he'd predicted his foray into this realm.

He tried to get up but was stopped by a pressure on his wrist. He looked down to see a skeletal hand grabbing his hand. His gaze came to rest on a human skeleton wearing plated armor lying motionless by his side.

Red was shocked. *Where did this come from?*

Rich ornamentation decorated its armor. He felt he'd seen this before, but no matter how much he concentrated, he couldn't recall when. All he could think about was the distress he'd felt back then.

It was as if a part of his memory had gone missing.

Wait...

Red's eyes widened. He felt eerily like his fellow Sect members who'd had their memory wiped after leaving the trial.

His blood ran cold. Had his memory also been messed with?

Red felt this was almost certainly what had happened. Yet who could have done this?

Was it the hawk spirit? What reason did it have to do something like that after he had been so open with his knowledge?

Was it the mist? Could it be trying to hide something?

Dread came over him. He freed himself from the skeleton's grip and sat cross-legged on the ground.

He closed his eyes and concentrated on his meditation technique. His awareness expanded, and he peered inside his own body.

Red's mind was shaken again. The mist, which had burrowed into almost every corner of his body, was nowhere to be seen. He checked again, but there was nothing.

Where did it go?

This was all so strange that Red almost fell into a panic again. The fact the mist had possibly altered his memories made him reassess his entire relationship with the demonic presence.

He took a deep breath, using the meditation technique to calm himself down again. Red recalled the hawk's words.

Analyze everything with an open and rational mind...

There was no point in panicking. There was so much that Red didn't and couldn't hope to understand, so he had to focus on what he knew.

First, he focused on himself.

Red had none of his belongings, predictably. But curiously enough, he was wearing the same clothes he wore when he had first entered this place —the garb Eiwin had provided him on his first night in the Sect. He hadn't noticed this before, and it confused him.

Red's hand moved up, feeling the side of his face which had undergone demonification. All he felt was smooth skin, which left him even more confused.

What happened to my scales?

He couldn't think of a reasonable explanation. Wasn't this supposed to be the Infernal Realm? Why was his demonification reversed in this place?

All Red could think of was that this wasn't his actual body, but rather a dream version of himself, or something similar.

Everything here still feels so real, though.

Red used his meditation technique to inspect his body. Was it still accurate in a dream? He didn't know, but upon finding nothing else after a thorough self-inspection, he turned his attention to the armored skeleton.

The skeleton had belonged to a man. There were no signs of rot on the bones, which meant that either things didn't decompose in this place, or that this corpse was very recent. Red searched the armor and body but found nothing. There were no signs of cracks or fractures either, which made the cause of death unclear.

Why was he grabbing onto me?

Red was unsure. His only guess was that he and the skeleton may have fought. Considering his own cautious nature, that seemed unlikely. But the more important question was... what was this person doing here?

Could it be another person who made a deal with the mist?

That would make sense. Red didn't know if he was the first person to bring this demonic presence out of the underground, so it might have already spread to the world before. But if that was the case, why was this individual right next to him?

Red had so many questions and no clear answers. It was frustrating, but he didn't lose spirit.

An explanation might not come quickly or easily, but one always had to start from somewhere. Conjecture was the first step toward true knowledge.

Red spotted the monumental bone he had been moving toward last time. The mountain-sized rib still looked impossibly far away, but it was the closest landmark in his vicinity.

He thought about taking the man's plate armor, but he changed his mind after feeling how heavy the equipment was. Instead, he took apart the skeleton, removing a few bones and ribs to use as improvised weaponry. This was unlikely to protect him against anything in this place, but it was better than walking unarmed.

Besides, Red had an idea.

He used one of the broken bones to stab his own hand. It was surprisingly difficult, as the skeleton was more brittle than Red was expecting, but eventually he succeeded. A fine stream of blood flowed down his palm before dripping onto the black sand below.

The fluid flowed between the grains before disappearing. No further reaction. It seemed his blood invoked no magic in this place.

Red's wound had yet to regenerate. That power seemed tied to the mist inside his body. He wondered whether his crimson sense would still work here, but even if it did, there was nothing for him to detect.

He tightened his fists, putting pressure on the bleeding to stop it. Then his gaze wandered back to the mountain in the distance.

Another endless journey, then?

Red was used to those at this point. He walked forward.

Once more, Red was uncertain how much time passed. It could have been a few hours, or it could have been a few days. To his surprise, he was making progress.

The jutting bone was expanding in his vision. This place wasn't some kind of spatial distortion like the inheritance ground. But even after walking for an eternity, Red had yet to reach the mountain, and he was already near the point of exhaustion.

This is strange... I shouldn't be this tired.

Red guessed this was another side effect of the mist leaving his body. His improved endurance was gone, and now he was back to being a ten-year-old child with three opened veins. His progress was inevitably slow.

Just as he contemplated sitting down to rest, he felt the ground rumble. He stood on guard.

Could it be that fiend?

Red recalled the first time he'd come to this place, when an impossibly large demon had burst from beneath the black sand. This rumbling was the prelude. Yet even as it continued, he couldn't see any signs of the creature.

Red frowned, wondering what was happening, before he felt it. A familiar sensation in some ways, yet this time it filled him with a once-unimaginable dread.

He shivered and looked up.

The blood-red sky trembled. The firmament drew ever so close to the boy. And there, in the center of it all, was the dark star.

It shimmered, and Red saw something on its surface.

He saw rage.

He saw violence.

He saw death.

He saw destruction.

He saw the end of everything.

Then he saw nothing.

CHAPTER 38
THE ART OF ASSASSINATION

RED WAS WOKEN up by the sound of knocking at his door.

"Huh?" He sat up dazed in his bed.

Red remembered staring at the sky one moment and being back in the real world the next. He couldn't recall what he had seen, but he had the distinct impression that it was a profoundly terrifying sight.

In fact, the more he tried to remember it, the more this dread settled in his gut. Red fought his own desire to understand this mystery and decided to let the matter go for now. He'd learned from his own experience and from the hawk's words that certain entities knew when they were mentioned in conversation or even thought about.

He couldn't afford that right now.

Another knock at the door.

"Come out, kid." It was Domeron's voice. "We need to talk."

Only now did Red register there was someone waiting for him at his door. He looked out his window with a frown. It was still the middle of the night.

He got up and opened his door. On the other side, Domeron was waiting with a smile.

Red's frown deepened. "What is it?"

"I said we need to talk," Domeron told him.

"What about?"

"Many matters."

"Is it so urgent that we need to do it in the middle of the night?"

"Well, not really." The swordsman shrugged. "However, you should get used to it. It's not convenient to do your training while others are watching, so we'll mostly train in the middle of the night."

"And you think the others won't notice it?"

"They probably will. But they'll know better than to stick their nose in my business. Besides, you have your power, don't you? You'll be able to tell if anyone's spying on us."

"Makes sense," Red agreed. "Where are we going?"

"To the training field." Domeron pointed behind him. "We can have our conversation there."

Domeron led the way, and soon they found themselves in the sand field. Red checked for his Sect members' fluctuations. Everyone had retired to their chambers. He did feel the curious absence of Rimold's presence in the Sect grounds and vicinity, but he didn't mention it.

The swordsman nodded at Red. "Go ahead."

Red blinked. "Go ahead with what?"

"With your questions."

"What questions?"

"Aren't you wondering why I didn't tell you that Hector knew about Allen's escape plan?"

"Not really. Hector's explanation was very clear."

"And aren't you angry that I tricked you?"

"Not angry, just surprised."

"Really?" Domeron narrowed his eyes.

"Well... yes," Red admitted. "I don't take much at face value, but I was actually convinced by your speech about the Empire and how Hector's attitude was helping them... Turns out the two of you are just really good at playing your parts."

Domeron grinned. "A good lie always has a bit of truth mixed in. I believed in what I said, and to a certain degree, I do think people like Hector were responsible for the rise of the Empire... But in that situation, I was just using that to convince you to take part in our plan."

"So it seems. I only hope it pays off for Allen in the long run."

The man sighed. "There's no way anyone can know that. We can only try to push him on the right path, but he is the only one that can walk it."

"And what is this right path, exactly?" Red asked. "Do you plan to have him start his own Sect and begin an uprising against the Empire?"

"That is more or less Hector's dream." Domeron nodded. "Although he's thinking more in the long term, too. As long as Allen can sow the seeds for the growth of a new Sect, then Hector will consider his work done."

"What about you? Do you have any thoughts of your own about this?"

The swordsman smirked. "Are you trying to probe for my real opinion?"

"Yes." Domeron was a mystery to him. He was apparently the strongest person in the Sect below Hector, and that was just with one arm. However, Red had never seen him in action outside of training. Then there was his attitude. He was the only person inside the Sect who seemed capable of reprimanding Hector, and the old man also respected his opinions. But most of it might have been pure theatrics, and maybe Domeron was actually completely deferential to Hector.

Red didn't think that was the case. He wasn't the best judge of character, but he didn't think Domeron's attitude and fearlessness in front of Hector could be faked. There was something about him that spoke to an unyielding and carefree attitude in the face of anything, despite his missing arm and nonexistent hopes of reaching the Lesser Ring Realm.

He found it admirable, and if Domeron could fake it, then he had to commend him.

The swordsman went on breezily. "I don't care much either way. I don't have any ambitions, and one of the few joys I can get from my day-to-day life is preparing the next generation to take on the world as I once did. If one day kids like you, Allen, Narcha and Eiwin leave their marks in this world, then I'll be satisfied."

Domeron turned and walked to the weapon rack. He picked out two wooden long swords, throwing one towards Red.

He stared at the boy with a widening grin. "Now I finally get to train an actual assassin. I'm quite excited myself."

"What's the difference between what you'll teach me and what you're teaching the others?" Red asked.

"Well, I teach them how to fight. You, I will teach how to kill."

Red frowned. "Is there a difference?"

"Sure there is." Domeron nodded as if it were the most obvious matter in the world. "You see, the fighting I normally teach is straightforward combat —how to defend yourself and defeat your opponents. It is obviously an extremely important skill, but fighting is not the most efficient way of killing. It requires too much effort and involves taking too many risks, and in cultivation, that is something you want to minimize whenever you can. The most efficient way of killing is ending the fight in a single blow before the enemy even knows what is happening."

"Isn't that obvious, though?"

"Of course it is, and yet, if it could be accomplished as easily as that, there would be no need for learning how to fight." Domeron shook his head. "It requires grasping and creating opportunity, as well as knowing how to act when the time comes. The mastery of that practice is called assassination, and it requires far more than just knowing how to fight."

"That makes sense. But why don't you teach the others about it, too? Wouldn't it be a useful skill to have?"

"Every skill is useful to have, but not everyone can learn every skill," Domeron said. "Assassination requires subtlety, cunning, and skullduggery. Do you think people like Narcha with her unruliness, Eiwin with her honest nature, and Allen with his naivety would be good fits for that?"

"I suppose not..."

"Indeed. Only someone devious like you—who's used to sneaking around, stealing things, and stabbing people in the back with no remorse—is suited for such a practice."

Red wasn't sure whether that was a compliment.

Domeron continued. "In any case, I'm not really here to teach you everything about assassination. I was never an accomplished assassin myself, so a lot of the fine details will be on you to learn."

"What are you here to teach me, then?" Red asked.

"I will teach you the most important part of assassination." Domeron pointed his sword at him. "Killing with one blow."

The swordsman approached one of the wooden dummies in the courtyard.

"You see, one of the more important matters of assassination is knowing where to strike, and for this you need knowledge of human anatomy." Domeron started to tap the dummy with his weapon. "The human being has a total of five vital organs, without which their body will die quickly. Those are the kidneys, the lungs, the heart, the liver, and the brain. Damaging any of those enough may cause instant death, or at the very least imminent death, which is what most assassinations focus on. Of course, when it comes to cultivators, you will often find that they can survive what would otherwise be fatal wounds..."

Red actually knew that from experience.

"Cultivators who have all their veins open can survive damage to their vital organs, and with healing pills, they may even recover in a matter of minutes. Therefore, you have target areas that can cause instant death, such as the heart and the brain..."

He went on to explain most human anatomy to Red and how to best kill a cultivator. He taught him how to locate an individual's heart properly, from which position to stab into someone's back, how to best penetrate a skull. It was all explained in fine and gory detail, without the man so much as swinging his sword once.

Apparently, Domeron was quite experienced. He told Red all about the difficulties and traps one might run into while trying to kill someone.

"Mind you, even if you're not perfect, that doesn't mean you can't kill someone," Domeron said. "It may often happen in your assassinations that you won't be able to kill someone in a single blow. However, the spirit of an assassin is to always strive to achieve that perfect killing blow, or else you give the opportunity for your opponent to retaliate and recover, and at that point, your assassination skills will avail you naught."

"... I never imagined you could put so much thought behind killing," Red remarked.

Domeron smiled. "You can put a lot of thought behind anything, kid. There is a science and principle behind any practice or art in the world, and a large part of cultivation is figuring out exactly what those principles are. Isn't that exciting?"

"I suppose." Red nodded without emotion. "I do have a question, though."

"What is it?"

"A lot of what you told me is useful, but do I have the strength to become an assassin as I am?" He had seen cultivators with twelve open veins in the past. They had far better senses than him, and could react much faster, too. He imagined trying to use these techniques on someone like Reinhart, and the results didn't look good for Red.

"If we're talking about ordinary combat strength, then there is no chance," Domeron acknowledged. "But assassination is the ultimate opportunist's art. A true master assassin can kill people many times stronger than them—as long as they have the right opportunity and technique. I can't really help you with finding opportunities, but I can teach you the right skills."

He pointed his sword at him. "So, do you want to learn the heron's way, kid?"

CHAPTER 39

TRANQUIL BEAK WEAPON ART

Would Red learn to be an assassin?

"You mean learn from the Great Heron School?" He frowned. "I thought I already agreed to it earlier."

Domeron snorted. "I was just asking for dramatic effect, kid. Either way, there are a couple of things we need to establish before we move on." He swung his sword in the air. "First, this 'assassination course' doesn't replace your combat training. Although a lot of the skills you learn in both practices are interchangeable, you can't really abandon one in favor of the other. After all, an assassin should still know how to fight."

"Does that mean I now have double the work?" Red asked.

"Yes. Combat training in the daylight and assassin training at night. Why? Do you think it's too much for you?"

"I'm not worried about the effort required," Red told him. "I'm just worried about if I'll have enough time in the day to attend all my practice sessions."

"I'm sure you'll settle into a rhythm eventually." Domeron shrugged. "Once you grasp initial proficiency in these skills, you will notice that improving becomes much more difficult and hard work alone won't suffice. By then, you'll just need to make sure you don't get rusty."

"Is that why you're always lazing about?" Red asked.

Domeron ignored him and turned to face the wooden dummy. "Now, let me show you the principle of this assassination art."

He twirled his sword around in his hand before putting it into a reverse grip with the blade flat against his extended arm. He brought his legs together and stood ramrod straight, setting his arm at his side, staring directly at the wooden dummy from three meters away.

His posture was strange, and rather than looking ready to kill, Domeron looked as if he were a soldier paying his respects to his superior.

"In assassination, you never want to give your hand away too early. This is why your combat stance needs to be subtle, so as not to raise any alarm in your target." Domeron seemed able to read his thoughts. "Of course, this is assuming it is a broad-daylight assassination. If you're doing it in the shadows, then you need not worry so much. It's still good practice, though."

"Can you even gather any power in that stance?"

Red couldn't imagine anyone manifesting enough strength and speed behind their blow to kill in one hit with that posture, much less from that far.

Domeron smiled. "This is where the heron weapon arts come in."

He burst into movement. Before Red even knew what was happening, he heard the impact of wood against wood. Splinters flew everywhere as Domeron's practice weapon exploded against the dummy. In the aftermath, Red noticed the training device had lost a huge chunk of wood from its chest.

His shocked gaze wandered back to Domeron, who now stood a meter behind the dummy, facing away. The man's body was almost parallel to the ground, as he had stretched his whole frame forward, front leg left bent as support while the shin of his back leg, outstretched, was almost touching the sandy ground. Domeron's upper body was bent forward over his left knee, and his arm stretched outwards and forwards, holding what remained of his sword.

Domeron's whole body was taut as a bowstring, and he held that position for a few seconds for Red to observe. Finally, he relaxed, standing back up.

He looked at Red with a grin. "How about it?"

"How did you do that?" Red asked, amazed.

The speed at which the swordsman moved, the power behind his blow, and all from that strange position... Even with all his experience, Red had yet to see someone with twelve open veins capable of such a feat—not even Viran.

Domeron seemed satisfied with his reverence. "This is the wonder of martial arts, kid. It gathers the potential within one's physical body and releases it all in a myriad of ways for a myriad of reasons. It requires skill, physical conditioning, and the right mental state."

"And you can do all that without Spiritual Energy?"

"Well, you can do most of it." Domeron shrugged. "You can think of Spiritual Energy as the key that unlocks the true potential behind these arts, but even without it, you can still do a lot. If you can master a proper martial art before opening your Spiritual Sea, you will stand head and shoulders above other cultivators at your level."

"I assume you mastered swordsmanship, then." Red stared at the ruined sword in his hand.

Domeron laughed. "What gave you that impression?"

"Well, you seem really skilled with a—"

"That was a rhetorical question. But yes, I have reached the level of mastery with the longsword. It's something a lot of cultivators at the Lesser Ring Realm can't claim to have done... Then again, I don't think I have the right to be proud, considering they can still kill me with a wave of their hand."

Red recalled a similar conversation with Rog while the two of them were out hunting. He was still curious to hear Domeron's thoughts.

"Who else in the Sect has reached that level?"

"Rog is the best archer I have ever seen in my life," Domeron said. "Likewise, Goulth is also the best blacksmith I have ever met. Hector is a master of water spells, too, but that's beyond my purview. As for the others, none of them are close to that level. Maybe Eiwin is the closest with her monk fist, or whatever she calls it, but she still has a long way to go."

"And you think I can do it before opening my Spiritual Sea?" Red asked, somewhat skeptical.

"Who knows? It depends equal parts on your hard work and talent."

"I see. Then can you teach me about this heron's art?"

"It's called the Tranquil Beak Weapon Art," Domeron said.

"Tranquil Beak? Are you sure this is an assassination art?"

The man smiled. "What, did you expect them to name it 'The Ruthless Assassination Weapon Art'? That's more of a devilish name. Orthodox Sects like to put pretty names on things, no matter how evil and violent they may be."

Red recalled the Rain Dance. Perhaps Domeron had a point.

"Either way, we can start with our lesson." He gave Red a serious look. "First, you need to think like a heron."

Red frowned. "Really?"

Domeron laughed. "I'm just joking. That's a more advanced chapter of this art."

Red still wasn't sure whether or not he was serious.

Two hours passed before Domeron called their practice to an end.

He had explained the initial posture of the Tranquil Beak Weapon Art, and how dozens of different attacks in the art all began from this same strange stance. Red tried to replicate the posture, but it was harder than expected.

Even by copying Domeron's movements perfectly, Red could not conjure up any significant power behind his blows. The man explained that the trick was in tensing his muscles a certain way, and even gave a thorough explanation of how to do it. Still, this seemed to be beyond Red's reach as of yet. But he wasn't too worried.

If it was easy to master, was there any point in practicing it in the first place?

Finally, when the training was over, Domeron asked him a question out of nowhere.

"Have you chosen a weapon?"

"Not yet," he said.

"Why not just go with a longsword?" Domeron said. "It's the only weapon I've mastered anyway, so it'll make our training much easier."

"Do I need to use a sword for this weapon art?"

"Not really. Anything with a pointy end and that doesn't stand out too much will work. As it turns out, though, that mostly includes swords and daggers."

Indeed, Red couldn't imagine a discreet assassin carrying around a spear. "Do I need to pick a weapon soon?" he asked.

"Hector would say the sooner the better, but as a responsible teacher, I say you shouldn't rush it. It might delay our training a bit, but when it comes to cultivation, no decision should be made in a rush."

"I understand. I'll speak with Goulth. He might be able to help me choose."

"Good idea," Domeron said. "Now, go to sleep. The sun will be rising in a couple of hours, and I imagine you must be tired from the trials and all the training."

Red nodded and left the field. He truly was tired, but in reality, he wasn't as spent as he expected. Another side effect of the mist, or so he thought.

Speaking of the mist...

As soon as Red returned to his room, he sat cross-legged on his bed and entered a meditative state. Domeron had interrupted him right after he woke up, so he hadn't had the time to check on the mist's condition after he left the dream world.

His awareness expanded, and he quickly noticed the crimson tendrils extending to every corner of his body.

It's still here.

The mist had only disappeared in the dream world. Not even the cut he had made on his palm there had been transferred to the real world, so clearly, as real as that dreamscape felt, nothing that happened there could affect his body.

Or so he hoped. He still remembered the hawk's advice.

Out of habit, Red reached towards the mist, hoping for a response. To his surprise, the entity stirred once his awareness touched it, the first time since the trial it had broken its silence. Their communication was nothing more than a jumbled mess of feelings and emotions, but he could still grasp what the mist was trying to say.

It was afraid.

No, not just afraid.

It was terrified.

And perhaps it had to do with that dread Red felt once he left his dream. He felt compelled to search his memories again, but he thought better of it.

Instead, he tried to communicate further with the mist. He tried to convey one feeling—safety.

Eventually he seemed to get it across, as the entity calmed down and returned to its silence. Red let out a sigh of relief, but he couldn't help but worry about his near future.

How was he supposed to deal with a problem he couldn't even think about?

I have to remain steady in my path. A way forward will eventually reveal itself as long as I seek it.

Nothing could comfort him more than the truth. These were his true thoughts and convictions, and since winning the trial, Red wouldn't entertain doubt any longer.

This was his path, and no matter how many difficulties he came across, he would not be toppled by them. Even if he didn't know what the danger was.

With these thoughts, Red eventually went back to sleep.

CHAPTER 40

DARK IRON ORE

RED WAS ONCE AGAIN WOKEN up by frenetic banging on his door.

"Wake up, kid! I need to show you something!"

A rough voice called out to him. Red sighed and looked out the window. It was already daytime.

He opened the door and was greeted by a giant of a man wearing workshop clothes and an apron full of coal and grease marks.

Goulth smiled upon seeing him. "You're finally awake! I was waiting the entire morning for you in the workshop, but you never came!"

"I was just too tired," Red said.

"That's fine, that's fine!" The blacksmith waved it off. "Just come quickly! I have something to show you!"

Goulth didn't wait for his response before running back the way he came. Red sighed again as he followed, watching him disappear ahead.

On the way over, he noticed Domeron sitting in his usual chair while Allen sat on the ground in front of him, the two having a discussion. The young master's eyes lit up when he spotted Red, and he seemed to want to go greet him. A stern gaze from Domeron was more than enough to stop Allen from even trying.

Their conversation seemed important, so Red didn't bother greeting them either. He soon arrived at the workshop and walked through the open door.

He smelled the coal burning in the forge, so he didn't need to guess where his smithing master was. He walked to the forge room, where the man bent over a mold he had put over the fire.

Goulth smiled at him and waved him over. "Come here! Quickly! You're going to miss it!"

Red ran over. A dark yet luminous material lay partially melted in the mold.

"Is it the Dark Iron?" he asked.

"It is." Goulth nodded eagerly. "Now, just watch it..."

Red observed the rock in silence. Even under this extreme heat that would have melted normal iron, this ore was still holding together. Almost an entire minute went by with nothing happening, but just as Red was wondering whether Goulth had made a mistake, there was a reaction.

A wisp of white smoke burst out of the rock, dissipating in the air. He was confused until a moment later, his skin tingled with a familiar sensation.

He looked back at Goulth in shock. "Was that Spiritual Energy?"

Goulth nodded with a huge smile. "It was! In its natural state, Dark Iron ore can attract and retain a lot of Spiritual Energy. It's how most of these magical ores are created in the first place!"

Red frowned. "Shouldn't you try keeping this energy inside the ore, then?"

"That's pretty much impossible, kid. We need to smelt the ore if we want to use it, and the Spiritual Energy will always escape. You shouldn't worry, though. You can think of smelting as a purification process. The amount of Spiritual Energy the metal can contain increases exponentially after the fact."

"How long does it take to smelt Dark Iron ore?"

Goulth shrugged. "Probably six to ten hours a piece."

Red's eyes widened. "And you need to keep watch over it the entire time?"

"Well, yes," Goulth said. "Sometimes the process of purification of these kinds of materials can be quite... explosive. I need to watch the forge temperature the entire time to prevent anything of the sort from happening." He turned around, patting the boy's shoulders with a smile. "At least I won't need to watch it alone this time around."

Red frowned. "Since when did I..."

"Shush, just pay attention and you might learn something..."

He fell silent and kept his eye on the forge.

Six hours passed by.

Red remained in the forge's constant heat, helping his smithing master raise and lower the temperature as requested. Although some might perceive him to be doing most of the hard work, Red knew this wasn't the case.

Goulth was constantly bent over the melting ore, touching it with all kinds of tools to check the consistency and temperature. He explained that this wasn't a process they could rush by just raising the temperature, since that could actually damage the properties of the metal and cause a violent reaction.

Red tasted a sample of that more than once. Sometimes the ore would release a pop of Spiritual Energy like an arrow shot from a bow, and both the boy and the blacksmith had to jump back so as not to get burnt. After witnessing this a few times, Red didn't feel so relaxed doing this seemingly menial task.

Finally, a bright-red liquid started to form at the bottom of the mold. The pure metal was separating from the slag.

"Quickly, bring me the other mold!" Goulth ordered, waving at him excitedly.

Red had already helped him smelt bars in the past, so he knew what to do. He brought the ingot mold right up to the furnace, holding it with a pair of pliers.

Goulth proceeded to dump the liquid metal into the mold. The molten fluid settled at the bottom, and to Red's amazement, he could already see signs of it solidifying. Barely thirty seconds passed before the metal lost its red fiery glow and turned dark and opaque.

Goulth laughed. "There, it's a success!"

Red squinted at the metal bar. "Is there supposed to be so little of it?"

He now realized that what metal remained was less than half the size of the original ore.

His master sighed. "Unfortunately, that's just the reality of smelting. You may receive a large piece of ore, only to be left with a bit of pure metal. That's even more common with these rare Spiritual Ores."

"Is there even enough with those three ore pieces to make anything?"

"By themselves? Of course not. But this is why we make alloys. The result will be worse than if it was pure Dark Iron, but it will be better than any steel weapon you can find."

Red nodded. "So you've decided to make a weapon out of this?"

Goulth smiled. "I have. Now I just need you to choose the kind of weapon you want."

The boy blinked. "You're making me a weapon?"

The blacksmith laughed. "Of course I am! I asked Hector, and he agreed to it. After all, you're the only one in this Sect without a proper weapon. Well, other than Rog and Eiwin, but one uses a bow and the other uses her fists, so there's not much point to that."

"I see..." Red recalled his conversation with Domeron. "When are you making it?"

"Whenever you've decided on the kind of weapon you want," Goulth said. "Ah, but I misspoke for a second there! I'm not the one making the weapon, you are!"

"... What?"

Goulth grinned. "Are you surprised? I didn't tell Hector about this, of course, but I thought this would be an appropriate test for you. After all, isn't it proper for a blacksmith to make his own weapon?"

"Isn't it risky having an apprentice handle such valuable material?"

"It is. But that's why you'll have enough time to prepare. The metal isn't going anywhere, after all."

"And how long do you think that will take?"

"Depends." The blacksmith shrugged. "I'll tell you when I feel you're ready. It might take a day, a week, a month, or maybe even more. It won't be just a matter of knowing how to handle the material, though. I want to see your creativity flow! I want you to create your own masterpiece and understand what that feels like! That will be the hardest part."

Red nodded reluctantly. "I understand."

He recalled where they had left his studies the last time. Goulth had admonished him for only knowing how to copy. It wasn't necessarily bad, but would bring him difficulty in the long run, as a crafter had to learn by creating. Red had never tried to create from imagination, so he wondered whether that creativity really was hidden somewhere inside his mind.

"Don't worry, kid." Goulth patted his shoulders. "We can walk through all your shortcomings step by step, and I'll help you overcome them."

"... I suppose so."

"Great." The blacksmith waved him off. "Then you can go eat something. I'm sure Domeron is still waiting for you to practice."

Red hesitated. "There is something else."

"Hm?" Goulth gave him a look. "Did you hide something from Hector and the others?"

Red was taken aback. "How did you know?"

"You think I'm stupid?! What kind of master would I be if I didn't know my own disciple well?"

"That's fair."

"You still had the good sense to tell your master, at least." Goulth nodded in satisfaction. "So, what is it?"

"I found a manual on Arcane Script," he said. "I would like to learn it."

"You what?!" The giant's eyes widened. "Are you being serious?"

Red nodded.

"May I see it?"

"There... might be sensitive information inside that manual."

"What do you mean?"

"I can't explain it," Red told him. "I just can't show it to you, though."

Goulth fell silent, looking him over. In the end, though, he agreed. "That's fine. I'll trust you on this matter. It's not like I need to read it, either. I know my own talent in that area... So, what is it that you need help with?"

"I would like to request the materials for practice," Red explained. "Preferably hidden from Hector and the others. I would also like to practice in your workshop, if possible."

"Why do you feel the need to hide it from them, though?"

"I don't want them to pry into the origin of this manual."

He meant it. This manual contained not only the Parting Storm formation, but also possible hints about the author's identity. If any of that was ever leaked outside the Sect, then all of them could die.

The only reason he revealed it to Goulth was because this smithing master of his seemed the most accommodating of his secrecy.

Goulth nodded in understanding. "I can help you with the materials, but it might raise some questions with Hector if there's a sudden influx of papers and special inks."

Red frowned. "Can you help me fool him?"

The blacksmith beamed. "Do you even need to ask?! I couldn't be more proud of my own disciple trying to learn Arcane Script! Of course, you need to promise me you won't neglect blacksmithing, is that clear?"

"I will," Red promised. He had taken a huge step in revealing a secret of his. He couldn't be more relieved at how it had turned out.

"Thank you," he said with all the sincerity he could muster. "For everything."

Goulth laughed. "There is no need for thanks, kid. I'm just doing my part! After all, I am your only master, isn't that right?"

Red froze for a second, but still nodded. "Yes, you are my only master in this world."

CHAPTER 41
WEIGHT

As soon as Red left the workshop, he saw Domeron sitting in his rocking chair and beckoning to him. The boy sighed and approached.

Domeron snorted. "What's with that face? Are you truly so reluctant to speak with your instructor?"

"That depends. Is it good news?" Red asked.

"It's not really news of any kind. I just wanted to praise you."

Red frowned. "Praise me for what, exactly?"

"For guiding Young Master Allen," Domeron said. "We didn't have the time to talk about it at the meeting, but he told me some of the things you told him. They left a mark on him."

"I said nothing important. Allen just didn't know much in the first place, so everything must've been helpful to him."

"That might be the case, but I don't think you understand how he feels." Domeron shook his head. "I see it in the way he talks about you. He trusts and admires you from the bottom of his heart. He even told me he wants to be more like you in combat—confident and unafraid."

"I don't think I'm a good example to follow."

Domeron shrugged. "I don't think so either, but Young Master Allen is just a kid. Actually, you're just a kid too, which is something I forget very often. In any case, I think you should keep that in mind when you interact with him. For better or for worse, he now thinks of you as both a companion and a role model of sorts, so you better not disappoint him."

Red's frown deepened. "Why is that my responsibility now?"

"It isn't your responsibility. However, keeping good relations with your companions is conducive to a better working environment. Shouldn't that be in your best interests too?"

"I suppose so," Red huffed.

Domeron smiled. "It's not as hard as it sounds, kid. You've impressed him by not pretending to be a different person, but just by being who you are. All I'm asking of you is to not turn your back on him when he needs you."

"I suppose I can do that."

Domeron's smile widened. "Good. Now, go to the library! Eiwin was asking for you earlier."

"Aren't we going to train?"

The man snorted. "Training after you've exhausted yourself helping that big oaf? No, leave that for tomorrow once Allen is feeling better. Just focus on resting for now."

Red soon found himself in front of the library building. The door was open, and he could see Eiwin at the table inside. As he approached, he saw several books open in front of her and stacks piled to the side.

Red announced his arrival. "You asked for me?"

"Oh." Eiwin looked up and smiled at him. "You're finally here. I thought you were never going to leave that workshop."

"I was helping Goulth smelt the Dark Iron ore," Red explained.

"Ah, I see. I asked you here to share our reports with you."

"Reports? About what?"

"About our preliminary investigation into the bandits, the imperials, and the forest in general," Eiwin said. "Master Hector insisted I share this information with you. I already planned on telling you about this, but seeing this request come from our Grand Elder himself made me both surprised and excited. I assume this means Master Hector is finally putting his trust in you."

Red was also surprised, but he supposed it made sense. A new position should come with some benefits, too.

"It seems like your conversation last night went better than you previously led us to believe," Eiwin said.

Red shrugged. "I just didn't imagine anything would come of it."

Of course, he couldn't tell Eiwin about the position Hector had arranged for him. Of all the people in the Sect, he was certain she would react the most negatively.

"I can see why. Master Hector's compliments aren't always very clear." She pointed him to the chair across from her. "Sit. There's a lot to go through."

Red sat down and examined the titles before him. The majority were tales and biographies of cultivators of the past, though a few of them talked about specific topics—such as inheritance grounds.

That phrase gave him a bad feeling.

"What are you researching?" he asked.

"I was looking to shed some light on our experience in that trial," Eiwin said. "This is not the first time in history a cultivator wiped the memories of a trial's participants. Of course, most cultivators do this because they fear their enemies hunting their inheritor in the outside world. I can only assume the person who set up that inheritance ground felt the same way."

Red frowned. "Do you think it's safe to look into this?"

"Well, I wasn't expecting to find many clues in these books." She shook her head. "There are too many cultivators in history, so it's impossible for me to find out which of them that inheritance trial belonged to, especially when I can't remember any of its details."

"Then what exactly are you looking for?"

"I was looking for any recordings of individuals who managed to recover their wiped memories. Seeing as the Empire took an interest in the hidden realm, it would serve us well to know the reason."

Somehow, that was even worse than Red's original assumption. "And did you find anything?"

"I did. Some people succeeded in recovering their memories, but they had the help of incredibly strong cultivators or medicines—neither of which we have right now."

"That's a shame." Red actually couldn't have been more relieved.

"It is." Eiwin sadly nodded. "But who knows? In the future, it might be within our reach."

I hope not.

Red decided to change the topic. "What did you want to report to me?"

"Ah, right!" Eiwin had forgotten why he was here in the first place. "The

Baron's men have been moving towards the bandits' hideout. However, they're still only finding abandoned camps and very light resistance."

Red was unsurprised. "The majority of them must have died in the trials."

"I think so too. We still don't know if Ricard is around, though. Of everyone in the trial, he is the one most likely to have won."

Red knew that all too well. He wondered whether the man had recovered from his wounds after their confrontation at the end of the trial.

"Either way, that's not the most important thing the Baron's men have found," Eiwin said. "They've seen signs of monsters in the forest."

This surprised him. "Really?"

Eiwin grinned. "Yes. We can only assume that their disappearance had to do with the trial, and now that it's finished, they've been seen reemerging from the tunnels. It seems we won't have an environmental collapse just yet."

"What about the tunnels? Have they explored those?"

"Not yet. There are still a lot of monsters in there, and their initial delves into the tunnel network showed that it might extend throughout the entire region, as Rimold told us. In any case, I doubt they'll find anything of value down there, or anything that might point us towards the trial's location, anyway."

Red had to agree. Someone as thorough as his master would never leave behind any obvious clues.

"And the imperials?" Red asked. "Any signs of them?"

Eiwin shook her head. "If any of them are still alive, they have yet to be spotted in the forest or in town."

Red knew that those people were dead, but he was more worried about what he'd heard from them before they died. The imperials had orders to kill or capture the slave who had escaped from the moonstone mines. "Do you think they have any more of their people in town?"

"If they do, they're very well-hidden. If our initial investigations failed to uncover them, I doubt they would give themselves away right now, particularly if they've won the inheritance as we think they did."

Red nodded, but his mind was spinning with the possibilities. If there was an imperial spy still in the region, they would know the Empire hadn't won the inheritance, seeing as none of their companions had returned. He could only imagine that person would try to get to the bottom of this matter if the inheritance was as important to the Empire as he thought.

Thankfully, Ricard would probably be their prime suspect. It wasn't far-fetched for their investigations to eventually lead them to their Sect, though. He had to be on the lookout.

"Reinhart hasn't returned to town either," Eiwin said, her tone bitter.

Red noticed her tense expression. "Are you afraid he'll do something? Even with Hector here?"

Eiwin sighed. "You were with us when he betrayed us. Did that look like a man concerned with the possibility of death?"

Red shook his head. "He gave up the Parting Sea Pill when we didn't agree to help him. He doesn't seem to care for riches or anything else other than revenge."

"Exactly. And he is a wise and patient man. Master Hector's presence here gives me some security, but what about when we're outside the Sect? He can't be there to protect us forever, and I don't think any of us can defeat Reinhart in combat. If he finds out about Allen too..."

"Then we stick together," Red told her. "He might be strong, but I doubt he could take all of us at once."

He actually wasn't confident about that, but it was the surest assertion he had at the moment.

Eiwin nodded with a troubled smile. "You're right. I can only hope we find him eventually, though. Until then, we will have to live with this sword above our heads."

Compared to what Red had to face, Reinhart's threat felt more like a dagger.

"Master Hector also told us to be prepared," Eiwin said. "Monster movement in the Skycrown Mountains has been increasing, so it's likely the horde could hit us within the year. He said it's a priority to increase the Sect's strength right now."

Red had almost forgotten about the monster horde with all the threats he'd been facing. "I'll do my best. Are you about to finish opening your veins?"

Eiwin let out a long sigh. "After what happened in the trial, I might need to delay for a bit longer."

Red recalled the power she had displayed in their fight against the parasite. She hadn't overcome its consequences just yet.

He considered asking Eiwin what her power was, but seeing her expression, he decided to forgo the idea. She had the right to keep a secret, and he would be a hypocrite if he put her in a position where she felt pressed to reveal it.

"Is that all?" Red asked.

"It should be. We can continue your reading and writing lessons tomorrow, if you wish. Although I don't think you'll be needing them for much longer."

"It's fine. There are still things I wish to study further." Now that Red was about to try his hand at Arcane Script, he needed his calligraphy to be perfect. His practice with Eiwin was sure to help.

"I'll be going then," he said before heading towards the exit.

"Wait!" Eiwin called out. "There's something else!"

"Hm?" He turned around.

"I never thanked you before," Eiwin said, sounding sincere. "So, thank you. For everything. It might not look like it, but since the day we decided to take you into this Sect, things have been changing for the better around here. Narcha, Allen, Goulth, even Hector... I believe they have all benefited from your presence, no matter what kind of risks they think you might have brought with you." She beamed at him. "Just know this, Red—you can always trust us, no matter what kinds of troubles you're facing. You are one of us now, and we would put our lives on the line for you."

Red fell silent. A few seconds later, he nodded. "I understand."

Then he turned around and left the room.

Narcha, Goulth, Domeron, and now Eiwin, too. Every kind word and note of trust thrown his way weighed more heavily on his back than the constant threat of death. Those words meant to raise his spirits up felt more like anchors to him, as much as he told himself they weren't.

Red wasn't sure he could live up to their faith. In fact, he wasn't even sure it was a good idea to.

The boy knew in his heart that one day he would need to leave this place.

He feared that by then, he would have made too many promises and would need to decide whether to live up to them or pursue his dreams and ambitions. It wasn't a choice he looked forward to making.

Yet there was still a long road ahead of him. For now, he would focus on each step.

He still was far from being a proper cultivator, after all.

CHAPTER 42
ADVANCING

Six months passed.

It was the middle of the night, and Red was performing his Rain Dance. At this point, he had engraved the steps of the technique on his mind. The movements flowed from him like never before, and there was a certain harmony and fluidity in each step he took.

No longer did the technique feel strange to him. Instead, Red felt at peace when he executed it, as if he were becoming part of something bigger. A few minutes, and he finally heard the sound of thunder right by his ear.

It's here.

Hurrying, he sat down cross-legged on his bed. He grabbed the insectoid crystal beside him before the tide of Spiritual Energy flowed into his veins.

Over the last half-year, Red had discovered the trick to manipulating this strange energy. Instead of trying to direct it with his limited control, he let it roam free through his veins, nudging it along as it traveled all over his body like a flowing river.

Soon the energy started to dissipate and lose strength, but he had solved this too. He swallowed one of the Vein Opening Pills the hawk spirit had given him.

Surprisingly enough, instead of wandering to open one of his acupoints, the Spiritual Energy from the pill merged with the strands of the Rain

Dance's energy. The two different powers became one, and a single new strand now flowed through his veins.

Red tried to direct it. As he had expected, the previously stubborn energy now followed his orders without resistance and traveled up towards his head.

Within moments, the energy stream clashed against the ninth and last acupoint in his Five Senses Vein. Red had already struck this obstacle multiple times, so it didn't take long for the wave of energy to break through.

Red felt a pop in his head. A terrible headache overcame him, but he had been bracing for it and held onto consciousness.

As the acupoint opened, the insectoid crystal in his hand glowed. Strands of green mist slipped into his veins, filling the newly opened acupoint.

It took just a few seconds for the Moonstone Energy to fill the acupoint, but Red was only able to collect himself and recover from the pain and exhaustion after three more minutes passed. When everything was done, he sighed in relief.

That should stave off the curse for a bit longer.

Just like the hawk had said, the draining of the creature on the moon had grown stronger over these last six months. Red barely had enough Moonstone Energy in his veins to feed the beast's appetite, and he was afraid of what would happen when it was no longer enough.

Thankfully, he had persevered. Now, after six months, he had finished opening his Five Senses Vein.

In retrospect, this vein alone had taken him longer to open than all his three other veins combined, but Red was more than satisfied with his speed.

The Five Senses Vein was the third-hardest vein to open, and it took most people almost half a decade to see it through. Yet not only had Red done it in six months, but he had also done it out of the proper order. If he'd had the support of all the previous nine veins, he was sure he could have opened it even quicker.

This technique is truly magical.

Combining the Rain Dance with the Vein Opening Pills had been a revelation. Once he learned that it would allow him to direct the energy, opening his acupoints became only a matter of time.

He didn't know if it was the intended solution, but it was the only solution he'd found. He didn't give up on the idea of controlling the Rain Dance energy by itself, but perhaps he could only achieve that once he opened more veins.

There was another discovery he'd made, too.

My crippled acupoint has healed.

For a long time, energy strands that passed through that area in his shoulder would cause a pang of pain. Yet during his experiments with the Rain Dance technique, that pain had disappeared.

Red had checked it many times before coming to a definite conclusion. He was joyful at the revelation, but it also left him quite confused.

He wasn't sure who, or what, had healed him. Was it the hawk? Was it the regenerative powers from the mist? If the latter, then that had deep implications.

It would mean his blood powers could heal even injuries in his veins. Didn't that mean that Red could absorb as many Spirit Stones through his acupoints as he wished? Of course, this was all under the presumption he was willing to absorb more blood to recover, which would incur much harsher consequences.

He wasn't willing to worsen his demonification.

The crimson mist inside his body had returned to normal, too. It was willing to communicate with Red through his meditation technique, and it even prompted him many times for "more." He could hazard a guess as to what it was referring to, and he obviously didn't provide it. Thankfully, the mist didn't push him on the matter.

He had also found himself back in that dream hellscape a handful of times over the last six months. Like he'd expected, his body in that place retained its own wounds and equipment. The scar of the cut in his hand was still there, and he was still carrying the bones.

He didn't know what that meant, but it was more information than he had before. Nothing of note had happened during those dreams, and Red always kept walking towards the bone monument.

He had yet to reach it.

I still don't know what happened back then.

He still recalled nothing about the "incident" and his lost memories. But it had not happened again, so it wasn't urgent for him to figure it out.

Another matter he'd made significant progress on was his crimson sense.

He had singled out many more peculiarities about the fluctuations he detected. Now he felt confident about detecting strong emotional fluctuations through his crimson sense, as well as age and general health.

This, by itself, wasn't too impressive, since most of these things were observable by the naked eye. But Red imagined other possibilities. If he could detect this much just through a single upgrade in his powers, who knew what he could detect in the future? It would be invaluable against subterfuge.

Of course, for that he would need to absorb more blood, which he still wasn't willing to do.

He sighed. *So much temptation. No wonder so many people resort to demonic arts.*

With such special powers and shortcuts, who wouldn't feel tempted? Red had held steady, though.

Since the monsters in the forest had returned, he had more than a few opportunities to absorb more blood. At times, he'd even had to be careful not to let spilled blood touch his skin.

It was a comical sight, actually. Now he had to avoid touching the blood of anything he killed. It wasn't always feasible, so he was trying to find a way to control the mist's absorption.

As Red was lost in thought, a fluctuation approached his room. He looked out of his window.

He's early. Red opened his door. He saw Domeron standing there, looking surprised.

The man smiled. "You know, sometimes I forget how you can feel when I'm approaching."

Red ignored his remark. "What happened?"

Domeron frowned. "What do you mean? We need to train, don't we?"

"You're early," Red pointed out.

The man shrugged. "I just felt like starting training early today."

"You've never been early since we started training at night."

Domeron sighed in defeat. "Just follow me, will you? We need to talk."

Soon enough, Red found himself back at the training field. He blinked. "Are we talking or training?"

"Do your stances first." Domeron threw him a wooden weapon. "I'll brief you on the situation."

246

Red nodded. He readied the shortsword in his hand before walking towards a wooden dummy.

Taking the weapon in a reverse grip, he changed his posture, standing ramrod straight. His breathing slowed, and he closed his eyes as he sought to tense his muscles in the way he had been taught.

Just as Red was getting ready to strike, Domeron spoke up.

"The horde might be here tomorrow."

He stumbled. He looked over at the swordsman in shock. "Tomorrow?"

"Probably tomorrow." Domeron nodded. "Might take a few days, though."

"Didn't you say we would know about the horde coming weeks before it happened?"

The man sighed. "That's what I thought too. However, something seems to have happened at the Skycrown Mountains. Hector just received news and he woke me up to inform me."

Red had a bad feeling about the situation. "What exactly happened?"

"The Sect cultivators at the border were engaged in battle against the first waves of the horde when they were ambushed from behind."

"Ambushed? By monsters?"

"No. By demonic cultivators."

Red's blood ran cold.

Domeron continued. "We have had many isolated cases of demonic cultivators running amok around the world. Yet this is the first time in almost a decade that they have organized in such numbers, not to mention striking at the Sects so blatantly."

"Did the Sect cultivators win?"

"Apparently there were some casualties, but they were able to force the demonic cultivators to retreat," Domeron said. "However, by then, the damage was already done. Thousands of monsters slipped through the Sect's barrier and they're now causing havoc around the Skycrowns' neighboring countries."

"And this includes us?" Red frowned.

"Indeed. We've received news from scouts across the river. They have already seen signs of foreign monsters appearing at the edge of the forest, with many of them in the Lesser Ring Realm. I wouldn't be surprised if we even saw a few in the Greater Ring Realm. The surrounding settlements will probably all start evacuating to our town tomorrow."

"What are we going to do then?"

"We're going to have an emergency meeting with the Baron tomorrow. Every person of power and influence in the town is going to be there to discuss our next course of action... Hector also wants to take some of our Sect members with him."

"I see..." Red's eyes widened in realization. "Wait—"

Domeron grinned. "That's right. That includes you."

CHAPTER 43
MAKING PLANS

RED DIGESTED the news in a prolonged silence.

I'm going to the meeting?

He stared at Domeron. "Why?"

The swordsman shrugged. "Might be a test, or he might just want you to learn what it feels like to be in one of those meetings. Trust me, there's nothing quite like being in a room full of cultivators who can kill you with a wave of their hand."

Red frowned. After his promotion six months ago, nothing had changed in his routine. He mostly trained, and sometimes he went hunting for troublesome monsters in the forest with Rog. Hector had never given him extra responsibilities, and since the collapse of the bandits, the region as a whole had been rather peaceful.

It was a period of bliss for Red, a time to focus on his training.

He hadn't expected this peace to last forever, but he was still taken off guard by the revelation.

"Is anyone else coming too?" he asked.

"Sure," Domeron said. "Allen and Eiwin are going too."

The Sect's talent base.

Yet he noticed the absence of one name in particular. "What about Narcha?"

Red knew she had a short temper, but she wouldn't disrupt such an important meeting with a tantrum.

"Gustav is going to be there too," Domeron said slyly.

That explained everything. This would be the first time Red would meet the head of the Adventurer's Guild. "What can I expect?" he asked.

Domeron sighed. "You can expect a lot of arguments and insults thrown between Hector and Gustav. The Baron will try to mediate, but he only succeeds about half the time. If things don't go too well, you might be in the meeting for a few extra hours."

Red nodded, but he had another concern. "I won't have to speak, will I?"

"You shouldn't have to. However, Gustav is a manipulative individual, so he might try to provoke you to probe your temperament. Since you're not the kind to respond to provocations, though, it should be fine."

Red was relieved. He had achieved the difficult task of remaining fairly inconspicuous in this large town—even with his red hair. The last thing he wanted to do was to draw the attention of important individuals.

Domeron continued. "That power of yours should be useful there, too. You might be able to tell if anyone is spying on the meeting."

"I'll keep that in mind."

The swordsman seemed satisfied with his response. "Then you should go back to sleep. Trust me, you will be thankful to be well-rested for tomorrow. Those kinds of meetings can be more draining than a dozen fights."

"I'll do that." Red trusted Domeron's advice on these matters. He had never been one for social meetings either, much less war councils.

After bidding the swordsman farewell, Red returned to his room.

He was about to go to sleep when he felt a fluctuation move.

Again? Red stared at the wall.

The person he felt was Rimold, and this wasn't the first time it had happened either. Over these last six months, the rogue had fallen into the habit of leaving the Sect many nights a week. Unfortunately for him, Red's nightly training had disrupted his schedule, and he always waited until Domeron and Red were done before sneaking out.

During his escapades, Rimold tried to stay as far as possible from Red's room, probably fearing his detection abilities. Of course, he was acting with outdated information, since with Red's upgraded crimson sense his detection range had doubled.

Red never followed Rimold or asked him about it. His outings didn't concern Red as long as they didn't affect him or the Sect at large.

He was just about to ignore the movement and settle down to sleep when he sensed something strange. Rimold was moving towards his room.

Red winced in suspicion. *What is he trying to do?*

Did he think Red had gone back to sleep already? No, something else had to be going on.

Red monitored his movements with his crimson sense. Sure enough, Rimold approached his room until he was standing right in front of his door.

Examining his fluctuation, he sensed the man was nervous. He waited for a knock at his door, but even after a minute, it didn't come. Rimold continued to stand in front of his room, doing nothing.

Red was tired of waiting. He stood up and approached the door with quiet steps.

With his improved senses from opening his Five Senses Vein, he could hear the rogue's heavy breathing clearly.

"What do you want?" he asked.

He heard a yelp on the other side. "Fuck! You brat... Why did you need to scare me like this?"

"I'm not the one standing in front of someone else's room in the middle of the night," Red retorted.

There was a long silence.

Rimold finally spoke up again. "... Ugh, just open the door, will you?"

"What do you want?" Red asked.

He felt hesitation behind the door. "I... need your help with something."

Red still didn't open up. "With what, exactly?"

"Listen, kid, can't we speak face-to-face?" Rimold snapped. "The more I stand right here, the more likely someone is going to notice us."

"Wait for me in the training field, then."

Rimold grunted. "Why not— Ugh, fine."

His fluctuation moved away. Red moved back from the door and picked up an iron shortsword he had been using as his replacement weapon these last few months. He had yet to craft anything using the Dark Iron.

Sheathing the sword at his waist, he walked outside.

Rimold was waiting for him in the training camp, leaning against the fence. He wore a dark robe, but with his night vision, Red could see the glint of armor beneath it.

The weapon on Red's waist gave Rimold pause. "What is that for?"

"That's for if you were trying to kill me."

Rimold glared at him. "You think you could stop me if I wanted to kill you?"

"Sure." Anyone else in the Sect would be a different story, but he felt confident about fighting Rimold.

"Ugh, you little..." Rimold swallowed his irritation. "Listen, we need to be quick before anyone else notices we're here."

"They're all in their rooms," Red pointed out.

"How do you— Oh, of course," Rimold sneered. "I forgot you are constantly monitoring everything people around the Sect do."

It's not like I have a choice in the matter.

Red sighed. "What is it that you want?"

Rimold looked troubled. "I need your help with something delicate."

"You mean something that you can't tell the others?"

"Ugh..."

Judging by Rimold's face, Red hit the mark.

The rogue collected himself. "Look, you're very discreet, aren't you? I heard about what you did for the others when you... stole things from other people."

Red frowned. This wasn't the reputation he was hoping to garner, and it was one reason he hadn't engaged in anything shady over the last half-year. "You want me to steal something?"

"Well... Yes, I do. I would do it myself, but this is a two-man operation."

"What do you want to steal?"

Rimold looked surprised. "Really? You're going to agree to it just like that?"

"I didn't say I would agree to it. I just need to know the details before making a decision."

"How can I just tell you all my plans before you agree to it? What if you tell the others about it?"

Red shrugged. "I'm not about to agree to something I know nothing about."

Rimold hesitated. In the end, he relented with a sigh. "Fine, but I need you to promise me you won't tell them about it."

"I can do that." He had no interest in screwing Rimold over, despite their less-than-amicable relationship.

"There is a merchant in town. He's carrying a lot of Spirit Stones with him... I need those stones."

"Why?"

Rimold scowled at Red. "Does it matter? It's not like you need to know the reason to make a decision."

Red supposed he was right. "Tell me about this merchant. Is he someone with influence? What kind of protection does he have with him?"

He couldn't imagine someone carrying such a fortune wouldn't have some strong bodyguards.

"As far as I know, he isn't anyone important," Rimold said. "That being said, the fact he's carrying so many Spirit Stones means he must be conducting business with important people."

Red was about to ask how the rogue even knew about these Spirit Stones in the first place, but this wasn't relevant information either.

"As for bodyguards..." Rimold breathed. "He has a Lesser Ring Realm cultivator with him."

Red's brow furrowed. He wasn't surprised by the revelation, but it did give him pause.

"You don't need to worry," Rimold insisted. "If everything goes well, there won't be any confrontation and they won't know anything happened until it's all said and done."

It sounded like wishful thinking on the rogue's part, but Red was at least willing to hear him out. "What's your plan?"

"I'll provide a distraction. I've already scouted where they're staying, so all that remains is for me to draw them away and for you to break in while they're not there."

"Would they really leave such precious merchandise unguarded?"

"They wouldn't. What matters the most is for me to drag the Lesser Ring Realm cultivator away. For the other bodyguards, you can use this." Rimold took a talisman from his pouch. "This is a sleeping spell. It can take out anyone in their room without making a sound."

Red's eyes widened. He reined in his curiosity, though, still weighing the matter. As much as Rimold seemed to have thought his plan through, there would still be an inherent risk that things could go wrong, and since they stood against a cultivator at the Lesser Ring Realm, the consequences could be dire.

Rimold noticed his hesitation. "You can also have a share of the Spirit Stones. We'll split it in half."

"How much is that?" Red asked.

"Should be about five Spirit Stones each."

Compared to what he had gotten in the hidden realm, five wasn't many. But Red was aware that opportunities like the ones in the trial came once in a lifetime. Five Spirit Stones were already a fortune in the outside world. He would need dozens of them, too, if he intended to buy the materials for his Parting Storm formation.

"Fine, I'll do it," Red told him. "But if things go wrong, don't blame me for not going forward with the plan."

Rimold smiled. "That goes without saying, of course."

"Where are they staying?"

"They're staying in an inn in town," Rimold said. "The Adventurer's Guild, to be exact."

Red frowned. That was Gustav's place. The same place he had stolen from before.

CHAPTER 44

STEALING AGAIN

RED STARED AT RIMOLD WARILY. "You know I stole from the Adventurer's Guild before, right?"

The rogue nodded. "That's why I'm asking for your help. Since you stole from them once, you shouldn't have much trouble stealing from them again."

"And you think they wouldn't be wiser to it?"

"Why would they? If I have it right, the last time you stole from them was six months ago. They might have been a bit more guarded right after that incident, but after six months, do you think they would still be so attentive?"

Red sighed. "You might have a point, but you know there are other reasons this is risky too."

Rimold snorted. "Gustav is just the owner. He might be angry, but as long as we don't target him directly, there's no need to worry about retaliation from him."

While that might be true, this wasn't the only thing Red was worried about. A merchant moving around with so many Spirit Stones might have a strong backer who would investigate a burglary. Of course, Red knew that if he wanted to gather enough stones to build his formation, he would probably need to resort to theft, and inevitably he would provoke the ire of many people.

In the end, he didn't press Rimold on the matter.

"Are we going right now?" Red asked.

Rimold nodded. "We'll meet in twenty minutes at the entrance to our street. I need time to prepare some things first."

Red agreed and the two parted ways.

Red returned to his room and prepared his equipment. There wasn't anything in particular he needed to take, but he wanted to have items he could rely on if things went south.

He opened his hidden stash stored below one of the floorboards, picking out one slip of paper in particular. It was a talisman he had received from Hector in recognition of his contributions over these six months.

After the trial, Red had recognized how useful talismans were to people like him who hadn't opened their Spiritual Seas. Talismans could mean the difference between life and death, and he made sure to stock up on them whenever he could.

This should be enough.

Best-case scenario, Red wouldn't have to use any talismans, but he knew to prepare for the worst.

After donning his uniform and equipment, Red checked his surroundings again with his crimson sense before sneaking out. He traveled down the uninhabited street before sensing Rimold's presence behind another ruined building.

He made sure to walk with heavy steps so as not to surprise Rimold. The man whirled around once he heard his approach, but right away he untensed.

He scowled at Red. "You know, it's a bit unfair..."

"What is?"

"How you can just tell where people are," Rimold grunted. "I've been sneaking around my entire life and have managed to stay unnoticed even by Hector. Yet a brat like you can spot me with little effort. Do you see how that's unfair?"

"I do."

"And I suppose you don't care, do you?"

Red didn't respond.

The rogue sighed. "How did you even get that power in the first place?"

"We should focus on the mission."

"Right," Rimold relented. "We all have our secrets."

Dropping the subject, he pointed forward. "You follow me. We'll climb a few buildings once we get near the guild so we can scout the area, and I can point out the room they're staying in. After that, we'll split up and you will wait for my distraction."

"It's already late at night," Red pointed out. "Won't they be inside their rooms? How are you going to drag them out?"

Rimold smirked. "You don't need to worry about that. I might not be as strong as the others, but when it comes to ingenuity, no one in our Sect can match me."

Red didn't know if the man was just boasting or not. Since returning to the Sect, he hadn't done much other than scout and gather information around the region. Red hadn't seen him training even once, which gave him no confidence in his strength. That being said, the Water Dragon Sect housed no ordinary people, so perhaps the rogue had reason to be cocky.

"Just stay close to me," Rimold said. "I know the best route."

To Red's surprise, he did indeed know his way around town.

Although it was the middle of the night, there were plenty of guards walking the streets on the lookout for thieves just like them. Rimold not only knew how to make his way through the ruins and buildings, but he also seemed to know the patrol's route by heart. They had an easy time making their way over to the Adventurer's Guild and climbing one of the nearby buildings.

As soon as they came within one hundred meters, Red's crimson sense covered the building. He felt at least thirty fluctuations within the guild, but one of them stood out.

Rimold squinted as he looked the building over. "The merchant should be—"

"In a back room on the second floor."

The rogue stared at Red. "How did you— Oh wait, is that your power again?"

He nodded. "I can feel the Lesser Ring Realm cultivator."

"So he's really here..." Rimold smiled. "I was hoping that maybe he could have left to take a walk."

"In the middle of the night? That seems unlikely."

"I know, I was just making a— Ugh, never mind. How many people are with him right now?"

"I can't tell exactly from here, but I can sense four other people nearby."

"The merchant and his three other bodyguards." Rimold nodded to himself. "That matches."

"How strong are the other ones?"

"I don't know, but they've probably all opened twelve veins," the rogue said. "Suffice it to say, you don't really want to face them in combat, so just stick to using the talisman."

Red nodded. That was what he'd been planning on doing.

Rimold continued. "I'll go create a distraction and as long as it works, you should sense the Lesser Ring Realm cultivator leaving the room. That will be your cue to break in and use the talisman."

"Won't they all be awake by then?" Red asked, not convinced by Rimold's flimsy plan. "How am I supposed to sneak in?"

The rogue snorted. "You don't need to sneak in. You can just break the window and throw the talisman inside. Trust me, there will be plenty of noise to cover your movement."

"What are you..." Red shook his head. "Never mind. Where are they keeping the Spirit Stones?"

"A strongbox, about the size of your head." Rimold demonstrated with his hands. "It will be hard to miss. The key is kept with the merchant at all times, so you'll need to search his body to find it. If you can't locate the key, just bring the box outside and we can figure out how to open it later."

"Where will we meet up after this?"

"Try to meet up back at the Sect's street when you can," Rimold said. "By that point, the town's guard might be on high alert, but they won't dare to come barging into our Sect's territory so easily, so we should be safe to reconvene... Of course, if things go wrong, just make sure to hide until everything calms down."

"As long as you can drag out the Lesser Ring cultivator and the talisman works as intended, we should be fine," Red confirmed. Despite his misgivings, Rimold seemed to know what he was doing.

The rogue chuckled. "Do you think I'd make that kind of mistake in planning? If the Lesser Ring cultivator doesn't come out, then there's no point in even continuing our heist."

Red sighed. "Whatever you say." He still wasn't sure how Rimold was going to pull that cultivator away from the room, but as the man said, if he didn't manage to do that, Red wouldn't dare to break into the room in the first place.

"You can scout the place while you're waiting." Rimold paused in thought. "I can't give you a signal for when I'll be acting, but it should be very obvious."

"How much time do I have to act?"

"It depends on how long I can keep that cultivator away... Probably no more than a few minutes."

This really wasn't much time, but Red supposed he wouldn't need that long if things worked as Rimold suggested.

"Ah yes, I forgot this." Rimold took something from his pouch and handed it to Red. "Here."

He accepted the piece of black leather. "A mask?"

"It will be useful to keep your identity hidden. Of course, if they spot you, a kid, running around in the crime scene, they'll probably suspect you immediately, but at least you'll have something to fall back on if things get complicated later."

Red frowned. If his identity were revealed during the heist, that would mean no end of troubles for him, but as Rimold said, it was best to have the mask on just to be safe.

Rimold wore his own mask, which only left two holes for his eyes. "Then I'll be going."

He walked to the edge of the building, about to go down. Then he paused and turned back to Red. "Oh, and don't screw this up, brat."

The rogue jumped down, disappearing from view.

Although Rimold had said his farewells, Red could still clearly sense his exact position, which made the whole interaction awkward for him. Either way, Red didn't stand idly by. He went on the move.

A few buildings stood between him and the Adventurer's Guild. He jumped, scaled, and crossed rooftops, a task he accomplished with surprising proficiency compared to the first time he'd sneaked through the town. Although he hadn't stolen anything for the last six months, that didn't mean he hadn't been out and about.

After all, Red still had many secrets he had to keep from his fellow Sect members.

Soon enough, he arrived at the back side of the guild. He stood across from it, on the rooftop of a building adjacent to the inn. Here he could clearly see into the rooms of the second floor, and he quickly identified the room of the Lesser Ring Realm cultivator, but he didn't let his gaze linger on the curtained window.

Red had learned to be more cautious since his encounter with Ricard in the trial. Cultivators possessed all kinds of strange and otherworldly abilities, so he couldn't discount the possibility that some of them could detect whether they were being spied on.

He lay down on the rooftop and waited for a signal.

He felt Rimold's fluctuation moving around the front of the building, but he couldn't see what the man was doing from his position. To his surprise, the rogue approached a handful of other fluctuations on the bottom floor, all of them awake.

Two belonged to horses, but one of them clearly belonged to a human.

He's at the stables.

Rimold continued to approach this human until he was only a few meters away from him. Red braced himself.

Is he going to kill them?

He waited, prepared to move, expecting this to be the signal. But to his surprise, nothing happened even after twenty seconds had gone by. Rimold continued to stay right next to this fluctuation.

Is he biding his time, or are they talking?

Finally Rimold moved again, having done nothing to the other presence as far as Red could tell. This time, he was moving towards the horses.

What is he doing—

A scream resounded from the first floor.

"There's a thief!" a man yelled. "They're stealing the carriage!"

The whole guild stirred awake, and Red heard cries of alarm coming from the merchant's room.

Horses neighed, and a heavy carriage, invisible from Red's position, went barreling down the street.

A rageful scream came from the merchant's room.

"DON'T LET THEM GET AWAY!"

The windows were thrown open, and Red saw a shadow jump from the second floor down to the street before running off. It was the Lesser Ring Realm cultivator, and before long, he was out of Red's senses.

Rimold had done as he promised.

Now it was Red's turn.

CHAPTER 45
SEEING RED

RED FELT fluctuations still inside the room. He stood up from his cover to look into the open window, knowing it was time to watch and wait.

The older merchant, whom Red recognized by his extravagant clothing, was pacing nervously. Two large men stood by the walls, equipped with scale armor and carrying weapons at their waists. They seemed ready to take on any invaders, even in the middle of the night.

Just one look at them told Red they weren't your common bodyguards.

The third bodyguard is not in the room.

A fourth presence was walking downstairs, perhaps to investigate the commotion.

Red began to worry. *Rimold told me nothing about the carriage.*

It was odd how nervous the merchant was. Wasn't the man's most valuable possession in his strongbox? Why would he be so anxious, then?

Red wasn't fond of receiving incomplete information, but this wasn't the time he'd cursed Rimold's name. There was only a brief window of time to act.

The merchant turned around to glare at his bodyguards. "Where is your other companion?!"

"He went downstairs to speak with Hubert," one of them said, steely-eyed.

The merchant sneered. "Are you sure he's not going to get lost on the way over?"

The bodyguard scowled but didn't respond.

"I don't know why I even pay the lot of you! Didn't you tell me you left someone to watch the carriage?! How did they even—"

"Wait." The bodyguard's eyes widened as he looked behind the merchant.

"What do you mean, *wait*? Are you out of your—"

"Get down!" The guard rushed forward to pull the merchant back.

His companion's hand went to his weapon, but it was too late. They saw a small shadow at the window. A pink light glowed in its hands before exploding in a flash.

Then there was only darkness.

Red was shocked by the scene. He never imagined Rimold's talisman would be so effective. One second, these men were standing ready to face an intruder, and the next, they had all fallen down like sacks of potatoes.

He made sure they were all truly unconscious before entering.

The first step—locate the strongbox.

Giving the room a cursory glance, he found no signs of it. The container was too big to be on the merchant's person, according to Rimold, so he went straight towards the wardrobe and chest of clothes, the only other places it could be hidden.

Nothing in the wardrobe.

He moved over to the chest and threw the clothes out, but still didn't find the strongbox. Red didn't panic, though.

He roughly measured the chest, noticing something strange. Red took out his shortsword and stabbed it into the chest's bottom. He heard the *ting* of his weapon hitting something metallic.

A hidden compartment.

Red didn't bother looking for the mechanism to open it. Instead, he opted for the tried-and-true method of brute force.

He slashed at the bottom of the chest, hacking the container to pieces.

Finally, he broke enough of the wood to take out a metallic strongbox. Red didn't bother examining it. If this wasn't what he was looking for, then he had to commend the merchant for fooling him.

Red focused on his crimson sense. No one was coming, so he still had time.

Next, the key.

He patted the merchant down and found a coin pouch, which he pocketed along with a handful of jewels. No signs of the key.

Red examined the man's neck, noticing he was hiding a handful of necklaces under his shirt. He pulled them out, and sure enough, there was a small key amidst the jewelry.

He was about to snap the chain off of the merchant's neck when something drew his gaze. One of the pendants.

A dark, opaque jewel hung from the necklace. It was a pure black color, darker than the night, and it seemed to draw all the light from its surroundings, threatening to swallow everything. It didn't fit with the other jewelry the merchant was wearing.

It looked demonic.

Yet no matter how much Red tried, he couldn't pull his eyes away. Slowly, something shifted in the endless darkness of the gem. An image formed on the surface of the pendant, and then he saw it.

A lizard-like crimson eye, staring back at him, holding the end of the world in its gaze.

Suddenly, Red remembered.

The rage.

The violence.

The death.

The destruction.

The chaos.

The dark star.

It had seen him.

Some floodgate was unlocked in the depths of his mind. A trembling came over his entire body as Red fell to the ground in horror.

No, I have to...

He tried standing up, but his body refused. He looked around, searching for some support, but he abruptly noticed his entire field of vision was crimson.

His hand went up to his eyes and felt a damp fluid running down under his mask. Panic overtook him as he fumbled around for anything to help him.

No, I can't... Not here.

By instinct, his mind went back to the meditation technique, trying to calm him down. But it was to no avail. It was as if every fiber of his being were consumed by fear and despair, and no matter what Red did, there was no getting rid of it.

His mind dug deeper, searching for something to help him. Then he remembered.

The first time he saw the crimson mist on the surface—he had felt the same way as he felt now. It was a force beyond his understanding, and he couldn't have faced it if not for that one image.

The white slate from one of his dreams.

As soon as Red pictured it, his fear and despair faded like dust blown away by the wind. He took a deep breath, noticing he'd been unable to breathe the entire time. The terror dissipated from his mind, but the effects it had on his body were still there.

I need to hurry.

Red didn't dare to contemplate what had just happened. He wiped at his eyes with his sleeves, clearing his vision somewhat, before stumbling, tripping, and finally standing upright again. That was when he felt an approaching fluctuation.

The other bodyguard is returning.

Red tried to hurry. He picked up the strongbox, ignoring the key, as he was too afraid to look anywhere near the merchant's neck. Then, like a drunk, he staggered towards the window.

He looked at the ground two stories below.

I can't climb down in this state.

As he pondered what to do, he heard footsteps drawing near. He frowned, but didn't hesitate any longer.

He threw the strongbox first and jumped down after it.

In a normal situation, someone like Red with a few open veins wouldn't have any trouble landing that jump. Yet his landing was not graceful. He fell hard on his side, and the breath was slammed out of his lungs.

Swallowing his pain, he stood as fast as he could, which wasn't fast at all.

He grabbed the strongbox and limped away, using his crimson sense to scout his surroundings.

Above him came a scream. He knew the bodyguard had entered the room. Red hurried even more, almost fainting, scrambling out of the alley before the man looked out the window.

Fearing the bodyguard might give chase, he was already fishing his talisman out of his pocket. Then, a few seconds later, he heard an inhuman shriek from above, followed by a scream of terror.

His blood ran cold. Looking back at the window, he couldn't see anything, but he heard rending flesh. More screams rang out, and he sensed a new presence appear in the room.

It was demonic.

Red shivered, running away without looking back. Thankfully, whatever had appeared in that room had plenty of other distractions in the Adventurer's Guild and didn't chase after him.

Soon he'd fled the scene of the crime, and the entire town seemed awoken by the death throes of the adventurers.

Red didn't immediately go to meet Rimold. The whole town was in a frenzy, and the guards were shouting, running towards the Adventurer's Guild.

Red hid in an alley until he had recovered and the majority of the guards had passed him by. Only then did he return to his Sect's street.

He approached with caution. He knew the rest of the Sect members would have woken up from the commotion, and it was likely they would find his and Rimold's rooms empty. How could they not suspect the two of them were responsible?

There was a bigger emergency at hand than their suspicions, though. As Red approached the Sect grounds, he sensed Rimold hidden behind a few ruined houses.

Rimold shot up as soon as he saw Red, even ignoring the strongbox in his hand. "What did you do?!"

Red shook his head, still shaken. "Something... happened."

Rimold's eyes widened, furious. "You're telling me?! What the fuck did you do to alarm the entire town?"

How could he explain it? "I was looking for the key... Then... Then there was a demon."

"... A d-demon? How was there a demon?"

"I don't know. I just looked at the merchant's necklace, and then—"

"Wait!" Rimold cried. "You said there was a necklace?"

Red nodded.

"Did it have a dark gem?" Rimold asked, troubled.

He nodded again, stunned. "How did you know?"

Rimold shivered. "Oh... Oh no."

"What is it?"

"We're doomed." Rimold shook his head in denial. "We're all doomed." He fell silent. Seconds later, he showed Red a terror-stricken face. "We've messed with demonic cultivators."

Red froze. This was indeed a reason to worry.

CHAPTER 46

TOWN ON ALERT

RED HELD BACK HIS WORRY. He needed to understand what had happened. "What does the necklace mean?"

"It's a symbol of a demonic cult," the rogue said with some apprehension.

"What do you mean by 'cult'? They also worship demons?"

"Of course they do, you brat!" Rimold looked at him as if he were an idiot. "Look, I don't feel like giving you a history lesson right now! We first need to figure out what we are going to do!"

Red winced, but he knew he was right. He restrained his curiosity. "Aren't we going back to the Sect?"

Rimold sneered. "And getting caught red-handed by Hector? I'd rather not!"

"What else would you suggest?"

"We go hide somewhere, of course!" Rimold said. "They'll kill that demon really quickly anyways, and once things have blown over in the morning, we can return to the Sect!"

Red was baffled. "Isn't that just delaying the inevitable? Besides, how are you so confident they'll kill the demon?"

He was actually aware, thanks to the demon's fluctuation, that it wasn't even in the Lesser Ring Realm, so the town's cultivators wouldn't have much issue killing it. But Rimold didn't know about that. Red didn't understand how Rimold could be so confident.

"You really don't know? There's an ancient formation covering the town that the Baron controls. As long as the demon isn't in the third realm or above, it won't survive within the town's borders."

Red faintly recalled hearing about that.

"What about the others?" he asked. "Won't they think something happened to us if they don't find us at the Sect?"

Rimold hesitated, then took a slip of paper from his pouch. It was a communication talisman—something they had in large supply since Red robbed that imperial agent.

"I'll send a message to them," he said.

"What are you going to say?"

"I don't know!" Rimold threw his hands up in exasperation. "I'll figure it out!"

The talisman glowed with a soft blue light. His whole countenance and air changed as he began to speak.

"It's Rimold..." he said. "Me and the kid are safe... By 'kid,' I mean Red. Uh... It's not convenient to come back to the Sect right now, but we'll be back in the morning... Bye."

The glow dissipated.

Red gawked at the rogue.

"What?!" Rimold glared back at him.

"I thought you were supposed to be good with words."

"Of course I'm good with words! I'm just not good when it comes to speaking to—"

The talisman flared again, and an enraged—and familiar—voice burst out. "WHAT HAVE YOU FUCKING DONE?! I SWEAR I'LL SKIN YOU ALIVE IF YOU DON'T COME BACK TO THE SECT RIGHT NOW!"

The glow disappeared, leaving Rimold's pale expression and a heavy silence behind.

"... Aren't you going to reply?" Red asked.

Rimold cleared his throat. "I don't think so. Either way, do you still think it's a good plan to go back to the Sect right now?"

Red shook his head. Even if they were going to be punished upon return, he would rather wait until Hector had calmed down somewhat. "Where should we go?"

"I have some hideouts around town prepared for this kind of occasion. We can wait there until things blow over." He examined the strongbox in the boy's hand. "Did you get the key, by the way?"

Red shook his head. "I got out of there as soon as I noticed something was wrong."

The rogue grunted. "That's fine. At the very least, you got the strongbox. Do you want me to carry it?"

Red hesitated, but agreed. He would rather not be weighed down by anything if they needed to flee.

Rimold took the box in his hands. "Now, follow me closely. The last thing we need is to be caught up with the guards."

Thankfully for them, the guards were too occupied with the demon appearing in the middle of the night to be on the lookout for a couple of thieves. Soon they made it to a patch of ruins and abandoned houses on the edge of town.

"It's here." Rimold singled one out.

He led Red into the ramshackle room. It seemed to have been abandoned for a long time—the roof had partially collapsed and the wooden furniture was in decay.

Red frowned. "Is this your hideout?"

Rimold glared back at him. "Do you really think I would just pick a random abandoned house for a hideout? Here, just hold the box for a second."

He did as he was told. Rimold, his hands now free, walked over to a corner where a wardrobe had toppled on the floor. He pushed the piece of furniture away, revealing a trapdoor underneath.

Rimold fished around at his waist before picking out a key and unlocking the hatch. He swung the trapdoor open, then looked back at Red with a cocky smile.

"See? I told you I had my means."

Red didn't respond.

The rogue climbed down the ladder. Red watched as he descended over five meters before finally hopping onto the floor. He lost sight of him as he wandered off, but soon enough, a white light illuminated the shaft.

"I've lit up the room," Rimold said. "You can come down now."

Red didn't need the light in the first place, but he saw no reason to comment on that. He climbed down carrying the strongbox.

When he reached the bottom, he was struck by what he saw.

This really is a hideout.

Red found himself in a small square room, no more than five meters across. Stone bricks lined the walls, and a large shelf full of sealed wooden boxes and all sorts of paraphernalia stood against the right side while a makeshift bed stood on the other. Countless tools were strewn about, and Red could barely walk without stumbling over something.

Rimold shot him a smug grin. "So, what do you think? I've built this myself."

"It's impressive." He was being honest. The room, of course, was a mess, but it served its purpose as a hideout, especially considering it was all set up by one person.

Rimold nodded in satisfaction. "Finally, you acknowledge my skills. Now, stand back, I need to close the hatch."

The rogue climbed back up and lifted the wardrobe over the trapdoor before slowly closing it down. A few seconds later, he was back.

He patted the dust off his clothes. "Now that we finally have some time, tell me exactly what happened. Oh, and take off your mask, will you?"

Red hesitated, but did so.

The rogue yelped at the dried blood running down his face. "What the fuck happened to you?"

"I'm not sure. I did everything as you told me, but when I was looking for the key, I felt my gaze drawn in by that dark pendant... After that, I was dizzy and barely made it out of the room before another bodyguard came in. When I was back in the alley, I felt that demon appear with my power, and I heard the screams of someone dying."

Red obviously omitted some details, but he saw no reason to lie otherwise.

"Did you ever see the demon? Or how it came to be?"

Red shook his head. "I got out of there as soon as I could."

Rimold was troubled. "I'm not a demon specialist, but even then, this whole story sounds weird to me."

"Why is that?"

"Well, there are two ways for demons to be created," the rogue said. "Either they're summoned in rituals, or someone becomes a demon over time. Neither of these happens spontaneously, though, and from what you told me, it didn't look like the merchant was in the middle of a summoning ritual, was he?"

Red shook his head.

Rimold grunted. "That's what confuses me. I've never heard of something like this, but then again, I suppose I don't know much about demons in the first place."

"What about the pendant?" Red asked, noticing Rimold had brushed over what he thought would be the most pressing matter. "You said it's a symbol of a demonic cult, didn't you?"

Rimold's frown deepened. "It is. They say it's crafted from obsidian mined from the Infernal Realm and that if you stare deeply into it, then something on the other side will look back. I thought it was all bullshit, of course, and I came across quite a few of those pendants in the past that belonged to demon worshipers that didn't do anything of the sort. However, if what you said is true..."

"Then it means they work."

And it also meant that the eye Red had seen belonged to a demon from the other side.

Rimold nodded slowly. "Maybe the ones I saw in the past were all fake... Or maybe they don't work all the time. I-I never imagined that this merchant... I'm sorry, kid."

"Should I be expecting anything else to happen?"

"I... I don't know. But just coming into contact with a demon worshiper... That can't mean anything good for any of us."

Red narrowed his eyes. "Those Spirit Stones... Do you think they were meant for a demonic cultivator?"

"That's my worry, yes..." Rimold hesitated. "Of course, it could be that the Spirit Stones and the demon-worshiping thing are unrelated, but even then, we've still messed with something we should have steered clear from."

"You think other demonic worshipers will investigate?"

"Probably, but not yet. A demon appearing in the middle of town is a pretty big deal, and I don't think the Baron will leave it alone."

Red realized something. "You think they could find out we were involved?"

Rimold shook his head. "They shouldn't be able to. We left no traces behind, and—"

He froze.

Red had a bad premonition. "What is it? Did you leave something behind?"

"N-no, but I... T-the bodyguard in the stables, he..." Rimold trailed off.

"You had a deal with him, didn't you?"

Rimold nodded. "I was supposed to give a cut of the profits from the items in the carriage to him. He didn't even know about the Spirit Stones we were trying to steal..."

Red asked the most vital question. "Does he know your identity?"

"I didn't reveal it to him, but... If he does some digging around, he might find some clues."

Red's blood ran cold. It didn't seem likely that this bodyguard would investigate the matter, considering it involved a demon, but leaving a loose end like this on such a serious issue didn't sit well with him. Not to mention, this bodyguard was likely to be questioned. Red didn't even know if the merchant was still alive.

Rimold's expression suddenly became determined. "We need to do something about it."

Red frowned. "You mean..."

The rogue nodded decisively. "We need to kill him."

CHAPTER 47

DEBT

ONCE AGAIN, Red was skeptical of Rimold's plan. "Kill the bodyguard? Just for that?"

Rimold gritted his teeth. "I don't want to do it either, but what choice do we have? If they figure out we were involved in this, we're completely screwed!"

Red sighed. "I understand where you're coming from, but think about it for a second. If we kill him, we'll be digging a deeper hole for ourselves. Right now, it's unlikely this bodyguard will look into this matter if he knows it involves demons. He'll probably just run away to avoid getting implicated with his employer."

Rimold glared at him. "No! You don't understand! We need to make sure we resolve everything here!"

Red went silent at this sudden bout of anger. He knew how dangerous this matter was, but he still found it odd for Rimold to react so violently about it.

There has to be something he's not telling me.

Rimold noticed he had gone too far with his words. He looked away in embarrassment.

"Before we proceed, I think I need you to clarify a few things for me," Red stated.

Rimold scowled at him, but still nodded.

273

"How did you escape from that Lesser Ring Realm cultivator?" Red asked.

"I used a talisman."

Vague. Red didn't comment on it. "What about the carriage? What did you do with it?"

Rimold hesitated. "I... abandoned it."

"That seems weird. Earlier, you told me that the bodyguard agreed to help you for a share of the goods in the carriage, but you just abandoned it?"

The rogue snorted. "I was obviously just lying to him."

"And the bodyguard just agreed to help someone he didn't know steal a carriage from his employee by himself while going against a Lesser Ring Realm cultivator? What made him so confident that things would go well?"

The more Red considered the situation, the more absurd it seemed.

Rimold had to notice this. His expression fell, defeated. "Fine, you win. I had other people that put me in contact with this bodyguard... I passed the carriage to them, and they helped me escape from the Lesser Ring Realm cultivator."

Red wasn't surprised. "So that's the connection you're afraid will get revealed... Do they know your true identity?"

"They do."

"So why aren't you worried about them revealing your involvement in this too?" Red asked.

"They have as much to lose about this coming to light as I do. Besides, even if I wanted to, I wouldn't be able to silence them."

That doesn't sound good.

"Did they know about the Spirit Stones?"

"No. I found out about them by chance while investigating the merchant. I made my plans with you on the side so we could split them between ourselves."

Red narrowed his eyes. "That sounds very risky. Wouldn't they have found out you acted behind their backs if the merchant asked about it?"

The rogue rolled his eyes. "These people don't care about loyalty. As long as I gave them a cut later, they wouldn't complain."

Red sighed. "Of course, but now that there's a demon involved, things get more complicated. They don't know about my involvement. You can claim to know nothing about it, but I doubt they would believe you."

Rimold's face became grim.

"Who are these people you were working with?" That was the most important matter to Red.

Rimold hesitated before shaking his head. "You don't need to know."

"That's for me to judge," Red argued. "I gave you the benefit of the doubt once I agreed to this job, considering you are my fellow Sect member, but you still hid information that may have future consequences for me."

Rimold was outraged. "You think I knew about the demon?!"

"No, I don't. But you still didn't tell me powerful people were involved in this operation, and thus implicated me in yet another issue, not even mentioning the possible demonic cultivators behind the merchant. That by itself is more than enough for me to demand more clarity moving forward."

"And what will you do if I don't tell you?"

"I would be forced to ask Hector for help," Red told him. "It would be my only choice in this matter."

He didn't say this to threaten Rimold; he was just being sincere. These people who had helped Rimold were active in this town, and powerful enough to help him escape from a Lesser Ring Realm cultivator. Unlike the force behind the merchant, this was a very clear and immediate threat.

Rimold's expression looked equal parts conflicted and annoyed. "I can tell you, but you must promise me you won't reveal it to Hector and the others."

Red was careful. "That depends. How likely is it that they could come after me?"

"They definitely won't come after you." Rimold shook his head. "I can promise you that, and if at any point you feel that might not be the case, I give you my permission to tell the truth to Hector."

Red nodded with some reluctance. "Fine. I promise I won't tell Hector as long as they don't threaten me."

"Good..." Rimold breathed. "I'm... working with Gustav's people."

Red regretted his promise. The silence grew heavy as he tried to digest this revelation. His gaze, once defiant, turned wary.

"I'm not betraying the Sect, if that's what you're worried about," Rimold added.

"You're working for Gustav. He's our enemy."

Rimold gritted his teeth. "I know! But it's not what you think! I only agreed to help him as long as it didn't involve acting against the Sect!"

"I find that hard to believe."

"Look, I'm not asking you to trust me right away, but think about it!" The rogue tapped the side of his head. "I've been working with him for the last six months, but did anything bad happen to the Sect in the meantime?"

"That doesn't prove anything," Red shot back. "As far as I know, you might just be biding your time."

"Biding my time for six months only to reveal my connection to the enemy to a fucking brat like you?!" Rimold glared at him.

Red sighed. "You just told me I don't need to trust you right away, so I'm doing just that. If you truly wish to convince me, tell me why you're working with Gustav."

"I'm trying to repay my debt."

"You borrowed money from Gustav?" Red was surprised.

"No, not from him. I borrowed it from someone else while I was in the kingdom's capital... I made a contract with them to repay this loan over time by providing my specialized services. They told me someone would approach me once I returned to town, but I never imagined they meant Gustav."

"You mean you borrowed money from the faction behind him?"

Rimold nodded, his head low. "I didn't figure it out at the time, but... I should have seen it coming."

"Didn't Gustav try to make you betray the Sect?"

"He did. But I told him I would rather they kill me then and there than make me betray our Sect..." Rimold grew angry. "In the end, he didn't push the matter, to my surprise, and neither did he threaten to reveal it to Hector... He just told me I would need to do jobs here and there for him. Stealing and spying on others—things I'm good at doing. Some of them were risky, but I knew what I was getting myself into when I took out that loan."

Red examined the man's face, looking for signs of a lie. There was nothing but guilt and remorse. Then he used his crimson sense. His fluctuation flared, a sign of great distress. That was to be expected, but it didn't tell him whether he was lying or not.

"How much do you owe them?" Red asked.

Rimold sighed. "Fifty."

"Fifty what?"

"... Fifty Spirit Stones."

Red stared at him in amazement. "How is that even possible?"

Fifty Spirit Stones was several times the worth of an average Lesser Ring

Realm cultivator. He just couldn't imagine why Rimold wanted to take out a Spirit Stone loan, much less why he needed such an exorbitant amount.

Rimold shook his head. "The amount I needed was lower, about fifteen Spirit Stones. Fifty is that plus the ridiculous interest they told me I had to pay... Of course, this isn't a debt I'm meant to be able to pay as long as I'm alive. It's pretty much just a slavery contract to Gustav and his faction."

"And they aren't afraid you would try to run?" Red asked.

"They aren't..." Rimold looked conflicted. "I left collateral with them back at the capital... I left something behind that I can't afford to lose."

"What did you borrow the money for?"

The rogue didn't answer, merely looking at Red. The man's gaze lingered on him as if pondering what to reveal.

A few seconds later, he relented. "I borrowed it for medicine. I have... Someone in the capital. They were sick with a rare disease, and they needed medicine. Expensive medicine... That's all you need to know."

If what the rogue said was true, it took little thinking to figure out what his collateral was.

Red tried to use all his senses and experience to see through Rimold's potential facade. Yet if the man was lying, then he couldn't detect it. This didn't reassure Red. He knew he wouldn't find out if the rogue was being genuine or not without investigating this matter—something he clearly couldn't do right now.

This made him hesitate, and Rimold was quick to pick up on it.

"I don't need you to believe me, kid," he sneered. "I just need you to keep your promise and not tell Hector about what happened."

Red nodded. "I have no reason to."

At least not yet.

This seemed to satisfy Rimold. "Good... I wanted to look for that bodyguard, but as you said, he might be long gone by now, and even then, killing him isn't a good idea. It's possible the guards or Gustav's people got to him first, but in either case, I doubt they would reveal my involvement in this, since it would implicate them too."

"So what do you plan on doing?" Red asked. "Waiting here until the morning?"

"Yes. It leaves us time for things to calm down and to come up with a good story to tell Hector. Besides... We haven't even opened the strongbox yet, have we?"

"Can you do it?" Red asked, skeptical.

"You're asking if I can do it?!" Rimold glared at him. "You brat, who do you think taught your precious Master Goulth how to pick locks?! As long as it's not locked by enchantments, there's nothing I can't open!"

He set the metal container on top of a crate.

"Just sit there and watch closely," Rimold said. "You might learn a thing or two!"

CHAPTER 48
A HEAD

FIVE MINUTES PASSED as Rimold fiddled with the strongbox, his confidence falling.

He grunted. "Ugh, what did they make this lock out of?"

"What's the problem?" Red asked.

"I have never seen a lock so complex before." Rimold shook his head. "I can't even begin to imagine how some of these mechanisms work."

Red frowned. "Does that mean you can't open it?"

"I'll need a few hours to study and do it properly, but I might still be able to do it."

"As long as you can still open it, it's fine." It wasn't like Red had much to do while locked up in this place.

As Rimold focused on his work, Red noticed a large assortment of equipment on one of the shelves. Tools for stealing, Red assumed. Nothing stood out to him, and he didn't dare to open any crates in front of Rimold.

"How did you learn about the Spirit Stones, by the way?" he asked.

"I have sources on the other side of the river," Rimold said without looking up from the strongbox. "When Gustav asked me to steal from that merchant, I looked a bit into who this guy was. Imagine my surprise when someone told me he might be carrying a large amount of Spirit Stones with him."

Red frowned upon learning yet another detail Rimold hadn't mentioned. "Might?"

Rimold snorted. "Well, he took out a large amount of Spirit Stones from his guild's coffers before setting out, and my source saw his strongbox. You just need to put two and two together."

"But how can you be so certain about it?" Red thought Rimold's information was little more than guesswork, no matter how likely.

"Look, I have experience with this, okay? Now, just sit there and let me work and we'll eventually find out if I'm right, will we not?"

Red sighed and went silent.

Just like the rogue said, it took him almost two hours to unlock the strongbox.

"Hah! Finally!" Rimold wiped the sweat from his forehead. "I was actually starting to doubt myself midway through there."

Red, who was sitting in a corner of the room meditating, opened his eyes and looked over. "Are there any traps in the box?"

Rimold grunted. "That's what I'm going to check now."

As Red had seen Goulth do before, Rimold lifted the lid slightly to search for any wires or trap mechanisms.

A few minutes later, he sighed in relief. "No traps."

"Really? They didn't put any traps in such an important container?"

"You're thinking about this all wrong." Rimold shook his head. "A merchant wouldn't rig a strongbox they were supposed to deliver, would they? Not only would it risk damaging the goods, but even if it was stolen, they would rather these goods remain intact so they can recover them in the future. Of course, if it was a sensitive object or something of the sort, then it would be a different story, but for Spirit Stones they probably thought just a sturdy lock would suffice. Too bad they met me."

He smirked, flipped the lid open, and looked inside. That wiped the grin off his face.

"What the fuck?!" He jumped back in shock.

Red shot up to his feet, half expecting an explosion to occur. Nothing happened.

He blinked. "What is it?"

"T-the box..." The rogue pointed with a trembling finger. "There's something in there!"

Red walked over to the strongbox. When he saw the contents, Rimold's shock made sense.

"It's a head," the boy told him.

A desiccated head. Its eye sockets were empty, its skin gray and pulled taut against its skull, its teeth poking out from between torn lips.

It turned out that when Rimold compared the strongbox's size to a human's head, the description was more fitting than he'd imagined.

Red squinted as he examined the disembodied head. "It looks human, but there's something weird about it."

"Get away from it, you lunatic!" Rimold pulled him back by his scruff. "You don't know what it does!"

"There are no Spirit Stones in there."

Rimold's eyes widened in anger. "I noticed! But we have more pressing concerns right now!"

Red sighed. "Why is there a head in that box?"

He just couldn't imagine why a merchant, even one in a cult, would need to put a desiccated head inside this kind of strongbox.

"He was a demon worshiper!" Rimold said. "They use all kinds of blood sacrifices and other unholy things in their rituals!"

"So you're saying this might have been for a ritual?"

"That's my guess. Nothing else would make sense!"

"Your explanation does work, but you do know what that means, right?"

"What do you—ugh!" Rimold was catching on.

Red completed his train of thought. "If the merchant was carrying this with him, then that means he was probably acting under the orders of other demon worshipers."

One good thing about the merchant being a demon worshiper was that he probably wasn't acting under the orders of a demonic cultivator. But that no longer seemed to be the case, and this revelation meant they had just interfered in the business of some very dangerous and insidious people.

Rimold looked grim. "Why did everything have to go so fucking wrong?!"

Red ignored him as he walked back over to the box.

"I mean, I just wanted to earn some money to repay my debts, so why— Hey, didn't I tell you to get away from that? You don't know if that head is cursed or carrying a disease or something!"

"It's strange..." Red said. "I feel like I recognize this head."

"You do?" Rimold looked shocked. He reluctantly walked over and likewise examined the head. As the seconds passed, he became intrigued.

Rimold's brow furrowed in thought. "Now that you mention it... Those large teeth do remind me of someone."

Red didn't respond. He was having his own revelation. Blood froze in his veins as he finally recognized who this head belonged to.

Isn't this Viran?

He couldn't believe it. How had these people gotten a hold of the old warrior's body? Wasn't it lost in the underground? More importantly, why had they done this to his head?

Red felt both indignant and terrified at the same time.

From the corner of his eye, he saw Rimold tremble. "This... No, it can't be." The rogue dropped down to his knees. "M-my mother..."

His words jolted Red out of his daze. He looked at the man in confusion. "Your mother?"

Rimold ignored him. "N-no, no way... How could they do this to you, Mother? H-how could they..."

The rogue was just about to reach into the box and touch the head. Red, however, realized what was happening.

"Rimold, no!" He tackled him to the ground.

Taken by surprise, Rimold glared at Red with fury in his eyes. "What are you doing, you fucking bastard?!"

He looked like he was about to attack him.

"It's not your mother!" Red warned him. "I'm seeing someone different in its face."

Rimold froze, baffled. "W-what do you mean?"

"I recognized someone else in the head's face... But it was a man."

The rogue shivered in horror.

"There's something wrong with it," Red explained. "We shouldn't look at it."

"R-right." Rimold nodded, still in a daze.

Red walked over to the box, not daring to even spare a glance at its contents. He closed the lid without hesitation, and only then did he let out a sigh of relief.

Rimold's face was pale, his composure shaken. "W-what was... What was that?"

Red shook his head. "I don't know."

Rimold looked down at his trembling hands. "When I looked at that head... I felt something change. I-it was like a creeping feeling... When I recognized my mother's face, I... I felt like I needed to touch it."

"We should tell Hector about this," Red insisted. "As quickly as possible."

"Y-you're right." To Red's surprise, Rimold agreed with him. "But should we bring it with us?" The man looked back at the box fearfully.

"No way. Let's leave it here." As far as they knew, the head only affected them if they looked at it, but Red would never risk bringing it back to their Sect. It was too dangerous.

Rimold got up and eyed the box with apprehension. "We should leave."

Red nodded. "Agreed."

Neither of them dared spend one more second close to that thing.

A few hours had passed since they had hidden away, and the town was calming down. They still saw quite a few guards running around, but the urgency was gone.

They killed the demon already.

This was the only conclusion that made sense to Red. Now they were probably looking around town for any other signs of demonic activity.

He looked back at the ruined hideout they had just crawled out from, feeling a shiver run up his spine. He hoped the head wouldn't result in another demonic summoning.

Rimold led the way back to the Sect as they sneaked under the night sky. It didn't take them long to arrive at the Sect's street.

The rogue stopped and turned to Red. "Let me do the talking, okay?"

Red nodded. If Rimold wanted to receive the brunt of Hector's anger, who was he to stop him?

They walked towards the Sect's courtyard, and Red already felt a handful of fluctuations moving about. Eiwin, Domeron, Allen, Goulth, and Hector.

He didn't feel Narcha or Rog's fluctuations.

They must have gone to investigate the scene.

Within a few dozen meters of the gate, the doors swung open. Hector walked outside, staring daggers at the two of them.

"You little shits!" The man shook with anger. "What the fuck have you done?!"

"Wait!" Rimold raised his hands up. "I know you're mad, but there's something really important we need to tell you! Whatever punishment you have in mind can wait until then!"

Red praised Rimold's approach in his mind. Hector's temper was explosive, but his bouts of anger disappeared just as quickly as they started. As long as the elder had something else to focus on, that is.

"You..." Hector gnashed his teeth.

It seemed he knew exactly what Rimold was doing, but he could do nothing to stop it.

"Fine!" He waved his sleeve. "To the hall!"

He spun on his heels and walked back into the courtyard. Two people had been standing behind him—Allen and Eiwin.

Allen's expression brightened. "Did you steal something?"

Eiwin frowned.

Red didn't respond to the question.

CHAPTER 49

DEMONIC INFLUENCE

EVERYONE WAS GATHERED inside the Sect hall except for Narcha and Rog. Goulth was glaring at Red, but Red ignored it for now.

Domeron rubbed his eyes. "What have you two done this time?" He looked more bothered by having been woken up in the middle of the night than anything else.

Goulth grunted. "Do you need to ask? They probably stole something again!" He glowered at Rimold. "I knew you would be a bad influence on my disciple!"

Rimold put his hands up in defeat. "Look, you can admonish me however you want after we're done reporting our situation, okay?"

Hector, weighing up the two of them in silence, now snorted loudly. "Then go ahead! Explain to me how the two of you managed to summon a demon in the middle of town!"

Allen's eyes widened. "So it was a demon?!"

One look from Hector was enough to silence him.

"We were, uh... Acquiring something from a merchant in the Adventurer's Guild." Rimold said it in the vaguest way possible, but that already earned him plenty of unfriendly looks. "Look, it doesn't matter! What matters is what the kid saw once he entered the merchant's room!"

Goulth's eyes twitched. "You sent him inside by himself?"

"Not the point. Tell them, kid!" Rimold looked at Red with pleading eyes.

Red sighed and turned to the others. "I was searching the merchant's body for a key when I found a dark pendant around his neck."

Everyone's faces fell. Everyone except for Allen, who squinted in confusion.

"A demon worshiper?" Domeron asked, voice heavy.

"Yes. I didn't know it at the time, but Rimold informed me afterwards. That's not all, though..."

Goulth could guess. "Did you look at it?"

Red nodded.

"This..." The blacksmith put a hand to his head. "Did it react?"

"It did. I felt dizzy and my eyes started to bleed... I saw something inside that pendant. It wasn't until I left that I heard the demon inside the room."

There was a long silence as Goulth paled. Eiwin looked anxious while Domeron pondered with his eyes closed. Hector was grimacing, studying Red.

Red was quick to understand there was more to this matter than Rimold first told him, but when he looked over at Rimold, the man seemed just as confused. Before Red could question them, Allen spoke up.

"What's with your faces?" The strange atmosphere was starting to worry him too. "Is Red not safe?"

Hector ignored his question, gazing at Red. "Do you remember what you saw inside that pendant?"

Red frowned, trying to remember the image, but before he could respond, Hector cut him off.

"Don't try to visualize it too much," he said. "Just tell me what you can remember off the top of your head."

"It... was a reptilian eye."

"So a draconic demon, then."

"Can you stop beating around the bush and tell us what the issue is?" Rimold looked nervous. "Why does it matter what the kid saw?"

Hector ignored him and continued to focus on Red. "Do you know why it's so dangerous to practice demonic arts, kid?"

Red hesitated. "... Isn't it because of demonification?"

"That is certainly one reason. But not the only one. In truth, practicing demonic arts makes you more susceptible to... Outside influence."

He understood where this was going.

Hector continued. "Some strong-willed cultivators can fight off demonification, and as such, they choose to rely on these demonic arts. They say that there is no such thing as an evil technique, only an evil cultivator. To some degree, they are right, but these people sadly miss the true danger of the demonic arts."

The mood grew heavier, and Red felt cold sweat running down his back.

"Throughout history, great cultivators have fallen victim to demonification and become horrible monsters," Hector said. "These people were extremely tenacious, even more so than any of us in this Sect, and yet they still fell to this dark curse. Why do you think that is?"

"Because of outside influence?" Red tried to guess.

"Indeed. Using demonic Spiritual Energy will inevitably open one up to the influence of demons from the Infernal Realm—creatures of primordial evil beyond our understanding. Intrusive thoughts, whispered words, strong bouts of unexplainable emotion—these demons can push a person to the brink of a mental breakdown without them noticing, and even if they do notice, sometimes there's nothing they can do to stop it. Under the pressure of such vicious beings, these cultivators find themselves unable to fight back against the demonification, and they all end up falling in the end."

"But Red doesn't practice any demonic arts!" Allen blurted out. "Why does that matter to him?"

"If these demons were only a risk to demonic cultivators, they wouldn't be as dangerous as they are." Hector shook his head. "In truth, even normal people can be influenced by demons if they're exposed to them."

Allen was stunned. "You mean..."

Hector nodded grimly. "When he looked into the pendant, it's highly likely a demon took notice of him."

So that's what happened...

This gave Red trepidation, but he didn't let it show.

Hector sighed. "Most of these pendants cultists carry with them are fake, and even the real ones don't work all the time when establishing connections to the Infernal Realm. However, you just so happened to stumble upon a real one. You're very unlucky, kid."

Somehow, Red felt this had nothing to do with being unlucky. "What does this mean for me, then?"

"It's hard to say. You see, there are many types of demons. Draconic demons in particular are very prone to bouts of anger and violence, so their influence is easily noticeable in other people. If you do end up suffering under one's influence, it won't be hard to notice."

Red winced. "And what can we do about it if something does happen?"

"I will call one of my colleagues," Hector said. "There are actually treatments for demonification in this world. As long as it's detected in the first phase, it can still be cured. So you don't need to lose heart yet—although your situation might be dangerous, it can still be remedied."

He nodded, but that wasn't his real worry. Red had the crimson mist inside his body, which, as far as he understood, actually prevented the demonification from affecting his mind, so even if this demon did try to affect him, perhaps he would be immune to it.

The same couldn't be said for his physical demonification. If Hector's colleague came to treat him and noticed he was already in the second phase of transformation, what would happen to Red? Would they kill him on the spot?

He couldn't let that happen, but he couldn't deny them outright, either.

"I'm feeling fine for now," he said. "But I will inform you if I feel something out of the ordinary."

"Red has excellent control of his mental state," Eiwin said, giving Goulth and Allen a look. "I doubt any sudden changes will pass unnoticed by him."

"R-right." Goulth nodded as her attempt at consoling him seemed to work. He turned to Red. "You are my disciple! No pesky demon will be able to bring you down!"

"Y-yeah!" Allen's expression lit up. "You already fought a demon before! What's one more?!"

Hector cleared his throat, interrupting their encouragement. Everyone turned to him.

"Previously, I was intent on punishing the two of you, but how can I after learning such dire news?" he said. "I wish I could say that you have already learned your lesson, but in truth, the problem is that the punishment is overly severe for your infractions. So instead, let this be a lesson to be more careful about how you approach complete strangers. Demon worshipers hide amongst common people all the time, so one should always be on their guard if they find any strange signs, much more so if they see those dark pendants."

"You're right." Rimold nodded, frowning. "But that isn't all..."

Hector's anger threatened to reignite. "What else did you do?!"

Everyone stared at Rimold and Red.

"Uh..." The rogue hesitated. "I did say we were trying to steal from this merchant. However, we found... Something strange in his possession."

"We found a decapitated head," Red added, cutting to the chase.

"You... You what?!" Hector's face fell.

"We found it in his strongbox," Red explained. "Rimold theorized it might be something they would use in a demonic ritual, but that's when something strange happened."

Red described the experience. How both he and Rimold felt they recognized the face of the desiccated head, and how Rimold felt compelled to touch it before Red stopped him.

By the end, Rimold looked embarrassed.

This time, there was confusion throughout the hall. No one seemed to have any idea what that thing was.

Domeron finally spoke up, shaking his head sadly. "There are all sorts of strange evil items in the world. By your account, it seems as if this 'head' was trying to compel you to touch it. It's not that uncommon for cursed items like these to exist, especially in possession of demonic worshipers."

Rimold cringed, but didn't say anything.

"You said this thing was inside a common strongbox, right?" Goulth asked.

Red nodded. "As far as I could tell, it was made of common steel and there were no traps or special locks to speak of."

"Hm, that is strange." Goulth scratched his beard. "Cursed items like these are generally capable of influencing people even if multiple walls are placed between them. Even if one was only affected by looking at it, I can't imagine what kind of idiot would feel safe locking it away in a common container."

This confused Red too, but he hadn't dared stay too close to the box to investigate it.

"Where did you say you left it?" Hector asked.

"In my hideout by the edge of town," Rimold said.

"At least you kept it hidden." The elder nodded and rose from his chair.

"What do you plan on doing, old man?"

"I will take the box and throw it into the river," Hector said. "It's too dangerous to keep something like that in town, and I don't feel confident in dealing with such a demonic item with only the resources I have on hand."

"Aren't you curious to know what that head is?" Red asked. He hadn't expected Hector to be so eager to get rid of the item.

"Of course I'm curious. But I know better than to meddle in things I neither understand nor am prepared to deal with. It's a useful survival skill, kid. You should try learning it someday."

Hector turned to look at Rimold. "Show me where the hideout is," he said.

Rimold nodded, and soon enough the two of them had left the hall, leaving behind a bewildered Red.

CHAPTER 50

NAMING EVIL

AFTER THE MEETING, Red went back to his room to reflect on what he'd seen in that pendant.

The dark star.

As soon as Red recalled that image, he felt a sharp headache. He gritted his teeth and stopped visualizing it. This time, it wasn't as easy.

The image of that dark star surrounded by the crimson sky lingered in the back of his mind, just like the ephemeral colors that remained in one's vision after staring at a bright light. It took almost a minute for Red to cleanse his mind of it.

I still can't think about it.

Despite that, he now remembered that his memory loss back in the dreamscape of the Infernal Realm was related to that star.

As soon as Red thought back on it, another headache struck.

"Ugh..."

He couldn't help but grunt in frustration and pain. Now that Red knew what caused his short-term amnesia, how could he stop his own thoughts from wandering back to that "thing"? It was instinctive, and trying to fight against it was almost like trying to stop your unconscious breathing. It was nigh impossible.

He had to admit things were better when he couldn't remember it at all.

This won't stop until I clear my doubts.

With no other choice, Red fought through his worsening headache to reflect on what he had learned. First, the dark pendant. It was apparently a portal to the Infernal Realm, and that demon had seen him through it. Red guessed this was what Hector had mentioned—a draconic demon—and that this wasn't the first time he had seen one. The demon in the trial also had lizard-like features. It was likely that the being that noticed him and the demon he'd killed were connected.

More importantly, though, what did any of this have to do with the dark star from his dreams? How was this draconic being connected in any way to that nightmare-inducing celestial body? Why did looking at that lizard eye remind him of it?

Red tried to recall what he'd seen in the depths of the dark star that one time. His eyes widened.

Could it be that I—

Another sharp headache, this time stronger than before. His vision darkened, and the image of the dark star was engraved even deeper in his mind. Red felt as if it were about to hop out of his imagination and take form in the real world.

And who was he to say that wasn't exactly what was happening?

Hector's warnings from earlier echoed in his head.

I have to stop. Red wasn't prepared to deal with this.

He closed his eyes and tried to draw his thoughts away from it. This time, it took ten minutes for the image to disappear from his mind. When it was finally gone, Red let out a sigh of relief.

Almost by instinct, he wondered how he could deal with this problem before he caught himself. If he tried to think about solutions, that was likely to draw the image back to his mind, and he didn't want that to happen.

So I can't even make a plan?

Red grimaced. For someone who meticulously overthought every aspect of his life, this was one of the hardest challenges he had yet faced.

To stop analyzing and contemplating plans and countermeasures and just let this enormous problem be. Was that even possible?

Maybe I should look for something to wipe my memories...

With no other choice, Red lay down on his bed and tried to go to sleep.

His mind, however, often wandered towards the image of the dark star over the course of the night, and a strong headache hit him every time. He didn't know if this was due to some cursed effect or just the result of his curious mind thinking what he shouldn't think. Either way, it was unsustainable.

Red soon gave up on sleeping and instead sat down cross-legged on his bed to meditate with his Radiant Current technique. His mind was wiped clean of any superfluous thoughts, and he concentrated solely on examining his body's condition with his expanded awareness.

This distraction worked, and the image didn't return to his mind while he focused on the technique.

An unknowable amount of time passed in this state before Red heard a knock at the door. The noise broke his concentration. He felt a fluctuation outside.

He frowned, left the bed, and opened the door.

Rimold was waiting for him on the other side, looking troubled.

"S-so..." The man stumbled over his words. "How are you doing?"

Red sighed. "If you're about to invite me on another heist, I'm not interested."

"Hey, there was no way I could have known he was a demon worshiper!" Rimold threw his hands up in defeat. "I know it might not look like it, but most times my jobs don't go this badly."

"And where do you assume it went wrong?"

"Uh... Perhaps I should have done a more thorough investigation into this merchant, but in my defense, this was our only opportunity to strike if we wanted those Spirit Stones."

"And yet there were no Spirit Stones," Red pointed out. "Only a cursed rotten skull."

"Yes, that was indeed the case..." Rimold scratched his head in embarrassment. "That has me very confused too. I'm certain that the information I got about the Spirit Stones was legitimate, and since the merchant did no big purchases with them, I thought it was reasonable to assume he was carrying them on his person. And yet..."

"Could he have been carrying them somewhere else?"

"I don't know," Rimold said. "You were the one in the room. Did you see anything else?"

Red shook his head. "I only found the strongbox in a hidden compartment."

Rimold sighed. "Then there's no point in thinking about it. If he did have another way to hide the Spirit Stones, we couldn't have found it in the short time we had to act."

Red agreed. "Is this all you wanted to talk about?"

The rogue scowled. "Are you telling me to go away?"

"Yes."

"Look, you..." Rimold groaned, but he held his anger back. "Argh, never mind. I brought you something."

He fished something from his pouch and handed it over to Red. A small box.

Red looked at him in bewilderment.

"Just open it!"

Red did so. Inside were three glowing white stones. "Spirit Stones?"

"It's all I can fork over at this moment," Rimold said sheepishly. "I still owe you two more."

Red's brow furrowed in confusion. "Why?"

The rogue snorted. "Because you got screwed over, obviously. We were business partners, and since my lack of information put you in a lot of danger for no reward, it's only reasonable that I repay what you're owed from my own pocket."

"That sounds reasonable."

Rimold frowned. "And? You're not even going to say thank you?"

"Didn't you say this was your repayment? Why should I thank you for it?"

"Ugh, you..." The rogue's eyes twitched. "You're lucky I have a reputation to maintain! Some people out there wouldn't even bother paying you out of pocket if something went wrong!"

Red knew he was right, but then again, the rogue wasn't the one being targeted by yet another demon.

"Oh yeah, Hector wanted me to deliver you a message!"

"Did you get rid of the head?" Red asked.

The man nodded. "We did, but it's not about that..." Rimold trailed off and looked around, suspicious.

"No one is spying on us, if that's what you're worried about."

The rogue sighed in relief. "Hector got some information from Narcha and Rog, as well as from other people. The demon was killed very quickly, but it still managed to take down twelve other people from the inn. Just like what you said in the hall, the demon was also lizard-like..."

Red wasn't surprised to hear this. "Did you figure out where it came from?"

"We did..." Rimold hesitated. "The merchant transformed into it."

"The merchant?"

"Yes. I was confused too. I never heard of any demonic transformation that sudden and fast. Not even Hector knows how it happened. It might be related to the pendant, though, since according to Narcha and Rog, the Baron's men found it in pieces in the room."

Red's mind started to wander towards certain possibilities, but he stopped himself.

No... I can't think about it.

"Is this what Hector wanted to tell me?" Red asked. "Doesn't seem to warrant the secrecy."

"That's not all," Rimold said. "You'll be happy to know that, at least for now, no one knows about your presence in the room. The demon also destroyed almost everything in there, so they can't even tell if something was stolen."

"That is reassuring," Red replied.

"Then there's the bad part... Hector doesn't think that's the only cultist in town."

"How does he know that?"

"The demonic group that attacked the Sect forces at the Skycrown Mountains was also related to the same demon that the merchant worshiped," Rimold explained. "It's too much of a coincidence for someone like the merchant to show up in town right before the horde is about to appear, so Hector thinks that there are probably more already in town or arriving soon."

"You mean they might investigate what happened?"

"Probably. Gustav is going to be the main target of this, since this all happened in a building he owns, but he's more than capable of defending himself. As for the two of us... Well, let's just say we better not wander around town alone if they do find out what happened."

Red understood how severe this was. "There's one thing that's confusing me, though," he said. "How do you know the merchant was related to that demonic group that attacked the Sects?"

"This..." Rimold hesitated. "I don't know for certain, but Hector said it was a fair assumption considering that the merchant transformed into a draconic demon. He said that demon worshipers will always transform into the type of demon they revere and pray to. The demonic cultivators in the Skycrown Mountains also worshiped the same damn type... Probably the same demon too, if I had to guess."

Red frowned. He felt he was getting close to a discovery and he needed to push through. "And what demon is that, exactly?"

Information on demons in the library was scarce, probably because people considered their study to be taboo and a form of temptation. Red's knowledge on the subject, as such, was still rather limited.

Rimold hesitated. "It's not wise to speak too much of Her."

"Her?"

The rogue nodded with some trepidation. "According to legend, She is one of the nine archdemons of the Infernal Realm, and also one of the beings responsible for invading our world thousands of years ago."

Red didn't like where this was heading.

"She has many titles... The Mother of Destruction, the Primordial Calamity, the Dark Sky. The one most people use, though, is the Chaos Dragon."

The boy shivered, a familiar image resurfacing in his head.

The next moment, everything went dark.

CHAPTER 51

TOWARDS THE CASTLE

RED'S DREAM was different this time. Or perhaps it was better to say his dream was normal instead. Images and feelings flashed by that made no sense to him, with only the slightest sliver of conscious thought to interpret them.

He saw himself towering above the world as lands unraveled beneath him. He saw everything crumble to dust, an ocean of blood and destruction washing away everything around him.

He felt helplessness and something he wasn't used to—sorrow. Then these sensations were blown away, and what came to fill their void was rage, unstoppable and insatiable.

So strong, so single-minded in its pursuit of revenge and retribution.

This rage was directed at something or someone at first. This the boy knew. Yet so much time passed—time lost in a fruitless pursuit, an objective that remained just as distant to him as when he first started seeking it.

It consumed him, this anger. So much so that his self was eventually lost in an unbridled sea of pure emotion. There was no longer a reason or aim behind it, no target or morality holding it back.

There was only rage and the desire to destroy, directed at existence itself.

The boy was no longer an individual. He no longer had a name or thoughts of his own.

He became an incarnation of something bigger, more primordial.

He became the end of everything.

The first thing Red felt when he came to was his back lying against a soft mattress. Then, as awareness returned, a lingering headache plagued him.

He stirred in the bed, scrunching his eyes.

"You're awake!" A surprised and relieved voice came from his side.

Red squinted in confusion and looked towards the sound. He saw Eiwin sitting next to his bed, smiling his way.

He frowned, focusing on his crimson sense. He could feel her fluctuation right there, but his detection power was being sluggish, taking longer to process information.

Even when Red was close to death in the past, his crimson sense always stayed fully functioning. This wasn't normal.

Then again, I suppose that much is obvious.

"What happened?" he asked Eiwin.

"Rimold called me after he saw you collapse," she said, wincing. "We put you on your bed and examined your condition, but we couldn't find anything wrong with you. You were just sleeping. It looked like you had just suddenly fallen asleep from exhaustion, but considering recent events, I was worried something beyond my understanding might have happened to you."

She wasn't wrong about that.

"Did you ask Hector to examine me?"

Eiwin shook her head. "Rimold wanted to call him, but I convinced him not to. We agreed that if you didn't awaken by the time the sun was up, we would tell Master Hector."

Red looked out of the window. The faintest traces of sunlight were coming through.

He nodded at Eiwin. "Thank you."

The last thing he wanted was for Hector to go snooping around his body. What if he found out about his healed acupoint and the being living inside his body? How would Red explain himself then?

Eiwin had proven yet again to be the most conscientious and considerate person he had ever known. She wasn't privy to most of his secrets, and yet she still respected his privacy and knew how important it was to him.

"It's nothing to worry about." She shook her head, her smile returning.

"If you had worse symptoms, then I would have asked Master Hector for help, but you looked fine, so I opted to wait. It seems I was right... Or was I?" She looked at Red with questioning eyes.

"I'm fine. Just a small headache."

Eiwin sighed in relief. "That's good. However, you must tell us if you feel anything strange, whether it's in your body or in your mind. Even experienced cultivators can't always predict how matters involving demons will develop, so we need to react to anything out of place with utmost urgency."

If only she knew...

"I'll let you know if I need help." He chose his words deliberately, and it didn't go unnoticed by Eiwin.

She hesitated for a moment before accepting. "Good. Then I'll be leaving you to rest." She made to get up.

"Wait," Red called out. "The meeting tomorrow... Or rather, today, with the Baron. Is it still happening?"

"It is. If anything, what happened with the demon yesterday only made the need for a meeting even more urgent. Of course, considering what happened to you, you don't need to come, should you not wish to."

He frowned. "Is that what Hector said?"

She grinned. "No, but I'm sure he will understand."

"I'll go."

Eiwin was unsurprised. "I will let the others know about it."

With that, she left the room, closing the door behind her. Red was alone again with his own thoughts, as well as the images from his dream.

No. I can't do that again...

He distracted himself by reading a book on the table. It seemed to work, and for many hours after, his mind didn't linger near the forbidden thoughts and memories, until eventually he had subconsciously thrown them to the back of his mind.

A few hours later, Red was called to meet with Hector in the main hall.

When he got there, Hector, Eiwin, and Allen were already waiting for him. The young master waved at him excitedly.

"I really can't wait for it!" Allen said. "I've never been part of a war council! I have some ideas that I want to—"

Hector cut him off. "You're not allowed to speak."

"What?!" Allen's eyes widened. "Then what's the point?"

"You will only go there to listen and learn," Hector said. "If you embarrass me in front of the Baron, I'll punish you myself when we get back to the Sect."

Allen frowned but bowed his head in defeat. "Fine."

Satisfied, Hector looked over at Red. "There are some things you should know before we go."

Red was surprised. "There are?"

"Of course. I don't intend for you to speak, but you should know Gustav is going to be there too. This is the first time you will meet with him, and since I know that bastard very well, I'm certain he'll try to speak to you to find out what kind of person you are. You must not answer his provocations, or any of his questions at all if possible, for that matter."

"I can do that."

"Good." Hector waved his hand towards the door. "Then we're off."

The group walked out of the Sect with the elder in the lead. As soon as they arrived at the main town streets, their whole surroundings became abuzz.

"It's the old man from the Water Dragon Sect!"

"It's the third time he's appeared out in public this year!"

"Do you think this has to do with the demon? Is another demon invasion coming?"

"I heard that the Sects fought with demonic cultivators at the Skycrown Mountains!"

Red continued to hear speculation and rumors as he walked through the streets. Most of the townsfolk's attention fell on Hector, but he felt quite a few gazes on him. It made him uncomfortable.

He could also tell through his crimson sense that these people were all anxious, which was understandable after what had happened yesterday. Yet in all their hubbub, one term continued to come up.

Red turned to Eiwin. "This demon invasion they're talking about... Should we be worried about it?"

This was yet another topic that wasn't available in the Sect's library. All he knew was that some thousands of years ago, a horde of demons invaded the world and almost wiped human life from its surface.

Eiwin shook her head. "Demonic worshipers have always been active since time immemorial. A demon appearing in the middle of town is hardly an indicator that another demon invasion is upon us."

Hector snorted. "Mortals' memories are too short-lived. Sometimes decades go by without any major appearances from demonic cultivators, and yet at the first sign of their presence, they believe it is a presage of the apocalypse. Those fiends have committed much greater atrocities in the past. Ambushing a couple of Sect forces is barely worth mentioning in our long history."

"But how can you be sure this time it's not for real?" Allen asked.

"Bah, do you know the first thing about the demon invasion, brat?!" Hector glared at the young master. "They established a connection to the Infernal Realm, a damn portal capable of crossing dimensions! People from the other side of the world saw the aftereffects of this phenomenon long before it was completed, so do you think it would go unnoticed this time around?"

"Uh... What if they're building it in secret? How can you be so sure they haven't found another way to do it?"

Hector was about to admonish him again before he paused. "That's... a surprisingly good question for someone like you."

"Really?" Allen looked surprised.

The elder grunted. "It is a valid concern, but you have to think clearly. How can they hide a portal to another world? Even if it's created in utmost secrecy, the Sects still have their ways to detect disturbances in space, and demons don't tend to be particularly stealthy, either. Not to mention, such an endeavor would probably require an enormous amount of resources, which I doubt those demon cultivators could move without being noticed."

"If that's the case," Red asked, "what do they want from attacking the Sects?"

"To undermine their forces, of course." Hector lowered his head. "Long gone are the times where demonic cultivators could act openly in the world. Now they are hunted down if the slightest sign of their presence is made known, so they stick to the shadows and search for opportunities to expand their influence. This obviously means that Sects are often taken by surprise when these demonic cultivators decide to act, but trust me, it is a much preferable state of affairs to when they had the strength to act in the open."

The elder explained further as they walked through the streets, oblivious to the gazes of the townsfolk. Red, on the other hand, now knew he had even more reasons to hide his demonic tendencies.

They continued to move up the hilly town, on a path that Red had seldom traveled before. The buildings became scarcer, leaving only the ruins of the temple that once stood in this place.

At the top of the hill was a large castle, an amalgamation of different kinds of building materials that stood as the symbol of the town of Fordham-Bestrem. The Baron's castle.

Red saw a contingent of guards waiting for them at the gate, and he sensed many others just inside with his crimson sense. He even felt three presences in the Lesser Ring Realm.

Hector looked back at them. "Remember—do not embarrass me."

The elder left these warning words behind before stepping forward.

CHAPTER 52
THE MEETING

THE GUARDS OPENED the large wooden gate before them, revealing a lavish patio inside. Unlike the castle's outside, everything in this courtyard was elegantly adorned, more befitting nobility as Red imagined them.

In the garden on each side of the paved path, unfamiliar flowers were bathed in the sunlight. Finely crafted stone statues of angelic figures dotted each corner of the patio, and even a few paintings hung off the walls. The path leading into the castle split further along, leading to many rooms and constant flows of servants and guards weaving in and out.

This courtyard alone was bigger than their Sect grounds, and Red knew even more awaited him further inside.

Allen grinned at him. "It's amazing, isn't it? Just looking at it from a distance doesn't do it justice. I hear the King's castle in the capital is even bigger than—"

Hector cleared his throat, glaring at Allen. The young master fell reluctantly silent.

An elegant servant, flanked by two guards, approached them inside.

The man bowed towards the elder. "The Baron is honored to welcome you to his castle, Master Hector."

He spoke reverently, yet his expression remained cold.

Hector grunted. "We both know the Baron wouldn't invite me here if there wasn't an emergency." He scrutinized the place. "Is everyone else already here?"

"Sir Gustav is already waiting inside the meeting hall," the servant replied, unbothered by his remark. "Would you like me to show you the way?"

Hector nodded. "No point in waiting."

"Then please. If you would follow me."

The two guards stepped aside, clearing a path, and the servant led Red and the others towards the large central building of the castle. Red was still looking everywhere, taking everything in, but above all else, he was paying attention to his crimson sense.

He counted more than a hundred people in this castle alone. Their fluctuations told him that these people, mostly servants and guards, were carrying themselves with a sense of urgency and concern. Red could make a good guess as to why.

Some people even looked at Hector with a degree of fear, which was extended to the other Sect members.

They were led through a long stone corridor, at the end of which two guards waited beside a large wooden door. The servant bowed and stepped aside, looking back at Hector.

"The Baron is waiting for you inside," he said.

Hector grunted and walked forward.

The guards pushed the door open, revealing a huge chamber. Light from a crystal chandelier hit them first, illuminating a room rich with lavish paintings depicting majestic creatures unfamiliar to Red's eyes. Beneath it stood an enormous round table, on which sat all sorts of foods and ornaments.

Red couldn't pay attention to any of it, though, since as soon as they entered the chamber, multiple gazes were thrown their way by the people at the table.

"Ah, so the old man finally deigns to grace us with his presence!" a loud and vibrant voice said.

An overweight man sat on the right side of the table, staring at Hector with a wide smile on his unblemished and rotund face. He wore sumptuous clothing, the style one might expect from a merchant except made much more extravagant, as jewels occupied almost every spot on his person. Most of all, he carried himself with a confidence and astuteness that befitted the best of con men, a type Red had become familiar with since arriving in this town.

It took little thought for Red to figure out that this was Gustav.

Red's attention shifted towards the two sitting at his sides. They wore plain white masks hiding their whole faces, and unlike Gustav, they sported sets of scale armor not unlike what Red had seen people from the Adventurer's Guild use.

The one on Gustav's left was a muscular man who towered over everyone else even from his sitting position. He must have been even bigger than Goulth—a first for Red. The person to Gustav's right didn't call as much attention to herself, being average in build with a reserved air. By simple observation, one couldn't discern her gender, but Red could tell through his crimson sense that she was a woman.

Both were in the Lesser Ring Realm.

Hector snorted. "I deliberately arrived late to avoid hearing your loud chewing."

Gustav laughed. "Oh, then I'm afraid you've failed! I've been waiting for you before digging into this feast!"

To underline his point, the merchant grabbed a chicken leg and took a massive bite, not breaking eye contact with Hector the whole time. The elder twitched in anger and looked ready to retaliate before the sound of a clearing throat interrupted him.

"Please, gentlemen," a man sitting at the head of the table said. "If you despise each other's presence so much, then you shouldn't extend this meeting with petty discussions."

This middle-aged man had a serene expression and sported short, glistening dark hair and a beard speckled with gray along its length. He wore fine dark-crimson clothing decorated with fine golden threads and a coat of arms depicting what looked like a mountain on his chest. His getup didn't seem as fancy as Gustav's, and yet the way he carried himself with such nobility and composure said it all.

This was the Baron, and to Red's surprise, the third fluctuation in the Lesser Ring Realm he felt belonged to this man.

Hector groaned. "You're right, Feron, but do not presume I will stand by and take in silence every insult this rogue throws at me."

Gustav laughed again. "Insult? We both know that if anyone so much as breathed too loud in your vicinity, you would take it as an insult!"

The elder glared at the guildmaster.

"Please, Hector," the Baron said. "Sit, so we may end this as soon as possible."

Hector quietly walked towards the free chairs on the other side of the room. Red and the others followed and sat beside him. Eiwin sat down calmly while Allen couldn't help but peer around, clearly affected by the heavy atmosphere.

He looked as if he wanted to speak to Red, but he caught himself.

"I see you've brought a few of your Sect members, Hector," Gustav said as he examined the group through narrowed eyes. His gaze lingered on Red. "I don't believe I recognize this one, though..."

"He's a new member," Hector said with a frown.

Gustav beamed, not shifting his gaze from Red. "Ah, is that so? I do feel like I recognize him, now that you mention it. Say, aren't you the little thief that has been stealing from me over the last year?"

The atmosphere changed. Hector's frown deepened, but he didn't respond. Much to Red's dismay, everyone's attention shifted to him, including the unfriendly eyes of Gustav's two bodyguards, felt even from underneath their masks.

He didn't panic and returned the guildmaster's gaze. He already expected Gustav to know about this, since Reinhart had already told Red as much.

He examined the man's mocking expression, a face that dared Red to respond, to lose his composure in front of the Baron by denying this accusation and embarrassing Hector.

Red didn't fall for it, so instead, he just agreed. "Yes, that's me."

Gustav looked bewildered, and the two bodyguards gave Red murderous glares. Hector twitched while both Allen and Eiwin stared at him, stunned.

An awkward silence followed until the Baron cleared his throat once more. "We should move on to the subject matter."

"You're right." Hector nodded, sparing an angry glance out of the corner of his eye for Red.

No one protested, not even Gustav. He was still staring at Red, but the gaze of provocation had changed to one of curiosity.

Gustav nodded with a smile. "You're correct, Baron. We should move on —but not before I eat a bit!"

He turned his attention to his plate, digging in with unexpected savagery. Hector stared at him with disgust, then turned to the Baron.

"What of the demon?" the elder asked. "Did you find out anything else about it?"

The Baron shook his head. "Nothing yet. We learned that the merchant had one more bodyguard looking after his carriage, but we didn't find him at the scene. He must have fled as soon as he noticed what happened."

Red's interest was piqued.

"Do you know where the merchant is from?" Hector asked.

"According to the documents Gustav provided, he should be from Illion, across the river."

Hector winced. "That's rather far."

The Baron sighed. "Indeed, and it will take us a while to get any information from them. And longer than usual, considering the horde is just about to hit us."

"Me and my guild can help you with the investigations, my dear Baron," Gustav interjected. "Of course, it will still take a while to receive information back, but we have more important matters to worry about right now, don't we?"

"More important than a demon appearing in the middle of town?" Hector said. "Aren't you just trying to avoid responsibility?"

The demon had appeared inside Gustav's Adventurer's Guild, after all.

"Oh, don't be like that, Hector." Gustav smiled ruefully. "Do you truly think I had anything to do with a demon appearing inside my own establishment and killing some of my trusted clientele? I would expect you to know better than that."

Hector snorted, but didn't reply. It was hard to imagine that Gustav would jeopardize his own reputation like this. Red knew better, since he was aware that Gustav had a habit of stealing from his own clients, but he couldn't reveal that to Hector, as he'd promised to keep Rimold's secret.

The Baron explained what they had learned from the demon and the merchant's belongings, information Red already knew. So instead, he scanned the chamber more carefully.

He hadn't paid much attention to it before, absorbed as he was, but there was a guard placed near each corner of the room, standing in perfect posture and complete silence. He was impressed that they kept such a solid composure, but he could tell through their fluctuations that inside they were also in a state of turmoil.

Red counted five guards with his crimson sense, but just when he was about to return his attention to the table, it hit him.

Five guards?

Since when did a square room have five corners? He looked around once again. He counted only four guards, and not a single other individual in the room.

How is that possible?

A shiver ran through him as he looked towards where he had felt this strange fifth fluctuation. It was right there, behind the Baron. Yet when he looked, he saw nothing but empty air.

He knew better than to doubt his crimson sense, so he arrived at a conclusion.

There was an invisible person inside this room.

CHAPTER 53
THE INVISIBLE MAN

RED'S EYES didn't linger on the spot where he'd felt this invisible being's presence. Instead, his focus returned to the meeting.

Is this one of the Baron's men?

Perhaps a hidden bodyguard—although when he thought about it further, the idea made little sense. Red hadn't noticed this fluctuation before because it was rather weak next to those of the Lesser Ring cultivators in the room, comparable to the fluctuations of the castle guards.

Would someone as strong as the Baron need that kind of weak protector?

No, I can't be hasty with my conclusions.

How could Red presume there were no ways to trick his crimson sense? That kind of overconfidence could spell his doom one day if he misjudged an enemy's strength.

Of course, there was another possibility. Maybe this invisible person was a spy. In which case Red needed to warn Hector about it.

He looked towards the elder without turning his head. Hector didn't seem to have noticed anything out of the ordinary. And Red didn't feel comfortable whispering in his ear, since he was in a room filled with people with superhuman hearing.

He needed a different approach.

Red poked Eiwin in the arm. She was taken by surprise, shooting Red a quizzical gaze.

"Do you have pen and paper?" he whispered.

Still confused, she nodded and reached for her pouch.

Eiwin handed him a small, leather-bound journal, accompanied by a special quill that, as Red had learned, could store ink in its tip that did not dry for months.

He took the items and mumbled, "Thank you."

His small interaction didn't go unnoticed, but the others didn't spare him a second glance and kept talking. More importantly, Red didn't feel the invisible fluctuation stir.

He opened the journal, flipped past several ledger-like entries, and reached a blank page. With the quill, he wrote a short sentence.

Then he turned to Hector, poking the elder in his arm when he wasn't speaking. The old man gave him a questioning frown, but didn't say anything.

Red handed him the journal under the table. Hector's eyes flicked down at the words.

There's an invisible person behind the Baron.

His expression didn't change. Red didn't know if this was because he wasn't surprised or because he was simply hiding it.

Hector extended his hand towards Red. The boy handed him the quill. He wrote in the journal before handing it back and refocusing on the meeting.

There was another short sentence.

Ignore it for now.

Red's face likewise didn't react. He could feel Eiwin silently paying attention to the whole interaction, so he handed the journal and quill back to her.

She read the two sentences, and a slight twitch in her eyebrows was all she showed before stowing the diary away. Red trusted Eiwin not to give away their discovery, and his trust was well-placed, it seemed.

Of course, this interaction didn't escape the eyes of Gustav.

He smiled at them. "Are your students passing you secret messages in the middle of a meeting, Hector?"

The elder snorted. "They were wondering how someone can fit that much food inside them."

Gustav laughed merrily before taking another bite of the bread.

The Baron massaged his temples. "Please, gentlemen. We were so close to arriving at a solution."

The guildmaster shrugged. "Isn't the solution obvious? We can try investigating all we want, but if anyone can dig out any demon worshipers out of hiding, it's the Sect cultivators."

"I have already informed the Crystal Sky Sect embassy in the capital," the Baron said. "Unfortunately, they are already stretched thin as it is with the horde, so they can't really send any demon specialists for the foreseeable future."

Red couldn't help but feel relieved.

"That might be so," Gustav said, "but don't we have someone in this room with some connections to a Sect that can help?"

He looked over at Hector. This time, the Baron didn't admonish him.

Hector frowned, and his fluctuation flared with anger.

"Is this the reason you called me here?" he said. "To ask me for a favor?"

"You know that is not true, Hector," the Baron said. "We had already scheduled this meeting before the demon accident... But yes, I did mean to ask for your help."

Hector grunted, bristling. "You know damn well I'm not part of that Sect any longer. When will it get through your thick skulls that I don't want to have to ask anything of them?"

Red frowned. Didn't the old man already promise him he would ask a friend for help with Red's potential demonification?

More theatrics.

The Baron nodded seriously. "I know that, Hector, but I wouldn't ask if it wasn't absolutely necessary. We will be dealing with a monster horde over the next few weeks, and that will leave our town vulnerable against attacks from the inside. If any demon worshipers choose to act during that time, we might not be able to stop them."

"Come on, Hector!" Gustav cried. "This is for your Sect's own good! You know it to be true!"

Hector glared at the guildmaster in silence. Of course, since Gustav was the one most affected by the demon accident, he stood to gain the most from a thorough investigation. Still, Red knew he had a point. The only problem was that none of this worked in Hector's favor.

"... I will ask," Hector said finally, after some consideration. "But don't hold your breath. You know that what remains of my old Sect is barely a fraction of its former power, so they might not be able to send anyone over that quickly either."

Gustav grinned, raising a wine glass. "I'm sure if the Great Elder Hector puts on his charm, tons of cultivators will stumble over themselves to fulfill his wishes."

Hector scowled, but stayed quiet.

Red was surprised at how tamely he was behaving. Was this out of respect for the Baron or because he knew he couldn't hurt Gustav? Was he afraid of those two bodyguards?

Red turned to them. The bodyguards had yet to speak a word throughout the entire meeting, sitting like statues by Gustav's sides. Red could tell by their fluctuations that neither of them were as strong as Hector. If anyone in the room could even slightly compare, it was the Baron, and even then, he was still a ways behind.

Red doubted Hector would be afraid of them.

There was still that one additional presence he was paying attention to, but nothing indicated any emotional distress in the invisible person, at least nothing that he could feel.

What are they doing here?

The Baron nodded towards Hector with a genuine smile. "Thank you, Hector. The town and I will not forget this favor."

The elder grunted.

"Since this matter is settled, we can move on to the original reason I sought to gather you here in the first place," the man said, his face becoming severe. "As you all have been made aware, the horde has already reached the borders of our province. Scouts tell us that they might reach the river in three days at most."

Every person in the chamber tensed.

The Baron continued. "I have already sent messages to the surrounding villages to evacuate with utmost urgency, so over the next couple of days, we will see a large influx of refugees. Gustav has also offered to help the evacuation efforts."

Gustav bowed slightly. "It's my pleasure to serve you, Baron."

The man returned the gesture with a nod. "Although we are evacuating all settlements beyond and around the river, my plans are to hold the horde at the river line and use the terrain to our advantage."

Hector frowned. "That sounds very optimistic. Do you already know what monsters we're dealing with?"

"The first wave is an assortment of mountain monsters," the Baron said.

"My men say they number in the hundreds, with a dozen or so at the Lesser Ring Realm. A force to be reckoned with, for sure, but nothing we haven't managed to defeat in the past."

Now Gustav looked concerned, leaning over the table. "You mean there's another wave behind it?"

"Indeed. The next wave is what worries me. It's a pack of Skycrown Wolves."

Red recognized the name. Weren't those the monsters he'd fought in the trial?

The atmosphere became heavier, and Gustav paled.

"H-how many?" he stuttered.

"Around three hundred or so... but that's not all..." The Baron hesitated.

"Hundreds?!" Gustav's eyes widened. "What could be worse than hundreds of fearsome pack monsters?"

"They're led by a Greater Ring Realm alpha."

The merchant almost choked out of shock, entering a coughing fit. The bodyguards shifted on their chairs, ready to help their boss, but he waved them off.

"I-I'm fine! I'm fine!" Gustav said, recovering. "No, wait! I'm not fine! How are we supposed to hold off a pack of Skycrown Wolves led by a Greater Ring Realm monster? We need to ask for help!"

"You know that isn't possible," the Baron told him. "Our province isn't the only place where the horde is attacking, and we are not even facing the worst of it. The kingdom can't afford to spare us reinforcements."

"So what do you suggest we do?" Gustav slammed the table. "Can any of us kill a monster like that?!"

The Baron didn't respond, looking towards Hector instead.

The elder snorted. "You know I'm not at the Greater Ring Realm. I can't kill a beast like that."

"Maybe not in direct confrontation, no. Yet there is no one else in the province more qualified than you to hold the monster's attention and remain alive. That much I know you can do."

"And what would you have me do? Distract it forever?"

"Until we can defeat the pack itself, yes. When that is done, we will reinforce you with utmost haste and dispose of their leader. Won't we, Gustav?"

Gustav nodded frantically. "Y-yes, yes! I will send all my men to assist you, so please, gods save you, Elder Hector!" He held his hands together and bowed towards Hector, as if worshiping him.

A wide smile appeared on the old man's face. "I suppose if no one else can do it, then I have to act."

The guildmaster sighed in relief.

"But I have some conditions," Hector said.

For the first time, anger flashed across Gustav's face.

CHAPTER 54

CONTRACT

THE DISPLEASURE that simmered behind Gustav's face disappeared in an instant. He continued to smile amicably. "And might I ask what these conditions might be?"

Hector grinned. "I want fifty Spirit Stones."

Gustav slammed his fist on the table. "Go to hell, you greedy bastard! If I had fifty Spirit Stones, do you think I would be in here asking for your help?!"

"I'm sure that your guild has that much," Hector laughed.

"Forget it, old man! They're never going to give me that much money, and even if they did, your help isn't worth it!" Gustav looked at the Baron. "I would rather just abandon the town, if this is how things are going to be!"

The Baron frowned. "Please, Hector, you have to be reasonable. If you wish for Spirit Stones as compensation, they can be provided, but even if I sold my entire castle, I would still be hard-pressed to provide you with fifty."

Hector grunted. "Fine. It would be remiss of me to be so greedy in a time of need for our town, but I still have other conditions that mostly concern our merchant friend here and my Sect."

"The number of Spirit Stones I can provide you is limited!" Gustav protested.

"I said nothing more about Spirit Stones." Hector shook his head, turning to the Baron. "You know my main concern is always the future of my Sect and its safety. By going to face such a powerful monster by myself, not only am I putting my own life at risk, but also the safety of my Sect and its members, since I won't be there to protect them. I need guarantees that they will be looked after during this time if something happens to me."

"You need not even ask that, my friend," the Baron said. "You act in service of the town, and I would not suffer anything happening to your people if you were to be wounded during that time."

"I trust you, Baron. However, this is something that I need to hear from another person too before I have peace of mind."

Gustav grimaced. "Do I look that unreasonable to you? I would not stoop so low as to take advantage of this situation."

"So you say," Hector sneered, "yet be that as it may, what about after the horde is dealt with? Will you still keep your promise?"

The guildmaster didn't respond, his face turning ugly.

"As I said, I know you too well, you fat bastard. If you want my help, I want you to make an official contract for me. It's the only way I know someone like you will keep your word."

Gustav narrowed his eyes. "What terms are you suggesting?"

Hector smiled. "It's simple. On top of not acting against any of my Sect members, you are to provide all of them with the necessary resources for training for the next five years."

The guildmaster remained skeptical. "I will not just agree to an arbitrary value."

"We can settle on something after doing calculations for each individual in our Sect," Hector said. "Trust me, though, when I say that I expect you to be willing to part with more than just the bare minimum."

Gustav scratched his chin. Ten seconds later, he nodded. "As long as the value is not detrimental to my business, I can provide it. It's only reasonable that I'd be willing to fork out that much if you were to be wounded."

Hector laughed. "Who said anything about being wounded? Those are my terms if everything goes well and I am able to return unscathed."

"What?!" Gustav's eyes widened. "You want me to just sponsor the growth of your Sect while you're still around?"

"I'm still not finished with my terms. If something does happen to me that prevents me from protecting my Sect, I want those terms extended to ten years instead of just five."

"Ten years?! I'm not even sure if I'll still be in this town in five years, much less ten!"

That surprised Red too. Ten years happened to be the elder's higher estimate of how long it would take Allen to open his Spiritual Sea.

"That's why I expect you to sign this contract in the name of your guild. That way, anyone that comes to replace you will still be obligated to fulfill it," Hector said. "I know you have the authority to do that much, at least."

Red was expecting Gustav to protest these terms, but to his surprise, the man fell silent with a sour look. An inner struggle was clearly evident on his face.

Almost half a minute later, though, Gustav sighed. "Let me see your numbers."

Although no reaction could be seen through their masks, the fluctuations of his two bodyguards trembled in surprise.

Hector grinned over at Eiwin, who pulled a handful of documents from her pouch. He grabbed them before waving his hand, sending the papers magically flying to settle right in front of Gustav.

The guildmaster took the papers and, hesitantly, began reading them. His eyebrows twitched a handful of times over the course of a few minutes.

Gustav sighed and handed the smaller bodyguard the documents. "Go back to our headquarters and tell them to draft the contract according to his terms."

Red could feel the reluctance in the bodyguard even without his crimson sense.

"Just do as I say, will you?!" Gustav cried through his teeth.

The bodyguard bowed, and the guards posted at the door let her out.

"It might take my men about an hour to write the contract up," Gustav said. "I want them to be thorough when it comes to these matters."

"That's fine." Hector grinned. "We can wait."

The Baron, who had been observing the interaction in silence, spoke up. "Then I assume this means you agree to our plan?"

Hector nodded. "Yes, I will deal with the big wolf for you."

"What about the rest of your Sect members? They would be of utmost help out there against the horde too."

"Hmm, I'll send a group too. However, I expect our friend here to remember that the terms of our contract should extend even outside of town."

Gustav's eyes twitched.

"I'm sure it will be no problem," the Baron said. "Such being the case, we should discuss the distribution of our forces."

The next hour was spent determining their strategy against the horde. As it so happened, a mob of angry monsters displaced from their homes wasn't so easily held back, and even if they planned to hold them at the river, there was no guarantee that they would be successful, so they needed to be prepared to retreat.

Not to mention the other effects of such a horde. It would devastate the local fauna, with monsters and animals still recovering from the trial. Some of the monsters might even join the horde's forces, bolstering their numbers. Others would be outright killed by the rampaging beasts.

They estimated that the forest wouldn't recover from the impacts of this stampede for many years to come. Yet in the grand scheme of the cultivation world, this wasn't all that uncommon.

Monsters too increased in strength, and the birth of a particularly powerful beast could, and most likely would, cause enormous disruptions in a biome. A territorial monster, for instance, could force local creatures to migrate elsewhere.

Displaced and deprived of their previous homes, these beasts would be driven into a rage. Sometimes they were led by other powerful beasts that had lost territorial disputes. This was the origin of hordes—monsters driven into desperation—and those were not uncommon either.

Nothing short of slaughter would stop them, and although many cultivators lamented that fact, this was still something they needed to do, or else the destruction could spread and threaten the human population.

Red also thought it was a shame they needed to massacre these monsters. Like many cultivators, he didn't hold a grudge against them, and he rather admired them for their special abilities that allowed them to thrive in nature. Yet sparing and relocating them wasn't an option either.

"My two bodyguards will be on the front line," Gustav said. "They will help kill any Lesser Ring Realm beasts that appear."

Hector snorted. "You would be willing to give up on your protection for the sake of the town?"

Gustav glared at him. "Yes, and unlike you, I won't be asking for compensation!"

Ignoring him, Hector asked, "What about you, Feron? Will you be joining the front line?"

"It would be negligent of me not to. We will need every Lesser Ring cultivator on the front if we hope to hold back these monsters."

Hector frowned. "Even they won't necessarily be safe out there."

"Your worry is misplaced in me, Hector," the Baron told him. "I have seen my fair share of battles in the past, even if it doesn't look like it, given my position. It's you that I am worried about. Even against a mindless monster, the difference in realms is something any cultivator would struggle to contend against."

"I can't claim to be able to kill it, but I have some tricks up my sleeve," Hector assured him. If I only need to distract it, then it shouldn't be a problem. However, if we do plan to kill it, we will need to be willing to spend no small amount of resources."

"There's no need to worry," the Baron said. "Once the other threats are dealt with, I have my own plans on how to deal with the alpha."

He refused to elaborate, leaving the rest of them confused. Still, neither Hector nor Gustav decided to press him about it, showing their trust in the Baron.

Right around this time, the bodyguard Gustav sent out returned to the meeting hall, carrying a stack of papers. One half she handed to the guildmaster and the other she gave to Hector.

Gustav didn't even bother reading his copy of the contract before signing it. Hector, however, read every line of the document with the utmost caution. A few minutes later, he even handed the document over to Eiwin for her to check.

Gustav frowned. "We don't have all day, you know!"

Hector didn't respond. Finally, Eiwin handed the contract back to Hector. "It is all in order," she said.

He smiled and likewise signed his own copy. He then exchanged documents with Gustav before they both set down their own signatures again. In this manner, they each had their own copy of the contract with both of the signatures. Neither Gustav nor Hector would be able to walk it back now.

The elder smiled widely once the deal was done. "It is always a pleasure doing business with you, Gustav."

CHAPTER 55

PREPARING FOR THE WORST

"THEN WE ARE SETTLED." The Baron looked over at Hector. "When are you planning on leaving, Hector?"

"Tomorrow morning at the latest," he said. "I need to settle some things within my Sect first. I'll be sending Domeron to coordinate things with your men tomorrow."

"Good. Then, with fate permitting, we shall triumph over this horde with no accidents or loss of lives."

After that, the Baron shared more details with Gustav and Hector. He provided them with communication talismans and decided where they would meet on the morrow. Orvin, the captain of the guard, would coordinate their defensive efforts while the Baron and Gustav's two bodyguards would act independently, ready to move wherever their powers were required.

They exchanged pleasantries before the Baron dismissed the meeting. Hector was the first at the door, with Red and the other Sect members following. Red took one final look back at the room, sensing that the invisible person's fluctuation was still there.

Still, he didn't let his gaze linger. Red planned on following Hector's advice on this matter, and he wouldn't mention this strange presence until the elder brought it up.

They soon left the castle and were back in the streets of town again.

Allen, who had been strangely quiet the entire meeting, gave Hector a worried look.

"You're not really going to put yourself in danger, are you?" he asked.

"Of course I am, it's what I agreed to."

"B-but what if the monster is too strong even for you?"

Hector shrugged. "It's entirely possible, but you shouldn't worry about it. If the monster is too powerful even for me, I don't intend to risk my life for a lost cause."

Allen frowned. "What will happen to the town then?"

"Nothing will happen to the town even if we lose against the horde," Hector explained. "The Baron has his own methods of defending this place. However, if we lose, it's likely that we'll be stuck inside the town for gods know how long until the Sects can send someone to get rid of that wolf."

Allen nodded, his confidence raised.

Hector continued through the streets as if nothing else had happened. Red studied him, trying to get his attention.

The elder shook his head. "Not now."

Red didn't say anything else. Very likely, Hector was worried about being heard even after they left the castle. He focused on his crimson sense, worried this invisible person could be following them, but the familiar presence wasn't nearby.

Since they couldn't talk about this right now, Red decided to ask about something else on his mind. "Why are you so confident Gustav will follow the contract's terms?"

"Because of the faction behind him," Hector stated. "You see, merchants like him are all backstabbing bastards, and yet how could they be successful in this world with such horrible reputations? No one would want to make deals with them and they wouldn't be able to conduct any business."

Red hadn't considered that before. "You mean the contracts are their assurance?"

Hector nodded. "His faction even encourages such skullduggery, and yet they have the inviolable rule that every one of its members should and will fulfill all the terms in any contract they sign of their own volition. Members that try to avoid these responsibilities are punished and most of the time expelled from the faction. It's the only way they can keep their reputation in the world and be so successful."

"What is this faction, exactly?"

321

"They're called the Golden Prestige Guild."

Soon enough, they were back on their Sect's street and away from the prying eyes of the townspeople. Hector froze and sent Red a questioning gaze.

"I sense no one."

"Good." Hector nodded gravely. "Then we need to talk."

"Huh?" Allen stared at the elder. "The Sect is right there! Why do we need to talk right outside?"

"We can't be sure there's no one else spying on us in there," Hector explained, "so it's safer to do it out here."

Allen paled. "There are spies in the Sect?"

"It's entirely possible, which is why it's better to be safe." Hector looked back at Red. "Now, tell me, what exactly did you sense?"

"A single individual in the meeting room," Red said. "They were standing behind the Baron the entire time without moving. At first I thought they were one of the guards."

"Wait!" Allen cried. "I'm sure there was no one behind the Baron!"

"That's the problem," Red pointed out. "I saw no one there either, but I'm certain I felt someone there with my powers."

"So they were invisible?"

"It's not that simple," Hector interjected. "It's more than just invisibility."

It was Red's turn to be confused. "What do you mean?"

"I have a technique that allows me to scout my surroundings using my Spiritual Energy," Hector said. "It works similarly to the echolocation of certain monsters. I send out a wave of energy into my surroundings and they bounce back to me, giving me an accurate layout of the closed space I'm in. It's nowhere near as powerful as the Spiritual Sense of cultivators in the Spirit Core Realm, but it's extremely useful in detecting hidden and invisible presences."

Eiwin frowned. "But you didn't detect anything there?"

"That's correct. I have a habit of using it in any place I stay for more than just a few minutes, and I had already used it even before the kid told me about the invisible presence. I'm certain there was no one there behind the Baron."

This revelation shocked everyone. Red even began to question himself and the accuracy of his crimson sense.

Could it be that there's something interfering with my power? After yesterday's incident, and the slowing of his sense, Red couldn't discount it.

Hector sensed his doubt. "I'm not questioning the veracity of your claim, kid. I don't know exactly how your power works, but I do know that there are plenty of techniques out there that can fool my own detection methods. The only issue is that for that to happen, the individual in question would most certainly be a high-level cultivator. At the very least, higher than me."

Red sighed. Back then, this invisible individual seemed no more powerful than a normal guard, but he couldn't trust what he felt so easily.

"W-wait!" Allen's eyes widened. "Could that have been one of those demonic cultivators?"

"We can't say for certain, but we have to consider the possibility," Hector said. "It could also be a cultivator sent by another Sect to spy on us or to keep things in order. They always had a habit of being secretive."

"There's also another possibility," Eiwin said. "This could just be a weaker individual armed with a treasure that can fool people's senses. Maybe they were even there under the Baron's own orders."

Hector grunted. "Hm... That could be true too, but even then, the mere fact someone could possess a treasure like that means their background is not to be underestimated, regardless of their power. In any case, I have the distinct feeling that this coming battle will not be as straightforward as it seems..."

Eiwin looked worried. "Do you think other forces might take this opportunity to attack us?"

He nodded. "What better occasion than when we're occupied fighting against a ravenous horde of monsters? Too many forces have remained quiet in this region for months already. The Empire—whose envoys remain in the capital for negotiations—Ricard, the demonic cultivators, the Cursebreakers, even that bloody necromancer who disappeared after the trial."

Red tensed at the last name.

Hector continued. "The Baron knows this as well, but the fact he remains so confident means he has some tricks up his sleeve. Perhaps that invisible individual is a guardian of sorts that can help us in case things go south."

"If that's the case, what reason does he have to keep it hidden from us?" Allen asked.

"It's probably out of fear of information leaking," Hector said. "Maybe this hidden protector means to use us as bait to draw out certain individuals, and if news of their presence was made public, then their planning would be for naught."

"T-they're using us as bait?"

Hector smiled. "Wouldn't be the first time. In any case, anything at this point is mere conjecture, but we need to be ready for the worst-case scenario."

Eiwin was taken aback. "You mean..."

The elder's face was grim. "Evacuation of the Sect."

"... B-but didn't you say that the town would be safe?" Allen asked, crestfallen.

Hector shook his head. "Only from outside attacks. If the enemy is already inside, of what use would these defenses be?"

A heavy silence followed his words.

"Goulth and Domeron will remain behind and make preparations," he finally said. "The rest will all be going out to fight against the horde."

"Including me?" Allen asked.

"Indeed. Inside the town might not be any safer than out there, and if something goes wrong near the front lines, I might still be able to rescue you from danger."

The young master looked both happy and nervous at the same time.

Hector turned to Eiwin. "I will leave you in charge of the group at the front lines."

She frowned. "Miss Valt has always been the one to lead us in these kinds of confrontations."

"If this was just combat, I wouldn't think twice about putting her in charge. However, if things go wrong—as I'm thinking they will—then you need to prioritize your fellow Sect members' safety, and I don't trust Narcha to make the best decision."

Eiwin was hesitant, but she still nodded.

"Good," Hector said. "I will brief all of our Sect members on this, but it's important for you to be prepared." He looked over at Red. "This includes you too, kid. Since you're the only person capable of detecting this invisible individual, your help might mean the difference between life or death for all of us."

This certainly isn't the kind of responsibility I would like to have.

Red accepted despite his misgivings. "I will do my best."

It was all he could do and all he had ever done.

CHAPTER 56
ARCANE PROGRESS

As soon as Hector returned to the Sect, he gathered the other members within the hall to share the results of the meeting. As Red had been there, he wasn't required to stay, but the elder did ask him to search the Sect grounds for any hidden presences. He found no one, to Hector's relief.

Eiwin told him she would bring him up to speed on what they decided later, so Red saw no reason to stay either. Now that he knew about the challenges that awaited him over the next few days, there was a certain matter he needed to attend to.

He walked into Goulth's workshop. The blacksmith wasn't here at the moment, but he had given Red permission to use the building even when he wasn't present.

Red opened the door to the forge. He considered getting it running, but then decided against it.

I don't know how long Goulth will be in the meeting.

Instead, Red approached a closed door in the back of the workshop. Goulth had set aside a former storage room for him to study and practice sensitive matters in peace.

When he opened it, a strong scent of paper and ink hit him. The room was an absolute mess of drawings and stacks of papers, with all kinds of ink bottles strewn about. Countless complex symbols and diagrams were affixed to the stone walls, with notes and references written alongside them. One could hardly move without knocking something over.

Yet Red knew where everything was in here. This was where he had been practicing Arcane Script over the last six months, after all.

Everything seems to be in order.

He could even tell that no one had messed with the room while he was gone. With Goulth's help, he could keep this practice of his a secret from his fellow Sect members. That was crucial, not because this was a dangerous matter like his demonification, but rather because he didn't want to give them any false hopes about his skills.

Indeed, after six months of practice, he was happy he'd kept it secret.

Out of the 496 basic symbols, Red could barely claim to have mastered a hundred of them. Goulth was impressed by this, since he said that a cultivator on average would require four years of study to memorize and master all of them, and this was in a proper learning environment. Red, on the other hand, was on track to accomplish this in half the time, all while practicing by himself in the back of the workshop.

Red couldn't be happy about it.

It's still too slow.

With so many dangers around him, how could he be satisfied with that speed? Not to mention, what he was studying right now was barely the beginning. It didn't cover applications, and Red could only imagine how hard that would become, and how much it would cost him to practice and experiment.

This all drew him to a single conclusion.

There's no way I can prepare the Parting Storm formation in time for Narcha.

She only had a handful of years left to break through, while it would take Red at least five years before he was comfortable enough to even try experimenting with that special formation. That, too, was only if he had the materials in hand, which wasn't likely.

Red had done his research, with Goulth's help. Overall, the basic construction materials would cost around twenty Spirit Stones, which was expensive, but still in the realm of possibility for him with enough time. The hardest and most essential material, though, was what troubled him.

Aspected Spirit Stones.

As the name implied, these were Spirit Stones that contained a specific type of Spiritual Energy. They could cost a dozen times the price of common

Spirit Stones, or more, depending on how rare the type of energy they contained. And Red needed three of them: one containing Lightning Energy, one containing Water Energy, and one containing Wind Energy.

The Water and Wind Stones would cost him around seven Spirit Stones each, while the rarer Lightning one could cost him more than fifteen. Of course, these prices assumed he could find someone willing to sell them to him, another difficult task.

Aspected Spirit Stones were specialty goods, things high-level cultivators and factions used by the hundreds, as he had come to learn. So any such items were quickly snapped up from the market, if they appeared in the market at all. Most of the time, suppliers would just directly sell them to known clients.

Suffice it to say, it wouldn't be easy for Red to acquire them. Thus, he wouldn't be able to help Narcha so soon either.

I wonder what she'll do.

Red frowned at the thought. Every day that went by, he could feel Narcha's desperation growing stronger. She was trying to hold it in, but the woman never had been good at hiding her emotions. What happened at the trial was still affecting her, too. She sought information about Reinhardt at every opportunity, to no avail.

I have to worry about myself right now.

It might have sounded cold to others, but Red was a realist. He had his own problems to worry about, and if he couldn't help Narcha right now, there was nothing more he could do. He could only hope some miracle happened soon to change her fate.

Red stepped over stacks of paper and equipment, heading towards the center of the room. Right there, in the middle of everything, was the free ground space that he used to work. He sat down in that spot and crossed his legs.

He was preparing to meditate.

Red could claim to have some talent in Arcane Script, work that required a calm and meticulous mind. But it wasn't that he was naturally two times faster than most students. In truth, his secret to success lay elsewhere.

Early in his training, Red sought to understand the source of this art's difficulty. It took little investigating. Even the basic arcane symbols were extremely complex. They took hours of single-minded focus to draw at first, and a simple mistake meant he needed to start again from scratch. Under such strains, even cultivators suffered from stress, becoming prone to mistakes.

Red, however, had a special method to eliminate stress—the Radiant Current meditation technique.

He could inspect and control the inside of his own body. It was perfect for calming his anxieties and worries, and it allowed him to work in complete serenity. Of course, that didn't mean he didn't make mistakes, but it certainly meant he made far fewer.

After six months of practice, Red didn't even need to repeat the mantras and mudras to enter this meditative state. Merely picturing the words and gestures in his mind was enough.

When Eiwin learned this, she was shocked. Apparently, only monks with dozens of years of training could achieve such a state, and not even she could do it. She told Red he had a strong aptitude in these arts, and that this would have made him a once-in-a-lifetime talent back in her temple.

He didn't let himself get any ideas. He wanted to be a cultivator, not a monk. Eiwin told him then that a monk could still be a cultivator, but he also knew that a monk had many other responsibilities beyond cultivating. How could Red allow himself to be bound like that?

He focused again on his body. There was nothing out of the ordinary from what he could feel. The crimson mist was also calm, which confused him. He thought this being would be distressed after what had happened yesterday, but nothing indicated that.

As soon as Red thought back on it, he felt a headache. He swiftly shifted his thoughts away from the subject.

After he calmed himself, he opened his eyes. He was ready to work.

He looked around for his stack of clean paper and grabbed a page. Then he set it on top of the smooth wooden board in front of him and picked up his ink and brush. Since he was still just practicing this symbol, there was no need to use expensive materials yet.

With no other immediate concerns, Red set about his task.

Almost two hours passed before he was finished. To his surprise, he managed to draw the symbol successfully in one go.

This wasn't uncommon. Sometimes an easy symbol could be done one time while the harder ones might take him a few days and multiple tries. Of course, replicating it the first time was just the initial success. Now Red needed to commit the image to memory over a few more attempts.

But he didn't continue his training. It was just about time for the meeting to be over, and Red knew Goulth would come back. He left the training room and entered the forge, sitting down to wait.

Sure enough, ten minutes later, the fluctuations in the meeting hall dispersed. The blacksmith in particular seemed nervous, rushing back to his workshop.

When Goulth entered the building and saw the boy waiting for him there like a ghost, he jumped in fright.

He glared at him. "Agh, you brat! Why are you trying to scare me?!"

"I'm not," Red pointed out. "You're the one who's nervous about something."

"Of course I'm nervous!" Goulth massaged his temples. "Imagine hearing from your boss that you need to be prepared to evacuate your entire workshop and the Sect's treasury in a matter of days! How would that make you feel?"

"So he already told you about it?"

"He did. He also told us about the... visitor at the Baron's castle."

"You can talk about it," Red assured him. "No one is around."

Goulth gave him a skeptical look. "Can you be sure?"

"I suppose not."

"Then it's best not to mention it." The blacksmith shook his head. "Anyway, what do you want?"

"How do you know I want something?"

Goulth smiled. "I told you already, I'm your master! Your emotionless expression might fool others, but I have my ways to tell what you're feeling or thinking about."

Red frowned. *Could it be that he has a crimson sense too?*

Upon further reflection, that was a ridiculous idea. He must have had a different power.

"I do want something," Red told him. "I want to make my weapon."

CHAPTER 57
AN IMPOSSIBLE CHALLENGE

GOULTH'S SMILE DISAPPEARED. "I thought we talked about this. You're not ready to forge your own weapon."

Red sighed. "I know, but I need all the help I can afford right now. You heard Hector yourself, didn't you? We don't know what will happen during these next few weeks, and having a good weapon at my disposal could make all the difference."

"That still doesn't change the fact you're not ready to make that weapon."

Red knew his master was right. This had been the single biggest point of frustration for Red over these last six months. All his other fields were going very well—his cultivation, his weapon training, his Arcane Scripture training. The only area in which he lacked was blacksmithing.

This wasn't because Red was a bad blacksmith. In fact, he had picked up many things at the forge, and he could confidently make almost any weapon to his master's specifications. The only problem came when creating something for himself.

Red lacked creativity. He couldn't help but fall back on the same designs he knew worked, and any foray into the original resulted in making nonsense or subconsciously copying Goulth's models.

At first, he and his master thought nothing of it. Goulth claimed that even creativity itself could be practiced and improved. But as months passed by, even Goulth realized the problem wasn't that simple.

Red's mind seemed to work differently than any mind the giant man had ever seen before, and this problem extended beyond just black-smithing.

"Since I'm not ready, couldn't you make the weapon for me?" Red asked.

Goulth grimaced. "If I do that, won't it mean we wasted these six months of training?"

"It will, but it will increase my chances of surviving."

He didn't deny Goulth's claim. But in truth, he wasn't any closer to creating something right now than he was six months ago.

Goulth still didn't relent. "You have no idea how much of an opportunity this is, kid. No words can describe the feeling of creating something of your own the first time."

Red indeed had no idea. To him, it didn't matter who made the weapon or what form it came in, as long as it was a good weapon. He was willing to take his master's word for it, but only to a point.

"I don't have a choice. If we don't make this weapon right now, then who knows when we'll be able to?"

His words gave Goulth pause. "... You're right."

"... I am?"

"Yes, you are." Goulth nodded. "We need to make the weapon right now, which is why you will do it."

Red was at a loss. "I thought you said I wasn't ready."

"You're not. However, nothing we try seems to improve your horrible sense of originality, so we'll try something else."

Goulth walked over to a small wooden box in the corner. He set it down on the table in front of Red.

The boy knew what this box contained. It was the Dark Iron ingot.

"You're going to use the Dark Iron and make yourself that weapon," Goulth said.

Red frowned. "Just like that?"

"Yes, but there are some conditions."

He knew that was coming.

"First of all, whatever you make here, you will need to take with you to the battlefield," Goulth said.

That sounds reasonable. If Red could copy Goulth's models, he wasn't afraid of making a faulty product.

"However, that is only if you make something original," the blacksmith said. "If I see so much as a hint of an imitation in your weapon, then I will throw it in the trash."

"Are you being literal?"

"I am. If you make a copy of my weapons, then I will throw it in the river."

This took Red by surprise. "You would be willing to throw such a precious metal away?"

Goulth smiled. "Of course I am! I'm not interested in riches at this stage in my life. Whether the metal costs a few gold coins or a hundred Spirit Stones doesn't matter to me. What I care about is raising a good disciple, and to me there is nothing more valuable than that!"

Red narrowed his eyes. "So that's your plan? You hope to squeeze something out of me under this pressure?"

"That's exactly it," Goulth said. "Since normal methods don't work, we'll try something else!"

"What if I refuse to do this?" Red couldn't bring himself to waste such a precious material.

"Well..." Goulth scratched his chin. "Then I guess I'll be very disappointed. Oh, and I'll still throw away the metal too."

Red's frown deepened. Somehow, this strategy of his was already working.

His face made Goulth smile. "Don't be afraid of failure, Red—no, wait! Actually, be very afraid of failure! If you fail, that's about five Spirit Stones' worth of precious metal going in the trash! You wouldn't want that, would you?"

Red could tell, despite the mixed signals, that Goulth was serious about his threat of throwing the Dark Iron away. How could Red, who valued these resources and his own safety so much, allow that to happen?

Goulth was giving him no choice either way.

Still, no matter how strong the pressure was, Red still tackled his problems with a calm and analytical mind. As such, he still wasn't too confident in his chances.

"I don't know what you want from me," he admitted. This originality Goulth asked of him made no sense to Red. Sure, even the same type of weapon had some differences depending on who made them, but even then, those were generally stylistic, and what made that weapon useful would always be the same. A longsword would still be a longsword no matter who made it.

A sharp edge would always be a sharp edge, no matter in what form or by whose hands it came to be.

So what did it matter if Red imitated Goulth's style? Did the man just want him to put his own decorations on the weapon? That didn't seem to be the case, so what could he possibly want him to do?

"How many times have I told you?!" Goulth glared at him. "Just put your own spirit into your creation!"

The same answer.

Yet it still wasn't any clearer to Red. Any past attempts to get Goulth to elaborate were unsuccessful too, so he didn't even bother asking any more questions.

Right now, he didn't have any choice but to try.

He rose from his chair and looked at his master. "Are you going to help me with the forge?"

"Of course," Goulth said. "Making a Dark Iron alloy is not easy, and this is not a test of your forge control anyway. I wouldn't want some stupid mistake to ruin the real test for you, so you can just focus on the creating part."

At least there was one less thing for him to worry about.

"Can you give me some time?" Red asked. "I just got done with my Arcane Script practice."

"Oh!" Goulth slapped the top of his head. "I almost forgot about that! Of course, rest for a bit. However, we don't have much time, and the forging process might take very long too, so try to be quick."

"I will." His script practice didn't drain him physically as much as it did mentally. He simply needed to rest his mind for a while until he could focus on the task ahead.

This was what he did for the next hour or so. He sat down, meditated, and ate so as not to work on an empty stomach.

In the meantime, Goulth tended to the forge, setting out the materials. Once he saw Red stand up, he looked at him in anticipation.

"Have you already decided what kind of weapon you want to make?" Goulth asked.

Red blinked. "I wasn't really thinking about that during my rest."

Goulth gritted his teeth. "Ugh, you... We need to at least know what kind of weapon you want to make before beginning the forging! I need to prepare the alloy, after all!"

Red hesitated. "... Something on the smaller side, then. Shortsword-sized."

"A wise decision." Goulth returned to his work.

Red didn't say that just because he was used to wielding shortswords. There was little Dark Iron at their disposal, and as such, they would need to make a mixture rather than just use the pure metal. Unlike some alloys, such as steel, this wouldn't make the resulting product stronger, but weaker than pure Dark Iron.

As such, the bigger the weapon, the more diluted the Dark Iron would be along its length, weakening it even further. Of course, compared to normal steel weapons, it would still be many times stronger, but Red would rather maximize the Dark Iron's advantage. This was why he opted for a smaller weapon.

Goulth set about heating up the ingots in their blast furnace, a process that would take many hours. This left Red with ample time to think and prepare for what was to come.

So, I just have to put my own spirit into my creation, then?

Red had already reflected on that sentence many times and thought of countless possibilities. He considered whether Goulth was being literal, and whether he would need to awaken some kind of hidden spirit in his body and fuse it into the weapon. In the end, though, it was clear the blacksmith intended a deeper and more personal meaning of "spirit."

Yet this discovery was no help, even back then. Red still failed every time to satisfy his master, no matter how much effort and "spirit" he put in. After all, wasn't it his own rational and cynical spirit that made it so hard for him to be creative in the first place?

It was a conundrum, and he didn't feel any closer to the answer, even under pressure. He thought back to all the weapons he'd seen in the past, even the ones he recalled from his dreams in the underground, where he was a soldier fighting against gods.

Perhaps he could use one of those models as reference. But would that truly be his creation? Would that even be able to fool his master? Further, did he want to fool his master?

No. I need to take this task seriously.

And so Red thought. He pondered for hours, considering every possibility, no matter how ridiculous or stupid they were. He came up with many plans and ideas, but when the alloy was finally ready for forging, he wasn't confident in any of them.

It was the first time in his life Red felt so frustrated by a challenge. He had faced certain death, curses he couldn't hope to fight against, and yet he was never this discouraged by their difficulty. It was this simple but elusively complex issue that brought him to his wit's end. A challenge that should have a simple solution, and yet Red failed to find it.

To put my own spirit into my creations...

Goulth called him to attention. "The metal is ready."

Red stood from his chair and approached the forge.

"Are you ready?" Goulth looked worried.

"No," Red admitted. "But I'll try it anyway."

CHAPTER 58
BITTER TRUTH

GOULTH NODDED SERIOUSLY. "Use my hammer. It's the best one for the job."

Red was surprised. The man had never allowed him to use his hammer before, claiming it was a personal gift he received a long time ago. Red didn't know what made his master change his mind, but he accepted Goulth's offer.

He knew the hammer's location by heart at this point, so he didn't have any trouble finding it in the workshop. It was heavier than what Red was used to, but he could tell it was an excellent tool.

"You'll need to fold the metal about ten times so the Dark Iron is evenly distributed along the length of the weapon," Goulth said. "However, you'll need to hammer the lump into the rough shape of the weapon first."

Red nodded. He knew all of this already, but this was also his first time doing it himself, so he appreciated the blacksmith's instruction.

With Red's approval, Goulth dragged out the lump of metal from the furnace and onto the anvil. Red was ready to hammer it down, but he suddenly hesitated.

What am I doing?

Goulth scowled at his hesitation. "You need to be quick! We don't want the metal to cool down!"

Red noticed how the man urged him on. Goulth could see the anxiety in his eyes, and he knew that success was more important for Goulth than for himself. It was at that point that he knew the answer.

It was no sudden enlightenment or anything of the sort. He'd known the answer to his problem the entire time, but he had chosen to ignore it, for one single reason.

Red was always searching for an answer that would make his master happy, and not for the truth.

He was always hoping to fulfill his master's expectations, but he couldn't fool either of them any longer. It wouldn't be fair to this man who had helped him so much.

"What are you waiting for, kid?! We need to move now!" Goulth's voice became frantic.

Red didn't hesitate any longer, and his hammer struck the lump.

The forging process lasted for more than four hours, and it was one of the most exhausting endeavors Red had ever taken part in. Even when heated to its utmost, the Dark Iron alloy was unyielding. It took every ounce of his strength to fold the metal onto itself, a task that only grew harder with every repetition.

When that was done, it was time for Red to shape the blade. He already had a weapon in mind, so he didn't hesitate putting his hammer to work.

Red was so focused on his task he couldn't turn to see Goulth's expression, but he could feel his fluctuation storming with heavy emotions. The man never said anything, though, and let Red do his work.

This was the first time he had ever tried to forge a shortsword, and his first time with this difficult metal. The task became much harder as it went along. To his surprise, Goulth began to speak up.

"The tip needs to be flatter."

Red froze for a second. Still, he followed his instructions. Goulth didn't stop there, either.

"This side is uneven."

"Strike here now."

"Flatten this part."

Every piece of advice was on point, as if the blacksmith knew exactly what kind of shortsword Red planned to make. Once they were done shaping the blade, it was time for the quenching and tempering.

Goulth also assisted with this process, and Red didn't protest. The sudden cooling of the quenching would give the blade hardness while the slow tempering process would give it flexibility, keeping it from breaking after severe impacts. Not that this metal seemed to suffer from either of these risks, but the blacksmith had always made it clear how important these two processes were in the forging of a good weapon.

So Red listened to him, and once they were through with this, the blade was finally ready.

It was a dark-gray shortsword, roughly fifty centimeters long, although one might confuse it with an oversized dagger. The blade was wide and heavy for a sword of this size, being five fingers wide at the pommel, but it tapered off on both sides at a sharp angle towards the point, forming a tall triangle. There were also two fullers along the wide sides of the blade, four total, which helped lighten the heavy weapon.

It looked unusual, and yet from Goulth's expression, he recognized it very well.

"A cinquedea," he said, looking saddened.

This was the weapon Red chose to make. A faithful recreation of an image his master had once shown him from that blacksmithing book of his.

"It's a heavier shortsword, proper for dealing deeper cuts," Red said, explaining his choice. "It might not be as swift as a normal shortsword, but I think it's a good fit for my combat style."

Goulth didn't say anything. Yes, Red had failed his task completely, but he wasn't disheartened.

He looked at Goulth. "I've always enjoyed learning new things, but I've never been a very passionate individual. My primary goal has always been to survive, and one of the few enjoyments I take out of life is the feeling of discovery and self-improvement as I move along with each day... I take an interest in learning new practices, but that interest only goes as far as it can help me reach these goals in the long run."

Goulth's face faltered, but he remained silent.

Red sighed. "I tried it. I watched you and how you spoke about your passions, how you seemed to become a different person every time you worked in this forge... Yet I wasn't able to spark that feeling you always seemed to talk about, no matter how interested I was in blacksmithing. I don't feel excited once I look at my work, or feel a drive to create something different, something that belongs to me. All I see when I'm done is a useful tool."

He could feel the man's emotions wavering even more through his fluctuation, but he knew he needed to say this. It was what Goulth was owed, after all.

"Maybe these emotions don't exist in me," Red said. "Maybe there is something out there I have yet to find that will spark that fire in my heart. Whatever the case, I know for certain that nothing I've done until now has been it." He shook his head. "I'm sorry, but I can't be the disciple you want me to be."

Deep down, perhaps Goulth always knew this but chose to ignore it, so eager was he to have someone finally show interest in his trade, a chance to pass on his knowledge. Maybe he hoped that with time he could awaken the passion in this emotionless disciple of his, but Red knew himself better in the end. He wasn't changing. He wasn't growing.

Ever since the day he awoke in that underground, the boy had been one calm lake—unchanged in his feelings and ideals. This didn't mean he was completely distant. He still felt a sense of responsibility and loyalty to the people who helped him. But Red never felt any kind of strong emotional attachment towards anyone or anything.

He didn't feel sad when he saw a dying Viran in the underground. He only thought it was a pity someone as strong as him would die in that kind of place.

He didn't feel bad about Narcha's struggles as a friend. He only felt sympathy for her as a fellow cultivator.

Red was still willing to be selfless and put his own best interests aside to help those close to him, but he could never pretend to feel the way people wanted him to feel.

This was his spirit—practical, cold, and cynical. An ugly face to show the world, and yet Red never shied away from accepting himself as he truly was.

This was the truth Goulth deserved to know.

The blacksmith gave him a defeated smile. "I see now that I have asked too much of you. I'm sure you have the capability to become a great blacksmith, yet I also tried to pass all my hopes and dreams onto you... It was unfair."

"I should have told you the truth sooner," Red confessed. "I took advantage of your eagerness to teach and became your disciple, and yet chose to ignore everything else that came with it. It was not something I should have done to someone who decided to help me."

Goulth gave a pitiful laugh. "Look at what you're saying, kid! You're barely ten, yet you speak as if you have lived tens of years more than me. Such worries and deep considerations aren't things a child should have to worry about. Just let me take the blame and be done with it!"

Red frowned but didn't offer any rebuke.

The blacksmith looked back at the dark sword. "I have always considered myself a failure to my predecessors. Possessed of the passion and talent for crafting, yet unable to continue in this path because of my poor aptitude in cultivation. It was my responsibility to find someone to carry on in my stead, to not let this knowledge die with me... Now that I say it out loud, how ridiculous does that sound? What kind of master looks for a disciple only to pass on the weight of his lifetime of hopes and dreams onto them? It's not right. This responsibility, this failure... It is mine to carry alone."

Goulth approached the newly crafted weapon. "You can come back tomorrow to collect your weapon. I'll have it sharpened and ready by then. I want to be alone for now."

He didn't look at Red.

Red hesitated but walked out. He still wasn't sure whether his choice was for the best, yet he believed in one thing.

It was always better to know the truth, no matter how much it might hurt.

Perhaps it was time he considered applying that line of thought to others in his Sect too.

CHAPTER 59
OFF TO WAR

THE NEXT MORNING came quickly for Red.

The sound of activity in the courtyard woke him up. Outside his window, the sun was barely up. It was unusual for so many people in his Sect to be awake at this hour, but then again, he supposed they had a long day ahead of them.

Red stood up from his bed and stretched. The forging process from the day before had taken its toll on him, even with his improved stamina, but after a good night's rest, he had managed to recover.

When he opened his door, he saw Eiwin and Allen in front of the main building, looking over an assortment of bags and equipment.

The young master lit up and waved at him. "Hey, Red! I'm coming too!"

"I know."

"How do you... Oh, right!" Allen slapped his forehead. "I forgot you were there!"

Red frowned. These last six months had shaped Allen into a skilled warrior, stronger and more reliable in a pinch. However, he was still just a child, naïve and slow on the uptake. Hector believed Allen would mature with time, but Red and many others in the Sect felt there were certain things that would probably remain the same no matter how many months passed.

Red turned to Eiwin. "Who's coming with us?" He hadn't had the opportunity to talk with her the night before, as tired as he was after the forging process.

"Everyone but Master Domeron and Master Goulth," she said.

"Hector's sending so many people out?"

"It's a necessary measure. It's possible we might have to take care of no small amount of Lesser Ring Realm beasts, so we need all the strength we can muster."

He remembered how the last fight with a Lesser Ring Realm monster went for him and his Sect members. Then again, this time, they would be prepared for it.

"What about Domeron and Goulth?" Red asked. "Will they be safe by themselves?"

Eiwin sighed. "There's always a risk, but there's no one I trust more to hold down the fort while we're away."

Red supposed they had no choice in the matter.

"Oh right, speaking of Master Goulth." Eiwin picked up a bundle of cloth from the top of the equipment pile. "He wanted me to give you this."

Red didn't need to guess what the item was. He unwrapped the cloth, revealing the sheathed shortsword they'd crafted the day before. Both the sheath and the hilt were made of unadorned dark-brown leather, with a simple iron cross guard. It would have looked like an unassuming weapon if it weren't for its peculiar triangular shape.

"What is that?" Allen asked.

"A weapon." Red strapped the sword to his belt.

The young master extended his hand. "Can I see it?"

"No."

"Oh..."

Eiwin cleared her throat. "Master Goulth also wanted me to leave you a message."

"Why not speak to me directly?" Red asked.

"He... said he's busy."

Red could tell there was something else to the matter, and he could guess what it might be, but he didn't push it.

She continued. "He told me to tell you that you did a good job, and he hopes the sword will serve you well."

He didn't know how to respond to this, so he just nodded.

Eiwin seemed satisfied with this. "Young Master, can you go fetch me another bag?"

"Hm?" Allen said. "But you said we had enough bags already."

She smiled. "It's just to make sure."

"Right, fine!" He nodded. "I'll be back in a second!"

Allen sought to make his claim true as he ran off like the wind.

"What is it?" Red looked at Eiwin with suspicion. Evidently, that was just an excuse to speak to him in private.

Her entire face became serious. "It's about Miss Valt."

Red frowned. "Did she not take the news about her not being the commander well?"

Eiwin shook her head. "She wasn't happy, but she would never jeopardize our mission because of that. I'm just worried that she might be considering doing something rash because of..."

"Because of the pill?" Red had noticed how Narcha hadn't been the same since their confrontation with Reinhart.

"Yes." She looked troubled.

"What makes you think so?" Red asked.

"I can just tell. Others might think this recent bout of anger from her is nothing unusual, something that will eventually pass, but I can tell something's different. The others... They don't know how important breaking through is to her, so I—"

"I'm back!" Allen broke into their conversation, running back with a leather bag in hand. "What were you talking about?"

"Nothing important," Eiwin said. But she gave Red a meaningful look.

Red nodded. "I'll keep it in mind."

Eiwin gave him a relieved smile.

Allen's cheer faded. "Keep what in mind?"

"Red, please help me check the supplies again. I'll hand you the list."

"Hey, don't ignore me!"

A few hours passed as everyone made their last preparations. The trip to the river would take days, but in truth, no one knew how long they would be out there fighting the horde.

Rog, who had the most experience with monsters, told them that the worst of the fight would come when the first waves hit. Then the beasts would be at their most ravenous, and the fight would be at its fiercest.

If they managed to beat back the horde at this point, then it was likely the few surviving beasts would run away and hide, and the group would need to hunt them down so they wouldn't disrupt the province. That task could take much longer, but it also wasn't as dire as surviving the first assault.

According to the information they'd received, the first wave of the horde would reach the river by tomorrow in the evening, which meant that Red and the others would need to walk through the night if they hoped to make it in time. Thankfully, they could stick to the road, which meant their trip would be much faster.

The second wave, the one with the Skycrown Wolves, would arrive three days after the first. This would give them time to recover and prepare before the biggest challenge. Of course, this was all assuming there would be no surprises along the way, and according to Hector, that was highly unlikely.

The elder gathered everyone at the front gate. Red noticed the absence of Goulth, who remained in his workshop, but he knew better than to approach the blacksmith right now.

Everyone carried different expressions as they prepared to set out. Rimold looked reluctant, Allen was excited, Rog acted indifferent and Eiwin appeared solemn. Narcha seemed to be in a bitter mood—more so than normal, that is. They were all carrying large bags of equipment and supplies, more than enough to last them a week. If even that wasn't enough, they would have the Baron's soldiers and Rog's hunting skills to provide for them.

As for other, more special items, they had a handful. More specifically, seven talismans in total and about a dozen pills of all sorts, easily more than half of the Sect's total treasure, or so Red had been told. He even had a few in his possession, including the fireball talisman he had intended to use during his heist with Rimold.

He had also brought all his sensitive items with him, including the insectoid crystal and his treasures from the trial. It just so happened that the new moon would arrive in ten days, so he might need to deal with his curse in the middle of their mission.

He only hoped that no one would notice it.

As for Hector, he actually had no bags. Red wondered if he had some other way to store treasures on his person, but the elder refused to answer any such questions.

"I have already told this to all of you, but I will do so again," Hector said. "We are going out there to help the province deal with the horde. However, if things go awry, I command you to prioritize your own survival. The Baron still has his own last line of defense in the form of this town, and it's pointless to throw our lives away for nothing out there."

Everyone nodded, except for Narcha, who snorted. Hector glared at her, but neither of them said anything.

A few seconds passed by before Eiwin spoke up. "We will do as you say, Master Hector. I promise I will make sure we all get out of this safe and sound."

"Good. The communication talismans we received from those imperials have a range limit of fifty kilometers, so it's quite possible we won't be able to communicate with each other, in which case Eiwin has absolute authority during my absence. She knows what needs to be done in case of any incidents."

Hector seemed to be directing these words specifically at Narcha, but she simply continued to silently stare into space.

"As for back here in the Sect, Domeron will be taking care of things while we're gone. You are to get in contact and meet with him as quickly as possible if something happens." He pointed at the swordsman, who was sitting in his rocking chair and drinking from his mug as if nothing were happening.

Domeron nodded back at them, then closed his eyes again as he sipped from his cup.

Hector continued. "I will walk with you to the outskirts of town. After that, we will part ways, and I will hurry east to meet with that big wolf."

"Do you know its location already?" Rimold asked, troubled.

"No, but I have a good eye. If there's really a horde of nearly a thousand snow-white wolves out there in the middle of the forest, I don't think they will be very hard to spot." Hector scanned over the others. "Any other last-minute questions?"

No one spoke up. Despite how dysfunctional and strange this group seemed at times, it was composed of strong and experienced warriors—including, to some extent, Red and Allen. They were cultivators raised and trained under masters of their craft, and each of them was probably worth ten normal soldiers. Of course the Baron would prize their presence in the front lines.

If the town had any chance of withstanding this attack, they would need the Water Dragon Sect's help. Unless the cause was lost from the beginning, in which case Hector had made it quite clear they were to flee.

"Then we're off." Hector nodded and waved his hand, turning to walk out the gate.

Red and the others followed. From their fluctuations, the boy could tell that some of them were more confident about this trip than others.

He himself didn't know into which camp he fell.

CHAPTER 60
ON THE ROAD AGAIN

THE ENTIRE TOWN was on high alert. The news about the coming horde had reached them, and refugees already lined the streets. At the same time, many merchants and visitors were leaving Fordham-Bestrem to take refuge elsewhere, where they thought it would be safer.

Uncertainty and fear could be seen in everyone. Families gathered on the sides of the road, disheveled and carrying their belongings on their backs, comforting their children and elders as the guards tried to institute order by force. It was a grim, heavy sight.

Only now did it dawn on many of them what was at play here.

Red, with his crimson sense, felt this even more clearly. The townspeople's emotions affected him to a degree it never had since the trial, and he found himself having a terrible headache in the middle of town.

This didn't go unnoticed by his companions.

"Are you okay, Red?" Eiwin asked.

He shook his head. "Too many people. Should be better once we're out of town."

Eiwin nodded, but she took one step closer to him, ready to act in case anything went wrong. Red didn't protest, and they continued on their way downhill.

Surprisingly, their group didn't get as much attention in the chaos the town had become. The townsfolk who recognized them, though, seemed more hopeful than before. "Hector and his guild are going to deal with the horde!"

"With Master Hector's help, we have nothing to fear!"

Red wondered how these people would feel if they knew Hector planned to abandon them at the slightest sign of trouble. Still, the Sect's appearance did lift the townspeople's spirits and give them some comfort, as fleeting as it might be.

The streets were crowded with carts and refugees, slowing their progress downhill. Still, with the help of the guards to clear the way, they eventually spotted the town's edge, where even more refugees could be seen huddling around the side of the road and building their own camps.

Allen looked at them with wonder and worry in his eyes. "This is a lot of people."

"Although our Fordham-Bestrem is the biggest settlement in the region, there are still dozens of villages and hamlets around the forest," Eiwin explained. "Everyone in the horde's path was forced to take refuge here."

"But there are still people arriving," Allen said. "Are they all going to make it in time?"

Even now they could see a trail of carts making their way up the road towards town. The suddenness of the horde had obviously required a fast evacuation.

Eiwin looked troubled. "I don't know, but the Baron's men are doing their best."

This didn't seem to comfort Allen, who stared sadly at the refugees.

As soon as they reached the town's edge, a guard on horseback approached them. Red could tell this was the one responsible for seeing movement in and out of town.

The man got off his horse and bowed. "Greetings, Master Hector. Our lord Baron told me to receive you and your Sect members as soon as you left town."

Hector frowned. "Why? Is there something I need to know?"

"Ah, not at all," the guard said. "I was told that the Baron was not made aware of how you and your group planned to travel, so me and my men were to provide you assistance if necessary. We have horses available for your use, should you so wish."

Hector snorted. "Horses? With how many people are on the road, horses would be more of a hindrance than anything. No, we'll be making our way on foot."

The man gulped. "I-is there any other help that I can provide you?"

Before Hector could respond, Eiwin spoke up. "Thank you for offering your assistance, but we have everything sorted here."

The guard relaxed. "Very well. Should you require something on your way over, make sure to approach our guards. The road to the river is long, but we have men stationed at various points to assure swift communication and support for our allies."

She smiled. "We will keep that in mind."

The guard bowed again before mounting his horse and trotting off.

Hector led the group to an empty area amidst all the refugees and the farmland, then turned to face them.

"This is where we part ways," he said. "I'll be going ahead of you."

Rimold scowled. "Wait, how exactly are you going to go ahead of us? Are you just going to run really fast?"

Red shared the same doubts. For some reason, he just couldn't imagine someone like Hector running around, or doing any kind of physical task, for that matter.

The elder scoffed. "Running? What do you think I am, a brute?" He shook his head. "No, I can't fly at my cultivation level, but I still have my ways."

As he spoke, he waved his hand. Bright-blue Spiritual Energy manifested from his fingers, transforming the ground in front of him into ice. Then he stepped onto this slippery ground before giving the rest of them one last glance.

"Remember—prioritize your safety above everything else."

With those words, Hector waved his hand again, and the ice began to extend in front of him, forming a raised path in the air. Without hesitation, he slid along this ice road, his movements leading him effortlessly along the continuously expanding path.

Pillars stretched beneath the narrow icy path and connected it to the ground, Hector conjuring it all with ease. Before long, he was moving almost ten meters above them. He skated along with extraordinary speed and quickly reached the tree line of the forest. This spectacle didn't go unnoticed by the people at the edge of town, who all pointed in wonder at this seemingly flying old man.

Red and the Sect also watched in awe as Hector disappeared completely from their view a few minutes later. He was in disbelief, but the raised ice path the elder left behind served as evidence that what just happened was indeed real.

"How long can he keep that up?" Red asked.

Rog scratched his beard. "A few hours. Then he has to land and run for a bit, or else he would spend all his Spiritual Energy."

He had recovered his scraggly hair and appearance after six months, and no one could tell he had almost died in flames.

"Wait, but I thought he didn't run!" Rimold said.

The hunter shrugged. "It's a funny sight."

The rogue ignored him and looked back at the ice path. "Can't we also use this path to—"

As soon as Rimold said that, a cracking sound erupted from the ice. It collapsed and melted in front of their eyes, leaving nothing but broken ice and a puddle of water to indicate it was ever there in the first place.

Eiwin smiled and shook her head. "Ice like this can't sustain itself for long, not to mention elemental structures created by Spiritual Energy have a certain impermanence too."

Narcha sighed. "Can we go already, or are you going to give us another lecture?"

Eiwin frowned at Narcha, but didn't reply. She glanced at the rest of the group. "Let's be on our way, then."

Red wasn't used to traveling on roads. Most of his forays into the forest were made among the trees and not on a clear walking path. He felt exposed out here, an easy target for an ambush by anyone hiding behind the heavy foliage.

Thankfully, he had the rest of his Sect members by his side. Rog and Rimold were experienced scouts, so they would notice if anything was amiss. Not to mention that with Red's crimson sense, he could detect ambushes from far away.

As they walked, they came across more guards, and more refugees rushing to reach the town. People became scarce as night arrived, but even then the group found a handful along the way, either walking through the night or camping on the roadside. This also meant they had plenty of torches and campfires to light their way.

Still, they had prepared a handful of lanterns in their bags. Not that Red needed them.

The atmosphere in the group itself was awkward. Narcha's brooding was obvious, except maybe to someone who was terrible at reading the room.

"When are we going to arrive?" Allen chirped.

"Probably in twelve more hours," Rog said. "Around when the sun is coming up again."

The young master brightened. "I can't wait! It's been so long since we've been on a trip together! I'll show you how much I've improved since then! I'll be fighting right by your side on the front lines!"

"You're going to stay in the back," Narcha said flatly.

"What?! No way!"

She grimaced. "This is not a joke, you brat. You have no idea how fierce a horde really is. The first clash is always the most dangerous, and none of us are going to have time to look after you in the thick of it." She turned to Red. "That goes for you too. I know you're capable, but this is something you haven't dealt with before."

I'm not sure if that's true. Red remembered his time in the underground dealing with waves of monsters. Of course, he was never in the front lines back then, so he supposed Narcha was right to some degree. He had grown stronger, but not to the point that he felt confident against dozens of monsters in melee combat.

Thankfully, he'd brought his bow along too.

"You will both have your chance to contribute, but that's after the initial attack has passed," Eiwin said, addressing Red and Allen. "For now, you will stick with Rimold and Rog in the back and support us from afar."

Rimold looked surprised. "I'm staying in the back?"

"Why? Is that a problem?"

"No, no! I mean, that's perfect for me!" he replied hastily. "I can definitely be more useful in the back."

Allen looked disheartened, but he didn't protest. That in itself was proof that he had indeed grown and matured, if only a little bit.

They continued to walk in the dark, and Red began to feel the familiar pressure of the lunar gaze set upon him. He was used to it, but its effects on his mind were impossible to ignore, much more so as they came closer to a new moon.

Right as Red felt the first pressure, he felt a flicker with his crimson sense.

"Hm?" He froze and looked between the trees.

The rest of the group froze with him.

"What is it?" Rog asked, his hand going to his bow.

"I felt something," he said. "It appeared and disappeared in a second."

His crimson sense didn't exclusively detect human or monster presences. It could also detect normal animals, which there were many in the forest. But their fluctuations were much weaker, barely registering in his senses.

This one, however, was clearly an animal, yet strong enough for him to detect, and the fact it immediately disappeared from his senses was doubly suspicious.

Narcha stared into the dark, her eyes narrowed. "Do you know what it was?"

"... I'm not sure."

Still, it felt familiar. A lingering feeling that he knew he couldn't ignore.

CHAPTER 61

FLOATING THOUGHTS

Narcha scanned the forest with a scowl. "You said this... thing appeared and disappeared instantly in your senses, right? And right on the edge? Do you think it knows about the range of your powers?"

Red frowned. "I can't imagine how it would know that."

Even his companions only knew his range to be two hundred meters. In truth, he'd counted a few meters higher than that and just rounded the number down. With that in mind, he didn't think anyone could be so precise as to enter and leave the edge of his detection range in an instant.

Something else was going on.

"Do you think we should investigate?" Allen asked the group.

"This seems too suspicious." Rimold shook his head. "I say we just continue on our way and ignore it. And we're on a tight schedule, so we can't afford to lose time."

Narcha was just about to speak before she caught herself. She nodded at Eiwin. "You're the leader. What do you think we should do?"

Eiwin hesitated. "It's... best if we look into it. I don't want to risk having a stalker or some other danger behind us during our trip. We should be quick, though, since we still need to worry about reaching the river in time."

Narcha and Allen nodded in approval while Rimold didn't look too happy. Rog, on the other hand, had already taken out his bow.

Red also agreed with Eiwin's decision. If they chose to ignore these strange signs, it could come back to haunt them in the future.

Eiwin motioned to Red. "Lead the way. We'll be right behind you."

Red did as much. He strayed from the road and walked into the sea of trees towards where he'd sensed the fluctuation.

Narcha and Eiwin flanked him, ready to strike if anything popped out, while the others watched their backs. They used Rog's lantern to illuminate their path, but Red's dark vision allowed him to see just as clearly in the pitch-black night.

They approached the area, inspecting their surroundings. Nothing stood out to them, even when they arrived at the spot where that fluctuation should have been.

Narcha looked around with caution. "Can you feel anything?"

Red shook his head. "Nothing..."

Eiwin looked back at Rog. "Can you discern anything?"

The hunter said nothing and approached them instead. He crouched down and beckoned Allen over to hold the lantern close while he inspected the ground for tracks.

Thirty seconds later, Rog stood up. "No tracks or anything as far as I can see."

"So there's nothing here?" Rimold turned to Red. "Are you sure about what you felt, kid?"

Allen scowled at the man. "Red's power has never been wrong before!"

Rimold threw his hands up. "I'm not saying he was wrong, but maybe it was just a coincidence! Maybe a flying monster could have dipped in and out of your detection range while it was gliding over, right?"

Red hesitated. "... I suppose that's possible."

Narcha frowned. "Yet you don't look too convinced. Is there something you're not telling us?"

"No. It's just a feeling. I felt like I recognized that presence, but it was too brief to make any conclusion."

"Couldn't it have been a monster you saw before?" Rimold asked.

"As I said, it's possible," he replied. "I just felt it was something worth investigating, but since there's nothing to follow up on, there's no point in lingering here."

"You were right to speak up," Eiwin said. "Hector warned us many times to expect something to happen during our foray into the forest, so we should remain alert."

Rog nodded in agreement. "I would prefer not to get ambushed by a demon or something else, so keep your eyes open, kid."

They prepared to return to the road. Red gave one last look over his shoulder, lagging behind.

That was when he felt it. The same fluctuation, a few meters behind him.

Red turned around in a hurry, and what he saw horrified him.

It was a familiar sight.

A decapitated head, floating in the air.

He froze.

Rog was the first to pick up on it. "What are you—"

"Stop! All of you, don't look!" Red howled as he turned his back to the head.

His warning alarmed them all. They all stopped in their tracks, not even shifting to look over. All except for one person.

Allen looked back. "What are you talking about, Red—"

His eyes grew wide. Red saw a mixture of terror and surprise on Allen's face as he saw the floating object.

"Allen, look away!" Red charged at him.

Allen didn't even notice his presence up until Red pushed him to the ground.

Finally, he snapped out of his daze, trembling. "Ah, R-Red, there is something..."

"I know!" Red shook his head. "Don't look at it!"

"Kid, what is going on?!" Narcha cried, still turned away.

The entire group was on edge, but no one else had disobeyed Red's instructions not to look back.

Rimold struggled to speak as a grim possibility seemed to cross his mind. "I-is it..."

"It's the head," Red said, confirming the man's suspicion. "It's right there by the tree."

Rimold paled. "H-how is that possible? Hector threw it in the river!"

"I don't know, but we need to—"

"A-Allen..."

A hoarse whisper came from the head. It was so low that it shouldn't have been audible, yet it seemed to have been spoken right next to his ear.

A chill ran down Red's spine.

Allen, still down on the ground, seized up. Recognition crossed his face. "... M-Mom?"

The voice spoke again, this time a bit louder and more feminine than before. "Yes... My dear Allen. How much you've grown, my dear, beloved son..."

Tears welled up in Allen's eyes. "B-but how? You're supposed to be—"

"Be quiet!" Red clamped a hand over Allen's mouth.

To his surprise, the young master struggled against him. Since Red had opened fewer veins than him, it took little effort for the boy to throw him off. Allen shot up and looked towards the head again.

Red warned the others. "Hold him back!"

Eiwin, eyes shut, was the first to dash towards Allen. But before she reached him, he had already laid eyes on the head again.

Renewed terror appeared on his face. "M-Mother, what happened to you—"

"Allen, no!" Eiwin pulled him back.

But at that point, he seemed too far gone.

"Allen, my dear Allen... I've missed you so much! Please, come and give me a hug!" The voice now sounded substantial and loud, almost deafening to their ears.

Red could sense its strange fluctuation growing ever closer to them. He still didn't dare to look back.

"It's coming for us! Run!"

This was all the prompting his group needed. They charged as one, back the way they came. Eiwin carried Allen under her arm. He was still struggling to get free.

"No! You don't understand!" He squirmed in despair. "It's her, I know it!"

"Allen, that is not your mother!" Eiwin shouted.

"You're wrong! It's her, I know it!"

It was to no avail. Allen continued to insist as if he were struck by a spell, and from what Red remembered of his own experience with the head, the young master might as well have been.

The voice continued to speak as if it were right behind them. "Allen! Don't let them take you away from me again!"

Red, however, could gauge the head's position with his crimson sense. "It's not here yet, but it's catching up!"

Rimold turned to his companions, panic in his voice. "What do we do?"

Narcha gritted her teeth. "Get ready to fight!"

She took something out of her pouch—a talisman. And she seemed ready to activate it at any moment.

That was when Red felt the fluctuation disappear. "It's gone! It—"

Before he could even complete his sentence, it manifested in front of them. The head appeared out of nowhere, and they all couldn't help but lay eyes on it.

Their steps slowed as they were drawn into its gaze. Eiwin dropped Allen, and he stood up to stare alongside them.

"Mom! I'm going to save you!"

Allen dashed forward, the only one unaffected by the malaise. Red quickly snapped out of it the same way he did when he first saw the head, wrenching himself away. At this point, though, he knew he couldn't stop Allen.

I need to do something!

Without much thought, he took his bow from his back and shot Allen's leg. His arrow struck true and impaled his calf.

"Agh!" Allen screamed in pain as he stumbled to the ground.

Even then, he continued to crawl towards the head, which was gently floating in the air, waiting for him.

"Closer, my son... You're almost back to me."

"Mom..." Allen moaned as he crawled. "I'm going to save you!"

"Yes, my son... Just a little bit closer—"

A dark sword cleaved into the side of its skull. Red, his eyes closed, felt his slash connect and dig into the bone and thanked his crimson sense.

Surprisingly, the head didn't go flying off from the force of his blow. Instead, the floating skull remained stationary even as his sword found purchase.

"No!" Allen screamed. "What have you done?!"

Red ignored his pleas and pulled his sword free. He kept his eyes closed and made to hack down again, but then the fluctuation disappeared.

He still didn't dare open his eyes and kept his guard up, waiting for the head's fluctuation to reappear. And reappear it did, right behind him.

"I see you, moonspawn..."

An inhuman chorus of voices whispered into his ears. Red's mind was flooded by an overwhelming force, and his entire world went dark.

The last things he heard before falling unconscious were the shouts of his companions as their weapons were drawn.

CHAPTER 62
UNEXPECTED SAVIOR

RED'S MIND stewed in the infinite darkness of unconsciousness. When he started coming to, he felt a strong fluctuation right by his side.

Crap!

On instinct alone, Red rolled away from it. His other senses returned to him, and a flood of light assaulted his vision. It was sunlight.

How long had he been unconscious? What happened to the others?

Red couldn't even stop to contemplate as he felt this strong presence stir. He struggled to his feet and began to run as fast as he could, not sparing a glance back.

A guttural and deep voice spoke. "Already leaving? No thanks?"

Red's steps slowed to a hesitant walk, and he looked back even as he distanced himself. A large tree-bark bear was sitting on the ground, staring at him with a surprisingly human expression. But what caught his attention were the parts where the beast's bark-like skin had rotted away, revealing flesh and bone underneath.

By no means should creatures have been able to live in this state. Yet the enormous bear sat there, gazing back at Red. As his mind recovered from its confusion, he recognized it as an undead. The fact it could speak only meant one thing.

It was the necromancer.

Red stared at the monster in wonder. "How?"

It made a loud noise that he assumed was a laugh. "How what? How I save you?"

He blinked. "How are you here?"

Red assumed that after the trial was over, the hawk spirit wouldn't allow the necromancer to roam free any longer. Yet here he was, still possessing another creature.

The bear scratched at its rotting skin. "Bird let me come help you—"

Red shook his head. "You're lying."

Not even mentioning the meager possibility that the hawk would trust the necromancer enough for this task, the spirit had made it clear that Red needed to walk this journey on his own. Why would it send the necromancer to help him now?

The beast grunted. "Left sliver of mind behind on surface. Bird couldn't stop me even if it tried... Still cut off from main body, though."

Red struggled to understand what the necromancer was saying. "What do you mean, 'cut off'? Aren't you the same individual? How could you be cut off from yourself?"

"Silly brat." The bear huffed. "Split little pieces of mind to make clone. Clone is connected to main mind—can feel and communicate with it. Still, stupid bird cut off way back... Can no longer feel main mind! Now all lost and wandering..."

He couldn't say this made the situation any clearer, but Red had the gist of it, at least.

A clone, separated from the main body...

Red wasn't knowledgeable enough about the subject to see what this meant. Still, the strange lack of the necromancer's old enthusiasm couldn't mean anything good.

Red had other matters to concern himself with, though.

"What happened?" he asked.

"Saved you." The bear shrugged.

He sighed. "I know you did, but tell me what happened to my companions and the floating head."

The beast scratched its decomposing chin. "Was stalking you from afar to stay hidden when suddenly heard battle noises. Undead energy, too. Very strong. Rushed over and saw your human friends fighting ghost head. Picked you up and ran away... Stupid woman tried to chase, but too slow for me."

Red tried to digest this deluge of information. For one, he didn't trust the necromancer, but he did hear a battle before he fell unconscious, and he couldn't think of any other way he could have been separated from his group.

"What happened to them?" Red asked. "My companions, that is."

The bear shrugged again. "Not sure. Didn't stick around."

He frowned and looked at his surroundings. They were in the middle of a forest clearing, but Red didn't know exactly where.

"Take me back to them," he said.

"No way. Too dangerous. Ghost will still be around. Besides, companions not dead yet..."

"And how can you be certain?"

"Head not looking to kill. Head looking for hosts."

Once again, Red was at a loss.

He stared at the necromancer's bear. "Explain to me."

"Head is prison. Necromantic treasure gone rogue," it said. "Meant to imprison ghosts, but with no master, they rebel. Probably hundreds inside. Only way they can escape is possession."

Red had heard the term before, but as with many other forbidden subjects, information about possession and ghosts in common books was limited. He knew what it meant for his companions, though.

"So the ghosts inside this head were trying to possess us?" Red asked.

"Yes. Tempts fools with voices and illusions. If you touch head, then you are gone. Probably succeeded already. Your friends probably all different people by now."

Red contemplated this. "This head was being carried by a demonic culti-vator inside of town. I stared at it directly, but I was still able to escape the illusion. So why did it only attack us now? Why did it choose to target us, of all people?"

"Your stench too strong." The bear waved its paw in front of its snout. "Can feel moonstone smell from miles away. Irresistible to undead—might have awakened the ghosts. Head probably wanted to take you then, but too scared to do it in town."

Red's brow furrowed. "Why was it scared?"

"Same reason as me. Formation covering town. Strange powers in ruins. If it reveals itself, it will get killed."

There's more to this...

From what he'd heard, Hector had promptly disposed of the head in the river. It could have attacked Hector at that point, but it chose not to, which meant that it probably also feared him. This added to the fact Red stabbed it with little resistance meant this head might be more fragile than it first seemed.

Red would have liked to know more about this strange treasure, but he knew he didn't have the time. The sun was in the middle of the sky. It was already midday, which meant the horde might have already struck, and yet his Sect members were nowhere to be found.

He snatched a talisman from his pouch. It was one of his communication talismans, and it would put him in direct contact with the others.

Red was about to activate it when the necromancer's bear interrupted him. "Shouldn't do that. If companion possessed, it can track you down by talisman."

His eyes widened. "That's possible?"

The beast nodded. "High-level skill, but totally possible. Some of the ghosts inside head really powerful, could know trick."

Red hesitated, but still put his talisman away. "In that case, help me find them."

"No way. Head still out there. Could find you any time."

"I'm going with or without your help," Red insisted. "Since you don't want to see me possessed, you should probably help me."

He was reluctant to ask the necromancer for help, but he had little choice. This was the only being that knew the head's capabilities, and if his companions were really possessed, he wouldn't be able to save them by himself.

"Was given order. Keep you safe. Could just hold you here until head left."

"You know that's not possible," Red replied. "If that head tracked me even after being thrown into the river, what's stopping it from doing it again?"

This was a bluff. He didn't actually know if the necromancer had a way to keep him hidden. According to the bear's words earlier, his "stench" was too strong, but the bear hadn't seemed too confident in the term.

The beast let out a guttural grunt. "Dangerous, stupid idea. If head catches you, can't guarantee safety."

"That's fine. It's afraid of the town, so as long as we can get there back in time, it won't be able to do anything to us."

He was already ignoring their earlier plans to help the town with the horde. This was exactly the kind of crisis Hector had told them to be wary about, and with such an insidious enemy out there, how could they guarantee their own safety?

The bear growled softly. "Hm, can help with companions, but there is problem... If they possessed, can't do anything about it."

Red frowned. That was one of the main reasons he wanted help. "Is there nothing that can be done?"

"Ghost possession too strong, too dangerous," the bear said. "Longer ghost is in body, harder to take out. Stronger ghost is, harder to take out too. Might be possible if I had powers, but... Too weak, too faint. Not sure how long form will last away from main body."

"So you mean you could do something if you had a connection to your main body?"

The bear nodded. "Can you do it?"

"Not possible."

It was obvious the necromancer was probing him. The hawk hadn't given him a means to communicate with it, and even if it had, he would never use it to help the necromancer. After all, Red still needed to consider that the necromancer wasn't telling him the truth.

Even if his companions were in trouble, he couldn't just throw caution to the wind.

The bear pondered in silence. "... Hm, in that case, there might still be way."

"How?" Red asked, suspicious.

"Learn necromancy and you can help them."

The bear's mouth curled up into what Red could only imagine was a smile.

ABOUT THE AUTHOR

Nameless Author is a writer inspired by xianxia, sci-fi, epic fantasy, and just about every genre out there. He enjoys reading, watching movies, and playing RPGs.

ABOUT TIMELESS WIND PUBLISHING

Founded in late 2020 by Lorne Ryburn and Silas Sontag, Timeless Wind Publishing is an up-and-coming indie publishing house. We love sci-fi and fantasy—progression fantasy, power fantasy, LitRPG, time loops, cultivation, system apocalypse—genre fiction of all kinds! We're prolific readers within these genres and endeavor to bring awesome books into the limelight.

We look forward to helping authors (aspiring and published alike) develop and expand an audience of readers who believe in their vision.

Our logo is an exotic cat from a Palmyrene ruin. The word along its back roughly translates to, "Alas!" or "What a shame!" This word is present on all gravestones in Palmyra. It's a recognition that all things come to an end... even the best people and stories. Alas!

We hope our readers will have "alas" moments when they finish our books.

Connect with Timeless Wind Publishing
TimelessWind.com
Facebook.com/timelesswind
Twitter.com/timeless_wind
Instagram.com/timelesswindpub